P9-DGQ-447

R·A·SALVATORE

THE TWO SWORDS

THE HUNTER'S BLADES TRILOGY

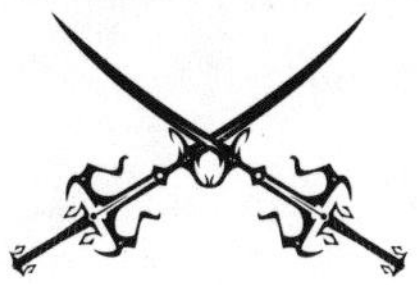

The Hunter's Blades Trilogy, Book III
THE TWO SWORDS

Distributed in the United States by Holtzbrinck Publishing.
Distributed in Canada by Fenn Ltd.

Distributed to the hobby, toy, and comic trade in the United States and Canada by regional distributors.

Distributed worldwide by Wizards of the Coast, Inc. and regional distributors.

Printed in the U.S.A.

Cover art by Todd Lockwood
First Printing: October 2004
Library of Congress Catalog Card Number: 2004106768

9 8 7 6 5 4 3 2 1

US ISBN: 0-7869-3360-7
UK ISBN: 0-7869-3361-5
620-17759-001-EN

U.S., CANADA,
ASIA, PACIFIC, & LATIN AMERICA
Wizards of the Coast, Inc.
P.O. Box 707
Renton, WA 98057-0707
+1-800-324-6496

EUROPEAN HEADQUARTERS
Wizards of the Coast, Belgium
T Hofveld 6d
1702 Groot-Bijgaarden
Belgium
+322 467 3360

Visit our web site at www.wizards.com/forgottenrealms

FORGOTTEN REALMS® NOVELS BY

R·A·SALVATORE

THE ICEWIND DALE TRILOGY

The Crystal Shard
Streams of Silver
The Halfling's Gem
The Icewind Dale Trilogy Collector's Edition

THE DARK ELF TRILOGY

Homeland
Exile
Sojourn
The Dark Elf Trilogy Collector's Edition

LEGACY OF THE DROW

The Legacy
Starless Night
Siege of Darkness
Passage to Dawn
Legacy of the Drow Collector's Edition

PATHS OF DARKNESS

The Silent Blade
The Spine of the World
Servant of the Shard
Sea of Swords
Paths of Darkness
Collector's Edition

THE CLERIC QUINTET

Canticle
In Sylvan Shadows
Night Masks
The Fallen Fortress
The Chaos Curse
The Cleric Quintet
Collector's Edition

THE HUNTER'S BLADES TRILOGY

The Thousand Orcs
The Lone Drow
The Two Swords

ALSO BY R.A. SALVATORE

THE HIGHWAYMAN

THE SPEARWIELDER'S TALES

The Woods Out Back
The Dragon's Dagger
Dragonslayer's Return

THE DEMONWARS SERIES

The Demon Awakens
The Demon Spirit
The Demon Apostle
Mortalis
Ascendance
Transcendence
Immortalis

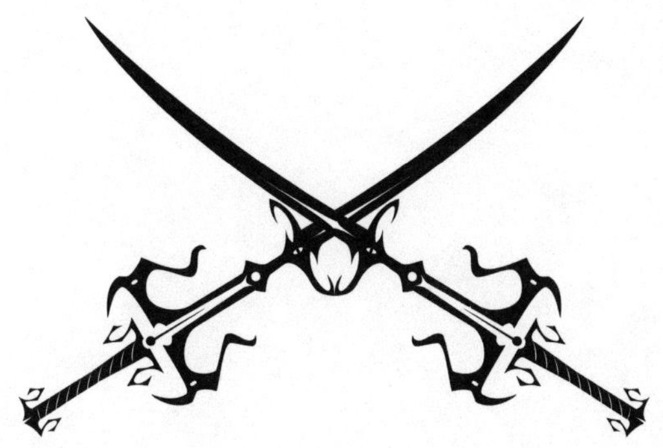

PRELUDE

The torchlight seemed such a meager thing against the unrelenting darkness of the dwarven caves. The smoky air drifted around Delly Curtie, irritating her eyes and throat, much as the continual grumbling and complaining of the other humans in the large common room irritated her sensibilities. Steward Regis had graciously given over a considerable suite of rooms to those seemingly ungrateful people, refugees all from the many settlements sacked by brutish King Obould and his orcs in their southern trek.

Delly reminded herself not to be too judgmental of the folk. All of them had suffered grievous losses, with many being the only remaining member of a murdered family, with three being the only remaining citizens of an entirely sacked community! And the conditions, as decent as Regis and Bruenor tried to make them, were not fitting for a human.

That thought struck hard at Delly's sensibilities, and she glanced back over her shoulder at her toddler, Colson, asleep—finally!—in a small crib. Cottie Cooperson, a spindly-armed woman with thin straw hair and eyes that drooped under the weight of a great loss, sat beside the sleeping toddler, her arms crossed tightly over her chest as she rocked back and forth, back and forth.

Remembering her own murdered baby, Delly knew.

That horrific thought sobered Delly, to be sure. Colson wasn't really Delly's child, not by birth. But she had adopted the baby girl, as Wulfgar had adopted Colson and in turn had taken on Delly as his traveling companion and wife. Delly had followed him to Mithral Hall willingly, eagerly even, and had thought herself a good and generous person in granting him his adventurous spirit, in standing beside him through what he had needed without regard for her own desires.

Delly's smile was more sad than joyous. It was perhaps the first time the young woman had ever thought of herself as good and generous.

But the dwarven walls were closing in on her.

Never had Delly Curtie imagined that she could harbor wistful memories of her street life in Luskan, living wild and on the edge, half-drunk most of the time and in the arms of a different man night after night. She thought of clever Morik, a wonderful lover, and of Arumn Gardpeck, the tavern-keeper who had been as a father to her. She thought of Josi Puddles, too, and found in those recollections of his undeniably stupid grin some measure of comfort.

"Nah, ye're being silly," the woman muttered under her breath.

She shook her head to throw those memories aside. This was her life now, with Wulfgar and the others. The dwarves of Clan Battlehammer were goodly folk, she told herself. Often eccentric, always kind and many times simply and playfully absurd, they were a lovable lot beneath their typically gruff exteriors. Some wore outrageous clothing or armor, others carried strange and ridiculous names, and most wild and absurd beards, but the clan showed Delly a measure of heart that she had never before seen, other than from Arumn perhaps. They treated her as kin, or tried to, for the differences remained.

Undeniably so.

Differences of preference, human to dwarf, like the stifling air of the caves—air that would grow even more stagnant, no doubt, since both exterior doors of Mithral Hall had been closed and barricaded.

"Ah, but to feel the wind and sun on my face once more!" a woman from across the common room shouted, lifting a flagon of mead in toast, as if she had read Delly's every thought.

From all across the room, mugs came up in response and clanged together. The group, almost all of them, were well on their way to drunkenness yet again, Delly realized. They had no place to fit in, and their drinking was as much to alleviate their helpless frustration as to dull the horrible memories of Obould's march through their respective communities.

Delly checked on Colson again and filtered about the tables. She had agreed to tend to the group, calling upon her experiences as a serving wench in Luskan. She caught bits of conversation wherever she passed, and every thought found a hold on her, and bit at what little contentment remained within her heart.

"I'm going to set up a smithy in Silverymoon," one man proclaimed.

"Bah, Silverymoon!" another argued, sounding very much like a dwarf with his rough dialect. "Silverymoon's nothing but a bunch of dancing elves.

Get ye to Sundabar. Ye're sure to find a better livelihood in a town of folk who know proper business."

"Silverymoon's more accepting," a woman from another table argued. "And more beautiful, by all tellings."

Those were almost the very same words that Delly had once heard to describe Mithral Hall. In many ways, the Hall had lived up to its reputation. Certainly the reception Bruenor and his kin had given her had been nothing short of wonderful, in their unique, dwarven way. And Mithral Hall was as amazing a sight as Luskan's harbor, to be sure. Yet it was a sight that quickly melted into sameness, Delly had come to know.

She made her way across the room, veering back toward Colson, who was still sleeping but had begun that same scratchy cough that Delly had been hearing from all the humans in the smoky tunnels.

"I'm right grateful enough to Steward Regis and King Bruenor," she heard one woman say, again as if reading her very thoughts, "but here's no place for a person!" The woman lifted her flagon. "Silverymoon or Sundabar, then!" she toasted, to many cheers. "Or anywhere else ye might be seeing the sun and the stars!"

"Everlund!" another man cried.

In the stark crib on the cold stone floor beside Delly Curtie, Colson coughed again.

Beside the baby girl, Cottie Cooperson swayed.

PART ONE

ORC AMBITIONS

I look upon the hillside, quiet now except for the birds. That's all there is. The birds, cawing and cackling and poking their beaks into unseeing eyeballs. Crows do not circle before they alight on a field strewn with the dead. They fly as the bee to a flower, straight for their goal, with so great a feast before them. They are the cleaners, along with the crawling insects, the rain, and the unending wind.

And the passage of time. There is always that. The turn of the day, of the season, of the year.

When it is done, all that is left are the bones and the stones. The screams are gone, the smell is gone. The blood is washed away. The fattened birds take with them in their departing flights all that identified these fallen warriors as individuals.

Leaving the bones and stones, to mingle and mix. As the wind or the rain break apart the skeletons and filter them together, as the passage of time buries some, what is left becomes indistinguishable, perhaps, to all but the most careful of observers. Who will remember those who died here, and what have they gained to compensate for all that they, on both sides, lost?

The look upon a dwarf's face when battle is upon him would argue, surely, that the price is worth the effort, that warfare, when it comes to a dwarven nation, is a noble cause. Nothing to a dwarf is more revered than fighting to help a friend; theirs is a community bound tightly by loyalty, by blood shared and blood spilled.

And so, in the life of an individual, perhaps this is a good way to die, a worthy end to a life lived honorably, or even to a life made worthy by this last ultimate sacrifice.

I cannot help but wonder, though, in the larger context, what of the overall? What of the price, the worth, and the gain? Will Obould accomplish anything worth the hundreds, perhaps thousands of his dead? Will he gain anything long-lasting? Will the dwarven stand made out here on this high cliff bring Bruenor's people anything worthwhile? Could they not have slipped into Mithral Hall, to tunnels so much more easily defended?

And a hundred years from now, when there remains only dust, will anyone care?

I wonder what fuels the fires that burn images of glorious battle into the hearts of so many of the sentient races, my own paramount among them. I look at the carnage on the slope and I see the inevitable sight of emptiness. I imagine the cries of pain. I hear in my head the calls for loved ones when the dying warrior knows his last moment is upon him. I see a tower fall with my dearest friend atop it. Surely the tangible remnants, the rubble and the bones, are hardly worth the moment of battle, but is there, I wonder, something less tangible here, something of a greater place? Or is there, perhaps—and this is my fear—something of a delusion to it all that drives us to war, again and again?

Along that latter line of thought, is it within us all, when the memories of war have faded, to so want to be a part of something great that we throw aside the quiet, the calm, the mundane, the peace itself? Do we collectively come to equate peace with boredom and complacency? Perhaps we hold these embers of war within us, dulled only by sharp memories of the pain and the loss, and when that smothering blanket dissipates with the passage of healing time, those fires flare again to life. I saw this within myself, to a smaller extent, when I realized and admitted to myself that I was not a being of comfort and complacency, that only by the wind on my face, the trails beneath my feet, and the adventure along the road could I truly be happy.

I'll walk those trails indeed, but it seems to me that it is another thing all together to carry an army along beside me, as Obould has done. For there is the consideration of a larger morality here, shown so starkly in the bones among the stones. We rush to the call of arms, to the rally, to the glory, but what of those caught in the path of this thirst for greatness?

Who will remember those who died here, and what have they gained to compensate for all that they, on both sides, lost?

Whenever we lose a loved one, we resolve, inevitably, to never forget, to remember that dear person for all our living days. But we the living contend with the present, and the present often commands all of our attention. And so as the years pass, we do not remember those who have gone before us every day, or even every tenday. Then comes the guilt, for if I am not remembering Zaknafein my father, my mentor, who sacrificed himself for me, then who is? And if no one is, then perhaps he really is gone. As the years pass, the guilt will lessen, because we forget more consistently and the pendulum turns in our self-serving thoughts to applaud ourselves on those increasingly rare occasions when we do remember! There is always the guilt, perhaps, because we are self-centered creatures to the last. It is the truth of individuality that cannot be denied. In the end, we, all of us, see the world through our own, personal eyes.

I have heard parents express their fears of their own mortality soon after the birth of a child. It is a fear that stays with a parent, to a great extent, through the first dozen years of a child's life. It is not for the child that they fear, should they die—though surely there is that worry, as well—but rather for themselves. What father would accept his death before his child was truly old enough to remember him?

For who better to put a face to the bones among the stones? Who better to remember the sparkle in an eye before the crow comes a'calling?

I wish the crows would circle and the wind would carry them away, and the faces would remain forever to remind us of the pain. When the clarion call to glory sounds, before the armies anew trample the bones among the stones, let the faces of the dead remind us of the cost.

It is a sobering sight before me, the red-splashed stones.

It is a striking warning in my ears, the cawing of the crows.

—Drizzt Do'Urden

1

FOR THE LOVE OF ME SON

"We must be quicker!" the human commented, for the hundredth time that morning, it seemed to the more than two-score dwarves moving in a line all around him. Galen Firth appeared quite out of place in the torchlit, smoky tunnels. Tall even for a human, he stood more than head and shoulders above the short and sturdy bearded folk.

"I got me scouts up ahead, working as fast as scouts can work," replied General Dagna, a venerable warrior of many battles.

The old dwarf stretched and straightened his still-broad shoulders, and tucked his dirty yellow beard into his thick leather girdle, then considered Galen with eyes still sharp, a scrutinizing gaze that had kept the dwarves of Clan Battlehammer ducking defensively out of sight for many, many decades. Dagna had been a well-respected warcommander for as long as anyone could remember, longer than Bruenor had been king, and before Shimmergloom the shadow dragon and his duergar minions had conquered Mithral Hall. Dagna had climbed to power through deed, as a warrior and field commander, and no one questioned his prowess in leading dwarves through difficult conflicts. Many had expected Dagna to lead the defense of the cliff face above Keeper's Dale, even ahead of venerable Banak Brawnanvil. When that had not come to pass, it was assumed Dagna would be named as Steward of the Hall while Bruenor lay near death.

Indeed, both of those opportunities had been presented to Dagna, and by those in a position to make either happen. But he had refused.

"Ye wouldn't have me tell me scouts to run along swifter and maybe give themselves away to trolls and the like, now would ye?" Dagna asked.

Galen Firth rocked back on his heels a bit at that, but he didn't blink and he didn't stand down. "I would have you move this column as swiftly as is possible," he replied. "My town is sorely pressed, perhaps overrun, and in the south, out of these infernal tunnels, many people may now be in dire jeopardy. I would hope that such would prove an impetus to the dwarves who claim to be our neighbors."

"I claim nothing," Dagna was fast to reply. "I do what me steward and me king're telling me to do."

"And you care not at all for the fallen?"

Galen's blunt question caused several of the nearby dwarves to suck in their breath, aimed as it was at Dagna, the proud dwarf who had lost his only son only a few tendays earlier. Dagna stared long and hard at the man, burying the sting that prompted him to an angry response, remembering his place and his duty.

"We're going as fast as we're going, and if ye're wanting to be going faster, then ye're welcome to run up ahead. I'll tell me scouts to let ye pass without hindrance. Might even be that I'll keep me march going over your dead body when we find yerself troll-eaten in the corridors ahead. Might even be that yer Nesmé kin, if any're still about, will get rescued without ye." Dagna paused and let his glare linger a moment longer, a silent assurance to Galen Firth that he was hardly bluffing. "Then again, might not be."

That seemed to take some of the steam from Galen, and the man gave a great "harrumph" and turned back to the tunnel ahead, stomping forward deliberately.

Dagna was beside him in an instant, grabbing him hard by the arm.

"Pout if ye want to pout," the dwarf agreed, "but ye be doing it quietly."

Galen pulled himself away from the dwarf's vicelike grasp, and matched Dagna's stare with his own glower.

Several nearby dwarves rolled their eyes at that and wondered if Dagna would leave the fool squirming on the floor with a busted nose. Galen hadn't

been like that until very recently. The fifty dwarves had accompanied him out of Mithral Hall many days before, with orders from Steward Regis to do what they could to aid the beleaguered folk of Nesmé. Their journey had been steady and straightforward until they had been attacked in the tunnels by a group of trolls. That fight had sent them running, a long way to the south and out into the open air on the edges of the great swamp, the Trollmoors, but too far to the east, by Galen Firth's reckoning. So they had started west, and had found more tunnels. Against Galen's protests, Dagna had decided that his group would be better served under cover of the westward-leading underground corridors. More dirt than stone, with roots from trees and brush dangling over their heads and with crawly things wriggling in the black dirt all around them, the tunnels weren't like those they'd used to come south from Mithral Hall. That only made Galen all the more miserable. The tunnels were tighter, lower, and not as wide, which the dwarves thought a good thing, particularly with huge and ugly trolls chasing them, but which only made Galen spend half his time walking bent over.

"Ye're pushing the old one hard," a young dwarf, Fender Stouthammer by name, remarked when they took their next break and meal. He and Galen were off to the side of the main group, in a wider and higher area that allowed Galen to stretch his legs a bit, though that had done little to improve his sour mood.

"My cause is—"

"Known to us, and felt by us, every one," Fender assured him. "We're all feeling for Mithral Hall in much the same way as ye're feeling for Nesmé, don't ye doubt."

The calming intent of Fender didn't find a hold on Galen, though, and he wagged his long finger right in the dwarf's face, so close that Fender had to hold himself back from just biting the digit off at the knuckle.

"What do you know of my feelings?" Galen growled at him. "Do you know my son, huddled in the cold, perhaps? Slain, perhaps, or with trolls all about him? Do you know the fate of my neighbors? Do you—"

"General Dagna just lost his boy," Fender interrupted, and that set Galen back a bit.

"Dagnabbit was his name," Fender went on. "A mighty warrior and loyal fellow, as are all his kin. He fell to the orc horde at Shallows, defending his king and kin to the bitter end. He was Dagna's only boy, and with a career as promising as that of his father. Long will dwarf bards sing the name of Dagnabbit. But I'm guessing that thought's hardly cooling the boil in old Dagna's blood, or hardly plastering the crack in his old heart. And now here ye come, ye short-livin', cloud-sniffin' dolt, demanding this and demanding that, as if yer own needs're more important than any we dwarves might be knowing. Bah, I tried to take ye in stride. I tried to see yer side of the fear. But ye know, ye're a pushy one, and one that's more likely to get boot-trampled into the stone than to ever see yer home again if ye don't learn to shut yer stupid mouth."

The obviously flabbergasted Galen Firth just sat there for a moment, stuttering.

"Are you threatening me, a Rider of Nesmé?" he finally managed to blurt.

"I'm telling ye, as a friend or as an enemy—choice is yer own to make—that ye're not helping yerself or yer people by fighting with Dagna at every turn in the tunnel."

"The tunnel. . . ." the stubborn man spat back. "We should be out in the open air, where we might hear the calls of my people, or see the light of their fires!"

"Or find ourselves surrounded by an army o' trolls, and wouldn't that smell wonderful?"

Galen Firth gave a snort and held up his hand dismissively. Fender took the cue, rose, and started away.

He did pause long enough to look back and offer, "Ye keep acting as if ye're among enemies, or lessers. If all the folk o' Nesmé are as stupid as yerself—too dumb to know a friend when one's ready to help—then who's to doubt that the trolls might be doing all the world a favor?"

Galen Firth trembled, and for a moment Fender half expected the man to leap up and try to throttle him.

"I came to you, to Mithral Hall, in friendship!" he argued, loudly enough to gain the attention of those dwarves crowded around Dagna in the main chamber down the tunnel.

"Yerself came to Mithral Hall in need, offerin' nothing but complaints and asking for more than we could give ye," Fender corrected. "And still Steward Regis, and all the clan, accepted the responsibility of friendship—not

the burden, but the responsibility, ye dolt! We ain't here because we're owing Nesmé a damned thing, and we ain't here asking Nesmé for a damned thing, and in the end, even yerself should be smart enough to know that we're all hopin' for the same thing here. And that thing's finding yer boy, and all the others of yer town, alive and well."

The blunt assessment did give Galen pause and in that moment, before he could decide whether to scream or to punch out, Fender rolled up to his feet, offered a dismissive, "Bah!" and waved his calloused hands the man's way.

"Ye might be thinking to make a bit less noise, yeah?" came a voice from the other direction, that of General Dagna, who glared at the two.

"Get along with ye, then," Fender said to Galen, and he waved at him again. "Think on what I said or don't—it's yer own to choose."

Galen Firth slowly moved back from the dwarf, and toward the larger gathering in the middle of the wider chamber. He walked more sidelong than in any straightforward manner, though, as if warding his back from the pursuit of words that had surely stung him.

Fender was glad of that, for the sake of Galen Firth and Nesmé Town, if for nothing else.

Tos'un Armgo, lithe and graceful, moved silently along the low corridor, a dart clenched in his teeth and a serrated knife in his hand. The dark elf was glad that the dwarves had gone back underground. He felt vulnerable and exposed in the open air. A noise made him pause and huddle closer to the rocky wall, his limber form melting into the jags and depressions. He pulled his *piwafwi*, his enchanted drow cloak that could hide him from the most scrutinizing of gazes, a bit tighter around him and turned his face to the stone, peering out of the corner of only one eye.

A few moments passed. Tos'un relaxed as he heard the dwarves back at their normal routines, eating and chatting. They thought they were safe back in the tunnels, since they believed they had left the trolls far behind. What troll could have tracked them over the last couple days since the skirmish, after all?

No troll, Tos'un knew, and he smiled at the thought. For the dwarves hadn't counted on their crude and beastlike enemies being accompanied by a pair of dark elves. Tracking them, leading the two-headed troll named Proffit and his smelly band back into this second stretch of tunnel, had been no difficult task for Tos'un.

The drow glanced back the other way, where his companion, the priestess Kaer'lic Suun Wett waited, crouched atop a boulder against the wall. Even Tos'un would not have seen her there, buried under her *piwafwi*, except that she shifted as he turned, lifting one arm out toward him.

Take down the sentry, her fingers flashed to him in the intricate sign language of the drow elves. *A prisoner is desirable.*

Tos'un took a deep breath and instinctively reached for the dart he held clenched in his teeth. Its tip was coated with drow poison, a paralyzing concoction of tremendous power that few could resist. How often had Tos'un heard that command from Kaer'lic and his other two drow companions over the last few years, for he among all the group had become the most adept at gathering creatures for interrogation, especially when the target was part of a larger group.

Tos'un paused and moved his free hand out where Kaer'lic could see, then answered, *Do we need bother? They are alert, and they are many.*

Kaer'lic's fingers flashed back immediately, *I would know if this is a remote group or the forward scouts of Mithral Hall's army!*

Tos'un's hand went right back to the dart. He didn't dare argue with Kaer'lic on such matters. They were drow, and in the realm of the drow, even for a group who was so far removed from the conventions of the great Underdark cities, females ranked higher than males, and priestesses of the Spider Queen Lolth, like Kaer'lic, ranked highest of all.

The scout turned and slid down lower toward the floor, then began to half walk, half crawl toward his target. He paused when he heard the dwarf raise his voice, arguing with the single human among the troop. The drow moved to a properly hidden vantage point and bided his time.

Soon enough, several of the dwarves farther along told the two to be quiet, and the dwarf near to Tos'un grumbled something and waved the human away.

Tos'un glanced back just once, then paused and listened until his sensitive ears picked out the rumble of Proffit's closing war party.

Tos'un slithered in. His left arm struck first, jabbing the dart into the dwarf's shoulder as his right hand came across, the serrated knife cutting a very precise line on the dwarf's throat. It could easily have been a killing blow, but Tos'un angled the blade so as not to cut the main veins, the same technique he had recently used on a dwarf in a tower near the Surbrin. Eventually his cut would prove mortal, but not for a long time, not until Kaer'lic could intervene and with but a few minor spells granted by the Spider Queen save the wretched creature's life.

Though, Tos'un thought, the prisoner would surely wish he had been allowed to die.

The dwarf shifted fast and tried to cry out, but the drow had taken its vocal chords. Then the dwarf tried to punch and lash out, but the poison was already there. Blood streaming from the mortal wound, the dwarf crumbled down to the stone, and Tos'un slithered back.

"Bah, ye're still a bigmouth!" came a quiet call from the main group. "Keep still, will ya, Fender?"

Tos'un continued to retreat.

"Fender?" The call sounded more insistent.

Tos'un flattened against the corner of the wall and the floor, making himself very small and all but invisible under his enchanted cloak.

"Fender!" a dwarf ahead of him cried, and Tos'un smiled at his cleverness, knowing the stupid dwarves would surely think their poisoned companion dead.

The camp began to stir, dwarves leaping up and grabbing their weapons, and it occurred to Tos'un that Kaer'lic's decision to go for a captive might cost Proffit and his trolls dearly. The price of the drow's initial assault had been the element of surprise.

Of course, for the dark elf, that only made the attack all the more sweet.

Some dwarves cried out for Fender, but the shout that rose above them all came from Bonnerbas Ironcap, the dwarf closest to their fallen companion.

"Trolls!" he yelled, and even as the word registered with his companions, so did the smell of the wretched brutes.

"Fall back to the fire!" General Dagna shouted.

Bonnerbas hesitated, for he was but one stride from poor Fender. He went forward instead of back, and grabbed his friend by the collar. Fender flopped over and Bonnerbas sucked in his breath, seeing clearly the line of bright blood. The dwarf was limp, unfeeling.

Fender was dead, Bonnerbas believed, or soon would be.

He heard the charge of the trolls then, looked up, and realized that he would soon join Fender in the halls of Moradin.

Bonnerbas fell back one step and took up his axe, swiping across viciously and cutting a deep line across the arms of the nearest, low-bending troll. That one fell back, stumbling to the side and toppling, but before it even hit the floor it came flying ahead, bowled over by a pair of trolls charging forward at Bonnerbas.

The dwarf swung again, and turned to flee, but a clawed troll hand hooked his shoulder. Bonnerbas understood then the frightful strength of the brutes, for suddenly he was flying backward, spinning and bouncing off legs as solid as the trunks of tall trees. He stumbled and fell, winding up on his back. Still, the furious dwarf flailed with his axe, and he scored a couple of hits. But the trolls were all around him, were between him and Dagna and the others, and poor Bonnerbas had nowhere to run.

One troll reached for him and he managed to swat the arm with enough force to take it off at the elbow. That troll howled and fell back, but then, even as the dwarf tried to roll to his side and stand the biggest and ugliest troll Bonnerbas had ever seen towered over him, a gruesome two-headed brute staring at him with a wide smile on both of its twisted faces. It started to reach down, and Bonnerbas started to swing.

As his axe flew past without hitting anything, the dwarf recognized the dupe, and before he could bring the axe back over him, a huge foot appeared above him and crashed down hard, stomping him into the stone.

Bonnerbas tried to struggle, but there was nothing he could do. He tried to breathe, but the press was too great.

As the trolls pushed past the two fallen dwarves, General Dagna could only growl and silently curse himself for allowing his force to be caught so unawares. Questions and curses roiled in his mind. How could stupid, smelly trolls have possibly followed them back into the tunnels? How could the brutes have scouted and navigated the difficult approach to where Dagna had thought it safe to break for a meal?

That jumble quickly calmed in the thoughts of the seasoned commander, though, and he began barking orders to put his command in line. His first thought was to move back into the lower tunnels, to get the trolls bent over even more, but the dwarf's instincts told him to stay put, with a ready fire at hand. He ordered his boys to form up a defensive hold on the far side of the cooking fire. Dagna himself led the countercharge and the push, centering the front line of five dwarves abreast and refusing to retreat against the troll press.

"Hold 'em fast!" he cried repeatedly as he smashed away with his warhammer. "Go to crushing!" he told the axe-wielding dwarf beside him. "Don't yet cut through 'em if that's giving them a single step forward!"

The other dwarf, apparently catching on to the reasoning that they had to hold the far side of the fire at all costs, flipped his axe over in his hand and began pounding away at the closest troll, smashing it with the flat back of the weapon to keep it at bay.

All the five dwarves did likewise, and Galen Firth ran up behind Dagna and began slashing away with his fine long sword. They knew they would not be able to hold for long, though, for more trolls crowded behind the front ranks, the sheer weight of them driving the force forward.

Thinking that all of them were doomed, Dagna screamed in rage and whacked so hard at the troll reaching for him that his nasty hammer tore the creature's arm off at the elbow.

The troll didn't seem to even notice as it came forward, and Dagna realized his error. He had over-swung the mark and was vulnerable.

But the troll backed suddenly, and Dagna ducked and cried out in surprise, as the first of the torches, compliments of Galen Firth, entered the fray. The man reached over and past the ducking Dagna and thrust the flaming torch at the troll, and how the creature scrambled to get back from the fire!

Trolls were mighty opponents indeed, and it was said—and it was true—that if you cut a troll into a hundred pieces, the result would be a hundred new trolls, with every piece regenerating into an entirely new creature. They had a weakness, though, one that every person in all the Realms knew well: fire stopped that regeneration process.

Trolls didn't like fire.

More torches were quickly passed up to Dagna and the four others and the trolls fell back, but only a step.

"Forward, then, for Fender and Bonnerbas!" Dagna cried, and all the dwarves cheered.

But then came a shout from the other side of "Trolls in the tunnels!" and another warning shout from directly behind Dagna.

All the tunnels were blocked. Dagna knew at once that his dwarves were surrounded and had nowhere to run.

"How deep're we?" the general shouted.

"Roots in the ceiling," one dwarf answered. "Ain't too deep."

"Then get us through!" the old dwarf ordered

Immediately, those dwarves near to the center of the tightening ring went into action. Two braced a third and lifted him high with his pickaxe, and he began tearing away at the ground.

"Wet one down!" Dagna yelled, and he knew that it was all he had to say to get his full meaning across to his trusted comrades.

"And tie him off!" came the appropriate addition, from more than one dwarf.

"Galen Firth, ye brace the hole!" Dagna roared at the human.

"What are you doing?" the man demanded. "Fight on, good dwarf, for we've nowhere to run!"

Dagna thrust his torch forward and the troll facing him hopped back. The dwarf turned fast and shoved at Galen.

"Turn about, ye dolt, and get us out o' here!"

A confused Galen did reluctantly turn from the fight just as daylight appeared above the area to the left of the cooking fire. The two dwarves supporting the miner gave a great heave, sending him up, where he caught on and scrambled onto the surface.

"Clear!" he reported.

Galen understood the plan then, and rushed to the hole, where he immediately began hoisting dwarves. After every one he had to pause, though, for

the dwarves up above began handing down more wood for the fire.

Dagna nodded and urged his line on, and the five fought furiously and brilliantly, coordinating their movements so that the trolls could not advance. But neither did the dwarves gain any ground, and Dagna knew in his heart that his two companions, Fender and Bonnerbas, were surely dead.

The tough old dwarf pushed the grim thoughts from his mind, and didn't even begin to let them lead him back down the road of grief for his lost boy. He focused on his anger and on the desperate need, and he forged ahead, warhammer and torch flailing. Behind him, he felt the heat increasing as his boys began to strengthen the fire. They'd need it blazing indeed if they meant to get the last of the group clear of the tunnels and up into the open air.

"Down in front!" came a call aimed at Dagna and his line.

As one the five dwarves sprang ahead and attacked ferociously, forcing the trolls to retreat a step. Then again as one they leaped back and dropped to the ground.

Flaming brush and logs flew over their heads, bouncing into the trolls and sending them into a frenzied scramble to get out of the way.

Dagna's heart fell as he watched the effective barrage, though, for beyond that line of confusion lay two of his kin, down and dead, he was sure. He and the other four fell back, then, moving right to the base of the hole, just behind Galen, who continued to ferry dwarves up.

The tunnel grew smokier and smokier with every passing second as more brush and logs came down the chute. A dwarven brigade carried the timber to the fire. The brush—branches of pine, mostly—flared up fast and furious to be rushed across to drive back whatever trolls were closest, while the logs were dropped onto the pile, replacing already flaring logs that were scooped up and hurled into the enemy ranks. Gradually, the dwarves were building walls of fire, sealing off every approach.

Their ranks thinned as more scrambled up to the surface, as Galen tirelessly lifted them into the arms of their waiting kin. Then the scramble became more frantic as the dwarves' numbers dwindled to only a few.

The dwarf beside Dagna urged him to go, but the crusty old graybeard slapped that notion aside by slapping the other dwarf aside—shoving him into Galen Firth's waiting arms. Up and out he went, and one by one, Dagna's line diminished.

Up came a huge flaming brand—Galen passing it to Dagna—and the old dwarf took the heavy log, handing back his hammer in exchange. He presented the log horizontally out before him and charged with a roar, barreling right into the trolls, the flames biting his hands but biting the trolls worse. The creatures fell all over each other trying to get back from the wild dwarf. With a great heave, Dagna sent the flaming log into them. Then he turned and fled back to where Galen was waiting. The human crouched, with his hands set in a clasp before him. Dagna hopped onto those waiting hands, and Galen turned, guiding him directly under the hole, then heaved him up.

Even as Dagna cleared the hole, and Galen instinctively turned to meet the troll charge he knew must be coming, dwarf hands reached into the opening and clasped tightly onto Galen's forearms.

The man went into the air, to shouts of, "Pull him out!"

His head and shoulders came out into the open air, and for a moment, Galen thought he was clear.

Until he felt clawed hands grab him by the legs.

"Pull, ye dolts!" General Dagna demanded, and he rushed over and grabbed Galen by the collar, digging in his heels and tugging hard.

The man cried out in pain. He lifted a bit out of the hole, then went back in some, serving as the line in a game of tug-of-war.

"Get me a torch!" Dagna cried, and when he saw a dwarf rushing over with a flaming brand he let go of Galen, who, for a moment, nearly disappeared into the hole.

"Grab me feet!" Dagna ordered as he went around Galen.

The moment a pair of dwarves had him securely about the ankles, the general dived face first into the hole behind the struggling Galen, his torch leading—and drawing a yelp from Galen as it brushed down behind him.

Galen frantically shouted some more as the torch burned him about the legs, but then he was free. The dwarves yanked both Galen and Dagna from the hole. Dagna held his ground as a troll stood up, reaching for the opening. The old dwarf whacked away with the torch, holding the creature at bay until his boys could get more substantial fire to the hole and dump it down.

Heavier logs were ferried into position and similarly forced down, blocking the opening, and Dagna and the others fell back to catch their collective breath.

A shout had them up and moving again, though, for the trolls had not been stopped by the clogged and fiery exit. Clawed hands rent the ground as the trolls began to dig escape tunnels of their own.

"Gather 'em up and get on the move!" Dagna roared, and the dwarves set off at a great pace across the open ground.

Many had to be helped, two carried even, but a count showed that they had lost only two: Fender and Bonnerbas. Still, not a one of them wanted to call that encounter a victory.

2
BONES AND STONES

Decay and rot had won the day, creeping around the stones and boulders of the bloody mountainside. Bloated corpses steamed in the cool morning air, their last wisps of heat flowing away to insubstantiality, life energy lost on the endless mitigating mourn of the uncaring wind.

Drizzt Do'Urden walked among the lower reaches of the killing field, a cloth tied across his black-skinned face to ward the stench. Almost all of the bodies on the lower ground were orcs, many killed in the monumental blast that had upended the mountain ridge to the side of the main area of battle. That explosion had turned night into day, had sent flames leaping a thousand feet into the air, and had launched tons and tons of debris across the swarm of monsters, mowing them flat under its press.

"One less weapon I will have to replace," said Innovindil.

Drizzt turned to regard his surface elf companion. The fair elf had her face covered too, though that did little to diminish her beauty. Above her scarf, bright blue eyes peered out at Drizzt and the same wind that carried the stench of death blew her long golden tresses out wildly behind her. Lithe and graceful, Innovindil's every step seemed like a dance to Drizzt Do'Urden, and even the burden of mourning, for she had lost her partner and lover, Tarathiel, could not hold her feet glumly to the stone.

Drizzt watched as she reached down to a familiar corpse, that of Urlgen, son of Obould Many-Arrows, the orc beast who had started the awful war. Innovindil had killed Urlgen, or rather, he had inadvertently killed himself by slamming his head at hers and impaling it upon a dagger the elf had snapped up before her. Innovindil put a foot on the bloated face of the dead orc leader, grasped the dagger hilt firmly in hand, and yanked it free. With hardly a flinch, she bent further and wiped the blade on the dead orc's shirt, then flipped it over in her hand and replaced it in the sheath belted around her ankle.

"They have not bothered to loot the field, from dead dwarves or from their own," Innovindil remarked.

That much had been obvious to Drizzt and Innovindil before their pegasus, Sunset, had even set them down on the rocky mountain slope. The place was deserted, fully so, even though the orcs were not far away. The couple could hear them in the valley beyond the slope's crest, the region called Keeper's Dale, which marked the western entrance to Mithral Hall. The dwarves had not won there, Drizzt knew, despite the fact that orc bodies outnumbered those of his bearded friends many times over. In the end, the orcs had pushed them from the cliff and into Keeper's Dale, and back into their hole in Mithral Hall. The orcs had paid dearly for that piece of ground, but it was theirs. Given the sheer size of the orc force assembled outside the closed door of Clan Battlehammer's stronghold, Drizzt simply couldn't see how the dwarves might ever win the ground back.

"They have not looted only because the battle is not yet over," Drizzt replied. "There has been no pause until now for the orcs, first in pushing the dwarves back into Mithral Hall, then in preparing the area around the western gates to their liking. They will return here soon enough, I expect."

He glanced over at Innovindil to see her distracted and standing before the remains of a particularly nasty fight, staring down at a clump of bodies. Drizzt understood her surprise before he even went over and confirmed that she was standing where he had watched the battleragers, the famed Gutbuster Brigade, make a valiant stand. He walked up beside the elf, wincing at the gruesome sight of shredded bodies—never had there been anything subtle about Thibbledorf Pwent's boys—and wincing even more when he caught sight of more than a dozen dead dwarves, all tightly packed together. They had died, one and all, protecting each other, a fitting end indeed for the brave warriors.

"Their armor . . ." Innovindil began, shaking her head, her expression caught somewhere between surprise, awe, and disgust.

She didn't have to say anything more for Drizzt to perfectly understand, for the armor of the Gutbusters often elicited such confusion. Ridged and overlapping with sharpened plates, and sprouting an abundance of deadly spikes, Gutbuster armor made a dwarf's body into a devastating weapon. Where other dwarves charged with pickaxes, battle-axes, warhammers, and swords held high, Gutbusters just charged.

Drizzt thought to inspect the area a bit more closely, to see if his old friend Thibbledorf might be among the dead, but he decided against that course. Better for him, he thought, to just continue on his way. Counting the dead was an exercise for after the war.

Of course, that same attitude allowed Drizzt to justify his inability to return to Clan Battlehammer and truly face the realization that his friends were all gone, killed at the town of Shallows.

"Let us get to the ridge," he said. "We should learn the source of that explosion before Obould's minions return here to pick the bodies clean."

Innovindil readily agreed and started toward the blasted line of stone.

Had she and Drizzt moved only twenty more paces up toward the lip of Keeper's Dale, they would have found another telltale formation of bodies: orcs, some lying three in a row, dead and showing only a single burned hole for injuries.

Drizzt Do'Urden knew of a weapon, a bow named Taulmaril, that inflicted such wounds, a bow held by his friend Catti-brie, whom he thought dead at Shallows.

The dwarf Nikwillig sat on the east-facing side of a mountain, slumped against the stone and fighting against such desperation and despair that he feared he would be frozen him in place until starvation or some wayward orc took him. He took comfort in knowing that he had done his duty well, and that his expedition to the peaks east of the battlefield had helped to turn the tide of the raging conflict—at least enough so that Banak Brawnanvil had

managed to get the great majority of dwarves down the cliff face and safely into Mithral Hall ahead of the advancing orc horde.

That moment of triumph played over and over in the weary dwarf's mind, a litany against the pressing fears of his current predicament. He had climbed the slopes higher than the combatants while the field of battle remained blanketed in pre-dawn darkness, had turned his attention, and the mirror he carried, to the rising sun. He had angled a reflected ray from that mirror back against the slope of the ridge across the way, until he had located the second mirror placed there, brilliantly illuminating the target for Catti-brie and her enchanted bow.

Then Nikwillig had watched darkness turn to sudden light, a flare of fire that had risen a thousand feet over the battlefield. Like a ripple in a pond or a burst of wind bending a field of grass, the waves of hot wind and debris had rolled out from that monumental explosion, sweeping the northern reaches of the battlefield where the majority of orcs were beginning their charge. They had gone down in rows, many never to rise again. Their charge had been all but stopped, exactly as the dwarves had hoped.

So Nikwillig had done his job, but even when he'd left, hoping for exactly that outcome, the Felbarran dwarf had known his chances of returning were not good. Banak and the others certainly couldn't wait for him to scramble back down—even if they had wanted to, how would Nikwillig have ever gotten through the swarm of orcs between him and the dwarves?

Nikwillig had left the dwarven ranks on a suicide mission that day, and he held no regrets, but that didn't dismiss the very real fears that huddled around him as the time of his death seemed near at hand.

He thought of Tred, then, his comrade from Felbarr. They, along with several companions, had started out on a bright day from the Citadel of King Emerus Warcrown not so long ago in a typical merchant caravan. While their route was somewhat different than the norm, as they tried to secure a new trading line for both King Emerus and their own pockets, they hadn't expected any real trouble. Certainly, they never expected to walk into the front scouts of the greatest orc assault the region had seen in memory! Nikwillig wondered what might have happened to Tred. Had he fallen in the vicious fight? Or had he gotten down into Keeper's Dale and into Mithral Hall?

The forlorn dwarf gave a helpless little laugh as he considered that Tred had previously decided to walk out of Mithral Hall and return home with the news to Citadel Felbarr. Toughened, war-hardened, and battle-eager Tred had thought to serve as emissary between the two fortresses and in the ultimate irony, Nikwillig had dissuaded him.

"Ah, ye're such the fool, Nikwillig," the dwarf said into the mournful wind.

He didn't really believe the words even as he spoke them. He had stayed, Tred had stayed, because they had decided they were indebted to King Bruenor and his kin, because they had decided that the war was about the solidarity of the *Delzoun* dwarves, about standing together, shoulder-to-shoulder, in common cause.

No, he hadn't been a fool for staying, and hadn't been a fool for volunteering, insisting even, that he be the one to go out with the mirror and grab those first rays of dawn. He wasn't a warrior, after all. He had walked willingly and rightly into this predicament, but he knew that the road ahead was likely to come to a fast and vicious ending.

The dwarf pulled himself to his feet. He glanced back over his shoulder toward Keeper's Dale, and again dismissed any thoughts of going that way. Certainly that was the closest entrance to Mithral Hall and safety, but to get to it meant crossing a massive orc encampment. Even if he somehow managed that feat, the dwarves were in their hole and those doors were closed, and weren't likely to open anytime soon.

So east it was, Nikwillig decided. To the River Surbrin and hopefully, against all odds, beyond.

He thought he heard a sound nearby and imagined that an orc patrol was likely watching him even then, ready to spring upon him and batter him to death. He took a deep breath. He put one foot in front of the other.

He started his dark journey.

Drizzt and Innovindil veered to the south as they headed for the blasted ridge, angling their march so that they came in sight of Keeper's Dale right near to the spot where the line of metal tubes had been placed by the dwarves. That line ran up from the ground to the entrance of the tunnels that wound

beneath what was once a ridgeline. Of course neither of them understood what that pipeline was all about. Neither had any idea that the dwarves, at the instructions of Nanfoodle the gnome, had brought natural gasses up from their underground entrapment, filling the tunnels beneath the unwitting giants and their catapults.

Perhaps if the pair had been granted more time to ponder the pipeline, to climb down the cliff and inspect it more closely, Drizzt and Innovindil would have begun to decipher the mystery of the gigantic fireball. At that moment, however, the fireball seemed the least of their issues. For below them swarmed the largest army of orcs either had ever seen, a virtual sea of dark forms milling around the obelisks that marked Keeper's Dale. Thousands, tens of thousands, moved down there, their indistinct mass occasionally marked by the larger form of a hulking frost giant.

As he scanned across the throng, Drizzt Do'Urden picked out more and more of those larger monsters, and he sucked in his breath as he came to realize the scope of the army. Hundreds of giants were down there, as if the entire population of behemoths from all the Spine of the World had emptied out to the call of King Obould.

"Have the Silver Marches known a darker day?" Innovindil asked.

Drizzt turned to regard her, though he wasn't sure if she was actually asking him or simply making a remark.

Innovindil swung her head to meet his lavender-eyed gaze. "I remember when Obould managed to rout the dwarves from Citadel Felbarr," she explained. "And what a dark day that was! But still, the orc king seemed to have traded one hole for another. While his conquest had played terribly on King Emerus Warcrown and the other Felbarran dwarves, never was it viewed as any threat to the wider region. The orc king had seized upon an unexpected opportunity, and so he had prevailed in a victory that we all expected would be short-lived, as it was. But now this. . . ." Her voice trailed off and she shook her head helplessly as she looked back to the dale and the massive orc army.

"We can guess that most of the dwarves of Clan Battlehammer managed to get back into their tunnels," Drizzt reasoned. "They'll not be easily routed, I assure you. In their chambers, Clan Battlehammer once repulsed an attack by Menzoberranzan. I doubt there are enough orcs in all the world to take the hall."

"You may be right, but does that even matter?"

Drizzt looked at the elf curiously. He started to ask how it might not matter, but as he came to fully understand Innovindil's fears, he held the question in check.

"No," he agreed, "this force Obould has assembled will not be easily pushed back into their mountain holes. It will take Silverymoon and Everlund, and perhaps even Sundabar . . . Citadels Felbarr and Adbar, and Mithral Hall. It will take the Moonwood elves and the army of Marchion Elastul of Mirabar. All the north must rally to the call of Mithral Hall in this, their hour of need."

"And even in that case, the cost will prove enormous," Innovindil replied. "Horrific." She glanced back to the bloody, carcass-ridden battlefield. "This fight here on the ridge will seem a minor skirmish and fat will the crows of the Silver Marches be."

Drizzt continued his scan as she spoke, and he noted movement down to the west, quickly discerning it as a force of orcs circling up and out of Keeper's Dale.

"The orc scavengers will soon arrive," he said. "Let us be on our way."

Innovindil stared down at Keeper's Dale a bit longer.

"No sign of Sunrise," she remarked, referring to the pegasus companion of Sunset, and once the mount of Tarathiel, her companion.

"Obould still has him, and alive, I am sure," Drizzt replied. "Even an orc would not destroy so magnificent a creature."

Innovindil continued to stare and managed a little hunch of her shoulders, then turned to face Drizzt directly again. "Let us hope."

Drizzt rose, took her hand, and together they walked down toward the north, along the ridge of blasted and broken stones. The explosion had lifted the roof of the ridge away, leaving a scarred ravine behind. Every now and again, the couple came upon the remains of a charred giant. In one place, they found a burned out catapult, somehow still retaining its shape despite the tremendous blast.

Their discoveries prompted more questions than they answered, however, leaving the pair no clue whatsoever as to what might have caused such a cataclysm.

"When we at last find our way into Mithral Hall, you can ask the dwarves

about it," Innovindil said when they were far from the field, on an open plateau awaiting the return of the winged Sunset.

Drizzt didn't respond to the elf's direct implication that he would indeed soon return to the dwarven stronghold—where he would have no choice but to face his fears—other than to offer a quiet nod.

"Some trick of the gods, perhaps," the elf went on.

"Or the Harpells," Drizzt added, referring to a family of eccentric and powerful wizards—too powerful for their own good, or for the good of those around them, in most cases!— from the small community of Longsaddle many miles to the west. The Harpells had come to the aid of Mithral Hall before, and had a long-standing friendship with Bruenor and his kin. Drizzt knew enough about them to realize that if anyone might have inadvertently caused such a catastrophe as befell the ridge, it would be that strange clan of confused humans.

"Harpells?"

"You do not want to know," Drizzt said in all seriousness. "Suffice it to say that Bruenor Battlehammer has made some unconventional friends."

As soon as he had spoken the words, Drizzt recognized the irony of them, and he managed a smile to match Innovindil's own widening grin as he glanced at her.

"We will know soon enough on all counts," she said. "For now, we have duties of our own to attend."

"For Sunrise," Drizzt agreed and he shook Innovindil's offered hand. "And for vengeance. Tarathiel will rest easier when Obould Many-Arrows is dead."

"Dead at the tip of a sword?" Innovindil asked, putting a hand to the hilt of her own weapon. "Or at the curve of a scimitar?"

"A scimitar, I think," Drizzt answered without the slightest hesitation, and he looked back to the south. "I do intend to kill that one."

"For Tarathiel, and for Bruenor, then," said Innovindil. "For those who have died and for the good of the North."

"Or simply because I want to kill him," said Drizzt in a tone so cold and even that it sent a shiver along Innovindil's spine.

She could not find the voice to answer.

3

PASSION

With a growl that seemed more anger than passion, Tsinka Shinriil rolled Obould over and scrambled atop him.

"You have put them in their dark hole!" the female shaman cried, her eyes wide—so wide that the yellow-white of her eyes showed clearly all around her dark pupils, giving her an expression that seemed more a caricature of insanity than anything else. "Now we dig into that hole!"

King Obould Many-Arrows easily held the excited shaman at bay as she tried to engulf him with her trembling body, his thick, muscular arms lifting her from the straw bed.

"Mithral Hall will fall to the might of Obould-who-is-Gruumsh," Tsinka went on. "And Citadel Felbarr will be yours once more, soon after. We will have them all! We will slay the minions of Bruenor and Emerus! We will bathe in their blood!"

Obould gave a slight shrug and moved the shaman off to the side, off the cot itself. She hit the floor nimbly, and came right back, drool showing at the edges of her tusky mouth.

"Is there anything Obould-who-is-Gruumsh cannot conquer?" she asked, squirming atop him again. "Mithral Hall, Felbarr . . . Adbar! Yes, Adbar! They will all fall before us. Every dwarven stronghold in the North! We will

send them fleeing, those few who we do not devour. We will rid the North of the dwarven curse."

Obould managed a smile, but it was more to mock the priestess than to agree with her. He'd heard her litany before—over and over again, actually. Ever since the western door of Mithral Hall had banged closed, sealing Clan Battlehammer into their hole, Tsinka and the other shamans had been spouting preposterous hopes for massive conquests all throughout the Silver Marches and beyond.

And Obould shared that hope. He wanted nothing more than to reclaim the Citadel of Many Arrows, which the dwarves had named Citadel Felbarr once more. But Obould saw the folly in that course. The entire region had been alerted to them. Crossing the Surbrin would mean engaging the armies of Silverymoon and Everlund, certainly, along with the elves of the Moonwood and the combined forces of the *Delzoun* dwarves east of the deep, cold river.

"You are Gruumsh!" Tsinka said. She grabbed Obould's face and kissed him roughly. "You are a god among orcs!" She kissed him again. "Gerti Orelsdottr fears you!" Tsinka shrieked and kissed him yet again.

Obould grinned, rekindling the memory of his last encounter with the frost giant princess. Gerti did indeed fear him, or she certainly should, for Obould had bested her in their short battle, had tossed her to the ground and sent her slinking away. It was a feat previously unheard of, and only served to illustrate to all who had seen it, and to all who heard about it, that King Obould was much more than a mere orc. He was in the favor of Gruumsh One-Eye, the god of orcs. He had been blessed with strength and speed, with uncanny agility, and he believed, with more insight than ever before.

Or perhaps that new insight wasn't new at all. Perhaps Obould, in his current position, unexpectedly gaining all the ground between the Spine of the World, the Fell Pass, the River Surbrin, and the Trollmoors with such ease and overwhelming power, was simply viewing the world from a different, and much superior, position.

". . . into Mithral Hall . . ." Tsinka was saying when Obould turned his attention back to the babbling shaman. Apparently noting his sudden attention, she paused and rewound the thought. "We must go into Mithral Hall before the winter. We must rout Clan Battlehammer so the word of their defeat and humiliation will spread before the snows block the passes. We will work the dwarven forges throughout the winter to strengthen our armor and weapons. We will emerge in the spring an unstoppable force, rolling across the northland and laying waste to all who foolishly stand before us!"

"We lost many orcs driving the dwarves underground," Obould said, trying to steal some of her momentum. "The stones are colored with orc blood."

"Blood well spilled!" Tsinka shrieked. "And more will die! More must die! Our first great victory is at hand!"

"Our first great victory is achieved," Obould corrected.

"Then our second is before us!" Tsinka shouted right back at him. "And the victory worthy of He-who-is-Gruumsh. We have taken stones and empty ground. The prize is yet to be had."

Obould pushed her back out to arms' length and turned his head a bit to better regard her. She was shaking again, though be it from passion or anger, he could not tell. Her naked body shone in the torchlight with layers of sweat. Her muscles stood on edge, corded and trembling, like a spring too tightly twisted.

"Mithral Hall must fall before the winter," Tsinka said, more calmly than before. "Gruumsh has shown this to me. It was Bruenor Battlehammer who stood upon that stone, breaking the tide of orcs and denying us a greater victory."

Obould growled at the name.

"Word has spread throughout the land that he lives. The King of Mithral Hall has risen from the dead, it would seem. That is Moradin's challenge to Gruumsh, do you not see? You are Gruumsh's champion, of that there is no doubt, and King Bruenor Battlehammer champions Moradin. Settle this and settle it quickly, you must, before the dwarves rally to Moradin's call as the orcs have rallied to Obould!"

The words hit Obould hard, for they made more sense than he wanted to admit. He wasn't keen on going into Mithral Hall. He knew that his army would suffer difficult obstacles every inch of the way. Could he sustain such horrific losses and still hope to secure the land he meant to be his kingdom?

But indeed, word had spread through the deep orc ranks like a windswept fire across dry grass. There was no denying the identity of the dwarf who had centered the defensive line in the retreat to the hall. It was Bruenor, thought dead at Shallows. It was Bruenor, returned from the grave.

Obould was not so stupid as to underestimate the importance of that development. He understood how greatly his presence spurred on his own warriors—could Bruenor be any less inspiring to the dwarves? Obould hated dwarves above all other races, even elves, but his bitter experiences at Citadel Felbarr had given him a grudging respect for the stout bearded folk. He had taken Felbarr at an opportune moment, and with a great deal of the element of surprise on his side, but now, if Tsinka had her way, he would be taking his forces into a defended and prepared dwarven fortress.

Was any race in all of Toril better at defending their homes than the dwarves?

The drow, perhaps, he thought, and the notion sent his contemplations flowing to events in the south, where two dark elves were supposedly helping ugly Proffit and his trolls press Mithral Hall from the south. Obould realized that that would be the key to victory if he decided to crash into Mithral Hall. If Proffit and his smelly beasts could siphon off a fair number of Bruenor's warriors, and any amount of Bruenor's attention, a bold strike straight though Mithral Hall's closed western door might gain Obould a foothold within.

The orc king looked back at Tsinka and realized that he was wearing his thoughts on his face, so to speak. For she was grinning in her toothy way, her dark eyes roiling with eagerness—for conquest, and for Obould. The great orc king lowered his arms, bringing Tsinka down atop him, and let his plans slip from his thoughts. He held onto the image of dead dwarves and crumbling dwarven doors, though, for Obould found those sights perfectly intoxicating.

The cold wind made every jolt hurt just a little bit more, but Obould gritted his teeth and clamped his legs more tightly against the bucking pegasus. The white equine creature had its wings strapped tightly back. Obould wasn't about to let it get him up off the ground, for the pegasus was not broken at all as far as the orcs were concerned. Obould had seen the elf riding the creature, so easily, but every orc who'd climbed atop the pegasus had been thrown far away, and more than one had subsequently been trampled by the beast before the handlers could get the creature under control.

Every orc thus far had been thrown, except for Obould, whose legs clamped so powerfully at the pegasus's sides that the creature had not yet dislodged him.

Up came the horse's rump, and Obould's body rolled back, his neck painfully whipping and his head turning so far over that he actually saw, upside down, the pegasus's rear hooves snap up in the air at the end of the buck! His hand grabbed tighter at the thick rope and he growled and clamped his legs against the mount's flanks, so tightly that he figured he would crush the creature's ribs.

But the pegasus kept on bucking; leaping, twisting, and kicking wildly. Obould found a rhythm in the frenzy, though, and gradually began to snap and jerk just a little less fiercely.

The pegasus began to slow in its gyrations and the orc king grinned at his realization that the beast was finally tiring. He took that moment to relax, just a bit, and smiled even more widely as he compared the pegasus's wild gyrations to those of Tsinka the night before. A fitting comparison, he lewdly thought.

Then he was flying, free of the pegasus's back, as the creature went into a sudden and violent frenzy. Obould hit the ground hard, face down and twisted, but he grunted it away and forced himself into a roll that allowed him to quickly regain some of his dignity, if not his feet. He looked around in alarm for just a moment, thinking that his grand exit might have lessened his image in the eyes of those nearby orcs. Indeed, they all stared at him incredulously—or stupidly, he could not tell the difference—and with such surprise that the handlers didn't even move for the pegasus.

And the equine beast came for the fallen orc king.

Obould put a wide grin on his face and leaped to his feet, arms wide, and gave a great roar, inviting the pegasus to battle.

The steed stopped short, and snorted and pawed the ground.

Obould began to laugh, shattering the tension, and he stalked right at the pegasus as if daring it to strike at him. The pegasus put its ears back and tensed up.

"Perhaps I should eat you," Obould said calmly, walking right up to the beast and staring it directly in the eye, which of course only set the pegasus even more on edge. "Yes, your flesh will taste tender, I am sure."

The orc king stared down the pegasus for a few moments longer, then swung around and gave a great laugh, and all the orcs nearby took up the cheer.

As soon as he was confident that he had restored any lost dignity, Obould turned back to the pegasus and thought again of Tsinka. He laughed all the louder as he mentally superimposed the equine face over that of the fierce and eager shaman, but while the snout and larger features greatly changed, it seemed to him that, other than the white about the edges of Tsinka's iris, their eyes were very much the same. Same intensity, same tension. Same wild and uncontrollable emotions.

No, not the same, Obould came to recognize, for while Tsinka's gyrations and sparkling eyes were wrought of passion and ecstasy, the winged horse's frenzy came from fear.

No, not fear—the notion hit Obould suddenly—not fear. It was no wild animal, just captured and in need of breaking. The mount had been ridden for years, and by elves, riders whose legs were too spindly to begin to hold if the pegasus didn't want them to stay on.

The pegasus's intensity came not from fear, but from sheer hatred.

"O, smart beast," Obould said softly, and the pegasus's ears came up and flattened again, as if it understood every word. "You hold loyalty to your master and hatred for me, who killed him. You will fight me forever if I try to climb onto your back, will you not?"

The orc king nodded and narrowed his eyes to closely scrutinize the pegasus.

"Or will you?" he asked, and his mind went in a different direction, as if he was seeing things from the pegasus's point of view.

The creature had purposefully lulled him into complacency up there on its back. It had seemingly calmed, and just when Obould had relaxed, it had gone wild again.

"You are not as clever as you believe," Obould said to the pegasus. "You should have waited until you had me up into the clouds before throwing me from your back. You should have made me believe that I was your master." The orc snorted, and wondered what pegasus flesh would taste like.

The handlers got the winged horse into complete control soon after, and the leader of the group turned to Obould and asked, "Will you be riding again this day, my god?"

Obould snickered at the ridiculous title, though he wouldn't openly discourage its use, and shook his head. "Much I have to do," he said.

He noted one of the orcs roughly tying the pegasus's back legs together. "Enough!" he ordered, and the orc gang froze in place. "Treat the beast gently now, with due respect."

That brought a few incredulous expressions.

"Find new handlers!" Obould barked at the gang leader. "A soft touch for the mount now. No beatings!"

Even as he spoke the words, Obould saw the error of distracting the crew, for the pegasus lurched suddenly, shrugging a pair of orcs aside, then kicked out hard, scoring a solid hit on the forehead of the unfortunate orc who had been tying its hind legs. That orc flew away and began squirming on the ground and wailing piteously.

The other orcs instinctively moved to punish the beast, but Obould overruled that with a great shout of, *"Enough!"*

He stared directly at the pegasus, then again at the orc leader. "Any mark I find on this beast will be replicated on your own hide," he promised.

When the gang leader shrank down, visibly trembling, Obould knew his work was done. With a sidelong look of contempt at the badly injured fool still squirming on the ground, Obould walked away.

The surprise on the face of the frost giant sentries—fifteen feet tall, handsome, shapely behemoths—was no less than Obould had left behind with his orc companions when he'd informed them, to the shrill protests of Tsinka Shinriil among others, that he would visit Gerti Orelsdottr alone. There was no doubt about the bad blood between Gerti and Obould. In their last encounter, Obould had knocked the giantess to the ground, embarrassing and outraging her.

Obould kept his head high and his eyes straight ahead—and he wasn't even wearing the marvelously protective helmet that the shamans had somehow fashioned for him. Giants loomed all around him, many carrying swords that were taller than the orc king. As he neared the entrance to the huge cave Gerti had taken as temporary residence far south of her mountain home, the giant

guards shifted to form a gauntlet before him. Two lines of sneering, imposing brutes glared down at him from every angle. As he passed them, the giants behind him turned in and followed, closing any possible escape route.

Obould let his greatsword rest easily on his back, kept his chin high, and even managed a grin to convey his confidence. He knew that he was surrendering the high ground, physically, but he knew, too, that he had to do just that to gain the high ground emotionally.

He noted a flurry of commotion just inside the cave, with huge shapes moving this way and that. And when he entered, his eyes adjusting to the sudden change of light as daylight diminished to the glow of just a few torches, he found that he didn't have to search far to gain his intended audience. Gerti Orelsdottr, beautiful and terrible by frost giant standards, stood at the back, eyeing him with something that seemed a cross of suspicion and contempt.

"It would seem that you have forgotten your entourage, King Obould," she said, and it seemed to Obould that she had weighted her voice with a hint of a threat.

He remained confident that she wouldn't act against him, though. He had defeated her in single combat, had, in effect, shamed her, and greater would her shame be among her people if she set others upon him in retribution. Obould didn't completely understand the frost giants, of course—his experiences with them were fairly limited—but he knew them to be legitimate warriors, and warriors almost always shared certain codes of honor.

Gerti's words had many of the giants in the room chuckling and whispering.

"I speak for all the thousands," the orc king replied. "As Dame Orelsdottr speaks for the frost giants of the Spine of the World."

Gerti straightened and narrowed her huge blue eyes—orbs that seemed all the richer in hue because of the bluish tint to the giantess's skin. "Then speak, King Obould. I have many preparations before me and little time to waste."

Obould let his posture relax, wanting to seem perfectly at ease. From the murmurs around him, he took satisfaction that he had hit just the right physical timbre. "We have achieved a great victory here, Dame Orelsdottr. We have taken the northland in as great a sweep as has ever been known."

"Our enemies have barely begun to rise against us," Gerti pointed out.

Obould conceded the point with a nod. "Do not deny our progress, I pray you," he said. "We have closed both doors of Mithral Hall. Nesmé is likely destroyed and the Surbrin secured. This is not the time for us to allow our alliance to . . ." He paused and slowly swiveled his head so that he spent a moment looking every giant in the room directly in the eye.

"Dame Orelsdottr, I speak for the orcs. Tens of thousands of orcs." He put added weight into that last, impressive, estimate. "You speak for the giants. Let us go to parlay in private."

Gerti assumed a pose that Obould had seen many times before, one both obstinate and pensive. She put one hand on her hip and turned, just enough to let her shapely legs escape the slit in her white dress, and she let her lips form into a pucker that might have been a pout and might have been that last moment of teasing before she reached out and throttled an enemy.

Obould answered that with a bow of respect.

"Come along," Gerti bade him, and when the giant nearest her started to protest, she silenced him with one of the fiercest scowls Obould had ever seen.

Yes, it was going splendidly, the orc king thought.

At Gerti's bidding, Obould followed her down a short corridor. The orc took a moment to study the walls that had been widened by the giants, obviously, with new cuts in the stone clearly showing. The ceiling, too, was much more than a natural formation, with all the low points chipped out so that the tallest of Gerti's minions could walk the length of the corridor without stooping. Impressive work, Obould thought, especially given the efficiency and speed with which it had been accomplished. He hadn't realized that the giants were so good at shaping the stone quickly, a revelation that he figured might be useful if he did indeed crash the gates into Mithral Hall.

The chamber at the end of the hall was obviously Gerti's own, for it was blocked by a heavy wooden door and appointed with many thick and lush bearskins. Gerti pointedly kicked several aside, leaving a spot of bare stone floor, and indicated that to be Obould's seat.

The orc king didn't question or complain, and was smiling still when he melted down to sit cross-legged, drawing out his greatsword as he descended. Its impressive length would not allow him to sit in that position with it still on his back. He lay the blade across his crossed legs, in easy reach, but he relaxed back and kept his hands far from it, offering not the slightest bit of a threat.

Gerti watched his every move closely, he recognized, though she was

trying to feign indifference as she moved to close the door. She strode across the room to the thickest pile of furs and demurely sat herself down, which still had her towering over the lower-seated and much smaller orc king.

"What do you want of me, Obould?" Gerti bluntly asked, her tone short and crisp, her eyes unblinking.

"We were angered, both of us, at the return of King Bruenor and the loss of a great opportunity," Obould replied.

"At the loss of frost giants."

"And orcs for me—more than a thousand of my kin, my own son among them."

"Are not worth a single of my kin to me," Gerti replied.

Obould accepted the insult quietly, reminding himself to think long-term and not jump up and slaughter the witch.

"The dwarves value their kin no less than do we, Dame Orelsdottr," he said. "They claim no victory here."

"Many escaped."

"To a hole that has become a prison. To tunnels that perhaps already reek with the stench of troll."

"If Donnia Soldou and Ad'non Kareese were not dead, perhaps we could better sort out information concerning Proffit and his wretches," said Gerti, referring to two of the four drow elves who had been serving as advisors and scouts to her and to Obould, both of whom had been found dead north of their current position.

"Do you lament their deaths?"

The question gave Gerti pause, and she even betrayed her surprise with a temporary lift of her evenly trimmed eyebrows.

"They were using us for their own enjoyment and nothing more, you know that of course," Obould remarked.

Again, Gerti cocked her eyebrow, but held it there longer.

"Surprised?" the orc king added.

"They are drow," Gerti said. "They serve only themselves and their own desires. Of course I knew. Only a fool would have ever suspected differently."

But you are surprised that I knew, Obould thought, but did not say.

"And if the other two die with Proffit in the south, then so much the better," said Gerti.

"After we are done with them," said Obould. "The remaining drow will prove important if we intend to break through the defenses of Mithral Hall."

"Break through the defenses?"

Obould could hardly miss the incredulity in her voice, or the obvious doubt.

"I would take the hall."

"Your orcs will be slaughtered by the thousands."

"Whatever price we must pay will be worth the gain," Obould said, and he had to work hard to keep the very real doubts out of his voice. "We must continue to press our enemies before they can organize and coordinate their attacks. We have them on their heels, and I do not mean to allow them firm footing. And I will have Bruenor Battlehammer's head, at long last."

"You will crawl over the bodies of orcs to get to him, then, but not the bodies of frost giants."

Obould accepted that with a nod, confident that if he managed to take the upper tunnels of Mithral Hall, Gerti would fall into line.

"I need your kin only to break through the outer shell," he said.

"There are ways to dislodge the greatest of doors," an obviously and suddenly intrigued Gerti remarked.

"The sooner you crack the shell, the sooner I will have King Bruenor's head."

Gerti chuckled and nodded her agreement. Obould realized, of course, that she was likely more intrigued by the prospect of ten thousand dead orcs than of any defeat to the dwarves.

Obould used the great strength in his legs to lift him up from his seated position, to stand straight, as he swept his sword back over his shoulder and into its sheath. He returned Gerti's nod and walked out, holding fast to his cocky swagger as he passed through the waiting lines of giant guards.

Despite that calm and confident demeanor, though, Obould's insides churned. Gerti would swing into swift action, of course, and Obould had little doubt that she would deliver him and his army into the hall, but even as he pondered the execution of his request, the thought of it gnawed at him. Once again, Obould envisioned orc fortresses dotting every hilltop of the region, with defensible walls forcing any attackers to scramble for every inch of ground. How many dwarves and elves and humans would have to lie dead

among those hilltops before the wretched triumvirate gave up their thoughts of dislodging him and accepted his conquest as final? How many dwarves and elves and humans would Obould have to kill before his orcs were allowed their kingdom and their share of the bounty of the wider world?

Many, he hoped, for he so enjoyed killing dwarves, elves, and humans.

As he exited the cave and was afforded a fairly wide view of the northern expanses, Obould let his gaze meander over each stony mountain and wind-blown slope. His mind's eye built those castles, all flying the pennants of the One-Eyed God and of King Many-Arrows. In the shadows below them, in the sheltered dells, he envisioned towns—towns like Shallows, sturdy and secure, only inhabited by orcs and not smelly humans. He began to draw connections, trade routes and responsibilities, riches and power, respect and influence.

It would work, Obould believed. He could carve out his kingdom and secure it beyond any hopes the dwarves, elves, and humans might ever hold of dislodging him.

The orc king glanced back at Gerti's cave, and considered for a fleeting moment the possibility of going in and telling her. He even half-turned and started to take a step that way.

He stopped, though, thinking that Gerti would not appreciate the weight of his vision, nor care much for the end result. And even if she did, Obould realized, how might Tsinka and the shamans react? Tsinka was calling for conquest and not settlement, and she claimed to hold in her ears the voice of Gruumsh himself.

Obould's upper lip curled in frustration, and he let his clenched fist rise up beside him. He hadn't lied to Gerti. He wanted nothing more than to hold Bruenor Battlehammer's heart in his hands.

But was it possible, and was the prize, as he had claimed, really worth the no-doubt horrific cost?

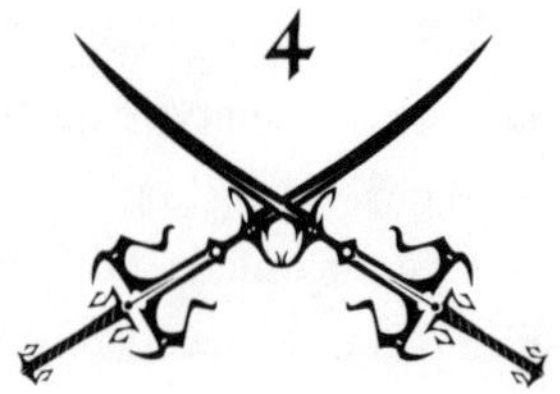

4

A KING'S EYE VIEW

To all in the chamber, the torchlight did not seem so bright, its flickering flames did not dance so joyously. Perhaps it was the realization that the doors were closed and that the meager light was all that separated the whole of the great dwarven complex of Mithral Hall from absolute darkness. The dwarves and others could get out, of course. They had tunnels that led to the south and the edge of the Trollmoors, though there had reportedly been some fighting down there already. They had tunnels that would take them as far west as Mirabar, and right under the River Surbrin to the east, to places like Citadel Felbarr. None of those were easy routes, though, and all involved breaking into that vast labyrinth known as the Underdark, the place of dark denizens and untold horrors.

So Mithral Hall seemed a darker place, and the torches less inviting, and less frequent. King Bruenor had already ordered conservation, preparing himself for what surely seemed to be a long, long siege.

Bruenor sat on a throne of stone, thickly padded with rich green and purple cloth. His great and wild beard seemed more orange than red under the artificial lighting, perhaps because those long hairs had become noticeably more infested with strands of gray since the dwarf king's ordeal. For many days, Bruenor had lain close to death. Even the greatest clerics of Mithral Hall had

only thought him alive through their nearly continual healing spells, cast upon a body, they believed, whose host had forsaken it. Bruenor, the essence of the dwarf, his very soul, had gone to his just reward in the Halls of Moradin, by the reckoning of the priests. And there, so it was supposed, Regis the halfling steward had found him, using the magic of his enchanted ruby pendant. Regis had caught what little flicker of life remaining in Bruenor's eyes and somehow used the magic to send his thoughts and his pleas for Bruenor to return to the land of the living.

For no king would lie so still if he knew that his people were in such dire need.

Thus had Bruenor returned, and the dwarves had found their way home, albeit over the bodies of many fallen comrades.

Those gray hairs seemed to all who knew him well to be the only overt sign of Bruenor's ordeal. His dark eyes still sparkled with energy and his square shoulders promised to carry the whole of Mithral Hall upon them, if need be. He was bandaged in a dozen places, for in the last retreat into the hall, he had suffered terrible wounds—injuries that would have felled a lesser dwarf—but if any of those wounds caused him the slightest discomfort, he did not show it.

He was dressed in his battle-worn armor, creased and torn and scratched, and had his prized shield, emblazoned with the foaming mug standard of his clan, resting against the side of his throne, his battle-axe leaning atop it and showing the notches of its seasons, chips from stone, armor, and ogre skulls alike.

"All who seen yer blast just shake their heads when they try to describe it," Bruenor said to Nanfoodle Buswilligan, the gnome alchemist from Mirabar.

Nanfoodle stepped nervously from foot to foot, and that only made the stout dwarf lean closer to him.

"Come on now, little one," Bruenor coaxed. "We got no time for humility nor nervousness. Ye done great, by all accounts, and all in the hall're bowing to ye in respect. Ye stand tall among us, don't ye know?"

Nanfoodle did seem to straighten a bit at that, tilting his head back slightly so that he looked up at the imposing dwarf upon the dais. Nanfoodle twitched again as his long, crooked, pointy nose actually brushed Bruenor's similarly imposing proboscis.

"What'd ye do?" Bruenor asked him again. "They're saying ye brought hot air up from under Keeper's Dale."

"I . . . *we* . . ." Nanfoodle corrected, and he turned to regard some of the others, including Pikel Bouldershoulder, the most unusual dwarf who had come from Carradoon on the shores of faraway Impresk Lake.

Nanfoodle nodded as Pikel smiled widely and punched his one fist up into the air, mouthing a silent, "Oo oi!"

The gnome cleared his throat and turned back squarely upon Bruenor, who settled back in his chair. "We used metal tubing to bring the hot air up from below, yes," the gnome confirmed. "Torgar Hammerstriker and his boys cleared the tunnels under the ridge of orcs and painted it tight with pitch. We just directed the hot air into those tunnels, and when Catti-brie's arrow ignited it all . . ."

"Boom!" shouted Pikel Bouldershoulder, and all eyes turned to him in surprise.

"Hee hee hee," the green-bearded Pikel said with a shy shrug, and all the grim folk in the room joined in on the much-needed laugh.

It proved a short respite, though, the weight of their situation quickly pressing back upon them.

"Well, ye done good, gnome," Bruenor said. "Ye saved many o' me kin, and that's from the mouth o' Banak Brawnanvil himself. And he's not one to throw praise undeserved."

"We—Shoudra and I—felt the need to prove ourselves, King Bruenor," said Nanfoodle. "And we wanted to help, any way we could. Your people have shown such generosity to Torgar and Shingles, and all the other Mirabarran—"

"Mirabarran, no more," came a voice, Torgar's voice, from the side. "We are Battlehammer now, one and all. We name not Marchion Elastul as our enemy, unless an enemy he makes of us, but neither are we loyal to the throne of Mirabar. Nay, our hearts, our souls, our fists, our hammers, for King Bruenor!"

A great cheer went up in the hall, started by the dozen or so formerly Mirabarran dwarves in attendance, and taken up by all standing around the room.

Bruenor basked in that communal glow for a bit, welcoming it as a needed

ray of light on that dark day. And indeed, the day was dark in Mithral Hall, as dark as the corridors of the Underdark, as dark as a drow priestess's heart. Despite the efforts, the sacrifice, the gallantry of all the dwarves, of Catti-brie and Wulfgar, despite the wise choices of Regis in his time as steward, they had been put in their hole, sealed in their tunnels, by a foe that Mithral Hall could not hope to overcome on an open field of battle. Hundreds of Bruenor's kin were dead, and more than a third of the Mirabarran refugees had fallen.

Bruenor had entertained a line of important figures that day, from Tred McKnuckles of Felbarr, stung by the loss of his dear friend Nikwillig, to the Bouldershoulder brothers, Ivan and the indomitable Pikel, giggling always and full of cheer despite the loss of his arm. Bruenor had gone to see Banak Brawnanvil, the warcommander who had so brilliantly held the high ground north of Keeper's Dale for days on end against impossible odds. For Banak could not come to him. Sorely wounded in the final escape, insisting on being the last off the cliff, Banak no longer had any use of his legs. An orc spear had severed his backbone, so said the priests, and there was nothing their healing spells could do to fix it. He was in his bed that day, awaiting the completion of a comfortable chair on wheels that would allow him a bit of mobility.

Bruenor had found Banak in a dour mood, but with his fighting spirit intact. He had been more concerned about those who had fallen than with his own wounds, as Bruenor expected. Banak was a Brawnanvil, after all, of a line as sturdy as Battlehammer's own, strong of arm and of spirit, and with loyalty unmatched. Banak had been physically crippled, no doubt, but Bruenor knew that the warcommander was hardly out of the fight, wherever that fight may be.

Nanfoodle's audience marked the end of the announced procession that day, and so Bruenor dismissed the gnome and excused himself. He had one more meeting in mind, one, he knew, that was better made in private.

Leaving his escort—Thibbledorf Pwent had insisted that a pair of Gutbusters accompany the dwarf king wherever he went—at the end of one dimly lit corridor, Bruenor moved to a door, gently knocked, then pushed it open.

He found Regis sitting at his desk, chin in one hand the other holding a quill above an open parchment that was trying to curl against the press of mug-shaped paperweights. Bruenor nodded and entered, taking a seat on the edge of the halfling's soft bed.

"Ye don't seem to be eatin' much, Rumblebelly," he remarked with a grin. Bruenor reached under his tunic and pulled forth a thick piece of cake. He casually tossed it to Regis, who caught it and set it down without taking a bite. "Bah, but ye keep that up and I'm to call ye Rumblebones!" Bruenor blustered. "Go on, then!" he demanded, motioning to the cake.

"I'm writing it all down," Regis assured him, and he brushed aside one of the paperweights and lifted the edge of the parchment, which caused a bit of the recently placed ink to streak. Noting this, Regis quickly flattened the parchment and began to frantically blow upon it.

"Ain't nothing there that ye can't be telling me yerself," Bruenor said.

Finally, the halfling turned back to him.

"What's yer grief then, Rumblebelly?" asked the dwarf. "Ye done good—damn good, by what me generals been telling me."

"So many died," Regis replied, his voice barely a whisper.

"Aye, that's the pain o' war."

"But I kept them out there," the halfling explained, leaping up from his chair, his short, stocky arms waving all around. He began to pace back and forth, muttering with every step as if trying to find some way to blurt out all of his pain in one burst. "Up on the cliff. I could have ordered Banak back in, long before the final fight. How many would still be alive?"

"Bah, ye're asking questions that ain't got no answers!" Bruenor roared at him. "Anyone can lead the fight the day after it's done. It's leading the fight *during* the fight that's marking yer worth."

"I could have brought them in," the halfling stated. "I should have brought them in."

"Ah, but ye knew the truth of the orc force, did ye? Ye knew that ten thousand would add to their ranks and sweep into the dale from the west, did ye?"

Regis blinked repeatedly, but did not answer.

"Ye knew nothing more than anyone else, Banak included," Bruenor insisted. "And Banak wasn't keen on coming down that cliff. In the end, when we learned the truth of our enemy, we salvaged what we could, and that's plenty, but not as much as we wanted to hold. We gived them the whole of the northland don't ye see? And that's nothing any Battlehammer's proud to admit."

"There were too many . . ." Regis started, eliciting another loud "Bah!" from Bruenor.

"We ran away, Rumblebelly! Clan Battlehammer retreated from orcs!"

"There were too many!"

Bruenor smiled and nodded, showing Regis that he had just been played like a dwarven fiddle. "Course there were, and so we took what we could get, but don't ye ever think that running from orcs was something meself'd order unless no other choice was afore me. No other choice! I'd've kept Banak out there, Rumblebelly. I'd've been out there with him, don't ye doubt!"

Regis looked up at Bruenor and gave a nod of appreciation.

"Questions for us now are, what next?" said Bruenor. "Do we go back out and fight them again? Out to the east, mayhaps, to open a line across the Surbrin? Out to the south, so we can sweep back around?"

"The south," Regis muttered. "I sent fifty to the south, accompanying Galen Firth of Nesmé."

"Catti-brie telled me all about it, and in that, too, ye did well, by me own reckoning. I got no love for them Nesmé boys after the way they treated us them years ago and after the way they ignored Settlestone. Bunch o' stoneheads, if e'er I seen a bunch o' stoneheads! But a neighbor's a neighbor, and ye got to help do what ye can do, and from where I'm seeing it, ye did all that ye could do."

"But we can do more now," Regis offered.

Bruenor scratched his red beard and thought on that a moment. "Might that we can," he agreed. "A few hundred more moving south might open new possibilities, too. Good thinking." He looked to Regis as he finished, and noted happily that the halfling seemed to have shaken off his burden then, an eager gleam coming back into his soft brown eyes.

"Send Torgar and the boys from Mirabar," Regis suggested. "They're a fine bunch, and they know how to fight aboveground as well as below."

Bruenor wasn't sure if he agreed with that assessment. Perhaps Torgar, Shingles, and all the dwarves of Mirabar had seen enough fighting and had taken on enough special and difficult assignments already. Maybe it was time for them to take some rest inside Mithral Hall proper, mingling with the dwarves who had lived in those corridors and chambers since the complex had been reclaimed from Shimmergloom the shadow dragon and his duergar minions years before.

Bruenor gave no indication to Regis that he was doubting the wisdom of the suggestion, though. The halfling had proven himself many times over in the last tendays, by all accounts, and his insight and understanding was a resource Bruenor had no intention of squashing.

"Come along, Rumblebelly," he said with a toothy grin. "Let's go see how Ivan and Pikel are getting on. Might be that they know allies we haven't yet considered."

"Cadderly?"

"Was thinking more of the elves of the Moonwood," Bruenor explained. "Seems them two came through there on their way to Mithral Hall. I'm thinking it'd be a good thing to get them elves putting arrows and magic across the Surbrin to soften our enemy's entrenchment."

"How would we get word to them?" Regis asked. "The elves, I mean. Do we have tunnels that go that far east and north?"

"How'd Pikel get him and Ivan there in the first place?" Bruenor replied with an exaggerated wink. "By Ivan's telling, it's got something to do with trees and roots. We ain't got no trees, but we got plenty o' roots, I'm thinking."

Regis put on his best Pikel voice when he replied, "Hee hee hee."

Tred McKnuckles emphatically raised a finger to his pursed lips, reminding the dwarven catapult team that silence was essential.

Bellan Brawnanvil mimicked the movement back to Tred in agreement and tapped his sideslinger pull crew to ease up on their movements as they worked to set the basket. Mounted on the side of the jamb of a hallway door, the sideslinger catapult served as the staple war engine of the outer defenses of Mithral Hall. Its adjustable arm length made it the perfect war engine to fit any situation, and in the east, so close to the great flowing river that the stones continually hummed with the reverberations of its currents, the catapults were front-line and primary. For just beyond the group's present position in the eastern reaches of the complex, the tunnels dived down into the wilds of the Underdark. Even in times of peace, the eastern sideslingers were often put to use, chasing back umber hulks or displacer beasts, or any of the other dark denizens of those lightless corridors.

By his own request, Tred had come down for duty right after the door to Keeper's Dale had been sealed, for the position oversaw those tunnels that connected Mithral Hall, through the upper Underdark, to Citadel Felbarr, Tred's home. From that very spot, a location where an ironbound door that could be quickly and tightly sealed, emissaries from Steward Regis had gone out to gain audience with King Emerus Warcrown of Citadel Felbarr, to tell Emerus the tale of Tred and Nikwillig, and his missing caravan.

Tred had remained there for many hours, taking double shifts, and staying even when he was not on watch. The only time he'd gone back to the main halls of Clan Battlehammer's complex had been that very day, for he had been summoned to meet with King Bruenor. He had just returned from that meeting, to find his companions all astir at reports of movement in the east.

Tred stood with them anxiously and thought, Is this the front end of yet another attack by Obould's masses? Some monstrous Underdark creature coming forth in search of a meal? The return of the emissaries, perhaps?

Beyond the door, the tunnel sloped down into a roughly circular natural chamber that branched off in several directions. Ready to turn that chamber into a killing ground, the dwarves opposite the sideslinger readied several kegs of highly flammable oil. At the first sign of trouble, the dwarves would lead, rolling the barrels down into the lower room, contents spilling on the floor, then the sideslinger would let fly a wad of burning pitch.

Bellan Brawnanvil signaled Tred and the barrel-rollers that the catapult was ready, and all the dwarves hushed, more than one falling to the floor and putting an ear to the stone.

They heard a sound below, from one of the tunnels off the circular chamber.

A barrel was silently brought into place at the top of the ramp and an eager young dwarf put his shoulder behind it, ready to send it bouncing down.

Tred peered anxiously around the door jamb above that barrel, straining his eyes in the darkness. He caught the flicker of torchlight.

So did the dwarf behind the barrel, and he gave a little yelp and started to shove.

But Tred stopped him before he ever began, waggling a finger at him and fixing him with a scowl. A moment later, all were glad that he did, for they heard, "Bah, ye great snorter of pig-sweat, ye turned us all about again!"

"Did not, yer mother's worst mistake! This ain't no chamber we been through."

"Been through and been out four times, ye dolt!"

"Ain't not!"

Tred and the dwarves around him grinned widely.

"Well, if ye been through four times, then ye been through with a lot less racket than ye're making now, ye fat-bellied bearded bunch o' archery targets!" Tred hollered.

Below him, the chamber went silent, and the light quickly flickered out.

"Oh, so now ye're the sneaky things?" Tred asked. "Step up and be recognized, be ye Warcrown or Battlehammer!"

"Warcrown!" came a shout from below, a voice that sparked some recognition in Tred.

"Battlehammer!" said another, and the dwarves in the room recognized it as Sindel Muffinhead, one of the emissaries sent out by Steward Regis, a young acolyte, and expert pie baker, who named the now famous Cordio as his older brother.

Torches flared to life below and several figures moved into sight, then began stomping up the ramp. As they neared, Tred noted an old friend.

"Jackonray Broadbelt!" he called. "Been a halfling's meal and more since I last seen ye!"

"Tred, me friend!" replied Jackonray, leading the way into the room for his seven companions, including Sindel, but not the other emissary.

Jackonray wore heavy armor with dark gray metal plates set on thick leather. His helm was bowl-shaped and ridged, and topped a shock of gray hair that reached out wildly from beneath its metal hem. Jackonray's beard was not so unkempt, though, and was streaked with hair the color of gold and lines the color of silver, braided together to give the dwarf a very distinctive and distinguished appearance. In accord with his surname, his girdle was wide and decorated with sparkling jewels. He rested the elbow of his weapon arm on it as he continued, "Sorry I am to hear o' yer brother." He patted Tred hard on the shoulder with a hand that seemed as hard as stone.

"Aye, Duggan was a good friend."

"And a loyal companion. A tribute to yer family."

Tred reached up and solemnly squeezed Jackonray's thick and strong arm.

"Ye come from King Emerus, then, and with good news, I'm thinking," Tred remarked a moment later. "Let's get ye to King Bruenor."

"Aye, straightaways."

The pair and Sindel moved off at a swift pace, the other Felbarran dwarves falling in line behind them. As they wound through the more populated reaches of Mithral Hall, more than a few Battlehammer dwarves took up the march, as well, so that by the time they crossed through the great Undercity and climbed along the main tunnels leading to Bruenor's chamber, nearly fifty dwarves formed the procession, many of them chatting amongst themselves, exchanging information about their respective strongholds. Other runners went far ahead to announce them to Bruenor long before they arrived.

"Where's Nikwillig, then?" asked Jackonray, rolling along at Tred's side.

"Still out there in the North," Tred explained, and there was no mistaking the sudden graveness to his tone. "Nikwillig went out to the mountains in the east to send back a signal, and he knew in doing it that he'd not easily get back into Mithral Hall. Felt he—we, owed it to Bruenor, since he done so much to help us avenge our lost kin."

"Seems proper," said Jackonray. "But if he's not in now, he's likely dead."

"Aye, but he died a hero," said Tred. "And no dwarf's ever asking more than that."

"What more than that might ye ask?" asked Jackonray.

"Here, here," added Sindel.

When the troupe arrived at Bruenor's audience chamber door, they found it wide open, with the dwarf king inside on his throne, awaiting their arrival.

"King Bruenor, I give ye Jackonray Broadbelt," Tred said with a bow. "Of the Hornriver Broadbelts, first cousins to King Emerus Warcrown himself. Jackonray here's King Warcrown's own nephew, and a favored one at that. Sixth in line for the throne, by last count, behind King Emerus's five sons."

"Sixth or twenty-fifth, depending upon King Warcrown's disposition," Jackonray said with a wink. "He's one for keeping us guessing."

"Aye, and a smart choice that's always been," said Bruenor.

"Yer ambassadors're telling me King Emerus that ye've come against Obould Many-Arrows," Jackonray said.

"One and the same, by all I'm hearing."

"Well, King Bruenor, know that Obould's a smart one, as orcs go. Ye take great care in handling this snortsnout."

"He sealed me and me kin inside the hall," Bruenor explained. "Shut the east door by the Surbrin."

"Felbarr scouts have seen as much," Jackonray said. "And them giants and orcs're building defenses all along the river's western bank."

"And they drove me kin in from the western door, in Keeper's Dale," Bruenor admitted. "I'd not thinked that Clan Battlehammer could be put underground by a bunch o' stinkin' orcs, but what a bunch it is. Thousands and thousands."

"And led by one that knows how to fight," said Jackonray. "Know in yer heart, King Bruenor, that if Obould's got ye in here, then Obould's thinking to come in after ye."

"That'll cost him."

"Dearly, I'm sure, good King Bruenor."

"They been fighting in the south tunnels a bit already," Bruenor reported. "With smelly trolls and not orcs, but the battling's not so heavy."

Jackonray stroked his silver and gold beard. "Lady Alustriel of Silverymoon's been sending out the word of a wide push from the Trollmoors. One that's threatened all the lands south of here. It's as big a fight as we thinked we'd ever be seeing, don't ye doubt. But know that Obould's not to let it sit, and not to let you sit. By all me experience in fighting that dog, and I've had more than ye know, if there's fighting in the south, then prepare for something bigger from the north, east, or west. Obould's got you in a hole, but he's not to let you stay, even if it costs him every orc, goblin, and giant he can find."

"Stupid orcs," Tred muttered.

"Aye, and that's just why they're so dangerous," Bruenor said. He looked from the two dwarves to his own advisors, then back at Jackonray directly. "Well, then, what's coming from Felbarr?"

"I appreciate yer bluntness," Jackonray said with another low bow. "And I'm here to tell ye not to doubt us. Felbarr's behind ye to the last, King Bruenor.

All our gold and all our dwarves. Right now we got hundreds working the tunnels under the Surbrin, securing the line all the way from Mithral Hall to Felbarr. We'll have them open and secure, don't ye doubt."

Bruenor nodded his gratitude, but at the same time motioned with his hand that he wanted to hear more.

"We'll set it as a trade and supply route," Jackonray went on. "King Emerus telled me to tell yerself that we'll work as agents for Mithral Hall in yer time o' need, no commission taken."

That brought a concerned look to Bruenor's face, and it was a look mirrored on all the Battlehammers in attendance.

"Ye're to need to get yer goods to market, and so we'll be yer market," Jackonray stated.

"Ye're sounding like we're to give Obould all that he's got and let him keep it," Bruenor voiced.

For the first time since the meeting commenced, Jackonray seemed a bit less than sure of himself.

"No, we're not for that, but King Emerus is thinking that it's to take some time to push the orcs back," Jackonray explained.

"And when time's come to do the pushing?"

"If it comes to fighting, then we'll shore up yer ranks, shoulder to shoulder," Jackonray insisted. "Know in yer Delzoun heart, King Bruenor, that Felbarr's with ye, dwarf to dwarf. When the fighting's starting, we'll be with ye. And not just Felbarr, don't ye doubt, though it'll take Citadel Adbar longer to mobilize her thousands."

The show of solidarity touched Bruenor deeply, to be sure, but he didn't miss the equivocation to Jackonray's remark. The other leaders of the region had taken note of the orc march, indeed, but there was apparently some discussion going on about what they should, or even could, do about it.

"In the meanwhile, we'll get those tunnels opened and safe for ye to move yer goods through to Felbarr and out to market," Jackonray offered, and Bruenor, who hadn't even entertained such a thought, who hadn't even begun to resign himself to that grim possibility, merely nodded.

"That orc was something . . . beyond any orc," Wulfgar remarked. With a frame closer to seven feet than six, and hardened in the wilderness of the tundra of Icewind Dale, the barbarian was as strong as any man, and so he thought, stronger than any orc. But the brutish creature who had cut Shoudra Stargleam in half had taught Wulfgar better, tossing the barbarian aside with a shrug. "It was as if I was pushing against a falling mountainside."

Catti-brie understood his shock and distress. It wasn't often that Wulfgar, son of Beornegar, had been bested in a test of sheer strength. Even giants had not thrown him aside with such seeming ease. "They're saying it was Obould Many-Arrows, himself," she replied.

"He and I will meet again," Wulfgar vowed, his crystalline blue eyes sparkling at the thought.

Catti-brie limped up beside him and gently brushed his long blond hair from the side of his face, forcing him to turn and look at her directly.

"You don't be doing anything foolhardy," she said softly. "We'll get Obould, don't you doubt, but we'll get him in the proper order of business. We'll get him as we'll get all of them, and there's no room for personal vengeance here. Bigger stakes than pride."

Wulfgar snickered and smiled. "True enough," he replied, "and yet, you're not believing the words any more than you're expecting me to believe them. You want that ugly one in your bow-sight again, as much as I want him now that I understand what to expect from him."

Catti-brie tried hard not to smile back at the barbarian, but she knew that her rich blue eyes were shining as brightly as Wulfgar's. "Oh, I'm wanting him," she admitted. "But not so much with me bow."

She led his gaze with her own down to the fabulous sword sheathed on her left hip. Khazid'hea, "Cutter," as it was called, a name that surely fit. Catti-brie had put that blade through solid stone. Could any armor, even the wondrous suit encasing Obould Many-Arrows, turn its keen edge?

Both of them seemed to realize then that they were but inches apart, close enough to feel the warmth of each other's breath.

Catti-brie broke the tension first, reaching up and playfully tousling Wulfgar's wild shock of hair, then hopping up to her tip-toes and giving him a kiss on the cheek—the kiss of a friend, and nothing more.

In its own way, that was a defining moment for her.

Wulfgar's reciprocating grin, though, seemed a bit less than certain.

"So we're thinking we should be getting scouts out through the chimneys," came a voice from behind Catti-brie, and she turned around to see her adoptive father Bruenor entering the room, Regis in tow. "We got to know what our enemies are thinking if we're to counter them properly."

"They're orcs," Wulfgar said. "Betting would say that they're not thinking much."

His attempt at humor would have been more successful if that last maneuver of the orc army had not been so fresh in all their minds, the deceptive swing behind the mountain spurs to the west that brought the bulk of their force in behind Banak's charges, nearly spelling disaster for the dwarves.

"We can't be knowing a thing about them orcs unless we're seeing it ourselfs," Bruenor remarked. "I'm not for underestimating this one again."

Regis shifted uncomfortably.

"I'm thinking that we scored a bigger victory than we realized," Catti-brie was quick to remark. "We won the day out there, though our losses surely hurt."

"Seems to me like we're the ones in our hole," Bruenor replied.

"But it's seeming to me that we could not've done better," reasoned the woman, and she looked directly at the halfling, her expression showing her approval. "If we'd've come right in, then we'd not now know what's come against us. What straights might we soon find ourselves in if you had acted otherwise, if we had run from the ridge straightaway? Would we truly understand the size and ferocity of the force that's arrayed against us? Would we have delivered so powerful a blow against our enemy? They've come to fight us, and so we'll be fighting, don't you doubt, and better that we understand what we're fighting, and better that we've laid so many low already. Thanks to Nanfoodle and the others, we've killed them as overwhelmingly as we could ever have hoped thus far, even if all the fighting had been in our own defended tunnels."

"Ye got the right way o' seeing things, girl," Bruenor agreed after a pause to digest the reasoning. "If they're thinking to come in against us, at least now we're knowing what they got to throw our way."

"So hold our heads high and hold our weapons all the tighter," Wulfgar chimed in.

"Oo oi!" said Regis, and everyone looked at him curiously.

"What's that meaning, anyway?" asked Catti-brie.

Regis shrugged. "Just sounded right," he explained, and no one disagreed.

5

TOO HIGH A CEILING

Galen Firth paced furiously, every stride showing his mounting impatience. He muttered under his breath, taking care to keep his curses quiet enough so that they wouldn't disturb the dwarves, who were huddled together in a great circle, each with his arms over the shoulders of those beside him. Heads down, the bearded folk offered prayers to Moradin for the souls of Fender and Bonnerbas. They had run a long way from the hole they had cut out of the tunnels to escape the troll ambush, but they were still outdoors, sheltered within a copse of fir trees from a heavy rain that had come up.

When the dwarves had finished—*finally* finished, to Galen's thinking—General Dagna wasted no time in marching over to the human.

"We'll be considering our course this night," the dwarf informed him. "More'n a few're thinking it's past time we got back into tunnels."

"We just got chased out of tunnels," Galen reminded him.

"Aye, but not them kind o' tunnels. We're looking for tunnels deep, tunnels o' worked stone—tunnels to give a dwarf something worth holding onto. No trolls're gonna push Battlehammer dwarves out of stone tunnels, don't ye doubt!"

"You're forgetting our course and our reason for being here."

"Them trolls're onto us," Dagna replied. "They'll catch up to us soon enough, and ye know it."

"Indeed, if we continue to stop and pray every . . ." Galen's voice trailed off as he considered Dagna's expression and realized that he was going over the line.

"I'll forgive ye that, but just this once," the dwarf warned. "I'm knowin' that ye're hurting for yer losses. We're all knowin' that. But we're running out o' time. If we're staying here much longer, then don't ye be thinking we'll find our way back to our home anytime soon."

"What do you mean to do?"

Dagna turned around slowly, surveying the landscape. "We'll head west, to that high ridge there," he said, pointing to a line of elevated ground some miles distant. "From there we'll take us the best look we can find. Might be that we'll see yer people. Might be that we won't."

"And if we don't, then you intend to turn back for Mithral Hall."

"No other choice's afore me."

"And where for Galen, then?" the man asked.

"Wherever Galen's choosing to go," Dagna answered. "Ye've proven yerself in a fight, to me and me boys. They'll keep ye along, and not a one's to complain. But it might be that ye cannot do that. Might be that Galen's got to stay and look, and die, if that's to be. Might be that Galen's doing better by his folk if he goes off to Silverymoon or some other town that's not being pressed by orcs and can spare more of an army. Choice is yer own."

Galen rubbed a hand over his face, feeling stubble that was fast turning into a thick beard. He wanted to yell and scream at Dagna, truly he did, but he knew that the dwarf was offering him all that he could under the present conditions. Somehow, the trolls were dogging them, and would find them again. How many times could Dagna and his small force hope to escape?

"We begin our march to the ridge this very night?"

"See no reason to be waiting," Dagna replied.

Galen nodded and let it go at that. He got his gear collected and his boots tightened as the dwarves formed up for their march. He tried to focus on the present, on the duty before him, for he knew that if he tried to think ahead, his resolve would likely crumble. For every question in Galen Firth's life at that point seemed to begin with, "What if?"

"I will not tolerate a retreat into the tunnels until we have discovered the disposition of my people!" Galen Firth grumbled as he pulled himself over the last rise of rock to the top of the windswept ridgeline. The man brushed himself off and stared at Dagna, looking for some reaction to his insistence, but found the dwarf strangely distracted, and looking off toward the southwest.

"Wha—?" Galen asked, the word catching in his throat as he turned to follow the dwarf's line of sight, to see the light of fires—campfires, perhaps—in the distance.

"Might be we done just that," Dagna said.

More dwarves came up around them, all hopping and pointing excitedly to the distant lights.

"Durn fools to be lighting so bright a burn with trolls all about," one dwarf remarked, and others nodded their agreement, or started to, until Dagna, noting the erratic movements of the flames, cut them short.

"Them fires're against the trolls!" the general realized. "They got themselves a fight down there!"

"We must go to them!" cried Galen.

"A mile. . . ." a dwarf observed.

"Of tough ground," another added.

"Mark the stars and run on, then!" General Dagna ordered.

The dwarves lined up the fires with the celestial constants, and began to stream fast down the back side of the ridge. Galen Firth sprinted off ahead of the pack, foolishly so, for his human eyes weren't very good in the darkness. Before he'd gone half a dozen strides, the man tripped and stumbled, then ran face long into a tree branch and staggered backward. He would have fallen to the ground had not Dagna arrived with open arms to catch him.

"Ye stay right beside me, long legs," the dwarf ordered. "We'll get ye there!"

With their short, muscled legs, dwarves were not the fastest runners in the Realms, but no race could match their stamina and determination. The force rolled past and over rocks and logs, and when one tripped, others caught him, up righted him, and kept him moving swiftly along his way.

They charged along some lower ground, splashed through some unseen puddles and scrambled through a tangle of birch trees and brush, a snarl that got so thick at one point that several dwarves brought forth their axes and began chopping with abandon. As they came through that last major obstacle, the lights of the fires clearly visible directly ahead, Galen Firth began to hear the cries of battle. Shouts for support and calls of pain and rage split the night, and Galen's heart sank as he realized that many of those calls were not coming from warriors, but from women, children, and elderly folk.

He didn't know what to expect when he and Dagna crashed through the last line of brush and onto the battlefield, though he surely expected the worst scenario, a helter skelter slaughter ground with his people trapped into small groups that could offer only meager resistance. He began to urge Dagna to form up a defensive ring, a shell of dwarves to protect his people, but when they came in sight of the actual fighting, Galen's words caught in his throat, and his heart soared with renewed hope.

His people, the hearty folk of Nesmé, were fighting hard and fighting well.

"They're in a double ellipse," one dwarf coming in behind remarked, referring to a very intricate defensive formation, and one, Galen knew, that the riders of Nesmé had often employed along the broken, tree-speckled ground north of the Trollmoors. In the double ellipse, two elongated rings of warriors formed end-to-end with a single joining point between them. Worked harmoniously, the formation was one of complete support, with every angle of battle offering a striking zone to more defenders than attackers. But it was also a risky formation, for if it failed at any point, the aggressors would have the means to isolate and utterly destroy entire sections of the defending force.

So far, it seemed to be holding, but barely, and only because the defenders employed many, many flaming torches, waving them wildly to fend off the trolls and their even more stupid partners, the treelike bog blokes.

"Dead trees must fall!" Galen shouted when he realized that the common allies of the wretched trolls were among the attackers. For bog blokes resembled nothing more than a small and skeletal dead tree, with twisted arms appearing as stubby limbs.

As he spoke, the man noted one part of the Nesmé line in serious jeopardy, as a pair of young men, boys really, fell back before the snarling and devastating charge of a particularly large and nasty troll. Galen broke away from the dwarves and veered straight for the troll's back, his sword leading. He hit the unwitting creature at a full run, driving his sword right through the beast and

making it lurch forward wildly. To their credit, the two young men didn't break ranks and flee, but just dodged aside of the lurching troll, then came right back in beside its swiping arms, smacking at it with their torches, the fires bubbling the troll's mottled green and gray skin.

Galen pulled his blade free and spun just in time to fend off the clawing hands of another troll, and another that came in beside it. Hard-pressed, and with the troll he had skewered behind him hardly out of the fighting, Galen feared that he would meet an abrupt end. He breathed a bit easier when the troll before him and to his left lurched over suddenly and tumbled away. As it fell, a heavy dwarven axe came up over its bending head and drove it down more forcefully. That dwarf pressed on, right past Galen to take on the wounded beast behind the man, while another dwarf leaped into view atop the fallen troll, using it as a springboard to launch him headlong into the other troll standing in front of Galen. His flying tackle took the beast around the waist, and as he swung about, the dwarf twisted his body to give him some leverage across the troll's lower half. The dwarf tugged mightily with his short, muscled arms, his momentum taking him right past the surprised troll. When the diminutive bearded warrior used that momentum, combined with his powerful arms, he compelled the troll to follow, the creature rolling right over him as he fell.

"Give me yer torch!" Galen heard the first dwarf cry to someone in the defensive line.

Galen turned and glanced over his shoulder to consider that scene, then fell back with a yelp as a torch flew right past his face. He followed the line of the fiery weapon, left to right, to the waiting hand of the complimenting dwarf, who caught it deftly and quickly inverted it. As the troll below that dwarf rolled around to counter the attack, the dwarf put that flame into its eye, and stuffed it right into the troll's mouth as the creature opened its jaws wide to let out an agonized roar. The troll flailed wildly and the dwarf went flying away, but he landed nimbly on his steady feet and brought a warhammer up before him in a single fluid movement.

Other enemies moved to engulf the dwarf and Galen, but Dagna and his boys were there first, fiercely supporting their comrades. They formed into a tight fighting diamond quickly to Galen's right, and to the man's left, the remaining dwarves similarly formed up. The two groups quickly pivoted to bring their lines together.

"Yer folks ain't no strangers to battle, I'm thinking!" General Dagna remarked to Galen. "Go on, then," Dagna offered, "join with yer folk. Me and me boys're here for ye, don't ye doubt!"

Galen Firth spun around and smashed the stubborn troll behind him yet again, then rushed past the falling beast to find a place in the human defensive line. He knew that at least some of the Riders must be among the group, for its coordination was too great for untrained warriors alone.

He spotted the central figure of the defenders even as that young man noted him, and Galen's gaze grew more stern. The young warrior seemed to melt back under that glare. Galen sprinted past his townsfolk, moving to the joint between the two coordinated defensive formations.

"I will assume the pivot," he said to the apparent leader.

"I have it secured, Captain Firth," the man, Rannek by name, replied.

"Move aside!" Galen demanded, and Rannek fell back.

"Tighten the ranks!" Galen called across the Nesmé position. "Bring it in closer so our dwarven allies can facilitate our retreat!"

"Good choice," muttered General Dagna, who had watched the curious exchange between the two men. Even with the arrival of two score dwarf warriors, the group of humans could not hope to win out against the monstrous attackers. Already the fires were dying low in several spots along the line, and wherever that happened, the fearsome trolls were fast to the spot, clawed hands striking hard and with impunity. For trolls did not fear conventional weapons. Cutting a troll to pieces, after all, only increased the size of its family.

"Form up, boys!" Dagna called. "Double ranks! Three sides o' chopping!"

With a communal roar, the disciplined dwarves spun, jumped, tumbled, and hopped into proper formation, forming a triangle whose each tip was tightly packed with the fiercest warriors. Clan Battlehammer called that particular formation the "splitting wedge" because of its ability to maneuver easily against weak spots in their enemy's line, shifting the focus of its offensive push. Dagna stayed in the middle of the formation, directing, rolling the dwarves like a great killing machine along the perimeter in support of the human line. They did an almost complete circuit, driving back the trolls with torches and splitting

bog blokes like firewood with great chops of heavy axes. On Dagna's sudden order, and with stunning precision, one tip broke away and rushed past the human line to the north, back toward the higher ground, pummeling the few trolls blocking that particular escape route.

"To the north!" Galen Firth cried to his charges, seeing the plan unfolding. He shoved those people nearest him that direction, urging them on.

Across from him, Rannek did likewise, and between the two, they had the bulk of the human force moving in short order.

Dagna watched the haphazard movements, trying hard to time his own pivots to properly cover the rear of the retreat. He noted the two men working frantically, one seeming a younger version of the other, but with the calm one would expect of a trained and veteran soldier. He also noted that Galen Firth pointedly did not glance at his counterpart, did not acknowledge the man's efforts at all.

Dagna shook his head and focused again on his own efforts.

"Damn humans," he muttered. "Stubborn lot."

"The rescue mission succeeds," Tos'un Armgo remarked as he and Kaer'lic watched the continuing battle from afar.

"For now, perhaps," the priestess replied.

Tos'un read the nonchalance clearly in her tone, and indeed, why should Kaer'lic, and why should he, really care whether or not a group of humans escaped the clutches of Proffit's monstrous forces?

"The dwarves will turn for home now, likely," the male drow said. As he finished, he glanced over his shoulder to the bound and gagged Fender. With a sly grin, the drow kicked the dwarf hard in the side, and Fender curled up and groaned.

"That is but a small number of Nesmé's scattered refugees, by all reports," Kaer'lic countered. "And these frightened humans know that they have kin in similar straights all across the region. Perhaps the dwarves will link with this force in an effort to widen the rescue mission. Would that not be the sweetest irony of all, to have our enemies gather together for their ultimate demise?"

"Our enemies?"

The simple question gave Kaer'lic pause, obviously.

"In a choice between humans and trolls, even dwarves and trolls, I believe that I would side against the trolls," the male drow admitted. "Though now, the promise of finding a vulnerable wayward human is a tempting one that I fear I will not be able to resist."

"Nor should you," the priestess said. "Take your pleasures where you may, my friend, for soon enough, striking at the enemy will likely mean crossing lines of wary and battle-ready dwarves."

"Perhaps that pleasure might involve a few vulnerable orcs, as well."

Kaer'lic gave a little laugh at the thought. "I would wish them all, orc, troll, dwarf, human, and giant alike, a horrible death and be done with it."

"Even better," Tos'un agreed. "I do hope that the dwarves decide to remain in the southland openly and with a widening force. Their presence will make it easier for us to persuade Proffit to remain here."

The words silenced Tos'un even as he spoke them, and seemed to have a sobering effect upon Kaer'lic, as well. For that was the gist of it, the unspoken agreement between the two dark elves that they really did not want to wander the tunnels leading back to the north and the main defenses of Mithral Hall. They had been sent south by Obould to guide Proffit through that very course, to urge the trolls on as the monsters pressured the dwarves in the southern reaches of the complex. But the thought of going against fortified dwarven positions and into a dwarven hall accompanied by a horde of stupid brutes was not really an appealing one, after all.

"Proffit will turn his eyes to the north, as Obould bade him," Tos'un added a moment later.

"Then you and I must convince him that the situation here is more important," Kaer'lic replied without hesitation.

"Obould will not be pleased."

"Then perhaps Obould will slay Proffit, or even better, perhaps they will slaughter each other."

Tos'un smiled and let it go at that, perfectly comfortable with the role that he and his three drow companions had made for themselves. Prodding Obould and Gerti Orelsdottr to war from the beginning, the drow had never really concerned themselves with the outcome. In truth, they hadn't a care as to which side emerged victorious, dwarf or orc, as long as the drow found

some excitement, and some profit, in the process. And if that process inflicted horrific pain and loss to the minions of Obould, Gerti, and Bruenor Battlehammer alike, then all the better!

Of course, neither Kaer'lic nor Tos'un knew then that their two missing companions, Donnia Soldou and Ad'non Kareese, lay dead in the north, killed by a rogue drow.

They found their first break in a shallow cave tucked into a rocky cliff behind a small pond more than an hour later, and there, too, their first opportunity to bandage wounds and determine who was even still among their continually thinning ranks. Nesmé had been an important town in the region for many generations, strong and solid behind fortified walls, the vanguard of the Silver Marches against intrusions from the monsters of the wild Trollmoors. That continual strife and diligence had bred a closeness among the community of Nesmians so that they felt every loss keenly.

The day had brought more than a dozen deaths, and had left several more people missing—a difficult loss for but one band of less than a hundred refugees. And given the seriousness of the wounds that many resting in that shallow cave had suffered, that number of dead seemed sure to rise through the remaining hours of the night.

"Daylight ain't no friend o' trolls, even in tracking," Dagna said to Galen Firth when he met the man at the cave entrance a short while later. "Me boys're covering the tracks and killing any trolls and blokes wandering too close, but we're not to sit here for long without them beasties coming against us in force."

"Then we move, again and again," Galen Firth said.

Dagna considered the man's tone—determination and resignation mingled into one—as much as his agreement.

"We'll cross shadow to shadow," Galen went on. "We'll find their every weakness and hit them hard. We'll find all the remaining bands of my townsfolk and meld them into a singular and devastating force."

"We'll find tunnels, deep and straight, and run headlong for Mithral Hall," General Dagna corrected, and Galen Firth's eyes flashed with anger.

"More of my people are out there. I will not forsake them in their time of desperation."

"Well, that's for yerself to decide," said Dagna. "I come here to see how I might be helping, and so me and me boys did. I left six more dead back there. That's eight o' fifty, almost one in six."

"And your efforts saved ten times the number of your dead. Are not ten of Nesmé's folk worth a single dwarf's life?"

"Bah, don't ye be putting it like that," Dagna said, and he gave a great snort. "I'm thinking that we're all to be slaughtered in one great fight if we make a single mistake. More than two score o' me boys and closer to a hunnerd o' yer own folk."

"Then we won't make a mistake," Galen Firth said in a low and even tone.

Dagna snorted again and moved past the man, knowing that he wouldn't be getting anything settled that night. Nor did he have to, for in truth, he had no idea of where the force might even find any tunnels that would take them back to Mithral Hall. Dagna knew, and so did Galen, that this band would be moving out of necessity and not choice over the next hours, and even days, likely, so arguing about courses that might not ever even become an option seemed a rather silly thing to do.

Dagna crossed by the folk of Nesmé, accepting their kind words and gratitude, and offering his own praise for their commendable efforts. He also found his own clerics hard at work tending the wounded, and he offered a solid pat on each dwarf shoulder as he passed. Mostly, though, Dagna studied the humans. They were indeed a good and sturdy folk, in the tough general's estimation, if a bit orc-headed.

Well, he supposed, orc-headed only if Galen Firth is an accurate representative of the community.

That notion had Dagna moving more purposefully among the ranks, seeking out a particular man whose actions had stood above the norm back on the battlefield. He found that man at the very back of the shallow cave, reclining on a smooth, rounded stone. As he approached, Dagna noted the man's many wounds, including three fingers on his left hand twisted at an angle that showed them to certainly be broken, and a garish tear on his left ear that looked as if the ear might fall right off.

"Ye might want to be seeing the priests about them fingers and that ear," Dagna said, moving up before the man.

Obviously startled, the warrior quickly sat up and straightened his battered chain and leather tunic.

"Dagna's me name," the dwarf said, extending his calloused hand. "General Dagna o' Mithral Hall, Warcommander to King Bruenor Battlehammer."

"Well met, General Dagna," the man said. "I am Rannek of Nesmé."

"One o' them Riders?"

The man nodded. "I was, at least."

"Bah, ye'll get yer town back soon enough!"

The dwarf noted that his optimism didn't seem to lift the man's expression, though he suspected, given the reception Galen Firth had offered Rannek back at the battlefield, that the dourness wasn't precipitated by the wider prospects for the town.

"Ye done well back there," Dagna offered, eliciting a less-than-resounding shrug.

"We fight for our very existence, good dwarf. Our options are few. If we err, we die."

"Ain't that the way of it?" asked the dwarf. "In me many years, I've come to see the truth in the notion that war's the time for determining the character of a dwarf. Or a man."

"Indeed."

Dagna's eyes narrowed under his bushy and prominent eyebrows. "Ye got nearly a hunnerd o' yer kin in here looking to ye. Ye're knowing that? And here ye be with a face showing defeat, yet ye got most o' yer folk out o' what them trolls suren thought to be the end o' yer road."

"They'll be looking to Galen Firth, now that he has returned," said Rannek.

"Bah, that's not a good enough answer."

"It is the only answer I have," said Rannek.

He slid off the rounded stone, offered a polite and unenthusiastic bow, and moved away.

General Dagna heaved a resigned sigh. He didn't have time for this. Not now. Not with trolls pressing in on them.

"Humans. . . ." he muttered under his breath, giving a shake of his hairy head.

"They are helpless and they are scattered," Kaer'lic Suun Wett said to the giant two-headed Proffit soon after the human band had temporarily escaped from the troll and bog bloke pursuit. "The hour of complete domination over all the region is at hand for you. If you strike at them now, hard and relentlessly, you will utterly destroy all remnants of Nesmé and any foothold the humans can dare hope to hold in your lands."

"King Obould wants us in the tunnels," one of Proffit's heads replied.

"Now!" the other head emphatically added.

"To help with Obould's victory in the north?" Kaer'lic said. "In lands that mean nothing to Proffit and his people?"

"Obould helped us," Proffit said.

"Obould showed Proffit the way out, with all the trolls behind him," the other head added.

Kaer'lic knew well enough what Proffit was referring to. It had been none other than Donnia Soldou, in fact, who had orchestrated the rise of Proffit, through the proxies of King Obould. All that Donnia had hoped was that Proffit and his force of brutish trolls would cause enough of a distraction closer to the major human settlements to keep the bigger players of the region, primarily Lady Alustriel of Silverymoon, from turning her eyes and her formidable armies upon Obould.

Of course at that time, Kaer'lic and the other dark elves had no idea of how fast or how high King Obould would rise. The game had changed.

"And Proffit helped Obould close the back door of Mithral Hall," Kaer'lic reminded.

"Tit," said one head.

"For tat," the other added with a rumbling chuckle.

"But dwarves are left," said the first.

"To," said the other.

"Kill!" they both shouted together.

"Dwarves of Mithral Hall to kill, yes," agreed Kaer'lic. "Dwarves who

are stuck in a hole and going nowhere. Dwarves who will still be there waiting to be killed when Proffit has done his work here."

The troll's heads looked at each other and nodded in unison.

"But the humans of Nesmé are not so trapped," Tos'un Armgo put in, right on cue, as he and Kaer'lic had previously decided and practiced. "They will run far away, out of Proffit's reach. Or they will bring in many, many friends, and when Proffit comes back out of the tunnels, he may find a huge army waiting for him."

"More."

"To."

"Kill!" the troll said, both heads grinning stupidly.

"Or too many to kill," Tos'un argued after a quick, concerned glance at Kaer'lic.

"The human friends of Nesmé will bring wizards with great magical fires," Kaer'lic ominously warned.

That took the stupid and eager smile from Proffit's faces.

"What to do?" one head asked.

"Fight them now," said Kaer'lic. "We will help you locate each human band and to position your forces to utterly destroy them. It will not take long, and you can go into the tunnels to fight the dwarves confident that no force will mobilize against you and await your return."

Proffit's two heads bobbed, one chewing its lip, the other holding its mouth open, and both obviously trying to digest the big words and intricate concepts.

"Kill the humans, then kill the dwarves," Kaer'lic said simply. "Then the land is yours. No one will bother to rebuild Nesmé if everyone from Nesmé is dead."

"Proffit likes that."

"Kill the humans," said the other head.

"Kill the dwarves," the first added.

"Kill them all!" the second head cheered.

"And eat them!" yelled the first.

"Eat them all," Kaer'lic cheered, and she motioned to Tos'un, who added, "Taste good!"

Tos'un offered a shrug back at Kaer'lic, showing her that he really had no idea what to add to the ridiculous conversation. It didn't really matter anyway, because both dark elves realized soon enough that their little ploy had worked, and so very easily.

"I remember when Obould was as readily manipulated as that," Kaer'lic said almost wistfully as she and Tos'un left Proffit's encampment.

Tos'un didn't disagree with the sentiment. Indeed, the world had seemed so much simpler a place not so very long ago.

6

FORWARD THINKING ORC

"All the anger of the day," Tsinka Shinriil said as she ran her fingers over Obould's massive shoulder. "Let it lead you now." Then she bit the orc on the back of his neck and began to wrap her sinewy arms and legs around him.

Feeling the tautness of her muscles against him, Obould was again reminded of the wild pegasus. Amusing images floated through his mind, but he pushed them away as he easily moved the amorous shaman aside, stepping out into the center of his tent.

"It is much more than a stupid creature," he remarked, as much to himself as to Tsinka. He turned to see the shaman staring at him, her bewildered expression so much in contrast to her trembling and naked form.

"The winged horse," Obould explained. Tsinka slumped down on a pile of furs. "More than a horse . . . more than the wings . . ." He turned away, nodding, and began to pace. "Yes . . . that was my mistake."

"Mistake? You are Gruumsh. You are perfect."

Obould's grin became an open snicker as he turned back to her and said, "I underestimated the creature. A pegasus, so it would seem, is much more than a horse with wings."

Tsinka's jaw drooped. Obould laughed at her.

"A horse might be clever, but this creature is more," said Obould. "It is wise. Yes! And if I know that . . ."

"Come to me," Tsinka bade him, and she extended her arm and struck a pose so exaggerated, so intentionally alluring, that Obould found it simply amusing.

He went to her anyway, but remained quite distracted as he thought through the implications of his insight. He knew the disposition of the pegasus; he knew that the creature was much more than a stupid horse with wings, for he had come to recognize its stubbornness as loyalty. If he knew that, then the pegasus's former masters surely knew it, and if they knew it, then there was certainly no way that they would let the imprisonment stand.

That thought reverberated through Obould, overshadowing every movement of Tsinka, every bite, every caress, every purr. Rather than diminish in the fog of lust, the images of elves sweeping down to rescue the pegasus only gained momentum and clarity. Obould understood the true value of the creature his minions had captured.

The orc king gave a great shout, startling Tsinka. She froze and stared at him, her eyes at first wild and showing confusion.

Obould tossed her off to the side and leaped up, grabbing a simple fur to wrap around himself as he pushed through the tent flap and out into the encampment.

"Where are you going?" Tsinka shrieked at him. "You cannot go!"

Obould disappeared behind the tent flap as it fell back in place.

"You must not go out without your armor!" cried Tsinka. "You are Gruumsh! You are the god! You must be protected."

Obould's head poked back in, his eyes and toothy grin wide.

"If I am a god . . ." he started to say, but he left the question there, letting Tsinka reason it out for herself. If he was a god, after all, then why would he need armor?

"Sunrise," Innovindil said breathlessly when at long last she saw the marvelous winged horse.

Behind her, over the rocky bluff and down the back slope of the mountain

spur, Sunset pawed the ground and snorted, obviously aware that her brother and companion was down there in the grassy vale.

Innovindil hardly heard the pegasus behind her, and hardly noticed her dark elf companion stirring at her side. Her eyes remained locked on the pegasus below, legs bound as it grazed in the tall brown grass. The elf couldn't block out recollections of the last time she had seen Sunrise, caught under a net, nor those images that had accompanied that troubling scene. The death of her lover Tarathiel played out so clearly in her mind again. She saw his desperate war dance against Obould and that sudden and stunning end.

She stared at Sunrise and blinked back tears.

Drizzt Do'Urden put a hand on her shoulder, and when Innovindil finally managed to glance over at him, she recognized that he understood very clearly the tumult within her.

"I know," the drow confirmed. "I see him, too."

Innovindil silently nodded.

"Let us find a way to take a giant stride toward avenging Tarathiel," Drizzt said. "Above all else, he would demand that we free Sunrise from the orcs. Let us give his spirit some rest."

Another silent nod, and Innovindil looked back down at the grassy vale. She didn't focus on the pegasus, but rather on the approach routes that would bring them near to the poor creature. She considered the orc guards milling about, counting half a dozen.

"We could swoop in fast and hard upon Sunset," she offered. "I drop you down right behind Sunrise and cover your movements as you free our captured friend."

Drizzt was shaking his head before she ever finished. He knew that the large enemy encampment was just over the low ridge on the other side of the vale.

"Our time will be too short," he replied. "If we alert them before we even arrive on the scene, our time to free Sunrise and be away will be shorter still. Frost giants can throw boulders a long, long way, and their aim is usually true."

Innovindil didn't argue the point. Her own thinking, in fact, had been moving along those same lines even as she was offering her suggestion. When she looked back at Drizzt, she rested more easily, for she could see the dark elf's eyes searching out every approach and weighing every movement. Innovindil had already gained tremendous respect for the dark elf. If anyone could pull off the rescue, it was Drizzt Do'Urden.

"Tell Sunset to be ready to come to your whistle," the drow said a few moments later. "Just as when we . . . when *you*, killed Obould's murderous son."

Innovindil slid back from the ridge, belly-crawling over the far side to Sunset. When she returned a few moments later, she was greeted by a smiling Drizzt, who was waving his hand for her to follow. He slithered over the stones as easily as a snake, Innovindil close behind.

It took the pair nearly half an hour to traverse the mostly open ground of the mountain's eastern slope. They moved from shadow to shadow, from nook to jag to cranny. Drizzt's path got them to the valley floor just north of the field where Sunrise grazed, but still with fifty yards of open ground between them and the pegasus. From that better vantage point, they noted two more orc guards, bringing the number to eight.

Drizzt pointed to himself, to Innovindil, then to the tall grass, and moved his hand in a slithering, snakelike fashion. When the elf nodded her understanding and began to crouch, the drow held up his hand to stop her. He started to work his fingers in the silent drow code, but stopped short in frustration, wishing that she could understand it.

Instead, Drizzt twisted his face and pushed his nose up, trying to look very orclike. Then he indicated the tall grass again and gave an uncertain shrug.

Innovindil winked in reply, to show that she had taken his meaning, and as she went back into her crouch, she produced a dagger from her boot and brought it up to her mouth. Holding it between clenched teeth, the elf went down to her belly and moved out of the trees and to the edge of the grass. She glanced back at Drizzt, indicating with her hand that she'd go out to the right, moving west of Sunrise's position.

The drow went into the grass to her left, similarly on his belly, and the two moved along.

Drizzt took his movements in bursts of ten elbow-steps, slowly and methodically creeping through the grass, then pausing and daring to lift his head enough to take note of the closest orc guard. He wanted to veer off and go right to that one, to leave it dead in the grass, but that was not the point

of their mission. Drizzt fought aside his instinctive rage, against the Hunter within him that demanded continual retribution for the death of Bruenor and the others. He controlled those angry instincts and reminded himself silently that Sunrise was depending on him, that the ghost of Tarathiel, another fallen friend, demanded it of him.

He veered away from the orc guard, swerving wide enough to avoid detection and putting himself back in line to approach Sunrise from the east. Soon he was inside the orc guard perimeter. He could hear them all around, chattering in their guttural language, or kicking at the dirt. He heard Sunrise paw the ground and was able to guess that he was still about twenty-five feet from the steed. That distance would likely take him longer than the hundred-plus feet he had come from the trees, he knew, for every movement had to be silent and carefully made so as to not disturb the grass.

Many minutes passed Drizzt by as he lay perfectly still, then he dared to place one elbow out in front of him and propel himself a foot forward. He moved slightly back to the west as he made his way, closing the ground, he hoped, between himself and Innovindil.

A footstep right before him froze him in place. A moment later, through the grass, he saw a strong, thick orc leg, wrapped in leather and furs.

He didn't dare draw breath.

The brutish creature called to its friends—something in its native language spoken too quickly for Drizzt to decipher. The drow did relax just a bit, though, when he heard other orcs respond with a laugh.

The orc walked along to the west, moving out of Drizzt's way.

The dark elf paused a bit longer, giving the creature time to completely clear and also making sure that it did not take note of Innovindil.

Satisfied, he started to move along once more, but then stopped in surprise at a sudden whinny from Sunrise. The pegasus reared and snorted, front hooves thumping the ground hard. The winged horse neighed again, loudly and wildly, and bucked, kicking the air so forcefully that Drizzt clearly heard the crack of hooves cutting the air.

The drow dared lift his head—and quickly realized his mistake.

Behind him, up in the trees from which he and Innovindil had just come, he heard the shout of an orc lookout. Before him, the eight guards began to close ranks, and one called out.

A noise to the side turned the drow that way—to see more orcs charging over the distant ridgeline.

"A trap," he whispered under his breath, hardly believing it possible.

To his other side, he caught a burst of movement as Innovindil came up fast behind an orc guard. Her hand, so deceptively delicate, flashed around the surprised creature's face and pulled its head back, while her other hand came around the other way, the knife's edge drawing a red line on the creature's exposed neck.

The next nearest orc gave a shout and charged as its companion tumbled down, clutching its mortal wound.

Innovindil's hand snapped forward, launching the already bloody dagger at the incoming orc. With wild gyrations, hands flailing, the orc managed to avoid the missile, but the clever elf was really just looking for a distraction. In a fluid movement, she drew forth her sword and dived into a forward roll, closing the ground between herself and the dodging orc. She came up to her feet gracefully, still moving forward, sword leading and scoring a solid strike into the orc's chest.

But three others charged in at her.

Drizzt called upon his innate drow abilities and put a globe of magical darkness in their path, then leaped up and raced to intercept. One of the orcs managed to stop short of the enchanted area, while another simply roared and charged in headlong, and the third veered off to the side.

"Coming through!" the drow warned his companion, and even as he finished, the charging orc burst out the other side of the darkness globe, barely two strides from the elf.

But Drizzt's warning was enough for Innovindil, and she had her sword angled up before her. As the orc came in hard, spear leading, she parried the tip aside.

The orc barreled on, trying to bury her beneath its larger frame, but at the last moment, Innovindil fell to all fours, turning sidelong to the brute. Despite all its efforts, the orc couldn't slow and couldn't turn, and it tripped against her and tumbled into a somersault over her.

Innovindil couldn't get back to her feet in time, though, and had to block the sword strike from the next incoming brute from one knee. The orc pressed in harder, chopping viciously at her from varying angles with the

sword. The elf had to work her blade frantically to deflect each strike.

She gave a shout as another form rushed past her, and it took her a long moment to even realize that it was Drizzt Do'Urden, and another moment to take a measure of the orc that had been pressing her. It was back a few steps suddenly, holding its sword in trembling fingers. As Innovindil watched, red lines of blood thickened on its face and neck.

"They were in wait for us!" Drizzt called to her, rushing past her again, moving behind her to meet the orc she had tripped up as it stood straight.

The orc thrust its spear at his new foe, and hit nothing but air. The perfectly-balanced, quick-moving drow easily slid back and to the side. Then Drizzt came ahead behind that stab, faster than the orc could begin to expect. The orc had never battled the likes of Drizzt Do'Urden before, nor had it ever seen a drow move in battle, let alone a drow wearing enchanted anklets that magically enhanced his foot-speed.

Rolling scimitars descended over the helpless creature, slashing line after line across its face and chest. It dropped its spear and tucked its arms in tight, trying somehow to fend off the attacks, but the drow's fine blades methodically continued their deadly work.

Drizzt had hit the retreating orc perhaps two dozen times, then he jumped up and kicked the creature in the chest for good measure, and also to use that movement to reverse his momentum and direction.

All thoughts of that orc flew from his mind as he turned around to see Innovindil backing from the remaining four guards. Many, many more orcs were closing ground left, right, and center across the field. Shouts from the trees told Drizzt that the humanoids were behind him as well, and there were louder shouts from not so far away.

"Get to Sunrise!" Innovindil shouted at Drizzt as he rushed up beside her, contacting her right arm with his left. He offered her an assuring look. He had seen Innovindil and Tarathiel fighting like that, and he and the elf had practiced the technique over the past few days.

Innovindil's doubting expression betrayed her.

"We have no choice," Drizzt pointed out.

He rolled ahead of the elf to meet the charge of the nearest orc. His scimitars worked furiously, batting at the creature's weapon, then cutting below its attempted parry, but at a shortened angle that could not reach the orc. The orc didn't realize that, however, as the drow spun past. In fact, the orc never began to understand the drow's intent, never began to recognize that the drow had worked his routine and sidelong retreat for no better reason that to set the orc up for the elf who was rolling in behind.

All the orc ever figured out was that an elven sword through the ribs hurt.

Already engaged with another orc, Drizzt hardly noted the grunt and fall of the first. He held complete confidence in Innovindil, though, and understood that if there was a weak link in the fighting chain that he and the elf had become, it was he. And so Drizzt fought with even more ferocity, scimitars working in a blur, batting away weapons and forcing awkward dodges, setting up the victims for Innovindil as she came in fast and hard behind him just as he was fast in behind her, going with all speed at those orcs Innovindil had left vulnerable for him.

Across the field the dancing duo went, moving in tight circles, rolling one upon the other and inexorably toward the trapped pegasus. But with every turn, every different angle coming clearly into his view, Drizzt understood that they would not rescue Sunrise that day. They had underestimated their enemy, had taken the scene of the pegasus grazing beside its handlers at face value.

Three more orcs were down. A fourth fell to Drizzt's double slash, a fifth to Innovindil's fast turn and stab at a creature that was still watching Drizzt turning aside.

When he came around the next time, Drizzt went down to his knees, avoiding an awkward cut from an orc sword. Rather than seizing the opportunity to strike at that overbalanced orc, the drow used the moment of respite to bring forth his onyx figurine. Guenhwyvar had not been gone from his side for long enough, he knew, but he had no choice and so he summoned the panther from her Astral home.

He went back to his feet immediately, blades working furiously to regain the edge against increasingly organized attacks. Behind him and Innovindil as they turned on their way, a gray mist began to take shape and solidify.

One orc noted that distinctive feline shape and slashed at the mist, its sword crossing through without finding a hold. The frustrated orc growled and reversed its cut, but the mist became more corporeal and a powerful cat's paw batted the sword aside before it could gain any momentum. Back

legs twitching easily, the panther flew into the orc's face, laying it low, and a quick rake left the brute howling and squirming on the field while mighty Guenhwyvar sprang away to find her next victim.

Even the panther would not be nearly enough, though, Drizzt knew, as many more orcs came into view, swarming the field from . . .

"Every angle," he said to his companion. "No clear route."

"Every angle but one," Innovindil corrected, and gave a shrill whistle.

Drizzt nodded his understanding at once, and as Innovindil went for the thin rope she kept hooked on her belt, the drow increased his tempo, fighting furiously beside her, forcing the orcs to fall back. He called for his panther to coordinate with him, to keep one flank clear while he assaulted the other.

Innovindil had a lasso up spinning hard a moment later, building momentum. Then Sunset appeared in a powerful stoop, coming over the rocky ridge from which Innovindil and Drizzt had first observed the captive Sunrise. The pegasus came down in a rush—a giant-thrown boulder hummed in the air, narrowly missing the equine beast—and leveled out fifteen feet above the grass, soaring past the surprised orcs too quickly for their clumsily thrown spears to catch up.

The well-trained pegasus lowered her head as she crossed above Innovindil, who launched her lasso perfectly, then held on, hooking her foot into a loop at the bottom of the twenty-foot length of rope. The pegasus immediately turned upward as she soared along, dragging the elf.

Innovindil took a stinging hit as she barreled through the nearest orcs, for one spear was angled just right to slice her hip. Fortunately for the elf, though, that was the only weapon that came to bear as she crashed among the scrambling brutes. Then she was up above them, spinning along as Sunset's mighty wings beat furiously to gain speed and height.

Dazed from slamming against so many, and with her hip bleeding, Innovindil kept the presence of mind to hold fast and begin her climb.

Drizzt was too engaged to follow her movements, and he winced more than once as more boulders cut the air above him. Rage propelling him, the drow went into a sudden charge, bursting through the orc ranks and finally getting beside Sunrise.

The pegasus's front hooves were firmly staked. There was no way Drizzt was going to easily free him. And no way for him to get away, it seemed, for the orcs had him fully ringed, shoulder to shoulder in an unbroken line. From somewhere behind those ranks, the drow heard Guenhwyvar cry out in pain, a call so plaintive that he quickly dismissed the panther.

He scrambled across the area around Sunrise, charging for the orc ranks, then reversing direction to come back to the pegasus. It all seemed too eerily familiar to him, even more so when the orcs began to chant, "Obould! Obould! Obould!"

The drow remembered Tarathiel's last fight, remembered the brutish warrior who had slain his elf friend. He had vowed to avenge that death. But he knew beyond all doubt that it was not the time nor the place. He saw the orcs parting at one point and caught a glimpse of the bone-white helm of his adversary.

Drizzt's knuckles whitened with eagerness as he clenched his scimitars. How he longed to put those fine blades to use on the skull of King Obould Many-Arrows!

But there were shamans among the orc ranks, he noted—if he gained advantage on Obould, could he hope to inflict a mortal wound that would not be quickly healed? If he drove the orc king back to disadvantage, would not the orc horde fall over him?

He didn't want to look up and tip his hand for his one hope, but his lavender eyes did glance upward more than once. He noted Innovindil, like a kite string as she and Sunset disappeared behind some trees, and knew beyond doubt that when he saw her again, she would be astride the pegasus.

The bone white helmet bobbed behind the front ranks, closer, and the volume and tempo of the chanting steadily increased.

Drizzt snapped his head around, as if nervously, but really so that he could cover another quick glance upward.

He caught the movement, the shadow. Again he tightened his hands on his scimitars, wanting nothing more than to sink one of those fine blades deep into Obould's chest.

He turned suddenly and leaped upon Sunrise's strong back, and the pegasus bristled and tried to stamp and turn.

"Will you kill me, Obould?" the drow cried as he stood tall upon the pegasus's back, and from that vantage point, he could see the orc king's head and upper body clearly, the bone helmet with its elongated eyes, the last vestiges

of daylight glinting off the translucent lenses. He saw the orc's magnificent black armor, all ridged, and that amazing greatsword, which Drizzt knew the orc king could cause to burst into flame with but a thought.

He saw the foe and Drizzt had to wonder if he could hope to beat Obould even in a different circumstance, even if he and the brute faced each other on neutral ground and without allies to be found.

"Are you mighty enough to defeat me, Obould?" he called in defiance anyway, for he knew that he had to make himself the focus, had to keep all eyes upon him and had to convince the orc king not to order its orcs to simply swarm him. "Come along, then," the drow boasted, and he flipped one of his scimitars in the air, deftly catching it by the hilt as it came around. "Long have I desired to see my blades stained red with your flowing blood!"

The last ranks of orcs parted then, leaving the line between Drizzt and Obould clear, and the drow had to consciously force himself to draw breath and to hold steady on his high perch. For the sheer presence of Obould assaulted him, the weight and balance of the creature, the solidity of form and the easy manner with which the king slowly moved his heavy sword with only one hand as if it was as light as an elven walking stick.

"I need you, Sunrise," the drow muttered quietly. "Lift me high, I beg, that I might find my way back to you."

A quick glance skyward showed Drizzt the return and dive of Innovindil and Sunset, but coming in much higher, the fine rope flowing below.

"Not now, Obould!" Drizzt screamed, startling many orcs, and he quick-stepped back to Sunrise's broad rump and kicked the pegasus.

Sunrise bucked on cue and Drizzt sprang away, using the lift to launch him high into the air. He snapped his scimitars away as he rose, twisting and turning to line himself up with the approaching rope.

"Another time, Obould!" he cried as he caught the rope with one hand some twenty feet from the ground. "You and I, another time!"

The orc king roared and his minions launched spears, stones, and axes up into the air.

But again they could not properly lead the swift-moving target, and Drizzt secured his hold, the wind snapping in his ears.

From his high vantage point he saw the giants, as did Innovindil and Sunset, obviously, for the pegasus veered as the boulders came sailing out.

They climbed higher into the fast-darkening sky, and avoided the barrage enough to get up over the ridge and to safety, both Drizzt and his elf companion having gained new respect for their cunning adversary.

Down on the field, Obould watched them disappear with as much amusement as disappointment.

Another time, indeed, he knew, and he was not the least bit afraid.

Around him, the orcs cheered and hooted.

Before him, Sunrise continued to buck and to whinny, and the pegasus's handlers moved in fast, whips in hand to control the beast.

Obould roared at them to steal their momentum.

"With ease and soft hands!" he demanded.

The next day, barely after the sun had cleared the eastern horizon, those handlers came to Obould.

"The beast was not hurt, god-king," the lead handler assured him. "The beast is ready to be ridden."

With Tsinka Shinriil on his arm, nibbling at his ear, Obould grinned widely at the handler.

"And if the beast throws me again, I will cut off your head," he promised, and Tsinka snickered.

The handler paled and shrank back.

Obould let him squirm uncomfortably for a few moments. The orc king had no intention of going to the captured pegasus that day, or ever again. He knew that he could never ride the beast safely, and knew, too, that he would never again be able to use the pegasus to lure his enemies in close. In short, the winged horse had outlived its usefulness to him—almost.

It occurred to the orc king that there might be one last service the captured pegasus could perform.

7

AS GRUUMSH WILLS

“They won’t come on, I tell ye, for them trolls in the south’ve run off,” said Cordio, who was fast being recognized as one of Mithral Hall’s leading priests, and leading voices in their difficult struggle.

“Moradin tell ye that, did he?” Bruenor came right back.

“Bah! Got nothing to do with that,” Cordio answered. “I’m using me own thinking here, and not needin’ more’n that. Why’d them trolls back out o’ the tunnels if them orcs’re meaning to press in? Even orcs ain’t that stupid. And this one, Obould, been showing himself smarter than most.”

Bruenor looked from the priest to Cordio’s patient, Banak Brawnanvil, still unable to walk or even stand after taking an orc spear in the back on his retreat from the ridge north of Keeper’s Dale.

“I ain’t so sure,” the wise old warrior dwarf answered. “Trolls could come back at any time, of course, and ye’re guessing that Obould even knows them trolls’ve left. We got no eyes out there, King Bruenor, and without them eyes, I ain’t for putting the safety o’ Mithral Hall on a guess.”

Bruenor scratched his hairy head and tugged on his red beard. His gray eyes went from Banak to Cordio, then back to Banak.

“He’s coming in,” Bruenor decided. “Obould’s not to let this stand. He took Felbarr once, and he’s wanting nothing more than to do it again. And he's knowing that he ain't to get there unless he comes through Mithral Hall. Sooner or later, he's coming in."

"I'm guessing sooner," said Banak, and he and Bruenor both turned to Cordio.

The dwarf priest held up his hands in surrender. "I'll argue all the day long on how ye might be bandaging a wound, but ye're the warcommanders. Cordio's just one to clean up after yer messes."

"Well, let's make this mess one for Obould's shamans to clean," said Bruenor.

"The boys're already making them top halls ready for defense," Banak assured him.

"I got an idea of how we might give Obould's shamans some extra work," the dwarf king remarked, heading for the corridor. He pulled Banak's door open wide, then looked back, grinning. "All the clan's owing to ye, Banak Brawnanvil. Them boys from Mirabar're thinking yerself to be a demigod."

Banak stared at his king stoically, though a bit of moisture was indeed beginning to glisten at the corners of his dark eyes.

Bruenor kept staring hard at the wounded warcommander. He reached down and snapped open his thick belt, and with one quick motion, pulled it off. He wrapped the leather around his hand locking the buckle, a thick, carved mithral clasp adorned with the foaming mug standard of the clan, across his knuckle. Still looking Banak in the eye, Bruenor grabbed and secured the door with his free hand then hit it with a solid left cross. He pulled the door open a bit wider, so that Banak and Cordio could see his work: the indent of the Battlehammer foaming mug.

"We're gonna fill that with silver and gold," Bruenor promised, which was the highest honor a king of Mithral Hall could bestow upon any of his subjects. With that, Bruenor nodded and left, closing the door behind him.

"I'm thinking that yer king's a bit fond of ye, Banak Brawnanvil," said Cordio.

Banak slumped back, resting flat on his back. "Or he's thinking I'm all done for."

"Bah!"

"Ye get me fixed then, ye durned fool," Banak demanded.

Cordio exhaled and took a long pause, then muttered, "By Moradin's blessing," under his breath.

And truly the priest hoped that Moradin was paying attention and would grant him the power to alleviate some of Banak's paralysis, at least. A dwarf as honored and respected as Banak should not be made to suffer such indignity.

Obould stood up high on the rocky bluff, overlooking the work. Orcs scrambled all around Keeper's Dale, sharpening weapons and practicing tight and fast strike formation, but the majority of the important work was being done not by orcs, but by Gerti's giants. Obould watched a procession of more than a dozen behemoths enter the western end of the dale, dragging a huge log with ropes as thick as an orc's chest. Other giants worked on the stone wall around the closed western doors, tossing aside debris and checking the strength of the mountain above the portal. Still other giants tied off and hammered logs on tall towers set on either side of the doors, and a third that rose up a hundred feet, which was located straight back from the iron-bound western gates of Clan Battlehammer's hall.

Obould scanned higher up on the mountain above the doors, at his many scouts scrambling over the stones. Foremost in his mind was the element of surprise. He didn't want any dwarf eyes peering out at the preparations in the dale. Tsinka and the other shamans had assured him that the dwarves would never expect the assault. The bearded folk were tied up in the south with Proffit's trolls, they presumed, and like those dwarves in Citadel Felbarr years before, they held too much confidence in the strength of their iron portals.

The orc king moved down the rocky slope, seeing Gerti standing among some of her giantkin, poring over parchments spread on a tall wooden table. The giantess looked from the parchments to the work on the towers and the huge log sliding across the stone floor of the dale, and grinned. The giant beside her pointed down to the parchment, nodding.

They were good at this, Obould knew, and he gained confidence with every stride.

"Mighty doors," he said to Gerti as he approached.

Gerti shot him a look that seemed somewhere between incredulity and disgust. "Anything a dwarf can build, a giant can knock down," she replied.

"So we shall soon see," the orc king responded with a low and respectful bow. He moved closer and those giants near to Gerti stepped aside, granting them some privacy.

"How far into Mithral Hall will your giants travel?" Obould asked her.

"*Into* Mithral Hall?" came her scoffing reply. "We are not built for dirty, cramped dwarven tunnels, Obould."

"The ceiling of the entry hall is high, by all that I have heard."

"I told you that we would knock down the door, and so we shall. Once the portal falls, let your orcs run into the killing chambers of King Bruenor."

"The treasures of Mithral Hall are considerable, so it is said," Obould teased.

"Treasures that I have already earned."

Obould bowed again, not as low, and not as respectfully. "Your giants will be of great help to my warriors in that entry hall," he said. "Help us to secure our foothold. From there, my warriors will spread like thick smoke throughout the tunnels, routing the dwarves."

Gerti's sly smile showed that she wasn't so sure of that.

"Then you and your kin can go to the Surbrin, as we agreed," said Obould.

"I will go to the Surbrin as *I* determine," Gerti retorted. "Or I will not. Or I will go back to Shining White, or to Silverymoon, if I feel so inclined to take the city of Lady Alustriel. I am bound by no agreements to Obould."

"We are not enemies, Dame Orelsdottr."

"Keep it that way, for your own sake."

Obould's red-streaked yellow eyes narrowed for just an instant, tipping off the giantess to the simmering rage within him.

"I wish for your giants to accompany the lead ranks through the entry hall," said Obould.

"Of course you do. You have no warriors who can approach their strength and skill."

"I do not ask this without recompense."

"You offer me the treasures of Mithral Hall?" asked Gerti. "The head of King Battlehammer, whom you already claimed dead?"

"The pegasus," Obould blurted, and for a brief moment, he saw a telltale flash of intrigue in Gerti's blue eyes.

"What of it?"

"I am not so foolish as to try to ride the creature, for it is not an unthinking beast, but a loyal friend to the elf I destroyed," Obould admitted. "I could eat it, of course, but would not any horse do as well? But you believe it to be a beautiful creature, do you not, Dame Orelsdottr? A fitting trophy for Shining White?"

"If you have no use for it—"

"I did not say that," Obould interrupted.

"You play a dangerous game."

"I make an honest offer. Send your giants in beside my orcs to crush the initial defenses of Mithral Hall. Once we have pushed the dwarves to the tighter tunnels, then leave the hall to me and go your own way, to the Surbrin or wherever you choose. And take with you the winged horse."

Gerti held a defiant pose, but the sparkle in her eyes betrayed her interest.

"You covet that creature," Obould said bluntly.

"Not as much as you believe."

"But your giants will charge into the hall beside my orcs."

"Only because they do so enjoy killing dwarves."

Obould bowed low once again and let it go at that. He didn't really care why Gerti sent her forces in there, as long as she did.

"Hee hee hee."

Ivan couldn't help but smile at his brother's continuing glee. Pikel hopped all about the upper western chambers of Mithral Hall, chasing behind Nanfoodle mostly. King Bruenor had come to the pair immediately following his discussion with Cordio and Banak. Convinced that the orcs would try to break into the hall, Bruenor had commissioned the two unconventional characters, the dwarf "doo-dad" as Pikel described himself, and the gnome alchemist, to help in setting unconventional and unpleasant surprises for the invaders. Of course, Nanfoodle had immediately set the best brewers of Mithral Hall to work in concocting specific formulas of various volatile liquids. All of the rarest and most expensive ingredients were even then being poured into vats and beakers. On Bruenor's instructions, Nanfoodle's team was holding nothing back.

Ivan followed behind the pair, carefully and gently carrying one such large pail of a clear liquid. He tried very hard not to let the volatile fluid slosh about, for in that pail was the same liquid that was held in a small vial in each of his hand crossbow darts. "Oil of Impact," it was commonly called, an exotic potion that exploded under the weight of concussion. Ivan's crossbow darts had been designed to collapse in upon themselves on impact, compressing the chamber and vial, and resulting in an explosion that would then drive the tip through whatever barrier it had struck. Given the force of those explosions using only a few drops of the oil of impact, the dwarf couldn't even begin to guess what clever Nanfoodle had in mind for so much of the potent mix.

"Right there," Nanfoodle instructed a pair of other dwarves who had been put in his charge. He pointed to a flat wall in the western entry chamber, to the side of the doors that led into the main upper level corridors. He motioned for Ivan to bring the pail up, which Ivan did, to the continuing "hee hee hee" of his brother Pikel.

"Would you be so kind as to go and inquire of Candles how he fares in his work?" Nanfoodle asked, referring to a thin, squint-eyed dwarf named Bedhongee Waxfingers, nicknamed Candles because of his family's line of work.

Ivan gently set the bucket on the floor before the wall and glanced back at the other two helpers, both of who were carrying brushes. "Aye, I'll go," he said, looking back at the gnome. "But only because I'm wanting to be far from here when one o' them dolts kicks the bucket."

"Boom!" said Pikel.

"Yeah, boom, and ye're not knowing the half of it," Ivan added, and he started away.

"What were the dimensions again?" Nanfoodle asked him before he had taken two strides.

"For Candles? Two dwarves abreast and one atop another," Ivan replied, which meant five feet wide and eight high.

He watched Nanfoodle motion to the pair with the brushes.

"Durned gnome," he muttered, and he left the chamber.

Barely in the hallway, he heard Nanfoodle lift his voice in explanation: "Bomblets, Pikel. No big explosions in here, of course—not like what we did outside."

"Boom!" Pikel replied.

Ivan closed his eyes and shook his head, then moved along more swiftly, thinking it prudent to put as much ground between himself and Nanfoodle as possible. Like most dwarves, Ivan applauded clever engines of war. The Battlehammer sideslinger catapults and "juicer," a rolling cart designed to flatten and crush opponents, were particularly impressive. But Nanfoodle's work assaulted Ivan's pragmatic dwarven sensibilities. Outside, in the battle for the ridge, the gnome had brought trapped subterranean gasses up under a ridgeline held by frost giants, and had blown the entire mountain spur to pieces.

It occurred to Ivan that while Nanfoodle's efforts might help secure Mithral Hall, it was also quite possible that he would destroy the whole complex in the process.

"Not yer business," the dwarf grumbled to himself. "Ye're the warrior, not the warcommander."

He heard his brother laughing behind him. More often than not, Ivan knew all too well, that laugh didn't lead to good things. Images of flames leaping a thousand feet into the air and the rubble of a mountain ridge flying wide filled his thoughts.

"Not the warcommander," he muttered again, shaking his head.

"Ye're doing great, Rumblebelly," Bruenor prompted.

Regis shifted at the unexpected sound, sending a small avalanche of soot tumbling back on his friend, who was climbing the narrow chimney behind him. Bruenor grumbled and coughed, but offered no overt griping.

"You're certain this will get us out?" Regis asked between his own coughs.

"Used it meself after ye all left me in here with the stinking duergar," Bruenor assured him. "And I didn't have the climbing tools, either! And carried a bunch o' wounds upon me battle-weary body! And . . ."

He rambled on with a string of complaints, and Regis just let them float by him without landing. Somehow having Bruenor below him, ranting and raving, brought the halfling quite a bit of comfort, a clear reminder that he was home. But that didn't make the climb any easier, given Regis's still-aching arm. The wolf that had bitten him had ground its teeth right into his bone, and even though tendays had passed, and even though Cordio and Stumpet had cast healing spells upon him, he was a battered halfling indeed.

He knew the honor Bruenor had placed upon him in asking him to lead the way up the chimney, though, and he wasn't about to slow down. He let the cadence of Bruenor's grumbling guide him and he reached up, hooked his fingers on a jag in the rough stone and hauled himself up another foot. Over and over, he repeated the process, not looking up for many minutes.

When he finally did tilt his head back, he saw at last the lighter glow of the nighttime sky, not twenty feet above him.

Regis's smile faded almost immediately, though, as he considered that there could be an orc guard out there, standing ready to plunge a spear down atop his head. The halfling froze in place, and held there for a long while.

A finger flicked against the bottom of his foot, and Regis managed to look down into Bruenor's eyes—shining whiter, it seemed, for the dwarf's face was completely blackened by soot. Bruenor motioned emphatically for Regis to continue up.

Regis gathered his nerve, his eyes slowly moving up to the starlight. Then, with a burst of speed, he scrambled hand over hand, not letting himself slow until he was within reach of the iron grate, one bar missing from Bruenor's climb those years ago. With a determined grunt, his courage mounting as he considered the feat of his dwarf friend in escaping the duergar, Regis moved swiftly, not pausing until his upper half was right out of the chimney. He paused there, half in and half out, and closed his eyes, waiting for the killing blow to fall.

The only sound was the moan of the wind on the high mountain, and the occasional scraping from Bruenor down below.

Regis pulled himself out and climbed to his knees, glancing all around.

An amazing view greeted him from up on the mountain called Fourthpeak. The wind was freezing cold and snow clung to the ground all around him, except in the immediate area around the chimney, where warm air

continued to pour forth from the heat of the great dwarven Undercity.

Regis rose to his feet, his eyes transfixed on the panoramic view around him. He looked to the west, to Keeper's Dale, and the thousands of campfires of Obould's great army. He turned around and considered the eastern stretches below him, the dark snaking line of the great River Surbrin and the line of fires on its western bank.

"By Moradin, Rumblebelly," Bruenor muttered when he finally got out of the hole and stood up to survey the magnitude of the scene, of the campfires of the forces arrayed against the goodly folk of the Silver Marches. "Not in all me days have I seen such a mob of foes."

"Is there any hope?" Regis asked.

"Bah!" snorted the toughened old king. "Orcs're all! Ten to one, me dwarves'll kill 'em."

"Might need more than that," the halfling said, but wisely under his breath so that his friend could not hear.

"Well, if they come, they're coming from the west," Bruenor observed, for that was obviously the region of the most densely packed opposition.

Regis moved up beside him, and stayed silent. They had an hour to go before the first light of dawn. They couldn't really go far, for they needed the warmth of the chimney air to help ward the brutal cold—they hadn't worn too many layers of clothes for their tight climb, after all.

So they waited, side by side and patiently. They each knew the stakes, and the bite of the wind was a small price to pay.

But the howls began soon after, a lone wolf, at first, but then answered again and again all around the pair.

"We have to go," Regis said after a long while, a chorus of howls growing closer by the second.

Bruenor seemed as if made of stone. He did move enough to glance back to the east.

"Come on, then," the dwarf prodded, speaking to the sky, calling for the dawn's light.

"Bruenor, they're getting close."

"Get yerself in the hole," the dwarf ordered.

Regis tugged his arm, but he did not move.

"You don't even have your axe."

"I'll get in behind ye, don't ye doubt, but I'm wanting a look at Obould's army in the daylight."

A howl split the air, so close that Regis imagined the wolf's hot breath on his neck. His arm ached from memory alone, and he had no desire to face the gleaming white fangs of a wolf ever again. He tugged more insistently on Bruenor's arm, and when the dwarf half-turned, as if moving toward the chimney, the halfling scrambled belly down to the ground and over the lip.

"Go on, then," Bruenor prompted, and he turned and squinted again to the west.

The air had grown a bit lighter, but Bruenor could still make out very little in the dark vale. He strained his eyes and prayed to Moradin, and eventually made out what looked like two great obelisks.

The dwarf scratched his head. Were the orcs building statues? Watch towers?

Bruenor heard the padded footsteps of a canine creature not far away, and still staring down into the dale, he bent low, scooped up a loose stone, and pegged it in the general direction of the noise.

"Go on, then, ye stupid puppy. Dog meat ain't to me liking, to yer own good!"

"Bruenor!" came Regis's cry from the chimney. "What are you doing?"

"I ain't running from a few skinny wolves, to be sure!"

"Bruenor. . . ."

"Bah!" the dwarf snorted. He kicked at the snow, then turned around and started for the chimney, to Regis's obvious relief. The dwarf paused and looked back one more time, though, concentrating on the tall, dark shapes.

"Towers," he muttered, and shook his hairy head. He hopped into the hole, catching the remainder of the grate to break his fall.

And it hit him.

"Towers?" he said. He lifted himself up and glanced to the side at a movement, to see the glowing eyes of a wolf not ten strides away. "O, ye clever pig-face!"

Bruenor dropped from sight.

He prodded Regis to hurry along all the way down the chimney, realizing then that his precious Mithral Hall was in more danger than he had imagined. He had wondered whether Obould would try to come in through lower tunnels,

or perhaps make one of his own, or whether he would try to crash through the great iron doors.

"Towers. . . ." he muttered all the way down, for now he knew.

The next morning, a tree appeared atop the mountain called Fourthpeak, except that it wasn't really a tree, but a dwarf disguised as a tree by the druidic magic of the strange Pikel Bouldershoulder. A second tree appeared soon after, farther down the mountain slope to the west, and a third in line after that. The line of "new growth" stretched down, dwarf after dwarf, until the leading tree had a clear vantage point of the goings-on in Keeper's Dale.

When reports began filtering back to Mithral Hall about the near-readiness of the giant towers and the ghastly, ram-headed battering pole that would be suspended and swung between those obelisks, the work inside the hall moved up to a frenetic pace.

There were two balconies lining the large, oval entry hall of the western reaches of the dwarven complex. Both had crawl tunnels connecting them back to corridors deeper within the complex, and both provided fine kill areas for archers and hammer-throwers. On the westernmost side of one of these balconies, the dwarves constructed a secret chamber, large enough to hold a single dwarf. From out its top, they ran some of the same metal pipes that Nanfoodle had used to bring the hot air up on the northern ridgeline, securing them tight against the ceiling and carrying the line out to the center of the large oval chamber. A heavy rope was then threaded through the piping, secured on a crank within the small secret chamber and dangling out the other end of the pipe, nearly to the floor, some thirty to forty feet below.

All across the reaches of that chamber, the dwarves built defensive positions, low walls over which they could fend off attackers, and which afforded them a continual line of retreat back into the main corridor in the east. They coordinated those junctures in the many walls with drop-points along the ledge above. Under the watchful eye of none other than Banak Brawnanvil, the teams practiced their timing continually, for those below knew that their brethren above would likely be their only chance of getting out of the chamber alive. To further hinder their enemies, the industrious Battlehammer gang placed hundreds of caltrops just inside the great doors, some fashioned purposely and many others nothing more than sharp pieces of scrap metal—waste brought up from the forges of the Undercity.

Outside that expected battlefield, the work was no less intense. Forges glowed, great spoons in brew barrels constantly stirred, sharpening stones whirred, smithy hammers pounded away, and the many pottery wheels spun and spun and spun.

The crowning moment came late one afternoon, when a procession of dwarves carried a large, layered circular bowl into the chamber. More than fifteen feet across, the contraption was all of beaten metal, layered in fans and hooked together on a center pole that rose up just a couple of feet and ended in a sturdy eyelet. Through this, the dwarves tied off the dangling rope.

Nanfoodle nervously checked the trip-spring mechanism on the center pole several times. The tension had to be just right—not so loose that the weight of the bowl's contents could spring it, and not so tight that the drop wouldn't trigger it. He and Ivan Bouldershoulder had done the calculations more than a dozen times, and their confidence had been high.

Had been.

In looking around at all the curious dwarves, Nanfoodle realized just how much was at stake, and the thought had his little knees clicking together.

"It'll work," Ivan promised him, the dwarf bending in low and whispering in his ear. He gently took Nanfoodle's shoulder and ushered the gnome back, then motioned to the helpers who had come in behind the pair, gently pushing a wide cart full of ceramic balls.

The dwarves began placing the delicate orbs inside the bowl of the contraption, along set ridges, all of which ended with a curled lip of varying angles.

When that work was done, the dwarves up above shoved a long handle into the crank in the secret cubby and began lifting the contraption from the floor, drawing the rope slowly and evenly. Other dwarves climbed ladders beside the bowl as it rose, slowly rotating it through its climb.

"Get a ladder and smooth the edges," Ivan ordered as the whole disk was locked into place up near the ceiling, for though the bottom of the bowl had been painted to make it look like the stone of the ceiling, once it was in place, he could see where improvements might be made.

"It'll work," the yellow-bearded Bouldershoulder said again to Nanfoodle, who was staring up nervously.

The gnome looked to Ivan and managed a meager smile.

Up on the ledge, Bruenor, Regis, Catti-brie, and Wulfgar watched the work with a mixture of hope and sheer terror. The two humans had already witnessed one of Nanfoodle's surprises, and both figured that one incident had made enough of an impression to foster grandiose stories for a lifetime.

"I'm not for liking yer choice," Bruenor said to Regis. "But I'm respecting yer decision, and respecting yerself more and more, little one."

"I'm not for liking my choice, either," Regis admitted. "But I'm no warrior, and this is my way of helping."

"And how are you to get out of there if we don't retake the hall?" Catti-brie asked.

"Would that question be any different if a dwarf was accepting the duty?" the halfling shot right back.

Catti-brie thought on that for a moment, then just said, "Maybe we can catch an orc and trick it into pulling the pin."

"Yeah, that'd work," Bruenor said. Beneath his sarcastic quip, the other three caught the slightest of quivering in his voice, a clear sign that he, like the others, realized that this might be the last time they saw their halfling friend.

But then, if they failed in this, they would all likely die.

"I'm wanting you two up on the other ledge," Bruenor said to his two human children. "Right near the escape corridor."

"I was thinking to fight on the floor," Wulfgar argued.

"The walls're too short for ye, and what a fine target ye'll be making for our enemies, standing twice a dwarf's height down there," Bruenor answered. "No, ye fight on the ledge, the two o' ye together, for that's when ye're at yer best. Hold all yer shots, bow and hammer, for any giants, should they come in, and keep yerselves at the escape tunnel."

"So that we might be the first to leave?" Catti-brie asked.

"Aye," the dwarf admitted. "First out and not bottlenecking the low crawl for me kin."

"If that's the reasoning, then shouldn't we be last?" Wulfgar asked, tossing a wink at Catti-brie as he did.

"No, ye go first and ye go early, and that's the end of it," said Bruenor. "Ye got to be near the tunnel, as ye'll both be needing that tunnel to fall back from sight, for ye can't get as low as me boys that'll be up there with ye. Now stop yer arguing with me and start sorting out yer tactics."

The dwarf turned to Regis and asked, "Ye got enough food and water?"

"Does he ever?" Catti-brie asked.

Regis grinned widely, his dimpled cheeks climbing high. He patted his bulging backpack.

"Should be today," Bruenor told him. "But ye might have a bit of a wait."

"I will be fine, and I will be ready."

"Ye know the signal?"

The halfling nodded.

Bruenor patted him on the shoulder and moved away, and with a grin and helpless shrug to his friend, Regis moved inside the secret cubby, pulled the stone-shaped door closed and bolted it on the inside. A pair of dwarves moved right up to the closed portal and began working its edges with mud and small stones, sealing the portal and also blending it in to the surrounding wall so perfectly that a trained elf thief would have a hard time spotting the door if he'd been told exactly where to find it.

"And you'll be on the floor, of course?" Catti-brie asked Bruenor.

"Right in the middle of the line's me place." He noted Catti-brie's scowl and added, "Ye might want to dip yer bow every now and then to clear the way if ye see that I'm attracting a bit too much orc attention."

That brought a light to the woman's face, a clear reminder that whether up on the ledge or down on the floor, they were in it together.

"We're gonna make 'em pay for every inch o' ground," Bruenor told his charges when word came down the chimneys that the towers were completed in Keeper's Dale, and that great lengths of rope were being strung. It took quite a while for that word to run up the dwarven "tree" line, down the chimney

to the Undercity, then back up the corridors to the entry hall, though, and so the words had just left Bruenor's mouth when the first thunderous smash hit the great iron doors. All the chambers shook under the tremendous weight of that blow, and more than one dwarf staggered.

Those closest to the doors immediately moved to inspect the damage, and with just that one blow, cracks appeared in the stone supporting the massive portals.

"Won't take many," the lead engineer closest the doors called.

He and his group moved back fast, expecting the second report—which shook the chamber even more. The doors cracked open under the great weight. More than one set of eyes went up nervously to the ceiling and the delicate bowl contraption.

"It'll hold," Bruenor shouted from the front rank in the center of the dwarven line, directly across the hall from the doors. "Don't ye be looking up! Our enemies're coming in through the doors in the next hit or two.

"Girl!" he called up to Catti-brie. "Ye set yer sights on that center line in the doors and if it opens and an ugly orc puts its ugly face against it, ye take it down hard! All of ye!"

The great ram swung in again, slamming the iron, and the doors creaked in some more, leaving a crack wide enough to admit an orc, if not a giant. Just as Bruenor had predicted, enemies did come against the portals, hooting, shouting, and pressing. One started through, then began to jerk in place as a barrage of arrows and crossbow bolts met it.

The orcs behind the unfortunate point pushed it in and to the floor, and hungrily crowded against the open slot.

More arrows and bolts met them, including a silver-streaking arrow that sliced right through the closest creature and several behind it, lessening the press for a moment.

Then the ram hit again, and the right-hand door busted off its giant top hinge and rolled inward, creaking and groaning as the metal of the bottom hinge twisted. Chunks of stone fell from above, smashing the first ranks of orcs, but hardly slowing the flood that followed.

The orcs poured in, and the dwarves howled and set themselves against the charge. The broken door twisted and settled back the other way, crashing down upon many of the unfortunate orcs and somewhat slowing the charge.

Missiles rained down from on high. A heavy warhammer went spinning among the throng, splitting the skull of one orc. As the charge neared the first of the newly-constructed low walls, dwarves sprang up from behind it, all of them leveling crossbows and blasting the closest rank of enemies. Bows fell aside, the dwarves taking up long spears and leveling them at the charging throng. Those orcs in front, pressed by the rolling wave behind, couldn't hope to slow or turn aside.

As one, Banak's well-drilled team let go of their spears and took up their close-combat weapons. Sword, axe, and hammer chopped away wildly as the orc wave came on. From above, a concentrated volley devastated the second rank of enemies, allowing the dwarves a chance to retreat back beyond the second wall.

The scene would repeat itself in ten-foot sections, wall to wall, all the way back to Bruenor's position.

"Wulfgar! Girl!" Bruenor cried when a larger form appeared in the broken doorway. Even as he spoke, a magical arrow from Catti-brie's Taulmaril zipped out for the hulking giant form, followed closely by a spinning warhammer.

The orcs made the second wall, where many more died.

But the monstrous wave rolled on.

Regis curled up and blocked his ears against the screaming and shouting that reverberated across the stones. He had seen many battles—far too many, by his estimation—and he knew well the terrible sounds. And it always sounded the same. From the street fights in Calimport to the wild battles he had seen in Icewind Dale, both against the barbarians of the tundra and the goblinkin, to the battles to retake and hold onto the coveted mines of Mithral Hall, Regis had been assailed by those same sounds over and over again. It didn't matter if the wails came from orcs or dwarves or even from giants. As one, they split the air, carrying waves of agony on their shrill notes.

The halfling was glad to be in his sealed compartment where he did not have to witness the flowing blood and torn bodies. He took faith that his role was an important one for the success of the dwarves' plan, that he was contributing in a great way.

For the time being, though, he wanted to put all those thoughts out of his head, wanted to put everything out of his mind and just lay in the near-absolute blackness of the sealed cubby. He closed his eyes and blocked his ears, and wished that it was all far, far away.

"Giant!" Wulfgar said to Catti-brie, who was kneeling on the balcony beside him. As he spoke, the huge form crossed over the lighter area of the fallen door and into the chamber, spurring orcs on before it. With a roar to his god of war, Wulfgar brought his warhammer up over his shoulder, then rolled his arms around to straighten them, putting the hammer directly in line behind his back.

"Tempus!" he cried again, and he leaned his tall frame back, then began a rolling movement that seemed to start as his knees, his back arcing and swaying forward, huge shoulders snapping ahead as his arms came up over his head, launching mighty Aegis-fang into an end-over-end flight across the room.

Catti-brie targeted quickly upon Wulfgar's call and let fly, her arrow easily outdistancing the warhammer to strike the giant first, right in the upper arm. The behemoth cried out and straightened, squaring up to the pair on the ledge right as the warhammer slammed in, taking it squarely in the face with a tremendous slapping sound.

The giant staggered. Another arrow hit it in the torso, then a third, and Wulfgar, the enchanted warhammer magically returned to his grasp, yelled out for Tempus again and launched the missile.

The giant turned and stumbled back toward the door.

The hammer pounded in right against its bending back, launching it forward and to the floor, where it crushed an unfortunate orc beneath its tumbling bulk.

"More of 'em," Catti-brie remarked as another, then another huge form crossed the leaning door.

"Just keep a line of arrows then," Wulfgar offered, and again his hammer appeared magically in his grasp. He started to take aim at one of the new adversaries, but then saw the wounded giant stubbornly trying to rise again. Wulfgar adjusted his angle, roared to his war god, and let fly. The hammer hit the giant right on the back of the skull as it tried to rise, with a crack that sounded like splitting stone. The behemoth went down fast and hard and lay very still.

Two other giants were in the foyer, though, the lead one accepting a hit from Catti-brie's devastating bow, and dodging fast as a second arrow sped by, the enchanted missile slicing right into the stone wall. Another behemoth appeared at the doorway and held there, and a moment later, the bombardiers on the balcony understood the tactic. For that giant turned fast and tossed something to the farthest one in the hall, who caught it and swiveled about, tossing it to the leading brute.

Another arrow from Catti-brie stung that behemoth but did not drop it, and when it turned around to face the ledge, its arms went up high, holding a huge boulder, and it let fly.

"Run away!" cried the dwarf to Wulfgar's left, and he grabbed the barbarian by the belt and tugged him aside.

Wulfgar twisted, off-balance, and tumbled to the balcony behind the dwarf. Only as he landed hard and managed to glance back did Wulfgar come to realize that the dwarf had saved his life. The giant-thrown boulder smashed hard against the front of the balcony and skipped upward, slamming into the wall at the side of the exit tunnel.

It rebounded from there back to the balcony, and Wulfgar could only look on in horror as it crushed down upon his dear friend.

"Clear the hall!" came a voice above the tumult of battle, the voice of Bruenor Battlehammer who centered the line of dwarves on the floor, ushering his retreating kin out. "Give us time, archers!"

"Special arrows!" cried dwarves all along both balconies.

As one the crossbowmen reached for their best quarrels, tipped with a metal that burned like a flaring star when touched to flame. Torchbearers ran the length of the archer lines, while cries went out to concentrate the killing area.

Flaring quarrel after quarrel soared down to the center rear of the entry hall, to the region just before the unmoving Bruenor Battlehammer and his

elite warriors, the Gutbuster Brigade, as they held the last line of retreat.

"Now go!" Bruenor cried as the orc ranks shook apart under the glare of the magnesium bolts and the shrieks of unbelievable agony from those who had been struck.

"Block it!" Bruenor cried.

Up on the ledge above him, a dwarf tugged hard at Wulfgar, pulling him away from the boulder that had fallen on Catti-brie.

"We need ye now!" the dwarf cried.

Wulfgar spun away, his blue eyes wet with tears. He was part of a team who were supposed to definitively finish the retreat, one of four assigned to lift the vat of molten metal and pour it down before the escape corridor, buying the fleeing Bruenor and the Gutbusters some time.

Wulfgar, full of rage, changed that plan. He pushed the dwarves aside and wrapped his arms around the vat, then hoisted it and quick-stepped to the edge of the balcony, roaring with every step.

"He can't be doing that," one dwarf muttered.

But he was.

At the edge, the barbarian dropped the vat and tipped it, glowing molten metal pouring down upon the orcs.

A boulder slammed the ledge right below him and the force of the blow threw him aside, stumbling, as pieces of stone broke away below him.

With one last look back to Catti-brie, Wulfgar fell from the ledge, tumbling right after the heavy metal vat.

8

GALEN'S STAND

General Dagna exhaled deeply, his whole body finally seeming to relax. Good news at last, he thought, for one of his scouts had returned with word that tunnels had been found leading straight and deep to the north, back to Mithral Hall, in all likelihood.

For more than a tenday, Dagna, his forty remaining dwarves, and Galen Firth and his human refugees had been moving fast across the muddy, scraggly terrain, collecting remnants of the scattered folk of Nesmé. They had more than four hundred Nesmians in tow, but less than half were battle-capable, and many were wounded.

Worse, their enemies had been dogging their every step, nipping at them in scattered attacks. The skirmishes had diminished to nothing over the past couple of days, but the nagging thought remained with Dagna that those fights had not been so haphazard, that perhaps they were a coordinated effort toward a larger goal. In fact, it occurred to Dagna, though he did not mention it to Galen Firth, that the last couple of bands of refugees, mostly women, children, and very old folk, had been left alone by the trolls purposely. The apparently cunning trolls seemed to recognize that Dagna and Galen would absorb the refugees, and that those less able would surely slow them all down and drain their resources. Dagna recognized

that he and his comrades were, in effect, being herded. The wise old dwarf warcommander understood the ways of battle enough to realize that time was working against him and his impromptu army. Tough as the humans were showing themselves to be, and determined as Galen Firth might be, Dagna believed in his heart that if they couldn't find their way out of there, they would all soon be dead.

Finally on that cold and rainy day had come the welcomed news of a potential escape route, and one through tunnels, where Dagna knew that he and his boys could be much more effective in slowing the powerful trolls. He found Galen Firth a short while later, and was surprised to see that the man was as excited as he.

"Me scouts're back," Dagna said in greeting.

"As are my own," Galen replied with equal enthusiasm.

Dagna started to explain about the tunnel, thinking that perhaps Galen had heard a similar tale, but the man wasn't listening, he realized, and indeed, Galen soon began talking right over him.

"Our enemies are weak between here and Nesmé," Galen explained. "A thin line, with no support to be found anywhere around the town."

"The *ruins* of Nesmé, ye mean," Dagna corrected.

"Not so ruined. Battered yes, but still defensible."

The dwarf paused for a moment and let those words digest. "Defensible?"

"Behind our walls, we are formidable, good dwarf."

"I'm not for doubting that, but are ye forgetting that yer enemy already chased ye out from behind those walls once?"

"We weren't properly prepared for them."

"Yer forces were many times yer present number!"

"We can hold the town," Galen insisted. "Word has gone out to Everlund, Mirabar, and Silverymoon. Surely help will soon arrive."

"To bury yer bones?" Dagna said, and Galen scowled at him. "Ye can't be thinking to move closer to the Trollmoors with an army o' bog blokes and trolls on yer heels."

"Army? The fighting has lessened since our escape from the trolls," Galen argued. "We have reason to believe that many of our enemies have gone into tunnels heading for Mithral Hall."

"Aye, tunnels to Mithral Hall," said Dagna. "Which is why I come to ye this day. We found the way back, deep and quiet. We can make the tunnels afore the morrow and be well on our way."

"Have you not listened to a word I've said?"

"Have ye yerself heared them words?" Dagna replied. "Ye're for walking out from the protection o' the mountains onto open ground where yer enemies can sweep upon ye. Ye're to get yer people slaughtered."

"I am to save Nesmé."

"Nesmé's gone!"

"And would you so quickly abandon Mithral Hall, General Dagna?"

"Mithral Hall's not gone."

It was Galen Firth's turn to pause and take a deep breath against the unrelenting pragmatism of General Dagna. "I am of the Riders of Nesmé," he explained slowly and calmly, as if reciting a vow he had made many times before. "My life has been given to the protection of the town, wholly so. We see a way back to our homes. If we get back behind our city wall—"

"The damned trolls'll catch ye there and kill ye."

"Not if many have turned their eyes to the north, as we believe."

"And ye'd be willing to risk all yer kinfolk on that belief?"

"Help will come," Galen declared. "Nesmé will rise again."

Dagna locked stares with the man. "Me and me boys're heading for the tunnels and back to Mithral Hall. Ye're welcomed to join us—Steward Regis's offered his hand. Ye'd be wise to take it."

"If we go home—to *our* homes, good dwarf!—will Mithral Hall not offer us the support we need?"

"Ye're asking me to follow ye on a fool's errand!"

"I am asking you to stand beside your neighbors as they defend their homes from a common enemy."

"You cannot be serious," came another voice, and both Dagna and Galen Firth turned to see Rannek moving to join them. The young man's stride was purposeful and determined. "We have a way to the north, underground where our allies can better protect us."

"You would abandon Nesmé?"

Rannek shook his head vigorously. "I would secure the wounded and those who cannot fight, first and foremost. They are the cause of the Riders, not empty buildings and walls that can be rebuilt."

"Rannek now determines the course of the Riders? Rannek the watchman?"

Dagna watched the exchange carefully, and noted how the younger man seemed to lose all momentum so suddenly.

"I speak for the Riders and I speak for all the folk of Nesmé," Galen Firth went on, turning back to the dwarf. "We see an opportunity to return to our homes, and we shall seize it."

"A fool's errand," said Dagna.

"Can you say with certainty that these tunnels you have found will be any less filled with enemies? Can you be so certain that they will even usher us to Mithral Hall? Or might it be that we go underground, flee from the region, only to have the armies of Mirabar, Silverymoon, and Everlund arrive? What then, General Dagna? They will find no one to rescue and no town to help secure. They will believe they are too late and turn for home."

"Or turn north to the bigger fight that's facing Clan Battlehammer."

"That would be your hope, wouldn't it?"

"Don't ye be talking stupid," Dagna warned. "We come all the way down here, I put ten of me boys in the Halls o' Moradin, and all for yer own sake."

Galen Firth backed off just a bit, and even dipped the slightest of bows.

"We are not unappreciative of your help," he said. "But you must understand that we are as loyal to our home as Clan Battlehammer is to Mithral Hall. By all reports, the way is nearly clear. We can fight our way to Nesmé with little risk and it is unlikely that our enemies will be able to organize against us anytime soon to try to expel us once more. By that time, help will arrive."

The dwarf, hardly convinced, crossed his hairy arms over his chest, his muscles tense and bulging around the heavy leather bracers adorning each wrist.

"And what of the remaining refugees who are still out there?" Galen Firth went on. "Would you have us abandon them? Shall we run and hide," he asked, turning quickly to Rannek, "while our kin cower in the shadows with no hope of finding sanctuary?"

"We do not know that more are out there," Rannek offered, though his voice seemed less than sure.

"We know not if there are none," Galen Firth retorted. "Is my life worth that chance? Is your own?" The fierce veteran turned back on Dagna. "It is,"

Galen answered his own question. "Come with us if you will, or run and hide in Mithral Hall if that is your choice. Nesmé is not yet lost, and I'll not see her lost!"

With that, Galen turned and stormed away.

Dagna tightened the cross of his arms over his chest and stared at Galen as he departed for a long while before finally turning back to Rannek.

"A fool's errand" he said. "Ye're not for knowing where them trolls're hiding."

Rannek didn't offer any answers, but Dagna understood that the man knew that it wasn't his place to answer. When Galen Firth declared that he spoke for the folk of Nesmé, he was speaking truthfully. Rannek had been given his say, short though it had been, but it was settled.

The young warrior's expression revealed his doubts, but he offered only a bow, then turned and followed Galen Firth, his commander.

A short while later, as twilight began its descent over the land, Dagna and his forty dwarves stood high on the side of a hillock, watching the departing march of Galen Firth and his four hundred Nesmians. Every bit of common sense in the old dwarf told him to let them go and be done with it. Turn about and head into the tunnels, he told himself over and over.

But he didn't give that command as the minutes passed and the black mass of walking humans receded into the foggy shadows of the marshland north of Nesmé.

"I'm not for liking it," Dagna offered to those dwarves around him. "The whole thing's not looking right to me."

"Ye might be thinking a bit too much favor on the cunning of trolls," a dwarf near the old veteran remarked, and Dagna certainly didn't dismiss the comment.

Was he giving the trolls too much credit? The patterns of the escape thus far and the disposition of those refugees they had acquired had led him to consider the trap he might be laying if he was the one chasing the fleeing humans. But he was a dwarf, a veteran of many campaigns, and his enemies were trolls, hulking, stupid, and never strong on tactics.

Maybe Galen Firth was right.

But still the doubts remained.

"Let's follow 'em just a bit, for me own peace o' mind," Dagna told his

fellows. "Put a scout left, put a scout right, and we'll all come up behind, but not close enough so that the durned fool Galen can see us."

Several dwarves grumbled at that, but not loudly.

"They coming, little dwarfie," an ugly troll, gruesome even by troll standards, said to the battered dwarf who lay on the ground below it. "Just like them drow elves said they would."

Another troll giggled, which sounded like a group of drunken dwarves forcing spit up from their lungs, and the pair leaned in close against the muddy bank, peering out through the scraggly brush that further camouflaged their position.

Below them, one heavy foot on his chest, poor Fender Stouthammer could hardly draw breath, let alone do anything to help. He wasn't gagged, but couldn't make any sounds other than a wet wheeze, the result of the male drow's clever work with his blade.

But neither could Fender just lie there. He had heard the drow telling the trolls that they would soon have all the refugees and the stubborn dwarves in their grasp. Fender had lain helpless throughout the last days watching those two dark elves orchestrate the movements of the trolls and the bog blokes. A clever pair, the dark elves had assured the biggest and ugliest of the trolls, a two-headed monstrosity named Proffit, that the stupid humans would walk right into their trap.

And there they were, not so far from the abandoned city of Nesmé, cleverly hidden in a long trench to the north of the west-marching humans, while on the right, their comrades, the treelike bog blokes, lay in wait.

The troll pinning Fender started laughing even harder and began jumping up and down, each descent crunching the dwarf a little deeper into the muck.

Reacting purely on instinct, thinking he would be crushed to death, Fender quickly reached out and grabbed an exposed tree root, then rolled back, pulling the soft wood out with him. As the troll came down the next time, its foot settled on the root instead of the dwarf, and to Fender's relief, the troll seemed not to notice—the root had about the same give, he figured.

Not pausing to savor in his minor victory, Fender bent the root so that it would remain sticking out far enough to accommodate the troll, then rolled back the other way, coming up to all fours as he wound about. He crept off quietly behind a line of equally distracted trolls, but couldn't begin to imagine how he might escape.

Because he could not, Fender Stouthammer admitted to himself. There was no way for him, battered as he was, to hold any hope of getting free of the wretched trolls.

"Next best thing, then," the dwarf silently mouthed and he moved into position at the base of the most gently sloping region of the trench, and near to a series of roots that climbed all the way to the crest, some eight feet from the muddy bottom. With a deep breath and a moment of regret for all those hearty friends and family he'd not ever see again, Fender exploded into motion, running up the root line, hand over hand.

He counted on surprise, and so he had it as he crossed out of the pit and away from the nearest, startled troll. Back behind him, he heard the hoots of his guards, and the growing rumble of outrage.

Fender sprinted for all his life, and more importantly for the lives of all those humans unwittingly approaching the designated kill zone. He tried to scream out to warn them off the trolls, but of course he could not, and he waved all the more frantically when several of the leading men began rushing his way.

Fender did not have to look behind him to know that the trolls had come out in pursuit, for he saw the humans blanch and skid to a stop as one. He saw their eyes go wide with shock and horror. He saw them start to backpedal, then turn and run off shouting in terror.

"Run on," Fender gasped. "Run far and run free."

He felt as if he had been punched hard in the back then, his breath blasted away. He didn't go flying away, though, and strangely felt no pain. When he looked down to his own chest, he understood, for the thick and sharpened end of a heavy branch protruded from between his breasts.

"Oh," Fender remarked, probably the loudest vocalization he had managed since his throat had been cut.

Then he fell over, hardly free, but satisfied that he had properly executed the next best thing.

Stupid trolls, Tos'un Armgo's fingers flashed to Kaer'lic in the silent hand code of the dark elves. *They cannot be trusted to guard a single wounded prisoner!*

Equally disgusted, Kaer'lic held her tongue and watched the unfolding events. Already, the humans were in full and furious retreat, running back to the east. From her high vantage point in the north, Kaer'lic began to nod with renewed hope as the human line predictably began to veer south, away from the charging trolls.

"Is he dead?" Kaer'lic asked, motioning toward the dwarf.

As she spoke, though, Fender squirmed.

"Run for the cover of the trees," the drow priestess said. The copse was comprised of three bog blokes—which very much resembled dead, wintry trees—for every real tree. "Yes, there you will find wood with which to burn the trolls!"

Kaer'lic's wide smile met a similarly knowing one from her partner, for he too recognized the certain doom looming before the ragtag bunch.

But Tos'un's growl stole her mirth, and she followed his scowl back to the east-northeast, where a second force appeared, sweeping down a rocky slope, whooping for war, rattling weapons, and calling out to the dwarf gods Moradin, Clangeddin, and Dumathoin.

Then, amazingly, the dwarves all joined voice in song, a single refrain repeated over and over again, "Along our wake ye people flee. We'll hold 'em back and get ye free!"

Over and over again they sang it out, more emphatically at every juncture when it seemed as if the folk of Nesmé wouldn't veer back to the northeast.

"They've seen the truth of the bog blokes," Kaer'lic observed.

Tos'un gave a derisive laugh and replied, "Of all the races on and under Toril, are any less adept at holding a simple trap than smelly trolls?"

"Any that were less adept than trolls likely were exterminated eons ago."

"What now?"

"Watch the fun," the priestess replied. "And go fetch that fallen dwarf.

Perhaps Lady Lolth will grant me the power I need to keep him alive, so that we might find more enjoyment from him before we kill him."

Dagna's scouts had picked the perfect route for intercepting the chase. The dwarves came down from on high, their short, strong legs gaining momentum as they rambled down the slope. They rushed past the fleeing Nesmians to the left, to a dwarf hollering angrily at those few human warriors who seemed ready to turn and join in the dwarves' charge.

Dagna led his boys right around the humans, hardly slowing as they met the charge of the trolls. Axes, swords, and hammers chopping, they slashed through the front ranks. Those leading trolls who were still standing turned around to fight their new, closer enemies.

Thus, by their own tactics, the dwarves found themselves surrounded almost immediately. There was no despair at that realization, however, for that was exactly as they, to a dwarf, had planned. They had stopped the troll charge in its tracks, and had given the Nesmians a free run.

They knew the cost.

And accepted it with a song of battle on their lips.

Not one of Dagna's boys came off that field alive.

"Look how easily Proffit's fools are distracted!" Kaer'lic said. "They turn on a force of two score, while twenty times that number run away!"

"They'll not escape," replied Tos'un, who had climbed a tree above Kaer'lic and the panting Fender, which afforded him a wider range of view. "The bog blokes outpace them from the south. Already the humans see that they will be caught. Many of their males are forming a defense."

Kaer'lic looked up to her companion, but her smile became a curious frown, for high above Tos'un, the priestess saw a line of fire streaking across the sky west to east, descending as it went. As the fiery object crossed over Tos'un, Kaer'lic began to make out its shape. It was some kind of a cart, a chariot perhaps, pulled by a team of fiery horses.

Tos'un glanced up, too, as did everyone on the field.

Down the chariot swooped, cutting low over the humans, many of whom fell to the ground in fear, but with others suddenly cheering.

Then, just south of the cluster of humans, great fireballs erupted, flames leaping into the night sky.

"The bog blokes!" Tos'un cried out.

East of his position, the humans started on their run once more.

Her long silvery hair flying out behind her, Lady Alustriel of Silverymoon held the reigns of her magically-created chariot of fire in one hand and waved the other hand in a series of movements that brought another tiny pill of glowing flame to her grasp. She veered the chariot for a run over the largest remaining cluster of bog blokes and tossed the pill upon them as she passed.

The fireball erupted in their midst, the hungry flames biting at the bark-like skin of the creatures.

Alustriel banked to get a view of the scene below, and saw that the humans were well on their way again, and that the remaining bog blokes seemed too busy getting away from burning kin to offer any more pursuit. Alustriel's heart sank more than a little when she glanced back to the west, for the battle was all but over, with the trolls overwhelming the dwarves.

Her admiration for Clan Battlehammer only grew that dark night, not only for the actions of that particular brave force, but for even sending any warriors south at such a dark time. Word had come to Silverymoon from Nesmé of the rise of the Trollmoors, and further information had filtered down through King Emerus Warcrown of Citadel Felbarr detailing the march of Obould Many-Arrows. Alustriel had set off at once to survey the situation.

She knew that Mithral Hall was under terrible duress. She knew that the North had been swept by the ferocious orc king and his swarm of minions, and that the western bank of the Surbrin had been heavily fortified.

She knew that she had done little to help that situation, but in looking at the fleeing, desperate Nesmians, she took comfort that she had helped a bit at least.

9

DISPUTING DIVINE INTERVENTION

Wulfgar flailed his arms and tried to twist as he fell from above, hoping to get away from the area of confusion, where orcs screamed in agony and ran all around, where molten metal glowed angrily, and where the vat bounced down hard. He couldn't change his angle of descent, but was fortunate to have instinctively pushed out when first he fell. He came down hard atop a group of unsuspecting orcs, burying them beneath his bulk.

They only partially broke the fall of nearly two dozen feet, though, and Wulfgar hit hard, twisting and slamming painfully as he and the orcs below him went down to the floor. Burning pain assailed him from many places—he figured that more than one bone had cracked in that fall—but he knew he had no time to even wince. Screaming indecipherably, the barbarian put his feet under him and forced himself up, flailing wildly with fist and hammer, trying to keep the closest orcs at bay.

He stumbled for the exit corridor where he knew Bruenor and the others were making their last stand in the great hall, but many orcs stood between him and that door. Any hopes he had that the confusion caused by the molten metal and the heavy vat would allow him to break free dissipated quickly as the orcs reacted to him, prodding at him from every direction. He felt a stab in his shoulder and twisted fast, snapping a flimsy spear's head right

off. Aegis-fang swung around hard, cracking an orc in the side with a blow heavy enough to send it flying into a second, and to send both of them tumbling over a third.

A spear hit Wulfgar in the buttocks, and one of the orcs lying on the floor near to him bit him hard on the ankle. He kicked and thrashed, he swung his hammer and shouldered his way forward, but against increasing resistance.

He couldn't make it, nor could the dwarves hope to get to him.

To the side of Wulfgar's position, a group of orcs moved cautiously toward a single door, not knowing whether it blocked yet another corridor or a second room. Fearing that enemies were waiting just beyond the closed portal, the orcs called to one of the frost giants, inviting it to crash through.

The giant wore a frown at first, lamenting that it could not get to the fallen human—the one, it knew, who had killed its friend with that terrible warhammer—in time to claim the kill. But when it noted the orcs pointing excitedly at the door, the behemoth curled up its lips and launched into a short run, bending low. The giant slammed into the door that was not a door, shouldering it, thinking to smash it into the room.

Except that there was no room, and it was no door.

It was wax, mostly, formed into the shape of a door and set not against a corridor or room opening, but against solid stone—a section of wall that had been thoroughly soaked with explosive oil of impact.

The fake door crashed in hard and the wax disintegrated under the force of the sudden and devastating explosion. The many pieces of sharpened metal concealed within the wax blew free, blasting outward in a line across the room.

The giant bounced back, what was left of its face wearing an expression of absolute incredulity. The behemoth held its arms wide and looked down at its shredded body, at the heavy clothing and flaps of skin wagging freely from head to toe, at the lines of blood dripping everywhere.

The giant looked back helplessly, and fell dead.

And all around it in that line of devastating shrapnel, orcs tumbled, shrieked, and died.

Across the eastern end of the great hall, the fighting stopped, dwarves and orcs alike turning back to gawk at the swath of death the exploding door cut through the line of orcs and another pair of unfortunate giants. Alone in the crowd, one warrior kept on fighting, though. Too blinded by pain and anger to even hear the blast and the screams, Wulfgar gained momentum, swatting with abandon, growling like an animal because he had not the sensibility remaining to even form the name of his god.

He stumbled as much as he intentionally moved forward, crashing through the lines of distracted orcs. He hardly heard the next loud report, though the sudden vibration nearly knocked him from his feet as a large rock crashed down behind him, clipping one orc and smashing a second. Had he turned back, had his sensibilities not been shattered by the pain, emotional and physical, Wulfgar would have recognized that particular boulder.

But he didn't look back, just drove forward. With the help of the distraction from the door blast, he managed to plow through to Bruenor's ranks. Dwarves surged out all around him, swarming behind him like a mother's loving arms and gathering him into the tunnel before them.

"Aw, get him to the priests," Bruenor Battlehammer said when he finally got the chance to take a good look at his adopted son.

Spear tips and orc arrows protruded from the barbarian in several places, and those represented only a fraction of the battered man's visible wounds. Bruenor knew well that Wulfgar likely had many more injuries he could not see.

The dwarf king had to move past his fear for his boy, and quickly, for the organized retreat reached a critical juncture that required absolute coordination. Bruenor and his warriors kept up the stubborn fight, but at the same time began to flow backward from the wider chamber, tightening the line appropriately as they melted into the single escape corridor.

Those in the first few ranks held tight their formations, but those farther back from the fighting broke and ran, clearing the way for the flight that would soon follow.

Farther back, in hidden side rooms, engineers held their positions at peg-and-crank mechanisms.

Bruenor stayed in the center of the trailing line of flight, face to face with the pursuing orcs. His axe added more than a few notches that day, creasing orc skulls. With every step he took backward, the dwarf king had to battle against his outrage that the filthy beasts had come into his sacred halls, and had to remind himself that he would fall back on them before the turn of day.

When his line passed the assigned point, Bruenor called out and his voice was joined by the shouts of all those around him.

The engineers pulled their pegs, literally dropping the ceiling of the corridor back toward the great entry hall. Two huge blocks of stone slid down, filling the corridor, crushing flat the unfortunate orcs beneath them and sealing off a score of their comrades, those closest to Bruenor's boys, from their swarming kin in the foyer.

The outraged dwarves made fast work of the trapped orcs.

Any joy that Bruenor had at the successful evacuation and upon learning that Wulfgar's injuries were not too serious, was short-lived, though. A few moments later, Bruenor's retreat route intersected with that of the dwarves fleeing the ledge, dwarves who carried Catti-brie tenderly in their arms.

Tucked into the secret cubby, Regis rubbed his chubby hands over his face, as if trying to brush away his mounting fear. He glanced up often to the light streaming in through a neatly-blown hole in the solid stone wall of his hiding place. Regis had heard the blast, and knew it to be the trapped wax door. Apparently, one of the projectiles had been deflected—off an orc skull, he hoped—and had rocketed up high, cracking through the outer stone wall of the cubby and splitting the air barely an inch in front of the poor halfling's face. Every so often, Regis glanced across at the other, far more substantial stone wall, where the projectile, a metal sling bullet, could be seen embedded in the rock.

The halfling fought hard to keep his breathing steady, realizing that the last thing he could afford was for orcs to discover him. And they had come up to the ledge, he knew, for he could hear their grunting and their large feet slapping on the stone behind him.

"Five hours," he silently mouthed, for that was the planned pause before

the counterattack. He knew that he should try to get some sleep, then, but he could smell the orcs nearby and simply couldn't relax enough to keep his eyes closed for any length of time.

The dwarves gathered around Bruenor could hear the tentativeness in his every word.

"But will it keep on rolling?" the dwarf king asked the engineers standing beside a modified version of a "juicer," a heavy rolling ram designed to squish the blood out of orcs and the like by pressing them against a wall. Unlike the typical Battlehammer juicers, which were really no more than a cylinder of stone on a thick axle with poles behind so the dwarves could rush it along, the new contraption had been given a distinct personality. Carved wooden likeness of dwarves upon battle boars, the handiwork of Pikel Bouldershoulder, stood out in front of the main body of the one-ton battering ram, and below them was a skirt of metal, fanning out like a ship's prow. An "orc-catcher," Nanfoodle had named it, designed to wedge through the throng of enemies like a spear tip, throwing them aside.

The whole of the thing was set upon well-greased metal wheels, lined in a thin, sharpened ridge that would simply cut through any bodies the catcher missed. Handles had been set for twenty dwarves to push, and as an added bonus, Nanfoodle had geared the boar-riding statues to an offset on the axle, so that the six wooden dwarf "riders" would seem to be charging, leaping over each other in a rolling motion.

"They'll stop it eventually," Nanfoodle reasoned. "More by the pile of their dead, I would guess, than by any concerted effort to halt the thing. Once the dwarves get this contraption rolling, it would take a team of giants to slow it!"

Bruenor nodded and kept moving, studying the device from every conceivable angle.

He had to keep moving, he knew. He had to keep studying and thinking of the present crisis.

His two children had been hurt.

Wincing with every movement, Wulfgar swung his wolf-hide cloak across his shoulders and managed to bring his right arm back far enough to get behind the mantle and wrap it around him, covering his strong chain shirt of interlocking mithral links.

"What're ye doing?" Delly Curtie asked him, coming back into the room after settling Colson in her bed.

Wulfgar looked back at her as if the answer should be obvious.

"Cordio said ye wasn't to be going back today," Delly reminded him. "He said ye're too hurt."

Wulfgar shook his head and clasped the wolf-hide surcoat closed. Before he finished, Delly was at his side, tugging at one arm.

"Don't go," she pleaded.

Wulfgar stared down at her incredulously. "Orcs are in Mithral Hall. That cannot hold."

"Let Bruenor drive them out. Or better, let us thicken the walls before them, and leave them in empty chambers."

Wulfgar's expression did not straighten.

"We can go out the tunnels to Felbarr," Delly went on. "All of the clan. They'll be welcomed there. I heard Jackonray Broadbelt say as much when he was talking to the folk chased down from the northland."

"Perhaps many of those folk would be wise to go," Wulfgar admitted.

"Not one's intending to make Felbarr a home. They're all for Silverymoon and Everlund and Sundabar. Ye've been to Silverymoon?"

"Once."

"Is it as beautiful as they say?" Delly asked, and the sparkle in her eyes betrayed her innermost desire, showing it clearly to Wulfgar, whose own blue eyes widened at the recognition.

"We will visit it," he promised, and he knew, somehow, that "visiting" wasn't what Delly had in mind, and wouldn't be nearly enough to assuage her.

"What are you saying?" he demanded suddenly.

Delly fell back from the blunt statement. "Just want to see it, is all," she said, lowering her gaze to the floor.

"Is something wrong?"

"Orcs're in the hall. Ye said so yerself."

"But if no orcs were in the hall, you would still wish to go to Silverymoon, or Sundabar?"

Delly kicked at the stone, her hesitance seeming so completely out of character that the hair on the back of Wulfgar's strong neck began to bristle.

"What kind of life is a child to get if all she's seeing are her parents and dwarves?" Delly dared to ask.

Wulfgar's eyes flared. "Catti-brie had such an upbringing."

Delly looked up, her expression hardly complimentary.

"I have no time to argue about this," Wulfgar said. "They are bringing the juicer into position, and I will hold my place behind it."

"Cordio said ye shouldn't go."

"Cordio is a priest, and always erring on the side of caution regarding those he tends."

"Cordio is a dwarf, and wanting all who're able up there killing orcs," Delly countered, and Wulfgar managed a smile. He figured that if it were not for Colson, Delly would be marching out beside him to battle.

Or maybe not, he realized as he looked at her more closely, at the profound frown that was hidden just below the surface of her almost-impassive expression. He had hardly seen her since the conflict had begun, since they had separated on the road from Icewind Dale back to Mithral Hall. Only then did he realize how lonely she likely was, down there with dwarves too distracted by pressing issues to hold her and comfort her.

"We will go see Silverymoon when this is over. And Sundabar," he offered.

Delly looked back down, but gave a slight nod.

Wulfgar winced again, and it was from more than physical pain. He believed his own words and had no time for petty arguments. He walked over and bent low, stiffly, from the pain, to give Delly a kiss. She offered only her cheek for the peck.

By the time he had crossed out of the room, though, Wulfgar the warrior, son of Beornegar, son of Bruenor, a champion of Mithral Hall, had put Delly and her concerns out of his mind.

"We have breached the hall!" Tsinka shrieked.

Obould smirked at her, thinking that the shaman had forgotten how to speak without raising her voice several octaves. All around them, orcs cheered and hopped about, punching their fists in defiance. The grand entry hall was theirs, as well as a complex of rooms both north and south of that huge foyer. The eastern corridor had been sealed by heavy blocks, but if they had been able to breach the magnificent western doors of Mithral Hall, could any of them believe the impromptu barriers would pose any substantial obstacle?

Lines of orcs marched past, dragging dead companions out into Keeper's Dale where they were tossing them onto a gigantic pyre for burning. The line seemed endless! In the few minutes of battle in the hall, the rain of death from above and the stubborn defensive stance of the dwarves, more than three hundred orcs had died. Traps, including that devastating explosion, the source of which Obould was still to discern, had taken more than a score. What other tricks might Bruenor Battlehammer have in store, the orc king wondered. Was this entire section of Mithral Hall rigged to explode, like the mountain ridge up the northern cliff beyond Keeper's Dale?

Had they even killed any dwarves in the fight? Obould was certain they had taken down a few, at least, but so coordinated was the dwarves' retreat that not a body had been left behind.

Beside him, Tsinka rambled on in her shrill tone, replaying the events with a heroic spin. She spoke of the glory of Gruumsh and the coming sweep of Clan Battlehammer from their ancient homeland, and all the orcs near to her screamed with equal glee and enthusiasm.

Obould wanted to throttle the shaman.

The voice of Gerti Orelsdottr, obviously not happy with events, distracted him from the maniacal cheering. Four giants had died in the fight, with two others seriously wounded and scarred, and Gerti never took well to losing one of her precious kin. While he was growing tired of Gerti's continual whining, Obould knew that he would need the giantess and her forces if they were to prod farther into the hall, and even if they were to continue to hold their position along the River Surbrin. As much as he hated to admit it, Obould's current vision of his kingdom included Gerti Orelsdottr.

The orc king looked back to Tsinka. Could she even grasp the trials ahead of them? Did she even understand that they could not lose orcs by the hundreds for every room's gain into Mithral Hall? Or that even if they managed to chase the Battlehammers out at such a horrendous cost, Citadels Felbarr and Adbar and the cities of Silverymoon and Everlund would certainly come back at them?

"Gruumsh! Gruumsh! Gruumsh!" Tsinka began to chant, and the orcs near to her took it up at the top of their lungs.

"Gruumsh! Gruumsh! Gruumsh!"

The sound poured in through the hole in the cubby and reverberated off the stones, filling the space and flooding poor Regis's ears. The whole orc nation seemed to be sitting on the halfling's shoulders, screaming in victory, and Regis reflexively curled and brought his hands up to cover his ears. The volume only seemed to increase despite his cover, though, as the orcs began to stamp their feet, the whole of the great hall shaking under their collective exultation.

Regis curled tighter to try to block it out. He almost expected Gruumsh to walk into the hall and reach through the small hole to pull him out. His jaw chattered so badly that his teeth hurt and his ears throbbed under the assault.

"Gruumsh! Gruumsh! Gruumsh!"

To his horror, Regis found himself yelling to counter the awful sound. His frightened reaction proved most fortunate for the defenders of Mithral Hall, for the halfling snapped his hands from his ears to his mouth just in time to hear a different sound behind the chanting.

Dwarven horns, low and throaty, winded from somewhere deeper in the complex.

It took Regis a long moment to even register them, and another moment to recognize the signal.

He grabbed the peg lever with both hands and yanked it back, releasing the crank. He held it back for a count of two, then shoved it forward.

The wheel spun for those two seconds, the rope winding out, through the top of the cubby and the metal piping set along the ceiling. Outside in the great entry hall, the umbrellalike contraption dropped, then stopped suddenly with an abrupt jerk as the halfling's movement re-pegged the crank. The jolt cracked the hinges holding the various layers of the bowl-shaped hopper, inverting them one after another even as the whole of the contraption, reacting to the untwisting of the heavy rope, began to turn.

Ceramic balls rolled out from the center, down prescribed tracks of metal that ended in upward curls of varying elevations. With the turning movement and the differing angles of release, the rolling balls leaped from the contraption in a manner well-calculated to spread the "bombing" out across the maximum area.

Each of the ceramic balls was filled with one of two potions. Some were filled with bits of sharpened metal and the same oil of impact that had blown apart the wax door, while others held a more straightforward concoction of volatile liquid that exploded upon contact with air.

Bursts of shrapnel and mini-fireballs erupted all across the orc throng.

Chants of "Gruumsh!" became muffled grunts as bits of metal tore through porcine lungs, and were surpassed by shrieks of agony as flames bit at other orcs.

"A thousand wounds and a few deaths." That was how Ivan Bouldershoulder and Nanfoodle the gnome had aptly explained the effects of the umbrella contraption to Bruenor and the others.

And that was exactly what Bruenor wanted. The dwarves of Clan Battlehammer knew orcs well enough to understand the level of confusion and terror they'd created. Farther back in the complex, great levers, larger versions of the one Regis had used, were yanked back, releasing massive counterweights chained to the blocks that had been dropped to seal the tunnels into the entry hall.

The first movement came far to the back of the dwarven line. Lowering their shoulders, the dwarves grunted and shoved, starting the massive juicer on its roll. How greatly their efforts increased when Wulfgar appeared among their ranks, taking his place on the higher handles that had been put in just to accommodate him.

"Go! Go! Go!" the warcommanders yelled to the leading line of dwarves as the rolling juicer came into view, rumbling down the hall. The lead unit, cavalry on fierce war pigs, swept out in front of the juicer and charged down the hall even as the blocks began to rise. Beside them, Pikel Bouldershoulder waggled the fingers of his one hand and waved dramatically, conjuring a mist that seemed to rise from the very stones, obscuring the air at the end of the corridor and in the closest areas of the great foyer.

Beyond the block, confusion dominated the hall, with dozens of small fires keeping the orcs rushing every which way. Others thrashed wildly in fear and pain. Some saw the coming charge, though, and shouted for a defensive stand.

The dwarves on the war pigs howled to Moradin and kicked their mounts into a swifter run, but then, as they neared the opening, they slowed suddenly, tugging back their reins. They turned aside as one, skidding into the many alcoves that lined the hall.

The orcs closest the corridor still saw cavalry charging, though, or thought they did, for in the mist they couldn't really discern the difference between real pigs and the carved figures on the front of the juicer. So they set their spears and grouped in tight formation against the charge . . .

. . . and were swept aside by the rolling tonnage of the dwarven war engine.

Into the hall went Wulfgar and the dwarves, plowing ahead and tossing orcs aside with abandon. Behind them came the war pig cavalry, fanning out with precision and to great effect against the supporting orcs, those that did not have the long spears to counter such a charge.

Up above, as similar blocking stones were lifted by counterweights, Bruenor and other dwarves roared out onto the ledges, finding, as they had anticipated, more orcs staring back dumbfounded into the chaos of the foyer than orcs ready to defend. Bruenor, and Pwent and his Gutbusters, gained a foothold on the main ledge. With sheer ferocity they dislodged the orcs one after another. Within moments, the balcony was clear, but Pwent and his boys had prepared for that foregone conclusion well. Some of the Gutbusters had come out onto the ledge already in harnesses, roped back to weighted cranks.

As soon as the ledge began to clear, the lead-liners, as Pwent had called them, simply leaped off, the counterbalanced cranks slowing their descent.

But not slowing them too much. They wanted to make an impression, after all.

The rest of the Gutbusters sprang upon the ropes to get down to the real action, and Bruenor did as well, turning the captured balconies over to lines of crossbow-armed dwarves pouring out through the small tunnels.

Confusion won those early moments, and it was something that Bruenor and his boys were determined to push through to the very end. More and more dwarves rolled in or came down from above, thickening and widening the line of slaughter.

Crossbowdwarves picked their targets carefully back by the entryway from Keeper's Dale, looking for any orcs barking orders.

"Leader!" one dwarf cried, pointing out to one orc who seemed to be standing taller than his fellows, perhaps up on a stone block so that he could better direct the fighting.

Twenty dwarves turned their crossbows upon the target, and on the order of "Fire!" let fly.

The unfortunate orc commander, shouting for a turn for defense, was suddenly silenced—silenced and shattered as a barrage of bolts, many of them packed with oil of impact, shredded his body.

The orcs around him howled and fled.

As Bruenor, Wulfgar, and all the floor fighters made their way across the foyer, out of the corridor came the most important dwarves of all. Engineers rambled out, bearing heavy metal sheets that could be quickly assembled into a killing pocket, a funnel-shaped pair of walls to be constructed inside the foyer near the broken doors. Lined on top with spear tips and cut with dozens of murder holes, the killing pocket would cost their enemies dearly if the orcs launched a counter charge.

But the work had to be done fast and it had to be done with perfect timing. The first pieces, those farthest back from Keeper's Dale, were set in place behind the leading edge of the dwarves' charge. If the orcs had countered quickly enough, perhaps with giant support, the dwarves caught in front of those huge metal wall sections would have been in a sorry position indeed.

It didn't happen, though. The orc retreat was a flight of sheer terror, taking all the surviving orcs right out of Mithral Hall, surrendering ground readily.

In the span of just a few minutes, scores of orcs lay dead and the foyer was back in Bruenor's hands.

"Turn them back! Lead them back!" Tsinka Shinriil pleaded with Obould. "Quickly! Charge! Before the dwarves fortify!"

"Your orcs must lead the way," Gerti Orelsdottr added, for she wasn't about to send her giants charging in to set off the no-doubt cunning traps the dwarves still had in place.

Obould stood outside of Mithral Hall's broken doors and watched his greatest fears come to fruition.

"Dwarves in their tunnels," he whispered under his breath, shaking his head with every word.

Tsinka kept shouting at him to attack, and he almost did it.

The visions of his kingdom seemed to wash away under rivers of orc blood. The orc king understood that he could counter the attack, that the sheer weight of his numbers would likely reclaim the entry hall. He even suspected that the dwarves were ready for such an eventuality, and would retreat again in a well-coordinated, pre-determined fashion.

Twenty orcs would die for every dwarf that fell, much like the first assault.

A glance to the side showed Obould the massive, still-smoldering mound of dead from the initial break-in.

Tsinka yelled at him some more.

The orc king shook his head. "Form defensive lines out here!" he shouted to his commanders and gang leaders. "Build walls of stone and hide behind them. If the dwarves try to come forth from their halls, slaughter them!"

Many of the commanders seemed surprised by the orders, but not a one had the courage to even begin to question King Obould Many-Arrows, and few of them wanted to charge back into the dwarven tunnels anyway.

"What are you doing?" Tsinka shrieked at him. "Kill them all! Charge into Mithral Hall and kill them all! Gruumsh demands—"

Her voice cut off suddenly as Obould's hand clamped hard around her

throat. With just that one arm, the orc king lifted the shaman from the ground and brought her up very close to his scowling face.

"I grow weary of Tsinka telling me the will of Gruumsh. I am Gruumsh, so you say. We do not go back into Mithral Hall!"

He looked around at Gerti and the others, who were staring at him skeptically.

"Seal the doors!" Obould ordered. "Put the smelly dwarves in their smelly hole, and let us keep them there!" He turned back to Tsinka. "I will not throw orcs onto dwarven spears for the sake of your orgy. Mithral Hall is an inconvenience and nothing more—if we choose to make it that way. King Bruenor is soon to be insignificant, a dwarf in a covered hole who cannot strike out at me."

Tsinka's mouth moved as she tried to argue, but Obould clamped just a bit tighter, turning her whispers into a gasp.

"There are better ways," Obould assured her.

He tossed her down and she stumbled back a few steps and fell onto her behind.

"If you wish to live to see those ways, then choose your words and your tone more wisely," Obould warned.

He turned on his heel and moved away.

PART TWO DWARF AMBITIONS

From a high ridge east of Keeper's Dale, I watched the giants construct their massive battering ram. I watched the orcs practice their tactics—tight lines and sudden charges. I heard the awful cheering, the bloodthirsty calls for dwarf blood and dwarf heads, the feral screams of battle lust.

From that same ridge, I watched the huge ram pulled back by a line of giants, then let loose to swing hard and fast at the base of the mountain on which I stood, at the metal doorway shell of Mithral Hall. The ground beneath my feet shuddered. The booming sound vibrated in the air.

They pulled it back and let fly again and again.

Then the shouts filled the air, and the wild charge was on.

I stood there on that ridge, Innovindil beside me, and I knew that my friends, Bruenor's kin, were battling for their homeland and for their very lives right below me. And I could do nothing.

I realized then, in that awful moment, that I should be in there with the dwarves, killing orcs until at last I, too, was cut down. I realized then, in that awful moment, that my decisions of the last few tendays, formed in anger and even more in fear, betrayed the trust of the friendship that Bruenor and I had always held.

Soon after—too soon!—the mountainside quieted. The battle ended.

To my horror, I came to see that the orcs had won the day, that they had gained a foothold inside Mithral Hall. They had driven the dwarves from the entry hall at least. I took some comfort in the fact that the bulk of the orc force remained outside the broken door, continuing their work in Keeper's Dale. Nor had many giants gone in.

Bruenor's kin were not being swept away; likely, they had surrendered the wider entry halls for the more defensible areas in the tighter tunnels.

That sense of hope did not wash away my guilt, however. In my heart I understood that I should have gone back to Mithral Hall, to stand with the dwarves who for so long had treated me as one of their own.

Innovindil would hear nothing of it, though. She reminded me that I had not, had never, fled the battle for Mithral Hall. Obould's son was dead because of my decision, and many orcs had been turned back to their holes in the Spine of the World because of my—of *our*, Innovindil, Tarathiel and myself—work in the north.

It is difficult to realize that you cannot win every battle for every friend. It is difficult to understand and accept your own limitations, and with them, the recognition that while you try to do the best you can, it will often prove inadequate.

And so it was then and there, on that mountainside watching the battle, in that moment when all seemed darkest, that I began to accept the loss of Bruenor and the others. Oh, the hole in my heart did not close. It never will. I know and accept that. But what I let go then was my own guilt at witnessing the fall of a friend, my own guilt at not having been there to help him, or there to hold his hand in the end.

Most of us will know loss in our lives. For an elf, drow or moon, wild or avariel, who will see centuries of life, this is unavoidable—a parent, a friend, a brother, a lover, a child even. Profound pain is often the unavoidable reality of conscious existence. How less tolerable that loss will be if we compound it internally with a sense of guilt.

Guilt.

It is the easiest of feelings to conjure, and the most insidious. It is rooted in the selfishness of individuality, though for goodly folks, it usually finds its source in the suffering of others.

What I understand now, as never before, is that guilt is not the driving force behind responsibility. If we act in a goodly way because we are afraid of how we will feel if we do not, then we have not truly come to separate the concept of right and wrong. For there is a level above that, an understanding of community, friendship, and loyalty. I do not choose to stand beside Bruenor or any other friend to alleviate guilt. I do so because in that, and in their reciprocal friendship, we are both the stronger and the better. Our lives become worth so much more.

I learned that one awful day, standing on a cold mountain stone watching monsters crash through the door of a place that had long been my home.

I miss Bruenor and Wulfgar and Regis and Catti-brie. My heart bleeds for them and yearns for them every minute of every day. But I accept the loss and bear no personal burden for it beyond my own emptiness. I did not turn from my friends in their hour of need, though I could not be as close to them as I would desire. From across that ravine when Withegroo's tower fell, when Bruenor Battlehammer tumbled from on high, I offered to him all that I could: my love and my heart.

And now I will go on, Innovindil at my side, and continue our battle against our common enemy. We fight for Mithral Hall, for Bruenor, for Wulfgar, for Regis, for Catti-brie, for Tarathiel, and for all the goodly folk. We fight the monstrous scourge of Obould and his evil minions.

At the end, I offered to my falling friends my love and my heart. Now I pledge to them my enduring friendship and my determination to live on in a manner that would make the dwarf king stare at me, his head tilted, his expression typically skeptical about some action or another of mine.

"Durned elf," he will say often, as he looks down on me from Moradin's halls.

And I will hear him, and all the others, for they are with me always, no small part of Drizzt Do'Urden.

For as I begin to let go, I find that I hold them all the tighter, but in a way that will make me look up to the imagined halls of Moradin, to the whispered grumbling of a lost friend, and smile.

—Drizzt Do'Urden

10

THE UNEXPECTED TURN

He heard a horn blow somewhere far back in the recesses of his mind, and the ground beneath him began to tremble. Shaken from Reverie, the elves' dreamlike, meditative state, Drizzt Do'Urden's lavender eyes popped open wide. In a movement that seemed as easy as that blink, the drow leaped up to his feet, hands instinctively going to the scimitars belted on each hip.

Around a boulder that served as a windbreak in their outdoor, ceilingless camp came Innovindil, quick-stepping.

Beneath their feet, the mountain itself trembled. Off to the side, Sunset pawed at the stone and snorted.

"The dwarves?" Innovindil asked.

"Let us hope it is the dwarves," Drizzt replied, for he didn't want to imagine the hellish destruction that rumbling might be causing to Clan Battlehammer if Obould's minions were the cause.

The two sprinted away, full speed down the side of the rocky slope. No other race could have matched the pace of the fleet and balanced elves, drow and moon. They ran side by side, leaping atop boulders and skipping over narrow cracks deep beyond sight. Arm-in-arm they overcame any natural barriers, with Drizzt hoisting Innovindil over one short stone wall, and she turning back to offer him a complimentary hand up.

Down they ran, helping each other every step. They came to one smooth and steeply declining slope that ended in a sheer drop, but rather than slow their swift run as they approached that cliff, they put their heads down and sped on. For at the base of that slope, overlooking the cliff, was a small tree, and the pair came upon it in turn. Drizzt leaped and turned, his torso horizontal. He caught the tree with outstretched arms and swung around it, using its strength to veer his run to the side.

Innovindil came right behind with a similar movement and the two ran on along the ledge. They moved to the same vantage point they had taken to witness Obould's break-in to Mithral Hall, a high, flat stone on a westward jut that afforded them a view of most of the dale, excepting only the area right near the great doors of the hall.

Soon the pair could hear screams from below, and Drizzt's heart leaped when he came to recognize that they were the cries of orcs alone.

By the time Drizzt and Innovindil got to their lookout spot, orcs were pouring from the broken doors, running back out into Keeper's Dale in full flight. Flames sprouted on some, flickering orange in the diminishing daylight, and others staggered, obviously wounded.

"The dwarves fight back," Innovindil observed.

Drizzt's hands went to his scimitar hilts and he even started away, but Innovindil grabbed him by the shoulder and held him steady.

"As you did for me when Tarathiel was slain," she explained into his scowl when he turned to regard her. "There is nothing we can do down there."

Looking back, Drizzt knew she was right. The area of the dale closest the doors was a swaying sea of orc warriors, shouting and shoving, some running for the broken doors, others running away. Giants dotted that sea, like tall masts of an armada, closing cautiously. Echoing from the entry hall came the unmistakable sounds of battle, a cacophony of screams and shouts, the clang of metal, and the rumble of stonework.

A giant staggered out, scattering orcs before it.

Up on the stone, Drizzt punched his fist in victory, for it quickly became apparent that the dwarves were winning the day, that Obould's minions were being rudely evicted from Mithral Hall.

"They are giving ground," Innovindil called to him. He turned to see that she had moved far to the side, even climbing down over the lip of the flat

stone perch to gain an even better vantage point. "The dwarves have gained the door!" she called.

Drizzt punched his fist again and silently congratulated the kin of King Bruenor. He had seen their mettle so many times up in the cold and harsh terrain of Icewind Dale, and in the war against his kin from Menzoberranzan. Thus, when he considered his former companions, he realized that he should not be surprised at the sudden turn of events. Still, it boggled even Drizzt to think that such an army as Obould's had been turned back in so efficient a manner.

Innovindil came up beside him a short while later, when the fighting had died down somewhat. She took his arm in her own and leaned in against him.

"It would seem that the orc king underestimated the strength of King Bruenor's kin," she remarked.

"I am surprised that they turned back against the orcs in this manner," Drizzt admitted. "The tunnels beyond the entry halls are tighter and more easily held."

"They do not want the stench of orcs in their halls."

Drizzt merely smiled.

For a long time, the pair stood there, and when they at last settled in for the remainder of the night, they did so right there on that flat stone, both eager to see what the orcs might do to counter the dwarves' charge.

As the slanting rays of the rising sun fell over them and past them to illuminate the dale below a couple of hours later, both elves were a bit surprised to see that the orcs had moved back from the doors, and seemed in no hurry to close in again. Indeed, from everything Drizzt and Innovindil could tell, it appeared as if the orcs and giants were taking up their own defensive positions. The elves watched curiously as gangs of orcs carted heavy stones in from the mountainsides, piling them near other teams who were fast at work in constructing walls.

Every now and then a giant would take one of those stones, give a roar of defiance, and launch it at the door area, but that, it seemed, was the extent of the monstrous counterattack.

"When have you ever known orcs to so willingly surrender ground, except in full retreat?" Drizzt asked, as much to himself as to his companion.

Innovindil narrowed her blue eyes and more closely studied the dale below, looking for some clue that there was something going on beneath the seemingly unconventional behavior by the brutish and aggressive monsters. For all she could tell, though, the orcs were not gathering for another charge, nor were they breaking ranks and running away, as so often happened. They were digging in.

Delly Curtie crept up to the slightly opened door. She held her boots in her hand for she did not want them to clack against the hard stone floor. She crouched and peered in and wasn't surprised, but was surely disappointed, to see Wulfgar sitting beside the bed, leaning over Catti-brie.

"We drove them back," he said.

"I hope more got killed than got away," the woman replied in a voice still weak. She had to swallow hard a couple of times to get through that single sentence, but there was little doubt that she was steadily and greatly improving. When they had first taken Catti-brie down from the ledge, the clerics had feared that her injuries could prove fatal, but instead they had all they could handle in keeping the woman in her bed and away from the fighting.

"I hit a few for you," Wulfgar assured her.

Delly couldn't see his face, but she was certain that the smile flashed on Catti-brie's face was mirroring Wulfgar's own.

"Bet ye did," Catti-brie replied.

Delly Curtie wanted to run in and punch her. It was that simple. The pretty face, the bright smile, the sparkle in her rich blue eyes, even in light of her injuries, just grated on the woman from Luskan.

"Talking like a dwarf again, pretty one?" Delly said under her breath, noting that Catti-brie's accent, in her stark time of vulnerability, seemed more akin to the tunnels of Mithral Hall than the more proper speech she had been using of late. In effect, Catti-brie was talking more like Delly.

Delly shook her head at her own pettiness and tried to let it go.

Wulfgar said something then that she did not catch, and he began to laugh, and so did Catti-brie. When was the last time Delly and Wulfgar had laughed like that? Had they ever?

"We'll pay them back in full and more," Wulfgar said, and Catti-brie

nodded and smiled again. "There is talk of breaking out through the eastern door, back toward the Surbrin. Our enemies are stronger in the west, but even there their ranks are diminishing."

"Swinging to the east?" Catti-brie asked.

Delly saw Wulfgar's shoulders hunch up in a shrug.

"Even so, they do not believe that they can get in that way, and they cannot expect that we can break out," Wulfgar explained. "But the engineers insist that we can, and quickly. They'll probably use one of Nanfoodle's concoctions and blow up half the mountain."

That brought another shared laugh, but Delly ignored that one, too intrigued by the possibilities of what Wulfgar was saying.

"Citadel Felbarr will support us across the Surbrin," he went on. "Their army now marches for the town of Winter Edge, just across the river and to the north. If we can establish a foothold from the eastern door to the river and establish a line of new warriors and supplies from across the river, Obould will not push us into the hall again."

And all those people from the north will get their wish and be gone from Mithral Hall, Delly silently added.

She watched as Catti-brie managed to prop herself up, wincing just a bit with the movement. She flashed that perfect smile again, the light of it searing Delly's heart.

For she knew that Wulfgar was similarly grinning.

She knew that the two of them shared a bond far beyond any she could ever hope to achieve with the man who called himself her husband.

"They will not break out without great cost," Obould told those gathered around him, the leading shamans and gang bosses, and Gerti Orelsdottr and a few of her elite frost giants. "They are in their hole, and there they will stay. We will not relent our efforts to fortify this dale. As the dwarves built their inner sanctum to cost an invader dearly, so this dale will become our first line of slaughter."

"But you will not go back in?" Gerti asked.

Across from her, Tsinka Shinriil and some of the other shamans growled at the thought, and King Obould gave them a sidelong glance.

"Let them have their hole," he said to Gerti. "I . . . we, have all this." He swept his muscular arm out wide, encompassing all the mountains and wide lands to the north.

"What about Proffit?" Tsinka dared to ask. "We put him into the southern tunnels to fight the dwarves. The trolls await our victory."

"May he find success, then," said Obould, "but we will not go in."

"You abandon an ally?"

Obould's scowl told everyone present that Tsinka was approximately one word from death at that moment.

"Proffit has found more gain that he could ever have hoped to achieve," said the orc king. "Because of Obould! He will fight and win some tunnels, or he will be pushed back to the Trollmoors where his strength has never been greater." Obould's red-streaked yellow eyes narrowed dangerously and a low growl escaped his torn lips as he added, "Have you anything more to say on this?"

Tsinka shrank back.

"You will end it here, then?" Gerti asked.

Obould turned to her and said, "For now. We must secure that which we have gained before we move further against our enemies. The danger now lies mostly in the east, the Surbrin."

"Or the south," Gerti said. "There are no great rivers protecting us from the armies of Everlund and Silverymoon in the south."

"If they come at us from the south, Proffit will give us the time we need," Obould explained. "The enemies we must expect are Adbar and Felbarr. Dwarf to dwarf. If they can breach the Surbrin, they will try to cut our lines in two."

"Do not forget the tunnels," one of Gerti's giant aides added. "The dwarves know the upper layers of the Underdark. We may find them climbing out of holes in our midst!"

All eyes went to the confident Obould, who seemed to accept and appreciate the warning.

"I will build a watchtower on every hill and a wall across every pass. No kingdom will be better fortified and better prepared against attack, for no kingdom is so surrounded by enemies. Every day that passes will bring

new strength to Obould's domain, the Kingdom of Dark Arrow." He stood up tall and stalked about the gathering. "We will not rest our guard. We will not turn our eyes aside, nor turn our weapons upon each other. More will join our ranks. From every hole in the Spine of the World and beyond, they will come to the power of Gruumsh and the glory of Obould!"

Gerti stood up as well, if for no better reason than to tower over the pompous orc.

"I will have the foothills to the Trollmoors, and you will have the Spine of the World," Obould assured her. "Treasure will flow north as payment for your alliance."

The ugly orc gave a toothy grin and clapped his hands together hard. A group of orcs soon approached from the side of the gathering, leading the hobbled pegasus.

"It is not a fitting mount," Obould said to Gerti. "An unreliable and stupid beast. A griffon, perhaps, for King Obould, or a dragon—yes, I would like that. But not a soft and delicate creature such as this." He looked around. "I had thought to eat it," he joked, and all the orcs began to chuckle. "But I see the intrigue in your eyes, Gerti Orelsdottr. Our perceptions of ugliness and beauty are not alike. I suspect that you consider the beast quite pretty."

Gerti stared at him skeptically, as if she expected him to then walk over and cut the pegasus in half.

"Whether you think it ugly or pretty, the beast is yours," Obould said, surprising all those orcs around him. "Take it as a trophy or a meal, as you will, and accept it with my gratitude for all that you have done here."

No one in attendance, not even Gerti's close frost giant friends, had ever seen the giantess so perfectly unnerved, excepting that one occasion when Obould had bested her in combat. At every turn, the orc king seemed to have Dame Orelsdottr off-balance.

"You think it ugly so you offer it to me?" Gerti balked, stumbling through the convoluted rebuttal, and without much heart, obviously.

Obould didn't bother to answer. He just stood there holding his smile.

"The winter winds are beginning to blow high up in the mountains," Gerti said clumsily. "Our time here is short, if we are to see Shining White again before the spring."

Obould nodded and said, "I would ask that you leave some of your kin at my disposal along the Surbrin through the season and the next. We will continue to build as the winter snows protect our flank. By next summer, the river will be impervious to attack and your giants can return home."

Gerti looked from Obould to the pegasus several times before agreeing.

The mountainside south of Mithral Hall's retaken western door was more broken and less sheer than the cliffs north of that door or those marking the northern edge of Keeper's Dale, so it was that approach Drizzt and Innovindil chose as their descent. Under cover of night, moving silently as only elves could, the pair picked their careful path along the treacherous way, inching toward Mithral Hall. They knew the dwarves had the door secured once more, for every now and then a ballista bolt or a missile of flaming pitch soared out to smash against the defenses of Obould's hunkering force.

Confident that they could get into the hall, Drizzt realized that he was out of excuses. It was time to go home and face the demons of sorrow. He knew in his heart that his hopes would be dashed, that he would learn what he already knew to be true. His friends were lost to him, and a few hundred yards away as he picked his path among the stones, lay the stark truth.

But he continued along, Innovindil at his side.

They had left Sunset up on the mountaintop, untethered and free to run and fly. The pegasus would wait, or would flee if necessary, and Innovindil held all confidence that she would find her again when she called.

About a hundred and fifty feet above the floor of Keeper's Dale, the pair ran into a bit of a problem. Leading the way, Drizzt found that he was out of easy routes to the bottom, and could see no way at all for him and Innovindil to get down there under cover.

"They've got a fair number of sentries set and alert," Innovindil whispered as she moved down in a crouch beside him. "More orcs and more alert than I'd have expected."

"This commander is cunning," Drizzt agreed. "He'll not be caught unawares."

"We cannot get down this way," Innovindil surmised.

They both knew where they had gone wrong. Some distance back, they

had come to a fork in the ravinelike descent. One path had gone almost straight down to the ridge above the doors, while the one they had opted to take had veered to the south. Looking at the doors, the pair could see that other trail, and it seemed as if it could indeed take them low enough for a final, desperate run to the dwarven complex.

Of course, they came to see the truth of it: if they went in, they wouldn't have an easy time getting out.

"We cannot backtrack and come back down the other way before the dawns light finds us," Drizzt explained. "Tomorrow, then?"

He turned to see a very serious Innovindil staring back at him.

"If I go in, I am abandoning my people," she replied, her voice even more quiet than the whispers of their conversation.

"How so?"

"How will we get back out when there seems no concealed trail to the valley floor?"

"I will get us out, if we have to climb the chimneys of Bruenor's furnaces," Drizzt promised, but Innovindil was shaking her head with every word.

"You go tomorrow. You must return to them."

"Alone?" Drizzt asked. "No."

"You must," said Innovindil. "We'll not get to Sunrise anytime soon. The pegasus's best chance might well be a parlay from Mithral Hall to Obould." She put her hand on Drizzt's shoulder, moved it up to gently stroke his face, then let it slip back down to the base of his neck. "I will continue to watch from out here. From afar, on my word. I know that you will return, and perhaps then we will have a means to retrieve lost Tarathiel's mount and friend. I cannot allow Obould to hold so beautiful a creature any longer."

Again her delicate hand went up to gently brush Drizzt's face.

"You must do this," she said. "For me and for you. And for Tarathiel."

Drizzt nodded. He knew that she was right.

They started back up the trail, thinking to return to a hidden camp, then take the alternate route when the sun began to dip below the western horizon once more.

The night was full of the sound of hammers and rolling stones, both inside the hall and outside in Keeper's Dale, but it was an uneventful night for the couple, lying side by side under the stars in the cool autumn wind.

To his surprise, Drizzt did not spend the hours in fear of what the following night might bring.

At least, not concerning his friends, for his acceptance was already there. He did fear for Innovindil, and he looked over at her many times that night, silently vowing that he would come back out as soon as he could to rejoin her in her quest.

Their plans did not come to fruition, though, for under the bright sun of the following morning, a commotion in Keeper's Dale brought the two elves to their lookout post. They watched curiously as a large caravan comprised mostly of giants—almost all of the giants—rolled out to the west away from them, moving to the exit of Keeper's Dale. Some orcs traveled along with them, most pulling carts of supplies.

And one other creature paced in that caravan, as well. Even from a distance, the sharp eyes of Innovindil could not miss the glistening white coat of poor Sunrise.

"They break ranks?" she asked. "A full retreat?"

Drizzt studied the scene below, watching the movements of the orcs who were not traveling beside the giants. The vast bulk of the monstrous army that had come to Keeper's Dale was not on the move. Far from it, construction on defensive barriers, walls low and high, continued in full.

"Obould is not surrendering the ground," the drow observed. "But it would seem that the giants have had enough of the fight, or there is somewhere else where they're more urgently needed."

"In either case, they have something that does not belong to them," said Innovindil.

"And we will get him back," Drizzt vowed.

He looked down at the path that would likely get him to the western doors of Mithral Hall, the path that he had decided to walk that very night so that he could settle the past and be on with the future.

He looked back to the west and the procession, and he knew that he would not take that path to the doors that night.

He didn't need to.

He looked to his companion and offered her a smile of assurance that he was all right, that he was ready to move along.

That he was ready to bring Sunrise home.

11

STUMBLING

Dizzy and weak with hunger, his extremities numb, his fingers scraped and twisted from a dozen falls as he tried to make his way down the difficult mountain terrain, Nikwillig stubbornly put one foot in front of the other and staggered forward. He wasn't even sure where he was going anymore—just forward. A part of him wanted to simply lie down and expire, to be rid of the pain and the emptiness, both in his belly and in his thoughts.

The past few days had not been kind to the poor dwarf from Citadel Felbarr. His food was gone, though there was plenty of water to be found. His clothing was torn in many places from various falls, including one that had him bouncing thirty feet down a rocky slope. That fall had left him senseless for nearly an hour, and had also left him weaponless. Somewhere in the descent, Nikwillig had dropped his short sword, and as luck would have it, the weapon had bounced into a narrow ravine, a deep crack really, between two huge slabs of solid stone. After he'd gathered his sensibilities, the dwarf retraced his steps and had actually found the weapon, but alas, it lay beyond his short reach.

He had fetched a small branch and tried again, using the stick to try to maneuver the sword at a better angle for grabbing. But the sword slipped from its unexpectedly precarious perch, clanking down to the deeper recesses of the cavity.

With a helpless shrug, Nikwillig, who had never been much of a fighter anyway, had let it go at that. He didn't much care for the idea of being unarmed in hostile territory, with ugly orcs all around him, but he knew there was nothing more he could do.

So as he had done after watching Nanfoodle's explosion and the dwarves' retreat, Nikwillig of Felbarr just shrugged with resignation. He continued on his way, moving generally east, though the trails were taking him more north than he had hoped.

A few days later, the dwarf just stumbled along almost blindly. He kept repeating "Surbrin" over and over as a reminder, but most of the time, he didn't even know what the word meant. A dwarf's stubbornness alone kept him in motion.

One foot in front of the other.

He was on flatter ground, though he hardly knew it, and his progress was steady if not swift. Early in his journey, he had moved mostly at night, hiding in shallow caves during the daylight hours, but eventually it all seemed the same.

It didn't matter. Nothing mattered, except putting one foot in front of the other and repeating the word, "Surbrin."

Suddenly, though, something else did matter.

It came to Nikwillig on the breeze. Not a sight, nor a sound, but a smell. Something was cooking.

The dwarf's stomach growled in response and he stopped his march, a moment of clarity falling over him. In mere seconds, his feet were moving again, of their own accord, it seemed. He veered to the side—he knew not whether it was left or right, or what direction. The aroma of cooking meat pulled him inexorably forward, and he leaned as he walked, and began licking his cracked, dirty lips.

His sensibilities clarified further when he came in sight of the cooking fire, and of the chef, with its sickly dull orange skin, shock of wild black hair, and protruding lower jaw.

Nothing could sober a dwarf like the sight of a goblin.

The creature seemed oblivious to him. It hunched over the spit, pouring some gravy from a stone bowl.

Nikwillig licked his lips again as he watched the thick liquid splatter over the juicy dark meat.

Leg of lamb, Nikwillig thought and it took every ounce of control the battered dwarf could muster to not groan aloud, and not rush ahead blindly.

He held his ground long enough to glance left and right. Seeing no other monsters about, the dwarf launched into a charge, lowering his head and running straight for the unwitting goblin chef.

The goblin straightened, then turned around curiously just in time to catch a flying dwarf in the shoulder. Over the pair flew, upsetting the spit and scattering bits of the fire. They crashed down hard, the hot gravy flying wildly, most of it splashing the goblin in the face. The creature howled from the burns and tried to cover up, but Nikwillig grabbed it by its skinny throat with both hands. He lifted up and slammed down several times, then scrambled away, leaving the goblin whimpering and curling in the dirt.

The leg of lamb, too, had landed on the ground and rolled in the dirt, but the dwarf didn't even stop to brush it clean. He grabbed it up in both hands and tore at it eagerly, ripping off large chunks of juicy meat and swallowing them with hardly a chew.

A few bites in, Nikwillig paused long enough to catch his breath and to savor the taste.

Shouts erupted all around him.

The dwarf staggered up from his knees and began to run. A spear clipped his shoulder, but it skipped past without digging in. Good sense would have told Nikwillig to throw aside the meat and run full out, but in his famishment, the dwarf was far from good sense. Clutching the leg of lamb to his chest as dearly as if it was his only child, he charged along, weaving in and out of boulders and trees, trying to keep as much cover between him and the pursuing monsters as possible.

He came out the side of a small copse and skidded to a stop, for he found himself on the edge of a low but steep descent. Below him, barely fifty feet away, the broad, shining River Surbrin rolled along its unstoppable way.

"The river . . ." Nikwillig muttered, and he remembered then his goal when he had left his perch high on the mountain ridge north of Mithral Hall. If only he could get across the river!

A shout behind him sent him running again, stumbling down the slope—one step, two. Then he went down hard, face first, and tucked himself just enough to launch himself in a roll. He gathered momentum, but did not let go of his precious cargo, rolling and bouncing all the way down until he splashed into the cold water.

He pulled himself to his feet and staggered to the bank and tried to run along.

Something punched him hard in the back, but he only yelled and continued his run.

If only he could find a log. He'd drag it into the river, and freezing water be damned, he'd grab onto it and push himself out from the bank.

Some trees ahead looked promising, but the shouts were sounding closer and Nikwillig feared he would not make it.

And for some reason he did not immediately comprehend, his legs were moving more slowly, and were tingling as if they were going numb.

The dwarf stopped and looked down, and saw blood—his own blood—dripping down to the ground between his widespread feet. He reached around and only then did he understand that the punch he'd felt had been no punch at all, for his hand closed over the shaft of a goblin spear.

"O Moradin, ye're teasing me," Nikwillig said as he dropped to his knees.

Behind him, he heard the hoots and shouts of charging goblins.

He looked down at his hands, to the leg of lamb he still held, and with a shrug, he brought it up and tore off another chunk of meat.

He didn't swallow as fast, though, but chewed that bite and rolled it around in his mouth, savoring its sweetness, its texture, and the warmth of it. It occurred to him that if he had a mug of mead in his other hand that would be a good way for a dwarf to die.

He knew the goblins were close, but was surprised when a club smacked him off the back of the head, launching him face down in the dirt.

Nikwillig of Citadel Felbarr tried to concentrate on the taste of the lamb, tried to block out the pain.

He hoped that death would take him quickly.

Then he knew no more.

12

FOOL ME ONCE, SHAME ON ME, FOOL ME TWICE . . .

"You cannot even think of continuing back toward Nesmé," Rannek scolded after he had taken Galen Firth off to the side of the main encampment.

They had run for many hours after the heroic intervention of General Dagna and his dwarves, going back to the foothills in the north near where the dwarves had found the tunnels that would take them to Mithral Hall.

"Would you make the sacrifice of those fifty dwarves irrelevant for the sake of your pride?" Rannek pressed.

"You are one to be speaking of pride," Galen Firth replied, and his adversary did back down at that.

But only for a moment, then Rannek squared his shoulders and puffed out his broad chest. "I will never forget my error, Galen Firth," he admitted. "But I will not complicate that error now by throwing our entire force into the jaws of the trolls and bog blokes."

"They were routed!" Galen yelled, and both he and Rannek glanced back to the main group to note several curious expressions coming back at them. "They were routed," he said again, more quietly. "Between the dwarves' valiant stand and Alustriel's firestorm, the enemy forces were sliced apart. Did they even offer any pursuit? No? Then is it not also possible that the monsters have gone home to their dung-filled moor? Are you so ready to run away?"

"And are you truly stupid enough to walk back into them? Care you not for those who cannot fight? Should our children die on your gamble, Galen Firth?"

"We do not even know where the caves are," Galen argued. "We cannot simply wander the countryside blindly and hope we find the right hole in the ground."

"Then let us march to Silverymoon," offered Rannek.

"Silverymoon will march to us," Galen insisted. "Did you not see Alustriel?

Rannek chewed his lip and it took all of his control not to just spit on the man. "Are you that much the fool?" he asked. "The ungrateful fool?"

"I am not the fool who put us out here, far from our homes," Galen answered without hesitation, and in the same calm tone that Rannek had just used on him. "That man stands before me now, errantly thinking he has the credibility to question me."

Rannek didn't blink and didn't back down, but in truth, he knew that he had no practical answer to that. He was not in command. The beleaguered folk of Nesmé would not listen to him over the assurances and orders of the proven Galen Firth.

He stared at the man a while longer, then just shook his head and turned away. He didn't allow his grimace to stop the smooth flow of his departure when he heard Galen Firth's derisive snort behind him.

The next dawn made the argument to Galen Firth that Rannek had been unable to make, for the scouts from the refugee band returned with news that a host of trolls was fast closing from the south.

Watching Galen Firth as he heard that grim report, Rannek almost expected the man to order the warriors to close ranks and launch an attack, but even the stern and stubborn Galen was not that foolhardy.

"Gather up and prepare to march, and quickly," he called to those around him. He turned to the scouts. "Some of you monitor the approach of our enemies. Others take swift flight to the northeast. Find our scouts who are searching for the tunnels to Mithral Hall and secure our escape route."

As he finished, the man turned a glare over Rannek, who nodded in silent

approval. Galen Firth's face grew very tight at that, as if he took the expression as a smarmy insult.

"We will lure our enemies into a long run, and circumvent them so that we might reclaim our home," Galen stubbornly told his soldiers, and Rannek's jaw dropped open.

Having grown adept at running, the Nesmé band was on the move in minutes, and in proper formation so that the weakest were well supported near the center of the march. Few said anything. They knew that trolls were in close pursuit, and that that day could mark the end of all their lives.

They came to higher and more broken ground by mid-morning, and from an open vantage point, Galen, Rannek, and some others got their first look at the pursuing force. It seemed to be trolls exclusively, for nowhere among the approaching mob did they see the treelike appendages of bog blokes. Still, there were more than a few trolls down there, including several very large specimens and some of those sporting more than one head.

Rannek knew that they had done right in retreating, as he had suggested many hours before. Any satisfaction he took from that was lost, though, in his fears that they would not be able to outrun that monstrous force.

"Keep them moving as fast as possible," Galen Firth ordered, his voice grave and full of similar fears, Rannek knew, whether Galen would admit them or not—even to himself. "Have we found those tunnels yet?"

"We've found some tunnels," one of the other men explained. "We do not know how deep they run."

Galen Firth pinched his lip between his thumb and index finger.

"And if we run in before we know for certain, and run into a dead end. . . ." the man went on.

"Hurry, then," Galen ordered. "Stretch lines of scouts into the tunnel. We seek one that will loop around and bring us out behind our pursuing enemies. We will have to either run by or run in—there will be no time to dally!"

The man nodded and rushed away.

Galen turned to regard Rannek.

"And so you believe that you were right," he said.

"For what that's worth," Rannek replied. "It does not matter." He looked back at the pursuing force, drawing Galen's eyes with his own. "Never could we have anticipated such dogged pursuit from an enemy as chaotic and undisciplined as trolls! In all my years . . ."

"Your years are not all that long," Galen reminded him. "Thus were you fooled that night you headed the watch."

"As you were fooled now into thinking the pursuit would not come," Rannek shot back, but the words sounded feeble even to him, and certainly Galen's smug expression did little to give him any thought that he had stung the man.

"I welcome their pursuit," Galen said. "If I'm surprised, it is pleasantly so. We run them off, farther from Nesmé. When we get behind our walls once more, we will find the time we need to fortify our defenses."

"Unless there are more trolls waiting for us there."

"Your failure has led you to a place where you overestimate our enemy, Rannek. They are trolls. Stupid and vicious, and little more. They have shown perseverance beyond expectation, but it will not hold."

Galen gave a snort and started away, but Rannek grabbed him by the arm. The Rider turned on him angrily.

"You would gamble the lives of all these people on that proposition?" Rannek asked.

"Our entire existence in Nesmé has been a gamble—for centuries," Galen replied. "It is what we do. It is the way we live."

"Or the way we die?"

"So be it."

Galen yanked himself free of Rannek's grasp. He stared at the man a while longer, then turned around and started shouting orders to those around him. He was cut short, though, almost immediately, for somewhere among the lines of refugees, a man shouted, "The Axe! The Axe of Mirabar is come!"

"All praise Mirabar!" another shouted, and the cheer was taken up across the gathering.

Rannek and Galen Firth charged through the throng, crossing the crowd to get a view of the source of the commotion.

Dwarves, dozens and dozens of dwarves, marched toward them, many of them bearing the black axe of Mirabar on their shields. They moved in tight and disciplined formation, their ranks holding steady as they crossed the broken ground in their determined advance.

"Not of Mirabar," one scout explained to Galen, huffing and puffing with every word, for he had run all the way back to precede the newcomers. "More of Clan Battlehammer, they claim to be."

"They wear the emblem of Mirabar's famed Axe," said Galen.

"And so they once were," the scout explained. He stopped and stepped aside, watching with the others as the dwarves closed.

A pair of battle-worn dwarves approached, one with a thick black beard and the other ancient and one of the ugliest dwarves either man had ever seen. He was shorter and wider than his companion, with half his black beard torn away and one eye missing. His ruddy, weathered face had seen the birth and death of centuries, the humans easily surmised. The pair approached Galen's position, guided by yet another of the scouts the Nesmians had sent forth. They walked up before the man and the younger dwarf dropped the head of his heavy warhammer on the stone before him, then leaned on it heavily.

"Torgar Delzoun Hammerstriker of Clan Battlehammer at yer service," he said. "And me friend Shingles."

"You wear the symbol of Mirabar, good Torgar," said Galen. "And glad we are to have your service."

"We were of Mirabar," Shingles offered. "We left to serve a king of more generous heart. And so ye see the end of that, for here we are, to support ye and support General Dagna, who came out here with ye."

Several of the nearby humans looked to each other with concern, expressions that were not lost on the dwarves.

"I will tell you of Dagna's fall when the time permits a tale that would do him justice," Galen Firth said, straightening his shoulders. "For now, our enemies close fast from behind. Trolls—many trolls."

Most of the dwarves mumbled to each other about "Dagna's fall," but Torgar and Shingles kept their expressions stoic.

"Then let's get to the tunnels," Torgar decided. "Me and me boys'll do better against the gangly brutes when they're bending low so as not to bump their ugly heads on the ceiling."

"We fight them there and push them back," Galen agreed. "Perhaps we can break them and gain a path through their lines."

"Through?" asked Torgar. "Mithral Hall's at the other end of them tunnels, and that's where we're for."

"We have word that Silverymoon will soon join in the fight," Galen explained, and no one around him dared point out that he was stretching the truth quite a bit. "Now is the day of our victory, when Nesmé will be restored and the region secured!"

The dwarves both looked at him curiously for a moment, then looked to each other and just shrugged.

"Not to matter," Shingles said to Torgar. "Either choice we're to make, we're to make it from the tunnels."

"So to the tunnels we go," the other dwarf agreed.

"Side run's open!" came a relayed shout along the dwarven line.

"Torch 'em!" Shingles cried.

Twenty dwarves from the second rank rushed forward, flaming torches in hand, and as one they threw the fiery brands over Shingles and the first line of fighters, who were engaged heavily with the leading lines of troll pursuit.

They had run down a long tunnel that spread into a wider chamber, and had made their stand at the funnel-like opening, allowing a score of dwarves to stand abreast, where only a few trolls could come through to battle them. The torchbearers aimed their flaming missiles at the narrower tunnel entrance, where several pieces of seasoned kindling, soaked with lamp oil, had been strategically placed.

The fires roared to life.

Trolls weren't afraid of much, but fire, which defeated their incredible regenerative powers, ranked foremost among that short list.

The torches loosened the pursuit considerably, and Shingles put his line, and those who had come behind, into a sudden, devastating charge, driving back those few trolls that had been caught on the near side of the conflagration. A couple were forced back into the flames, while others were chopped down and stabbed where they stood.

The dwarves broke and ran in perfect formation. The side passage had been declared open, and the refugees were already well on their way.

Yet again, for the third time that afternoon, Torgar's boys had fended off the stubborn troll pursuit.

The monsters would come on again, though, they all knew, and so those dwarves leading the line of retreat were busy inspecting every intersection and every chamber to see if they could find a suitable location for their next inevitable stand.

From the rear defensive ranks of the human contingent, Rannek watched it all with admiration and gratitude. He knew that Galen Firth was stewing about it all, for they had already eschewed a route that likely would have put them back outside ahead of the trolls, possibly with open ground to Nesmé.

But it was Torgar, not Galen, who was in control. Rannek and all the folk of Nesmé understood that much. For after hearing the details of Dagna's fall, Torgar had explained in no uncertain terms that the humans could run away from the dwarven escort if they so chose, but they would do so at their own risk.

"All glory to Dagna and Mithral Hall," Torgar had said to Galen and the others after hearing the sad story. "He goes to join his son in the Halls of Moradin, where a place of honor awaits."

"He tried to help us reclaim our home," Galen put in, and those words had drawn a look from Torgar that dwarves often reserved for orcs alone.

"He saved yer foolish arse," Torgar retorted. "And if ye're choosing to try to make that run again, then 'twas his mistake. But know ye this, Galen Firth o' Nesmé, Torgar and his boys ain't about to make that same mistake. Any ground we're holding, we're holding with tunnels to Mithral Hall at our back, don't ye doubt."

And that had been the end of it, and even overly proud Galen hadn't argued beyond that, and hadn't said a word of rebuttal to the other Nesmian warriors, either. Thus, Torgar had taken complete control, and had led them on their desperate chase. They ran until pursuit forced a stand then they shaped every encounter to be a quick-hitting deflection rather than a head on battle.

Rannek was glad of that.

13

DIVERGING ROADS

"Are we to follow the commands of an orc?" a large, broad-shouldered frost giant named Urulha asked Gerti as the procession of nearly a hundred of the behemoths made its way around the northern slopes of Fourthpeak, heading east for the Surbrin.

"Commands?" Gerti asked. "I heard no commands. Only a request."

"Are they not one and the same, if you adhere to the request?"

Gerti laughed, a surprisingly delicate sound coming from a giantess, and she put her slender hand on Urulha's massive shoulder. She knew that she had to walk gently with him. Urulha had been one of her father's closest advisors and most trusted guards. And Gerti's father, the renowned Orel the Grayhand still cast a long shadow, though the imposing jarl hadn't been seen among the frost giants in many months, and few thought he would ever leave his private chambers. By all reports, Orel was certainly on his deathbed, and as his sole heir, Gerti stood to inherit Shining White and all his treasures, and the allegiance of his formidable giant forces.

That last benefit of Orel's death would prove the most important and the most tentative, Princess Gerti had known for some time. If a coup rose against her, led by one of the many opportunistic giants who had climbed Orel's hierarchical ladder, then the result, at best, would be a split of the nearly unified forces. That was something Gerti most certainly did not want.

She was a formidable force all her own, skilled with her sword and with her arcane magic. Gerti could bring the power of the elements down upon any who dared stand against her, could blast them with lightning, fire, and storms of pelting ice. But just putting her hand on Urulha's massive shoulder reminded her pointedly that sometimes magic simply would not be enough.

"It is in our interest, at present at least, that Obould succeed," she explained. "If his army were to shatter now, who would stop the forces of Mithral Hall, Felbarr, Adbar, Silverymoon, Everlund, Sundabar, perhaps Mirabar, and who knows what other nation, from pressing the war right to our doorstep at Shining White? No, my good Urulha, Obould is the buffer we need against the pesky dwarves and humans. Let his thousands swarm and die, but slowly."

"I have grown weary of this campaign," Urulha admitted. "I have seen a score and more of my kin killed, and we know not the disposition of our brethren along the Surbrin. Might the dwarves of Felbarr have already crossed? Might another twenty of our kin lay dead at the smelly feet of the bearded creatures?"

"That has not happened," Gerti assured him.

"You do not know that."

Gerti conceded that point with a nod and a shrug. "We will go and see. Some of us, at least."

That surprising caveat got Urulha's attention and he turned his huge head, with its light blue skin and brighter blue eyes, to regard Gerti more directly.

Gerti returned his curious look with a coy one of her own, noticing then that Urulha was quite a handsome creature for an older giant. His hair was long, pulled back into a ponytail that left him a fairly sharp peak up high on his forehead, his hairline receding. His features were still strong, though, with high cheekbones and a very sharp and definitive nose. It occurred to Gerti that if her verbal persuasion did not prove sufficient to keep Urulha in line, she could employ her other ample charms to gain the same effect, and that, best of all, it would not be such an unpleasant thing.

"Some, my friend," she said quietly, letting her fingers trace up closer to the base of the large giant's thick neck, even moving her fingertips to brush the bare skin above his chain mail tunic. "We will send a patrol to the river—half our number—to look in on our missing friends, and to begin collecting them. Slowly, we will rotate the force north and back home. Slowly, I say, so that Obould will not think our movement an outright desertion. He expects that he will need to secure the river on his own, anyway, and with his numbers, it should be of little effort to convince him that he does not need a few giants.

"I wish to hold the alliance, you see," she went on. "I do not know what the response from the communities of our enemies will yet be, but I do not wish to do battle with twenty thousand orcs. Twenty thousand?" she asked with a snicker. "Or is his number twice or thrice that by now?"

"The orcs breed like vermin, like the mice in the field or the centipedes that infest our homes," said Urulha.

"Similar intelligence, one might surmise," said Gerti as her fingers continued to play along her companion's neck, and she was glad to feel the tenseness ease from Urulha's taut muscles, and to see the first hints of a smile widen on his handsome face.

"It is even possible that our usual enemies will come to see a potential alliance with us," Gerti added.

Urulha scowled at the notion. "Dwarves? You believe the dwarves of Mithral Hall, Citadel Felbarr, or Citadel Adbar will agree to work in concert with us? Do you believe that Bruenor Battlehammer and his friends will forget the bombardment that tumbled a tower upon them? They know who swung the ram that breached their western door. They know that no orc could have brought such force to bear."

"And they know they might soon be out of options," said Gerti. "Obould will dig in and fortify throughout the winter, and I doubt that our enemies will find a way to strike at him before the snows have melted. By then. . . ."

"You do not believe that Silverymoon, Everlund, and the three dwarven kingdoms can dislodge orcs?"

Gerti took his incredulity in stride. "Twenty thousand orcs?" she whispered. "Forty thousand? Sixty thousand? And behind fortified walls on the high ground?"

"And so Gerti will offer to aid the countering forces of peoples long our enemies?" Urulha asked.

Gerti was quick to offer a pose that showed she was far from making any such judgment.

"I hold open the possibility of gain for my people," she explained. "Obould is no ally to us. He never was. We tolerated him because he was amusing."

"Perhaps he feels the same way toward us."

Again the disciplined Gerti managed to let the too-accurate-for-comfort comment slide off her large shoulders. She knew that she had to walk a fine line with all of her people as they made their way back to Shining White. Her giants and Obould had achieved victory in their press to the south, but for the frost giants had there been any real gain? Obould had achieved all he had apparently desired. He had gained a strong foothold in the lands of the humans and dwarves. Even more important and impressive, his call to war had brought forth and united many orc tribes, which he had brought into his powerful grasp. But the army, for all its gains, had found no tangible, transferable plunder. They had not captured Mithral Hall and its treasuries.

Gerti's giants were not like the minions of Obould. Frost giants were not stupid orcs. Winning the field was enough for the orcs, even if they lost five times the number of enemies killed. Gerti's people would demand of her that she show them why their march south had been worth the price of dozens of giants' lives.

Gerti looked at the line ahead, to the pegasus. Yes, there was a trophy worthy of Shining White! She would parade the equine creature before her people often, she decided. She would remind them of the benefits of removing the pesky Withegroo and the folk of Shallows. She would explain to them how much more secure their comfortable homeland was now that the dwarves and humans had been pushed so far south.

It was, the giantess realized, a start.

He was surprised by the softness as his consciousness began to creep forth from the darkness, for the dwarf had always expected the Halls of Moradin to be warm with fires but as hard as stone. Nikwillig stirred and shifted, and felt his shoulder sink into the thick blanket. He heard the crackle of leaves and twigs beneath him.

The dwarf's eyes popped open, then he squeezed them shut immediately against the blinding sting of daylight.

In that instant of sight, that snapshot of his surroundings, Nikwillig realized that he was in a thick deciduous forest and as he considered that, the poor dwarf became even more confused. For there were no forests near where he fell, and the last thing he ever expected in the Halls of Moradin were trees and open sky.

"En tu il be-inway," he heard, a soft melodic voice that he knew to be an elf's.

Nikwillig kept his eyes closed as he played the words over and over in his jumbled thoughts. A merchant of Felbarr, Nikwillig often dealt with folk of other races, including elves.

"Be-inway?" he mouthed, then, "Awake. *En tu il bi-inway* . . . he is awake."

An elf was talking about him, he knew, and he slowly let his eyelids rise, acclimating himself to the light as he went. He stretched a bit and a groan escaped him as he tried to turn in the direction of the voice.

The dwarf closed his eyes again and settled back, took a deep breath to let the pain flow out of him, then opened his eyes once more—and was surprised to find himself completely surrounded by elves, pale of skin and stern of face.

"You are awake?" one asked him, speaking the common language of trade.

"A bit of a surprise if I be," Nikwillig answered, his voice cracking repeatedly as it crossed through his parched throat. "Goblins got poor old Nikwillig good."

"The goblins are all dead," the elf on his right explained. That elf, apparently the leader, waved all but one of the others away, then bent low so that Nikwillig could better view him. He had straight black hair and dark blue eyes, which seemed very close together to the dwarf. The elf's angular eyebrows pinched together almost as one, like a dark V above his narrow nose.

"And we have tended your wounds," he went on in a voice that seemed strangely calm and reassuring, given his visage. "You will recover, good dwarf."

"Ye pulled me out o' there?" Nikwillig asked. "Them goblins had me caught at the river and . . ."

"We shot them dead to a goblin," the elf assured him.

"And who ye be?" asked Nikwillig. "And who be 'we'?"

"I am Hyaline of the Moonwood, and this is Althelennia. We crossed the river in search of two of our own. Perhaps you of Mithral Hall have seen them?"

"I ain't of Mithral Hall, but of Citadel Felbarr," Nikwillig informed them, and he took Hralien's offered hand and allowed the elf to help him up gingerly into a sitting position. "Got whacked by that Obould beast, and was Bruenor that rescued me and me friend Tred. Seen nothing of yer friends, sorry to say."

The two elves exchanged glances.

"They would be upon great flying horses," Althelennia added. "Perhaps you have seen them from afar, high in the sky."

"Ah, them two," said Nikwillig, and both elves leaned in eagerly. "Nope, ain't seen them, but I heard of them from the Bouldershoulder brothers who came through yer wood on the way to Mithral Hall."

The crestfallen elves swayed back.

"And the hall remains in Bruenor's hands?" asked Hralien at the very same time that Althelennia inquired about "a great fire that we saw leap into the western sky."

"Aye and aye," said the dwarf. "Gnomish fire, and one to make a dragon proud."

"You have much to tell us, good dwarf," said Hralien.

"Seems I'm owin' ye that much at least," Nikwillig agreed.

He stretched a bit more, cracked his knuckles, his neck, and his shoulders a few times, and settled in, putting his back to a nearby tree. Then he told them his tale, from his march with the caravan out of Citadel Felbarr those tendays before, to the disastrous ambush, and his aimless wandering, injured and hungry, with Tred. He told them of the generosity of the humans and the kindness of Bruenor Battlehammer, who found the pair as he was returning home to be crowned King of Mithral Hall once more.

He told them of Shallows and the daring rescue, and of the unexpected help from Mirabarran dwarves, moving to join their Battlehammer kin. He described the standoff above Keeper's Dale, going into great detail in painting a mental image of the piled orc bodies.

Through it all, the elves remained completely attentive, expressions impassive, absorbing every word. They showed no emotion, even when Nikwillig jumped suddenly as he described the explosion Nanfoodle had brought about, a blast so complete that it had utterly decapitated a mountain spur.

"And that's where it stands, last I noted," Nikwillig finished. "Obould put Bruenor in his hole in the west, and trolls, orcs, and giants put Bruenor in his hole in the east. Mithral Hall's a lone jewel in a pile o' leaden critters."

The two elves looked at each other.

Their expressions did not comfort the battered dwarf.

After more than a tenday, Drizzt and Innovindil found themselves along the higher foothills of the Spine of the World. Gerti and her nearly three-score giants had taken a meandering path back to the higher ground, but they had moved swiftly along that winding road. The journey had given the two elves a good view of the work along the Surbrin, and what they had seen had not been reassuring. All along the bank, particularly at every known ford and every other area that seemed possible for crossing, fortifications had been built and were being improved on a continual basis.

The pair tried to focus on their present mission to rescue Sunrise, but it was no easy task, especially for Innovindil, who wondered aloud and often if she should divert her course and cross the river from on high to warn her kinfolk.

But of course, the elves of the Moonwood carefully monitored the Surbrin, and they already knew what was afoot, she had to believe.

So she had kept to the course with Drizzt, the two of them holding close watch on Gerti's progress and looking for some opening where they could get to Sunrise. In all that time, though, no such chance had presented itself.

Once they were in the mountains, in more broken terrain, keeping up with the giants grew more difficult. On several occasions, Drizzt had brought in Guenhwyvar to run fast ahead and locate the band just to ensure that he and Innovindil were keeping some pace, at least.

"It is folly, I fear," Innovindil said to Drizzt as they camped one night in the shadows of a shallow overhang, with just enough cover for Drizzt to

chance a small fire. Normally, he would not have done so, but though autumn had barely begun down in the south near Mithral Hall, up there, at so high an elevation, the wind was already carrying its wintry bite. "And while we run the fool's errand my people and your dwarves are under siege."

"You will not desert Sunrise while a hope remains," Drizzt replied with a wry grin, his expression as much as his words acting as a rather uncomplimentary mirror to the elf lass.

"You are just frustrated," Drizzt added.

"And you are not?"

"Of course I am. I am frustrated, I am angry, I am sad, and I want nothing more than to take Obould's ugly head from his shoulders."

"And how do you fight past such emotions, Drizzt Do'Urden?"

Drizzt paused before he answered, for he saw a shift in Innovindil's eyes as she asked that question, and noted a distinct shift in her tone. She was asking him as much for his own sake as for hers, he realized. So many times in their tendays together, Innovindil had turned to Drizzt and said something along the lines of, "Do you know what it is to be an elf, Drizzt Do'Urden?" Clearly, she expected to be a bit of a mentor to him concerning the elf experience, and they were lessons he was glad to learn. He noticed too, for the first time with her last question, that whenever Innovindil began her subtle tutoring, she finished the question by referring to him with his full name.

"In moments of reflection," he answered. "At sunrise, mostly, I talk to myself aloud. No doubt anyone listening would think me insane, but there is something about saying the words, about speaking my fears and pain and guilt aloud that helps me to work through these often irrational emotions."

"Irrational?"

"My racist beliefs about my own kind," Drizzt replied. "My dedication to what I know is right. My pain at the loss of a friend, or even of one enemy."

"Ellifain."

"Yes."

"You were not to blame."

"I know that. Of course I do. Had I known it was Ellifain, I would have tried to dissuade her, or to defeat her in a non-lethal manner. I know that she brought her death upon herself. But it is still sad, and still a painful thing to me."

"And you feel guilt?"

"Some," Drizzt admitted.

Innovindil stood up across the way and walked around the campfire, then knelt before the seated Drizzt. She brought a hand up and gently touched his face.

"You feel guilt because you are possessed of a gentle nature, Drizzt Do'Urden. As am I, as was Tarathiel, as are most of elvenkind, though we do well to hide those traits from others. Our conscience is our salvation. Our questioning of everything, of right and wrong, of action and consequence, is what defines our purpose. And do not be fooled, in a lifetime that will last centuries, some sense of purpose is often all you have."

How well Drizzt had known that truth.

"You speak your thoughts after the fact?" Innovindil asked. "You take your experiences and play them out before you, that you might consider your own actions and feelings in the glaring and revealing light of hindsight?"

"Sometimes."

"And through this process, does Drizzt internalize the lessons he has learned? Do you, in reaffirming your actions, gain some confidence should a similar situation arise?"

The question had Drizzt leaning back for a minute. He had to believe that Innovindil had hit upon something. Drizzt had resolved many of his internal struggles through his personal discussions, had come almost full circle, so he believed—until the disaster at Shallows.

He looked back at Innovindil, and noticed that she had moved very close to him. He could feel the warmth of her breath. Her golden hair seemed so soft in that moment, backlit by the fire, almost as if she was aglow. Her eyes seemed so dark and mysterious, but so full of intensity.

She reached up and stroked his face gently, and Drizzt felt his blood rushing. He tried hard to control his trembling.

"I think you a gentle and beautiful soul, Drizzt Do'Urden," she said. "I understand better this difficult road you have traveled, and admire your dedication."

"So you believe now that I know what it is to be an elf?" Drizzt asked, more to alleviate the sudden tension he was feeling, to lighten the mood, than anything else.

But Innovindil didn't let him go so easily.

"No," she said. "You have half the equation, the half that takes care to anticipate the long-term course of things. You reflect and worry, ask yourself to examine your actions honestly, and demand of yourself honest answers, and that is no small thing. Young elves react and examine, and along that honest road of self-evaluation, you will one day come to react to whatever is found before you in full confidence that you are doing right."

Drizzt leaned back just a bit as Innovindil continued to press forward, so that her face was barely an inch from his own.

"And the half I have not learned?" he asked, afraid his voice would crack with each word.

In response, Innovindil pressed in closer and kissed him.

Drizzt didn't know how to respond. He sat there passively for a long while, feeling the softness of her lips and tongue, her hand brushing his neck, and her lithe body as she pressed in closer to him. Blood rushed through him and the world seemed as if it was spinning, and Drizzt stopped even trying to think and just . . . felt.

He began to kiss Innovindil back and his hands started to move around her. He heard a soft moan escape his own lips and was hardly even conscious of it.

Innovindil broke the kiss suddenly and fell back, her arms coming out to hold Drizzt from pursuing. She looked at Drizzt curiously for just a moment, then asked, "What if she is alive?"

Drizzt tried to question the sudden shift, but as her inquiry hit him, his response was more stutter than words.

"If you knew that Catti-brie was alive, then would you wish to continue this?" Innovindil asked, and she might as well have added, "Drizzt Do'Urden," to the end of the question.

Drizzt's mind spun in circles. He managed to stammer, "B-but . . ."

"Ah, Drizzt Do'Urden," Innovindil said. She twirled, rising gracefully to her feet. "You spend far too much time in complete control. You consider the future with every move."

"Is that what it is to be an elf?" Drizzt asked, his voice dripping with sarcasm.

"It might be," Innovindil answered. She came forward again and bent low, looking at Drizzt mischievously, but directly. “In your experience, stoicism is what it is to be an elf. But letting go sometimes, my friend, that is what it is to be alive.”

She turned with a giggle and stepped away.

“You pulled back, not I,” Drizzt reminded, and Innovindil turned on him sharply.

“You didn’t answer my question.”

She was right and Drizzt knew it. He could only begin to imagine his torn emotions had they gone through with the act.

“I have seen you reckless in battle,” Innovindil went on. “But in love? In life? With your scimitars, you will take a chance against a giant or ten! But with your heart, are you nearly as brave? You will cry out in anger against goblinkind, but will you dare cry out in passion?”

Drizzt didn’t answer, because he didn’t have an answer. He looked down and gave a self-deprecating chuckle, and was surprised when Innovindil sat down again beside him and comfortably put her arm around his shoulders.

“I am alone,” the female elf said. “My lover is gone and my heart is empty. What I need now is a friend. Are you that friend?”

Drizzt leaned over and kissed her, but on the cheek.

“Happily so,” he answered. “But am I your friend or your student, when you so freely play with my emotions?”

Innovindil assumed a pensive posture and a moment later answered, “I hope you will learn from my experiences, as I hope to learn from yours. I know that my life is enriched because of your companionship these last tendays. I hope that you can say the same.”

Drizzt knew he didn’t even have to answer that question. He put his arm around Innovindil and pulled her close. They sat there under the stars and let the Reverie calm them.

14

REGROUPING

A pall hung over the audience chamber at Mithral Hall. The orcs had been pushed out, the western entry seemingly secured. And because of their cleverness and the explosive potions of Nanfoodle, few dwarves had fallen in either the initial assault that had brought the orcs into the hall or the counterattack that had pushed them out.

But word had come from the south, both hopeful and tragic.

Bruenor Battlehammer stood tall in front of his throne then, commanding the attention of all, from the guards lining the room to the many citizens and refugees standing by the doors awaiting their audience with the king.

To the side of Bruenor stood Cordio and Stumpet, the two principle clerics of the clan. Bruenor motioned to them, and Cordio quickly dipped a large mug in the barrel of dwarven holy water, a very sweet honey mead. Attendants all over the hall scrambled to disseminate the drink, so that everyone in attendance, even the three non-dwarves—Regis, Wulfgar, and Nanfoodle—had mug in hand when Bruenor raised his in toast.

"And so does General Dagna Waybeard of Adbar and Mithral Hall join his son in the Halls of Moradin," Bruenor proclaimed. "To Dagna and to all who served well with him. They gave their lives in defense of neighbors and in battle with smelly trolls." He paused, then raised his voice to a shout as he finished, "A good way to die!"

"A good way to die!" came the thunderous response.

Bruenor drained his entire mug in one great gulp, then tossed it back to Cordio and fell back into his seat.

"The news was not all bad," said Banak Brawnanvil, sitting at his side in a specially constructed chair to accommodate legs that would no longer support him.

"Yeah?" said Bruenor.

"Alustriel was seen at the fight," said Banak. "No small thing, that."

Bruenor looked to the young courier who had brought the news from the south. When Bruenor had sent out the Mirabarran dwarves, he had stretched a line of communication all the way from Mithral Hall, a relay team of couriers so that news would flow back quickly. With the orcs back out of Mithral Hall, the dwarf king expected a very fluid situation and had no intention of being caught by surprise from any direction.

"Alustriel was there?" he pressed the courier. "Or we're *thinking* she was there?"

"Oh, they seen her, me king," said the dwarf, "come in on a flaming chariot, down from the sky in a ball of fire!"

"Then how did they know it to be her, through the veil of flames?" Nanfoodle dared to ask. He blanched and fell back, showing everyone that he was merely thinking aloud.

"Aye, that's Alustriel," Bruenor assured the gnome and everyone else. "I'm knowing a thing or two about the Lady of Silverymoon's fiery chariot."

That brought chuckles from the others around Bruenor, especially from the normally quiet Wulfgar, who had witnessed first-hand Bruenor's piloting of Alustriel's magical cart. Far to the south and out on the sea, Bruenor had brought Alustriel's conjured chariot of flame streaking across the deck of a pirate ship, to ultimate disaster—for the pirates, of course.

"So she's knowing that a fight's afoot," Bruenor said, and he looked to the emissary from another outside kingdom.

"Citadel Felbarr would surely've telled her," Jackonray Broadbelt agreed. "We've got a good flow o' runners to Silverymoon and to Sundabar. Alustriel's knowing what's afoot, to be sure, if she joined in the fight in the south."

"But will she come on to the north with her forces, as she did when the drow marched against Mithral Hall?" asked Wulfgar.

"Might be that we should send Rumblebelly to her to find out," Bruenor said, throwing a wink at the barbarian as they both turned their looks over Regis.

The halfling didn't catch it, obviously, for he sat very still and very quiet, head down.

Bruenor studied him for just a moment, and recognized the source of his apparent dismay. "What'd'ye think, Rumblebelly?" he bellowed. "Ye think ye might use yer ruby there on Alustriel and get all o' Silverymoon marching to help us?"

Regis looked up at him and shrugged, and his eyes widened as he apparently only then registered the absurd question.

"Bah, sit yerself back," Bruenor said with a laugh. "Ye won't go using that magical pendant o' yers on the likes of Alustriel!"

Everyone around the dwarf king joined in the laughter, but Bruenor's expression took on a more serious look as soon as he had the cover of the mirth.

"But we'll be needin' to talk about Silverymoon, and yerself and me girl're the two who're best knowing the place. Ye go and sit with her, Rumblebelly. I'll get by to talk with ye two as soon as I'm done here."

Regis's relief at being dismissed from the large gathering was evident to anyone who bothered to glance his way. He nodded and hopped up, then swiftly walked out of the room, even breaking into a trot as he reached the doorway.

Regis found Catti-brie sitting up in bed, a sizable plate of food set out before her. Her smile at him as he entered was among the sweetest sights he had ever known, for it was full of eagerness and acceptance. It was a smile that promised better days and another fight—something that Regis had feared Catti-brie would never be able to hope for again.

"Stumpet and Cordio have been hard at work, I see," he remarked as he moved into the room and pulled up a small chair to sit beside the woman's bed.

"And Moradin's been good enough to hear their call, for healing the likes of me. Do ye . . . *you* think perhaps I have more dwarf in me than either of us are knowing?"

The halfling found her answer somewhat ironic, given her own mid-sentence correction of her dwarven dialect.

"When do you think you'll be out of here?"

"I'll be out of bed in less than a tenday," Catti-brie answered. "I'll be fighting again in two—sooner if I find I'm needed, don't you doubt."

Regis looked at her skeptically. "Is that your guess or Cordio's?"

Catti-brie waved the question away and went back to eating, and so Regis understood that the priests had likely given estimates of at least a month.

As she finished with one piece of fruit, Catti-brie leaned over the opposite side of the bed, where a pail sat for the refuse. When she did, the movement caused the blanket to ride up on the side closest Regis, affording him a clear view of her torn hip and upper leg.

The woman settled back before the halfling could replace his pained expression.

"The rock hit you good," Regis said, knowing there was no way to avoid it.

Catti-brie tucked the blanket back down under her side. "I'm fortunate that it bounced off the ledge and the wall first," she admitted.

"How serious was the damage?"

Catti-brie's face went blank.

Regis met that stare and pressed on, "How far will you recover, do they say? That hip was crushed, the muscles torn through. Will you walk again?"

"Yes."

"Will you run?"

The woman paused a bit longer, her face growing tight. "Yes."

It was an answer more of determination than expectation, Regis knew. He let it go and stiffened his resolve against the wave of pity that wanted to flood out of him. He knew very well that Catti-brie would hear none of that.

"Word has come from the south," Regis said. "Lady Alustriel has joined the fight, albeit briefly."

"But Dagna has fallen," Catti-brie replied, surprising Regis.

"Word of such things passes quickly through a dwarven community," she explained.

Regis quieted for a few moments so that they could both offer a silent prayer for the soul of the fallen dwarf.

"Do you think it will ever be the same?" he asked.

"I don't," replied Catti-brie, and the halfling's head snapped up, for that was not precisely the answer he had expected and wanted from the normally optimistic woman. "As it was not the same when we drove the dark elves back underground. This fight's sure to leave a scar, my friend."

Regis considered that for a moment, then nodded his agreement. "Obould stuck it in deep, and stuck it hard," he said. "Bruenor will be glad when he has that one's head piked out beyond the western door."

"It is not all bad, these changes . . ." said Catti-brie.

"Torgar's here with his boys," Regis was quick to put in. "And we're talking with Felbarr as never before!"

"Aye," said the woman. "And sometimes tragedy is the catalyst for those who are left behind, to change in ways they knew they should, but never found the courage to grasp."

Something about her tone and the faraway look in her eye told the halfling that many things were stirring behind the blue eyes of Catti-brie, and not all of them in accordance to that which he and the others would normally expect of her.

"We're trying to get some scouts out and about, up through the chimneys," he said. "We're hoping for word from Drizzt."

Catti-brie's face twitched a bit at the mention of the drow. Not a grimace, but enough of a movement to tell Regis that he had hit a sensitive subject.

Again Regis quickly changed the topic. What use in speculating about Drizzt, after all, when none of them knew anything definite, though all of them held the same hopes? Instead Regis talked of better days to come, of the inevitable defeat of Obould and his stupid orcs and the good times they'd have with the brave dwarves of Mirabar, the newest members of the clan. He talked of Tred and Citadel Felbarr, and promises of allegiance that ran deep on both sides of the Underdark tunnels. He talked of Ivan and Pikel, and of the Spirit Soaring, their cathedral home set high in the Snowflake Mountains above the town of Carradoon on Impresk Lake. He would go and see that wondrous place, he prompted repeatedly, drawing smiles from Catti-brie, and finally coaxing her into talking about it, for she and Drizzt had once visited Cadderly and Danica.

After an hour or so, there came a sharp knock on the door, and Bruenor came bounding in.

"Word's in from Felbarr," he announced before he even bothered to say hello. "Jackonray's runners come back with the news that Emerus Warcrown's marching!"

"They will arrive through the eastern tunnels?" Regis asked. "We must set a proper feast for a visiting king."

"Ain't about food this time, Rumblebelly," said Bruenor. "And not through any tunnels. King Emerus's got his boys spilling out aboveground. A great force, marching to the River Surbrin. Already their front runners are setting up camp at Winter Edge, just across the river. Townsfolk there ain't never had such company as they're seeing today!"

"You're breaking out the eastern door," Catti-brie said.

"We're crossing Garumn's Gorge with everything we've got," Bruenor replied, referring to the cavern and ravine that separated the eastern end of Mithral Hall from the rest of the complex. "We'll blow the side o' the mountain away before us, and come out in such a rush that them stupid orcs'll be jumping into the river to get away from us!"

"And we'll wave at each other across the river?" Regis remarked.

Bruenor scowled at him and said, "We're gonna set a hold on our side, and smash those orcs back to the north. Emerus is coming across—they're building the boats as they march. From the eastern doors to the river will become a part of Mithral Hall, walled and strong, and with a bridge that'll cross over and give our growing allies a clean route to join in the fight."

The bold plan stole any quips from Regis, and had both he and Catti-brie sitting quietly attentive.

"How long?" the halfling finally managed to ask.

"Three days," said Bruenor, and Regis's jaw dropped open.

"I'll be ready to go," Catti-brie remarked, and both dwarf and halfling turned to her in surprise.

"No ye won't," said her father. "Already been talking to Cordio and Stumpet. This is one ye're missing, girl. Ye get yerself healthy and ready to fight. We'll be needing ye, don't ye doubt, when we've got the hold and're

trying to get the damn bridge built. Yer bow on a tower's worth a legion of ground fighters to me."

"Ye're not keeping me out o' the fight!" Catti-brie argued.

Regis nearly giggled at how dwarflike the woman suddenly seemed when her ire went up.

"No, I'm not," Bruenor agreed. "It's yer wound that's doing that. Ye can't even stand, ye unbearded girl gnome."

"I will stand!"

"And ye'll hobble," said Bruenor. "And ye'll have me and me boy Wulfgar, and Rumblebelly there, looking back for ye as often as we're looking ahead at the damned orcs!"

Catti-brie, sitting so bolt upright then that she was leaning forward at Bruenor, started to argue, but her words dissipated as she seemed to melt beck into her pillows. The intensity didn't leave her eyes—she so dearly wanted to fight—but it was clear that Bruenor's appeal to her on the grounds of how her stubbornness would affect those she loved had done the trick.

"Ye get well," Bruenor said quietly. "I promise ye girl that there'll be plenty more orcs looking for an arrow when ye're ready to come back in."

"What do you need me to do?" Regis asked.

"Ye stick with Jackonray," the dwarf king instructed. "Ye're me eyes and ears for Felbarr's worries. And I might be needing ye to look in on Nanfoodle and them Bouldershoulders, to tell me straight and without the gnome's winding words and Pikel's 'Boom!' what's really what in their progress on opening up that durned door. Them giants've put a hunnerd tons o' rock over them doors when we closed them, and we're needing to break through fast and strong to drive right to the Surbrin."

Regis nodded and hopped up, starting out of the room. He skidded to an abrupt halt even as he began, though, and turned back to regard Catti-brie.

"Better days are coming," he said to her, and she smiled.

It was the smile of a friend, but one who, Regis understood, was beginning to see the world through a different set of eyes.

15

DWARVEN FORTITUDE

The mob of trolls receded down the hill, sliding back into the bog and mist to lick their wounds, and a great cheer went up along the line of warriors both dwarf and human. They had held their ground again, for the third time that day, stubbornly refusing to be pushed back into the tunnels that loomed as black holes on the hillside behind them.

Torgar Hammerstriker watched the retreat with less excitement than his fellows, and certainly with less enthusiasm than the almost-giddy humans. Galen Firth ran along the human lines, proclaiming yet another victory in the name of Nesmé.

That was true, Torgar supposed, but could victory really be measured in terms of temporary advances and retreats? They had held, all three fights, because they had washed the leading trolls with a barrage of fiery logs. Looking back at their supply of kindling, Torgar hoped they had enough fuel to hold a fourth time. Victory? They were surrounded, with only the tunnels offering them any chance of retreat. They couldn't get any more fuel for their fires, and couldn't hope to break out through the ranks and ranks of powerful trolls.

"They're grabbing at every reason to scream and punch their fists in the air," Shingles McRuff remarked, coming up to stand beside his friend. "Can't say I blame 'em, but I'm not seeing how many victory punches we got left."

"Without the fires, we can no hold," Torgar agreed quietly, so that only Shingles could hear.

"A stubborn bunch o' trolls we got here," the old dwarf added. "They're taking their time. They know we got nowhere to run except the holes."

"Any scouts come back dragging logs?" Torgar asked, for he had sent several runners out along side tunnels, hoping to find an out of the way exit in an area not patrolled by their enemies, in the hope that they might be able to sneak in some more wood.

"Most're back, but none with any word that we've got trees to drag through. We got what we got now, and nothing more."

"We'll hold them as long as we can," Torgar said, "but if we don't break them in the next fight it'll be our last battle out here in the open."

"The boys're already practicing their retreat formations," Shingles assured him.

Torgar looked across his defensive line, to their partners in the struggle. He watched Galen Firth rousing his men once more, the tall man's seemingly endless supply of energy flowing out in one prompting cheer after another.

"I'm not thinking our boys to be the trouble," Torgar said.

"That Galen's no less stubborn than the trolls," Shingles agreed. "Might be a bit harder in convincing."

"So Dagna learned."

The two watched Galen's antics a bit longer, then Torgar added, "When we get the last line o' fires out at the trolls, and they're not breaking, then we're breaking ourselves, back into the tunnels. Galen and his boys can come if they want, or they can stay out here and get swallowed. No arguing on this. I'm not giving another o' Bruenor's war bands to Moradin to defend a human too stubborn or too stupid to see what's plain afore him. He runs with us or he stands alone."

It was a sobering order, and one that Torgar issued in a raised voice. There was no compromise to be found, all those dwarves around him understood. They would not make a gallant and futile last stand for the sake of Galen Firth and the Nesmians.

"Ye telled that all to Galen, did ye?"

"Three times," said Torgar.

"He hearing ye?"

"Dumathoin knows," Torgar answered, invoking to the dwarf god known as the Keeper of Secrets under the Mountains. "And Dumathoin ain't for telling. But don't ye misunderstand our place here in the least. We're Bruenor's southern line, and we're holding for Mithral Hall, not for Nesmé. Them folks want to come, we'll get them home to the halls or die trying. Them folks choose to stay, and they're dying alone."

It couldn't be more clear than that. But neither Torgar nor Shingles believed for a moment that even such a definitive stand would ring clearly enough in the thick head of Galen Firth.

The trolls wasted little time in regrouping and coming on once more as soon as the fires from the previous battle had died away. Their eagerness only confirmed to Torgar that which he had suspected: they were not a stupid bunch. They knew they had the dwarves on the edge of defeat, and knew well that the fiery barrage could not continue indefinitely.

They charged up the hill, their long legs propelling them swiftly across the sloping ground. They kept their lines loose and scattered—an obvious attempt to present less of an opportunity for targeting fiery missiles.

"Ready yer throws!" Shingles ordered, and torches were put to brands across the dwarven line.

"Not yet," Torgar whispered to his friend. "That's what they're expecting."

"And that's all we're giving."

But Torgar shook his head. "Not this time," he said. "Not yet."

The trolls closed ground. Down at the human end of the defensive line, fiery brands went flying out.

But Torgar held his missiles. The trolls closed.

"Running wedge!" Torgar shouted, surprising all those around him, even Shingles, who had fought so many times beside his fellow Mirabarran.

"Running wedge?" he asked.

"Send 'em out! All of 'em!" Torgar shouted. He lifted his warhammer high and yelled, "With me, boys!"

Torgar leaped out from behind the stony barricade, Shingles at his side. Without even bothering to look left or right, the dwarf charged down the hill, confident that his boys would not let him down.

And that confidence was well placed. The dwarves poured out like water, tumbling and rolling right back to their feet. In a few short strides, they were

already forming their running wedge and by the time they hit the leading trolls, their formations were tight and well supported.

Torgar was, fittingly, first to engage. He led with a great sweep of his hammer, and the troll standing before him hopped back out of range, then came in fast behind the swipe. Apparently thinking it had the aggressive little creature vulnerable, the troll opened wide its mouth and lunged forward to bite at the dwarf.

Just as Torgar had hoped, for as his hammer cut the air before the beast, the dwarf, who hadn't put half the weight behind that swing as he had made it appear, yanked against the momentum and reversed the flow of the weapon, bringing it in close. He slid one hand up the shaft of the hammer as he moved one foot forward, turning almost sidelong to the troll, then thrust weapon's head straight out into the diving mouth of the troll. Teeth splintered and Torgar heard the crack of the troll's jawbone.

Not one to sit on his laurels, the dwarf yanked his hammer back, snapping it into a roll over his trailing right shoulder and letting go with his left hand. He caught the weapon down low with his left hand again as it came spinning up over his head, then chopped down with all his strength, every muscle in his body snapping, driving the hammerhead into the troll's brain.

The creature fell straight to the ground, squirming wildly, and Torgar just kicked it in the face as he barreled by.

"Clever dwarves," Kaer'lic Suun Wett remarked.

With Tos'un beside her, the drow priestess stood on a high, tree-covered bluff off to the side of the main action.

"They saw that the trolls were coming up widespread and gradually, trying to draw out their flaming brands," Tos'un agreed.

"And now they've sent those leading decoys running or to the ground, and not a brand have they thrown," said Kaer'lic.

The contrast between the dwarves' tactics and those of the humans standing beside them came crystal clear. While the dwarves had come out in a wild charge, the humans held their ground, and had indeed launched many of their fiery brands against the leading troll line.

"Proffit will exploit the human line and drive around to flank the dwarves," Kaer'lic said, pointing up that way.

Lower on the field, the disciplined dwarves had already turned around, having scattered the leading trolls. Their wedge retreated without a pivot, so that the dwarves at the trailing, widespread edges were the first back over the wall, and those dwarves wasted no time in stoking the fires and readying the barrage.

Kaer'lic growled and punched her fist into her open palm when she noted Proffit's forces closing in on the dwarves' retreat. The trolls had been clearly enraged by the brash charge of the bearded folk, and were rolling up the hill behind the retreating point of the wedge, grouped tightly.

Before those running dwarves even got over the wall, the barrage began, with dozens and dozens of burning logs spinning over the wall and out over the dwarves. So closely grouped, the trolls took hit after hit, and when the flames stuck on one, sending it up in a burst of fire, its close-standing comrades, too, felt the fiery bite.

"Fools," Kaer'lic grunted, and the priestess began muttering the words of a spell.

A moment later, a small geyser of water appeared among the trolls, dousing fires and buying them some freedom from the dwarves' volley. Kaer'lic finished her spell, muttered under her breath, and began to conjure some more water. How much easier it all would have been, she thought, had Proffit not allowed the pursuit and had instead sent the bulk of his minions at the western, human end of the defensive line. . . .

Even with the magical interference of an unexpected burst of water, the firestorm proved considerable and highly effective, sending troll after troll up in a blaze. But Torgar saw the truth of the situation before him. They had stung their enemies again, but their time of advantage was over. Their fuel was exhausted.

Torgar looked past the flames and flaming trolls, to the horde of enemies behind, lurking down the hill, patiently waiting for the fires to diminish.

"Ye hold 'em here as long as ye can, but not a moment longer," Torgar instructed Shingles.

“Where’re ye going, then?” the old dwarf asked.

“Galen Firth’s needing to hear this from me again, so that there’s no misunderstanding. We’re going when we’re going, and if they’re not going, then they’re on their own.”

“Tell him, and let him see yer eyes when ye tell him,” Shingles said. “He’s a stubborn one.”

“He’ll be a dead one, then, and so be it.”

Torgar patted his old friend on the shoulder and trotted along to the west, moving behind his boys and encouraging them with every step. He soon came to the human warriors, all readying their weapons, for their fires were burning low out on the hill before them. The dwarf had little trouble finding Galen Firth, for the man was up on a stone, shouting encouragement and pumping his fist.

“Well fought!” he said to Torgar when he spotted the approaching dwarf. “A brilliant move to go out and attack.”

“Aye, and a smarter move’s coming soon,” Torgar replied. “The one that’s putting us back in the tunnels, not to come out again.”

Galen’s smile remained as he digested those words, coming down from the stone. By the time he was standing before Torgar, that smile had been replaced by a frown.

“They have not breached our line, nor shall they!”

“Strong words, well spoken,” said Torgar. “And true in the first and hopeful in the second. But if we’re waiting to see if ye’re right or wrong on what’s to come, and ye’re wrong, then we’re all dead.”

“I long ago pledged my life to the defense of Nesmé.”

“Then stand yer ground if that’s yer choice. I’m here to tell ye that me and me boys’re heading into the tunnels, and there we’re to stay.” Torgar was well aware of the many frightened looks coming in at him from all around at that proclamation.

“Ye’ll want to tighten yer line, then,” said Torgar. “If ye’re that stubborn. Me thinking’s that ye should be going into the tunnels with us—yer old ones and young afore us, and yer fighters beside us. That’s me thinking, Galen Firth. Take it as ye will.”

The dwarf bowed and turned to leave.

“I beg you to stay,” Galen surprised him by saying. “As General Dagna decided to fight for Nesmé.”

Torgar turned on him sharply, his heavy eyebrows furrowing and shadowing his dark eyes. "Dagna gave his life and his boys gave theirs because ye were too stubborn to know when to run," he corrected. "It's not a mistake I'm planning on making. Ye been told that we're going. Ye been invited to come. Choice is yer own, and not mine."

The dwarf was quick in moving off, and when Galen called to him again, he just continued on his way, muttering, "Durn fool," under his breath with every step.

"Wait! Wait!" came a cry from behind, one that did turn Torgar around. He saw another of the Nesmé warriors, Rannek, running along the line toward Galen Firth and pointing up at the sky. "Good dwarf, wait! It is Alustriel! Alustriel has come again!"

Torgar followed his finger skyward, and there in the dark sky the dwarf saw the streaking chariot of fire, coming in hard and fast.

At the same time, drumbeats filled the air, booming in from the southeast, and horns began to blow.

"The Silver Guard!" one man cried. "The Silver Guard of Silverymoon is come!"

Torgar looked at Galen Firth, who seemed as surprised as any, though he had been saying that such help would arrive from the beginning.

"Our salvation is at hand, good dwarf," Galen said to him. "Stay, then, and join in our great victory this night!"

"Lady Lolth, she's back," Tos'un groaned when he saw the telltale flash of fire sweeping out of the night sky.

"Obould's worst nightmare," Kaer'lic replied. "Alustriel of Silverymoon. A most formidable foe, so we have been told."

Tos'un glanced at Kaer'lic, the tone of her words showing him that she had taken that reputation as a challenge. She was staring up at the chariot, eyes sparkling, mouthing the words of a spell, her fingers tracing runes in the empty air.

She timed her delivery perfectly, casting just as Alustriel soared past, not so far overhead. The very air seemed to distort and crack around the flying

cart, a resonating, thunderous boom that shook the ground beneath Tos'un's feet. Alustriel's disorientation manifested itself to the watching drow through the erratic movements of the chariot, banking left and right, back and forth, even veering sharply so that it seemed as if it might skid out of control in the empty air.

Kaer'lic quickly cast a second spell, and a burst of conjured water intercepted Alustriel's shaky path.

The chariot dipped, its flight disturbed. For a moment, the flames on the magical horse team winked out, and down they all went.

"To the glory of Lolth," Tos'un said with a grin as the chariot plummeted.

The two anticipated a glorious wreckage, the enjoyable screams of horses and driver alike, and indeed, when the flying carriage first hit, they realized more disaster than even they could imagine.

But not in the manner they had expected.

The flames came alive again when Alustriel's chariot touched down, bursting from the carriage and horses alike, and leaping out in a fireball that swept out to the sides, then rolled up over the chariot as it charged along.

Both drow had their mouths hanging open as they watched the driver regain control, as her chariot—rolling along instead of flying—cut a swath of destruction and death through Proffit's ranks. Alustriel banked to the south, a wide sweep that both drow understood was intended to turn her around so that she could find her magical attackers.

"She should be dead," Kaer'lic said, and she licked her suddenly dry lips.

"But she's not," said Tos'un.

The chariot went up in the air, then continued its turn, completing a circuit. The dark elves heard the sound of a larger battle to the east, and the sound of horns and drums.

"She brought friends," said Kaer'lic.

"Many friends," Tos'un presumed. "We should leave."

The dark elves looked at each other and nodded.

"Get the prisoner," Kaer'lic instructed, and she didn't even wait as Tos'un moved off toward the small hole where they had concealed poor Fender.

The two dark elves and their captive started away quickly to the west, wanting to put as much ground as possible between themselves and the fierce woman in the flying chariot.

From the joyous cries among the line of dwarves and humans in the north, to the gathering sounds of a great battle erupting in the east, to the sheer power and control of the woman in the chariot up above, they knew that the end had come for Proffit.

Lady Alustriel and Silverymoon had come.

The Silver Guard of Silverymoon charged into the troll ranks in tight formation, spears leveled, bows firing flaming arrows from behind their ranks. Watching from the higher ground, Torgar could only think of the initial engagement as a wave washing over a beach, so fully did the Silver Guard seem to engulf the eastern end of the troll ranks.

But then that wave seemed to break apart on many large rocks. They were trolls, after all, strong and powerful and more physically resilient than any creature in all the world. The roar of the charge became the screams of the dying. The tight formations became a dance of smaller groups, pockets of warriors working hard to fend off the huge, ugly trolls.

Fireballs erupted beyond the leading edge of the Silver Guard, as Silverymoon's battle wizards joined in the fray.

But the trolls did not break and run. They met the attack with savagery, plowing into the human ranks, crushing warriors to the ground and stomping them flat.

"Now, boys!" Torgar yelled to his dwarves. "They came to help us, and it's our turn to repay the favor!"

From on high came the dwarven charge, down the barren, rocky slope at full run. To their right, the west, came Galen and the humans, sweeping in behind the trolls as the monsters pressed eastward to do battle with the new threat.

Blood ran—troll, dwarf, and human. Troll roars, human screams, and dwarven grunts mingled in the air in a symphony of horror and pain. The drama played out, minute by minute, a hundred personal struggles within the greater overall conflict.

It was the end for so many that day, lives cut short on a bloody, rocky slope under a pre-dawn sky.

As the lines tightened, the wizards became less effective and it became a contest of steel against claw, of troll savagery against dwarf stubbornness.

In the end, it wasn't the weapons or the superior tactics that won the day for the dwarves and humans. It was the care for each other and the sense that those around each warrior would stand there in support, the confidence of community and sacrifice. The willingness to stand and die before abandoning a friend. The dwarves had it most of all, but so did the humans of Nesmé and Silverymoon, while the trolls fought singly, self-preservation or bloodlust alone keeping them in battle.

Dawn broke an hour later to reveal a field of blood and body parts, of dead men, dead dwarves, and burned trolls, of troll body pieces squirming and writhing until the finishing crews could put them to the torch.

Battered and torn, half his face gouged by filthy troll claws, Torgar Hammerstriker walked the lines of his wounded, patting each dwarf on the shoulder as he passed. His companions had come out from Mirabar behind him, and had known nothing but battle after vicious battle by the end of the first tenday. Yet not a dwarf was complaining, and not one had muttered a single thought about going back. They were Battlehammers now, one and all, loyal to kin and king.

The fights, to a dwarf, were worth it.

As he moved past the line of his fighters, Torgar spotted Shingles talking excitedly to several of the Silverymoon militia.

"What do ye know?" Torgar asked when he came up beside his old friend.

"I know that Alustriel's not thinking to move north against Obould," came the surprising answer.

Torgar snapped his gaze over the two soldiers, who remained unshaken and impassive, and seemed in no hurry to explain the surprising news.

"She here?" Torgar asked.

"Lady Alustriel is with Galen Firth of Nesmé," one of the soldiers asked.

"Then ye best be taking us there."

The soldier nodded and led them on through the encampment, past the piled bodies of Silverymoon dead, past the lines of horribly wounded men, where priests were hard at work in tending the many garish wounds. In a tent near the middle of the camp, they found Alustriel and Galen Firth, and the man from Nesmé seemed in as fine spirits as Torgar had known.

The two dwarves allowed the soldiers to announce them, then walked up to the table where Lady Alustriel and Galen stood. The sight of Alustriel did give stubborn Torgar pause, for all that he had heard of the impressive woman surely paled in comparison to the reality of her presence. Tall and shapely, she stood with an air of dignity and competence beyond anything Torgar had ever seen. She wore a flowing gown of the finest materials, white and trimmed in purple, and upon her head was a circlet of gold and diamonds that could not shine with enough intensity to match her eyes. Torgar could hardly believe the thought, but it seemed to him that next to Alustriel, even Shoudra Stargleam would be diminished.

"L-lady," the dwarf stuttered, bowing so low his black beard brushed the ground.

"Well met, Torgar Hammerstriker," Alustriel said in a voice that was like a cool north wind. "I was hoping to speak with you, here or in the inevitable meetings I will have with King Bruenor of Mithral Hall. Your actions in Mirabar have sent quite an unsettling ripple throughout the region, you must know."

"If that ripple slaps Marchion Elastul upside his thick skull, then it's more than worth it," the dwarf answered, regaining his composure and taciturn facade.

"Fair enough," Alustriel conceded.

"What am I hearing now, Lady?" Torgar asked. "Some nonsense that ye're thinking the battle done?"

"The land is full of orcs and giants, good dwarf," said Alustriel. "The battle is far from finished, I am certain."

"I was just told ye weren't marching north to Mithral Hall."

"That is true."

"But ye just said—"

"This is not the time to take the fight to King Obould," Alustriel explained. "Winter will fast come on. There is little we can do."

"Bah, ye can have yer army—armies, for where's Everlund and Sundabar?—to Keeper's Dale in a tenday's time!"

"The other cities are watching, from afar," said Alustriel. "You do not understand the scope of what has befallen the region, I fear."

"Don't understand it?" Torgar said, eyes wide. "I been fighting in the middle of it for tendays now! I was on the ridge with Banak Brawnanvil, holding back the hordes. Was me and me boys that stole back the tunnels so that damned fool gnome could blow the top off the mountain spur!"

"Yes, I wish to hear all of that tale, in full, but another time," Alustriel said.

"So how can ye be saying I'm not knowing? I'm knowing better than anyone!"

"You saw the front waves of an ocean of enemies," Alustriel said. "Tens of thousands of orcs have crawled out of their holes to Obould's call. I have seen this. I have flown the length and breadth of the battlefield. There is nothing the combined armies can do at this time to be rid of the vermin. We cannot send thousands to die in such an effort, when it is better to secure a defensive line that will hold back the orc ocean."

"Ye came out to help Galen here!"

"Yes, against a manageable enemy—and one that still tore deeply into my ranks. The trolls have been pushed back, and we will drive them into the moors where they belong. Nesmé,"—she indicated the map on the table—"will be raised and fortified, because that alone is our best defense against the creatures of the Trollmoors."

"So ye come to the aid of Nesmé, but not of Mithral Hall?" said Torgar, never one to hold his thoughts private.

"We aid where we can," Alustriel answered, remaining calm and relaxed. "If the orcs begin to loosen their grip, if an opportunity presents itself, then Silverymoon will march to Mithral Hall and beyond, gladly beside King Bruenor Battlehammer and his fine clan. I suspect that Everlund will march with us, and surely Citadels Felbarr and Adbar will not forsake their Delzoun kin."

"But not now?"

Alustriel held her hands out wide.

"Nothing ye can do?"

"Emissaries will connect with King Battlehammer," the woman replied. "We will do what we can."

Torgar felt himself trembling, felt his fists clenching at his sides, and it was all he could do to not launch himself at Alustriel, or at Galen, standing smugly beside her, the man seeming as if all the world had been set aright, since Nesmé would soon be reclaimed.

"There is nothing more, good dwarf," Alustriel added. "I can not march my armies into the coming snow against so formidable an enemy as has brought war against Mithral Hall."

"It's just orcs," said Torgar.

No answer came back at him, and he knew he would get none.

"Will you march with us to Nesmé?" Galen Firth asked, and Torgar felt himself trembling anew. "Will you celebrate in the glory of our victory as Nesmé is freed?"

The dwarf stared hard at the man.

Then Torgar turned and walked out of the tent. He soon made it back to his kinfolk, Shingles at his side. Within an hour, they were gone, into the tunnels and marching at double-pace back to King Bruenor.

16

SHIFTING SANDS AND SOLID STONE

"The boys from Felbarr're in sight across the river," Jackonray Broadbelt excitedly reported to King Bruenor.

For several days, the dwarf representative from Citadel Felbarr had been watching intently for the reports filtering down the chimneys for just such word. He knew that his kin were on the march, that Emerus Warcrown had agreed upon a Surbrin crossing to crash a hole in the defensive ring the orcs were preparing and link up aboveground with Mithral Hall.

"Three thousand warriors," Jackonray went on. "And with boats to get across."

"We're ready to knock out the hole in the east," Bruenor replied. "We got all me boys bunched at Garumn's Gorge, ready to charge out and chase the stinkin' orcs from the riverbank."

The two dwarves clapped each other on the shoulder, and throughout the audience hall other dwarves cheered. Sitting near to Bruenor's dais, two others seemed less than enthusiastic, however.

"You'll get them out fast?" Regis asked Nanfoodle.

The gnome nodded. "Mithral Hall will come out in a rush," he assured the halfling. "But fast enough to destroy the river defenses?"

The same question echoed in Regis's thoughts. They had won over and over again, and even when they'd lost ground, the cost had been heavier for their enemies. But all that had been achieved through *defensive* actions.

What they planned was something quite different.

"What do ye know, Rumblebelly?" Bruenor asked a moment later, and Regis realized that he wasn't doing a very good job of keeping his fears off of his face.

"There are a lot of orcs," he said.

"Lot o' dead orcs soon enough!" declared Jackonray, and the cheering grew even louder.

"We have the hall back, and they're not coming in," Regis said quietly. The words sounded incredibly inane to him as he heard them come from his mouth, and he had no idea what positive effect stating the obvious might bring. It was simply a subconscious delaying tactic, he understood, a way to move the conversation in another, less excitable direction.

"And they're soon to be running away!" Bruenor shot back at him, and the cheering grew even louder.

There was no way to go against it, Regis recognized. The emotions were too high, the anger bubbling over into the ecstasy of revenge.

"We should take no chances," Regis said, but no one was listening. "We should move with care," he said, but no one was listening. "We have them held now," he tried to explain. "How long will their forces hold together out there in the cold and snow when they know that there is nowhere left for them to march? Without the hunger of conquest, the orc momentum will stall, and so will their hearts for battle."

Nanfoodle's hand on his arm broke the halfling's gaining momentum, for it made Regis understand that Nanfoodle was the only one who even realized he was talking, that the dwarves, cheering wildly and leaping about, couldn't even hear his whispered words.

"We'll get out fast," the gnome assured him. "These engineers are magnificent. They will make wide tunnels, do not fear. The Battlehammer dwarves will come against the orcs before the orcs know they are being attacked."

Regis nodded, not doubting any of those specifics, but still very uneasy about the whole plan.

A clap on his other shoulder turned him around, to see Wulfgar crouching beside him.

"It is time to turn the orcs back to the north," the big man said. "It is time to put the vermin back in their mountain holes, or in the cold ground."

"I just . . ." Regis started.

"It is the loss of Dagna," said Wulfgar.

Regis glanced up at him.

"You struck out forcefully and the cost was heavy," the barbarian explained. "Is it so surprising that you would be less eager to strike out again?"

"You think it was my fault?"

"I think you did the right thing, and everyone here agreed and agrees still," Wulfgar answered with a reassuring smile. "If Dagna could reach out from the Halls of Moradin, he would pick you up by the collar and send you running to lead the charge out the eastern doors." Wulfgar put his hand on the halfling's shoulder—and from shoulder to neck, Regis disappeared under that gigantic paw.

The halfling tuned back in to the wider conversation then, in time to hear Bruenor shouting orders to send signalers up the chimneys to the mountain-top, to tell the Felbarr boys across the river that it was time to send Obould running.

The cheering drowned out everything, and even Regis and Nanfoodle were swept up in it.

It was time to send Obould running!

"Before winter!" came the shout, and the roar that was heard in the common room of the human refugees was as loud as that of the dwarves above vowing vengeance on King Obould. Word had filtered down the corridors of Mithral Hall that Citadel Felbarr had come, and that King Bruenor and his dwarves were preparing to burst out of their imprisonment.

The River Surbrin would be secured—that much seemed certain—and the dwarves had promised to set up passage over the river to the lands still tamed. They would cross the Surbrin before winter.

"Never again will I be crawling into any tunnels!" one man shouted.

"But huzzah to King Bruenor and his clan for their hospitality!" shouted another and a great cheer went up.

"Silverymoon before the snow!" one shouted.

"Everlund!" argued another.

"There's word that Nesmé's looking for hearty souls," added another, "to rebuild what the trolls tore down."

Each city mentioned drew a louder cheer.

Each one stung Delly as acutely as the bite of a wasp. She moved through the crowd nodding, smiling, and trying to be happy for them. They had been through so much turmoil, had seen loved ones die and houses burned to the ground. They had trekked across miles of rocky ground, had suffered the elements and the fear of orcs nipping at their heels all the way to Mithral Hall.

Delly wanted to be happy for them, for they deserved a good turn of fortune. But when the news had come down that the dwarves were preparing the breakout in earnest, and that they expected to open the way for the refugees to leave, all Delly could think about was that soon she would again be alone.

She had Colson of course, and Wulfgar when he was not up fighting—which was rarely of late. She had the dwarves, and she cared for them greatly.

But how she wanted to see the stars again. And bask in the sun. And feel the wind upon her face. A wistful smile crossed her face as she thought of Arumn and Josi at the Cutlass.

Delly shook the nostalgia and the self-pity away quickly as she approached a solitary figure in the corner of the large room. Cottie Cooperson didn't join in the cheers that night, and seemed hardly aware of them at all. She sat upon a chair, rocking slowly back and forth, staring down at the small child in her arms.

Delly knelt beside her and gently put her hand on Cottie's shoulder.

"Ye put her to sleep again, did ye, Cottie?" Delly quietly asked.

"She likes me."

"Who would not?" Delly asked, and she just knelt there for a long time, rubbing Cottie's shoulder, looking down at the peaceful Colson.

The sounds of eager anticipation continued to echo around her, the shouts and the cheers, the grand plans unveiled by man after man declaring that he would begin a new and better life. Their resilience touched Delly, to be sure, as did the sense of community that she felt there. All those refugees from various small towns, thrown together in the tunnels of dwarves, had bonded in common cause and in simple human friendship.

Delly held her smile throughout, but when she considered the source of the cheering, she felt more like crying.

She left the room a short while later, Colson in her arms. To her surprise, she found Wulfgar waiting for her in their room.

"I hear ye're readying to break free of the hall and march to the Surbrin," she greeted.

The bluntness and tone set Wulfgar back in his chair, and Delly felt him watching her closely, every step, as she carried Colson to her small crib. She set the baby down and let her finger trace gently across her face, then stood straight and took a deep breath before turning to Wulfgar and adding, "I hear ye're meaning to go soon."

"The army is already gathering at Garumn's Gorge," the big man confirmed. "The army of Citadel Felbarr is in sight above, approaching the Surbrin from the east."

"And Wulfgar will be there with the dwarves when they charge forth from their halls, will he?"

"It is my place."

"Yer own and Catti-brie's," Delly remarked.

Wulfgar shook his head, apparently missing the dryness of her tone. "She cannot go, and it is difficult for her. Cordio will hear nothing of it, for her wounds have not yet mended."

"Ye seem to know much about it."

"I just came from her bedside," said Wulfgar as he moved toward Colson's crib—and as Delly moved aside, so that he did not see her wince at that admission.

Bedside, or bed? the woman thought, but she quickly shook the preposterous notion from her mind.

"How badly she wishes that she could join in the battle," Wulfgar went on. So engaged was he with Colson then, leaning over the side of the crib and waggling his finger before the child's face so that she had a challenge in grabbing at it, that he did not notice Delly's profound frown. "She's all fight, that one. I think her hatred of the orcs rivals that of a Gutbuster."

He finally looked up at Delly and his smile disappeared the moment he regarded the stone-faced woman, her arms crossed over her chest.

"They're all leaving," she answered his confused expression. "For

Silverymoon and Everlund, or wherever their road might take them."

"Bruenor has promised that the way will be clear," Wulfgar answered.

"Clear for all of us," Delly heard herself saying, and she could hardly believe the words. "I'd dearly love to see Silverymoon. Can ye take me there?"

"We have already discussed this."

"I'm needing to go," Delly said. "It's been too long in the tunnels. Just a foray, a visit, a chance to hear the tavern talk of people like meself."

"We will break through and scatter the orcs," Wulfgar promised. He came up beside her and hugged her close in his muscular arms. "We will have them on the run before winter and put them in their holes before midsummer. Their day is past and Bruenor will reclaim the land for the goodly folk. Then we will go to Silverymoon, and on to Sundabar if you wish!"

He couldn't see Delly's face as he held her so closely.

He wouldn't have understood anything he saw there, anyway, for the woman was just numb. She had no answers for him, had not even any questions to ask.

Resignation smacked hard against impatience, and the woman couldn't find the heart to start counting the many, many days.

Feeling refreshed and confident that he would rouse Citadel Felbarr to Mithral Hall's aid, Nikwillig walked out of the Moonwood to the south, escorted by Hralien. They would strike southwest, toward the Surbrin, to gather needed information, and Hralien planned to return to the Moonwood after seeing Nikwillig safely on his way back to his dwarven home.

When the pair reached the Surbrin, they saw their enemies across the way, still building on the already formidable defenses. Picket walls of huge sharpened logs lined the western bank and piles of stones could be seen, ready to be thrown by the few giants they saw milling about, or by the many catapults that had been constructed and set in place.

"They're thinking to hold it all," Nikwillig remarked.

Hralien had no response.

The two moved back to the east soon after, marching long into the night

and far from the riverbank. The next morning, they set off early, and at a swift pace. At noon, they came to the crossroads.

"Farewell, good dwarf," Hralien offered. "Your enemy is our enemy, of course, and so I expect that we might well meet again."

"Well met the first time," Nikwillig replied. "And well met the second, by Moradin's blessing."

"Yes, there is that," Hralien said with a grin. He clapped the dwarf on the shoulder and turned back to the north and home.

Nikwillig moved with a spring in his step. He had never expected to survive the battle north of Keeper's Dale, had thought his signaling mission to be suicidal. But, at long last, he was going home.

Or so he thought.

He came upon a high bluff as twilight settled on the hilly landscape, and from that vantage point, Nikwillig saw the vast encampment of an army far to the south.

An army he knew.

Citadel Felbarr was already on the march!

Nikwillig punched his fist in the air and let out a growl of support for his warrior kinfolk. He considered the ground between him and the encampment. He wanted to run right out and join them, but he knew that his weary legs wouldn't carry him any farther that night. So he settled down, thinking to get a short rest.

He closed his eyes.

And awoke late the next morning, with the sun nearing its apex. The dwarf leaped up and rushed to the southern end of the bluff. The army was gone—marching east, he knew. East to the river and the mighty defenses that had been set in place there.

The dwarf glanced all around, studying the ground, looking for some sign of his kin. Could he catch them?

He didn't know, but did he dare try it?

Nikwillig hopped in circles for many minutes, his mind spinning faster than his body ever could. One name kept coming back to him: Hralien.

He ran off the bluff soon after, heading north and not south.

17

OVEREAGER

Bruenor Battlehammer stood on the eastern gatehouse of the bridge at Garumn's Gorge, overseeing the preparations for the coming assault. The couriers scrambled, relaying messages and information from the engineers and the many scouts working the eastern slopes of the mountain, who shouted the information down the cooled chimneys to the great Undercity. The dwarf king was arrayed in full battle regalia, his shield emblazoned with the foaming mug standard of his clan and his well-worn, often chipped battle-axe slung casually over one shoulder—but without his signature helmet, with its one horn remaining.

Regis and Wulfgar were there by his side, as was Banak Brawnanvil, seated and strapped into a carriage set upon two sturdy poles. Four strong dwarves attended Banak, ready to carry him out onto the battlefield and into position where he could help direct the movements of the various dwarven regiments.

"Girl's gonna miss the fun this day," Bruenor remarked, referring to the notably absent Catti-brie. She had argued and argued to be a part of the battle, but Cordio and the other priests would hear none of it, and in the end, Wulfgar and Bruenor had quietly pointed out that her presence would more likely jeopardize those attending her than anything else.

"Fun?" Regis echoed.

He continued to stare to the east, where three high platforms had been built, each holding a train of ore carts, cranked up and locked in place at the top of a high rail ramp. The rails swept down across the remaining distance of the gorge ledge, then into the exit tunnels. The doors to those tunnels had been reopened, but the orcs, trolls, and giants had done a fair job of bringing down that side of the mountain, leaving the dwarves trapped in their hole. And so while the engineers had constructed the rails, miners had dug extensions on the escape tunnels, scraping right to the very outer edge of the landslide, so close to the open air that they often had to pause in their work and let noisy orc guards wander by.

"Fun in a Pwent kind o' way," Bruenor remarked with a snicker. "Durned crazy dwarf's arguing to sit atop the middle train instead of inside!" Bruenor offered a wink at Banak.

"He'd lead with his helmet spike, and probably take half the mountain with him," Banak added. "And he'd love every tumble and every rock that fell upon his too-hard head."

"Not to doubt," said Bruenor.

"The middle tunnel will prove the widest," Wulfgar said more seriously.

"Me and yerself'll lead the charge right behind the carts out that one, then," said Bruenor.

"I was thinking to go on the left," said Wulfgar. "The scouts report that the watchtower is well defended by our enemies. Taking that, and quickly, will be crucial."

"To the left, then. The both of us."

"You'll be needed in the center, directing," Regis said.

"Bah!" Bruenor snorted. "Pwent's starting the fight there, and Pwent don't take no directions. These boys'll get Banak out fast enough, and he'll call the orders to the river."

All three, dwarf, human, and halfling, looked to the injured Banak as Bruenor spoke, and none of them missed the expression of sincere gratitude the old warrior wore. He wanted to see the fight through, wanted to complete what he had started on the high ridge north of Keeper's Dale. As they all had learned with Pikel Bouldershoulder after the green-bearded dwarf had lost an arm, the physical infirmity would be minimized if the wounded could still contribute to the cause.

The conversation rambled along for some time, the four really talking about nothing important, but merely trying to pass away the tense minutes until the final words came up from the Undercity. Everyone at Garumn's Gorge wanted to just go, to burst out and be on with the battle. Seasoned veterans all, the Battlehammer dwarves knew well that those moments before a battle were usually the most trying.

And so it was with hopeful eyes that the four turned to see the courier running to them from the depths of Mithral Hall.

"King Bruenor," the dwarf gasped, "the scouts're saying that Felbarr's ready to cross and that most o' the damned orcs've gone down to the river."

"That's it, then," Bruenor told them all.

He gave a shrill whistle, commanding the attention of all nearby dwarves, then lifted his battle-axe into the air and shook it about.

Cheering started near him and rolled out to the edges of the gorge like a wave on a pond. Up above, warriors scrambled into the ore carts, packing in tightly, and pulled the thick metal covers over them, and just below them, engineers moved to the locking pins.

Wulfgar bounded off toward the left-hand tunnel, nearly running over Nanfoodle as the gnome rushed to join Bruenor, who was offering last-minute instructions to Banak.

"I wish we had some of that oil of impact remaining," the gnome moaned.

"Bah, the dwarves'll knock them walls out!" said Regis, using his best Bruenor imitation, and when Bruenor turned to regard him curiously, the halfling tossed him a reassuring wink.

It seemed that Regis had put his doubts aside, or at least had suppressed them since they were moot in any case, but before Bruenor could begin to discern which it might be, the pins were yanked free and the three large trains began to rumble down the tracks.

They came down from a height of more than fifty feet, picking up speed and momentum as they shot along the oiled rails into the low, narrow tunnels. So perfectly timed was the release, and so minimal the tolerance of each set of rails, that they rolled along side-by-side into their respective tunnels and all hit the outer shell of the mountain blockade within a blink of each other.

The screech of metal grinding on metal and stone, and the thunder of

tumbling boulders, echoed back into the main chambers, eliciting a great war whoop from the gathered forces, who took up the charge.

Wulfgar led the way on the left, though he had to stoop nearly double to pass through the tight corridor. Before him lay bright daylight, for the train had blasted right through and had gone skidding and tumbling down beyond the exit. Already dwarves were scrambling out of that wreckage, weapons ready.

The barbarian came out into the open air and saw immediately that their surprise was complete. Few orcs were in the area, and those that were seemed more frightened than ready to do battle. Wulfgar ignored his instincts to go to the seemingly vulnerable train-riders, and instead cut a fast left and sprinted up a rocky slope toward the watchtower. The door was partially ajar, an orc moving behind it just as Wulfgar lowered his shoulder and barreled into it.

The orc grunted and flew across the room, arms and legs flailing. Its three companions in the room watched its flight, their expressions confused. They seemed hardly aware that an enemy had burst in, even when Aegis-fang swept down from on high, smashing the skull of the closest.

Wulfgar pivoted around that dead orc as it fell, and in his turn, sent his warhammer sweeping out wide. The targeted orc leaped and turned, trying to twist out of the way, but the warhammer clipped it hard enough to launch it into a spin, around and around, into the air, its flight ending abruptly at the tower's stone wall. Wulfgar strode forward, chopping at the third orc, who rushed away and out of reach. But the barbarian just turned the momentum of the hammer, launching it out left to right so that it cracked into the back of the orc who was pressed face-up against the wall, crushing its ribs and splitting its sides. The creature gasped and blood fountained from its mouth.

Wulfgar wasn't watching, though, certain that his hit had been fatal. He let go of Aegis-fang, confident it would return to his call, and charged ahead, swatting aside the spear of the remaining orc as it clumsily tried to bring the weapon to bear.

The huge barbarian stepped close and got his hand around the orc's neck, then pressed ahead and down, bending the creature over backward and choking the life out of it.

"Above ye!" a dwarf called in a raspy voice from the doorway.

Wulfgar glanced back to see Bill HuskenNugget, the lookout who had been in there when the tower had been taken. Bill had been downed with a poisoned dart, and simultaneously, his throat had been expertly cut, taking his voice, which was only beginning to heal. The retreating dwarves had thought Bill dead, but they'd dragged him along anyway, as was their custom—and a good thing they had, for he had awakened cursing in a whisper soon after.

Wulfgar's gaze went up fast, in time to see an orc in the loft above him launching a spear his way. The orc jerked as it threw, Bill's crossbow bolt buried in its side.

Wulfgar couldn't dive out of the way, so he reacted with a twist and a jerk, throwing his arm, still holding the dying orc by the throat, coming up to block. The dying orc took the spear in the back, and Wulfgar tossed the creature aside. He glanced back to Bill, who offered a wink, then he ran to the ladder and leaped, reaching up high enough to catch the lip of the loft. With his tremendous strength, the barbarian easily pulled himself up.

"Aegis-fang!" he cried, summoning the magical hammer into his hands.

Roaring and swinging, he had orcs flying from the loft in short order. Down below, the dwarves, including Bill and Bruenor, finished them up even as they hit the ground.

Wulfgar ran for the ladder to the roof, and nearly tripped as a small form came rushing past him. He wasn't even surprised to see Regis go out the loft's small window, nor was he surprised when he charged up the ladder and shouldered through the trapdoor—a trapdoor that had been weighted down with several bags of supplies—to see Regis peeking at him over the lip of the tower.

As soon as Wulfgar got the attention of all three orcs on the tower top, the halfling came over and sat on the crenellation. Regis picked out a target and let fly his little mace, the weapon spinning end-over-end to smack the orc in the face. The creature staggered backward, nearly tumbling over the parapet, and as it finally straightened, the halfling hit it with a flying body block. The orc went over the edge, to be followed by a second, thrown out by Wulfgar, and a third, leaping of its own volition in the face of the raging barbarian.

"Good place to direct!" Bruenor yelled, coming through the trapdoor. He ran to the southern edge of the tower top, overlooking the battlefield.

The wide smile on the fierce dwarf's face lasted until he looked to the east, to the river.

The jolt when they hit the stone wall rattled their teeth and compressed all eight of the dwarves in the ore cart into an area that two had fully occupied just a moment before. They weathered it, though, to a dwarf. And not just in that cart and in the other nine in the same train, but in the twenty carts of the other two trains as well.

Ivan and Pikel Bouldershoulder stretched and shoved with all their might, trying to keep the dwarves in their cart from crushing each other. The jolts continued, though, the iron carts twisting and straining. Rocks bounced down as the train rumbled about.

When it finally settled, Ivan was first to put his feet under him and strain his back against the dented cover of the cart. He pushed it open a bit, enough so that he could poke his head out.

"By Moradin!" he cried to his companions. "All of ye boys, push now and push hard!"

For Ivan saw that the plan had not worked quite so well, at least with their particular train. They had hardly cracked through the mountain wall, instead beginning an avalanche over them that had left the train half buried, twisted, and still blocking the tunnel exit so that the soldiers running behind could not easily get out.

Ivan grabbed at the twisted metal cart cover and shoved with all his strength. When that did nothing, he reached out over it and tried to pry away some of the heavy stones holding it down.

"Come on, lads!" he shouted. "Afore the damned orcs catch us in a box!"

They all began shoving and shouldering the metal cover, and it creaked open a bit more. Ivan wasted no time in squeezing out.

The view from that vantage point proved no more encouraging. Only two of the other nine carts were open, and the dwarves coming out were bleeding and dazed. Half the mountainside had come down upon them, it seemed, and they were stuck.

And to the east, Ivan saw and heard the charge of the orcs.

The yellow-bearded dwarf scrambled atop his damaged cart and pushed aside several stones, then reached back and tugged the cover with all his strength.

Out popped Pikel, then another and another, with Ivan shouting encouragement all the while.

The orcs closed.

But then a second roar came down from just north of their position, and Ivan managed to get a peek over a pile of rubble to see the countering charge of the Battlehammer dwarves. The center train and the northern one had pounded right through, exactly as planned, and the army was pouring out of Mithral Hall in full force, sweeping east and fanning south to form a perimeter around the catastrophe of the southernmost train. The fierce dwarves met the orc charge head on, axe against spear, sword against sword, in such a violent and headlong explosion that half the orcs and dwarves leading their respective charges were down in the first seconds of engagement.

Ivan leaped from the rubble and led the charge of those few among the dwarves of the southern train who could follow. Of the eighty in the carts of that southern train, less than a score came forth, the others out of the fight either because of serious injury or because they simply could not force open their twisted and buried carts.

By the time Ivan, Pikel, and the others joined in the fray, that particular orc charge had been stopped in its tracks. More and more dwarves poured forth; formations gathered and marched with precision to support the flanks and to disrupt the in-flow of orc warriors.

"To the river, boys!" came a shout from the front of the dwarven line, and Ivan recognized the voice of Tred. "The boys of Felbarr have come and they're needing us now!"

That, of course, was all the ferocious Battlehammers needed to hear, and they pressed all the harder, driving back the orcs and raising their cheers in the common refrain of, "To the river!"

The progress in the center and south proved remarkable, the dwarves crushing the resistance and making good speed, but from the tower top in the north, Bruenor, Wulfgar, and Regis were granted a different perspective on it all.

Regis winced and looked away as a giant boulder crashed into a raft laden

with Felbarr dwarves, sending several sprawling into the icy waters and driving the side of the craft right under, swamping it.

The boats were putting in upstream, obviously, the Felbarr dwarves trying to ride the current with their own rowing to get them to the bank at the point of conflict. But the orcs and giants had some tricks to play. Sharpened logs met the dwarven rafts in the swift river current, catching against the sides of the craft and disrupting the rowing. And the barrage of boulders, giant thrown and catapult launched, increased with every passing second. Rocks hit the water with tremendous *whumps!* and sent up fountains of spray, or crashed into and through the dwarven boats.

Dozens of boats were in the water, each carrying scores of dwarves, and the three observers on the tower had to wonder if any of them would even get across.

Bruenor shouted down to his commanders on the ground, "Get to the durned river and turn to the north! We got to clear the bank along the north. Take 'em over the ridge," the dwarf king instructed Wulfgar. "We got to stop those giants!"

Wulfgar nodded and started down the ladder, but Regis just shook his head and said, "Too many," echoing all their fears.

Within minutes, the main thrust of the dwarven army had split the orc forces in half, spearheading right to the bank of the Surbrin. But as more and more dwarves rushed out to support the lines, so too were the orcs reinforced from the north. A great swarming mass rushed down over the mountain spur to join in the fight.

Bruenor and Regis could only look on helplessly. They would take the riverbank and hold it south of that spur, Bruenor could see, but they'd never get up north enough to slow the giant barrage and help the poor dwarves of Citadel Felbarr and their ill-advised crossing.

Another boulder smashed a raft, and half the dwarves atop it tumbled into the water, their heavy armor tugging them down to the icy depths.

Regis rubbed his plump hands over his face.

"By the gods," he muttered.

Bruenor punched his fist against the stone, then turned to the ladder and leaped down to the loft. In moments, he was outside with Wulfgar, calling every dwarf around him to his side, and he and the barbarian led the charge straight north, up the side of the mountain spur and beyond.

Regis screamed down to him, but futilely. The halfling could see the force over that ridge, and he knew that Bruenor and Wulfgar were surely doomed.

Out in the water, another boat capsized.

18

THE SKIN OF A DWARF'S TOOTH

Nikwillig groaned and shouted as another of the rafts overturned, dumping brave dwarves to a watery death. He looked to his companion for some sign of hope.

Hralien, as frustrated as the dwarf, looked away, back to his warriors as they sprinted along the stones. They had located the sight of the most devastating volleys, where a trio of giants were having a grand time of it, throwing boulder after boulder as the defenseless dwarven crafts floated past.

Many times did the elf leader wave at his warriors for patience, but all of them, even Hralien, were anxious and angry, watching good dwarves so easily slaughtered. Hralien held them together in tight formation, though, and had them holding their shots until the giant trio was right below them.

The elf nodded and all his charges, three-score of the Moonwood's finest warriors, bent back their bows. Silent nods and hand signals had the groups split evenly among the respective targets, and a shout from Hralien set them in motion.

A score of arrows reached out for each of the unsuspecting giants, and before that devastating volley struck home, the skilled elves had put the next arrows to their bowstrings.

Sixty more streaked out, the hum of elven bows drowned out by the howls of screaming giants.

One of the three went down hard under that second volley, grasping at the shafts sticking from its thick neck. The other two staggered, but not toward their attackers. The behemoths had seen enough of the elven war party already. One ran flat out, back to the west, while the other, hit many times in the legs, struggled to keep up. The straggler caught the full force of the next volley, three-score arrows reaching out to sting it hard and send it tumbling to the stones.

All around the western riverbank, where there had been only glee at the easy slaughter of dwarves, came tumult and confusion. Giants howled and orcs, dozens and dozens of the creatures, scrambled to and fro, caught completely unawares.

"Press forward!" Hralien called down his line. "None get close enough that we must draw swords!"

Grim-faced to an elf, each adorned with identical silver helmets that had flared sides resembling the wings of a bird, and silver-trimmed forest green capes flapping in the breeze behind them, the moon elf brigade marched in a perfect line. As one they set arrows to bowstrings, as one they lifted and leveled the bows, with permission to seek out the best targets of opportunity.

Few orcs seemed interested in coming their way, however, and so those targets grew fewer and fewer.

The elves marched south, clouds of arrows leading their way.

Wulfgar led the charge over the mountain spur, where he and the dwarves were met immediately by a host of orcs rushing south to reinforce their line.

With Aegis-fang in hand the mighty barbarian scattered the closest monsters. A great one-armed swing of the warhammer, and he clipped a pair of orcs and sent them flying, then stepped ahead and punched out, launching a third into the air. Beside him, the dwarves came on in a wild rush, weapons thrusting and slashing, shouldering orcs aside when their weapons didn't score a hit.

"The high ground!" Wulfgar kept shouting, demanding of his forces that they secure the ridgeline in short order.

Up went Wulfgar, stone by stone. Down went the orcs who tried to stand

before him, crushed to the ground or tossed aside. The barbarian was the first to the ridge top, and there he stood unmovable, a giant among the dwarves and orcs.

He called for the dwarves to rally around him, and so they did, coming up in scattered pockets, but falling into perfect position around him, the first arrivals supporting the barbarian's flanks, and those dwarves following supporting the flanks of their kin. Lines of dwarves came on to join, but the orcs were not similarly bolstered, for those monsters farther down the northern face of the mountain spur veered east or west in an effort to avoid this point of conflict, to avoid the towering and imposing barbarian and his mighty warhammer.

From that high vantage point, Wulfgar saw almost certain disaster brewing, for farther to the east, down at the riverbank, such a throng of orcs had gathered and were streaming south that it seemed impossible for the dwarves to hold their hard-fought gains. The dwarves, too, were at the river then, south of the spur, trying hard to fortify their tentative position.

If they lost at the riverbank, the brave Felbarrans in the river would have nowhere to land their rafts.

Looking out at the river, at the splashes of giant boulders and the flailing dwarves in the water, at the battered craft and the line of missiles reaching out at them, Wulfgar honestly wondered if holding the riverbank would mean anything at all. Would a single Felbarran dwarf get across?

Yet the Battlehammers had to try. For the sake of the Felbarrans, for the sake of the whole dwarven community, they had to try.

Wulfgar glanced back behind him, and saw Bruenor leading another force straight east along the base of the mountain spur, driving fast for the river.

"Turn east!" Wulfgar commanded his troops. "We'll make a stand on the high ground and make the orcs pay for every inch of stone!"

The dwarves around him cheered and followed, rushing down the rocky arm toward where it, too, spilled into the river. With only a hundred warriors total in that group, there was no doubt that they would lose, that they would be overwhelmed and slaughtered in short order. They all knew it. They all charged on eagerly.

They made their stand on a narrow strip of high, rocky ground, between the battleground south, where Bruenor had joined in the fighting and the dwarves were gaining a strong upper hand and the approaching swarm from the north.

"Bruenor will protect our backs!" Wulfgar shouted. "Set a defense against the north alone!"

The dwarves scrambled, finding all of the best positions which offered them some cover to the north, and trusting in King Bruenor and their kin to protect them from those orcs fighting in the south.

"Every moment of time we give those behind us is a moment more the Felbarrans have to land on our shore!" Wulfgar shouted, and he had to yell loudly to be heard, for the orc swarm was closing, screaming and hooting with every running stride.

The orcs came to the base of that narrow ridge in full run and began scrambling up, and Wulfgar and the dwarves rained rocks, crossbow bolts, and Aegis-fang upon them, battering them back. Those who did reach the fortified position met, most of all, Wulfgar the son of Beornegar. Like an ancient oak, the tall and powerful barbarian did not bend.

Wulfgar, who had survived the harshness of Icewind Dale, refused to move.

Wulfgar, who had suffered the torment of the demon Errtu, denied his fears, and ignored the sting of orc spears.

The dwarves rallied around him, screaming with every swing of axe or hammer, with every stab of finely-crafted sword. They yelled to deny the pain of wounds, the broken knuckles, the gashes, and the stabs. They yelled to deny the obvious truth that soon the orc sea would wash them from that place and to the Halls of Moradin.

They screamed, and their calls became louder soon after, as more dwarves came up to reinforce the line, dwarves who fought with King Bruenor—and King Bruenor himself, determined to die beside his heroic human son.

Behind them, a Felbarran raft made the shore, the dwarves charging off and swinging north immediately. Then a second slid in, and more approached.

But it wouldn't be enough, Bruenor and Wulfgar knew, glancing back and ahead. There were simply too many enemies.

"Back to the hall?" Wulfgar asked in the face of that reality.

"We got nowhere to run, boy," Bruenor replied.

Wulfgar grimaced at the hopelessness in the dwarf's voice. Their daring breakout was doomed, it seemed, to complete ruin.

"Then fight on!" Wulfgar said to Bruenor, and he yelled it out again so that all could hear. "Fight on! For Mithral Hall and Citadel Felbarr! Fight on for your very lives!"

Orcs died by the score on the northern face of that ridge, but still they came on, two replacing every one who had fallen.

Wulfgar continued to center the line, though his arms grew weary and his hammer swings slowed. He bled from a dozen wounds, one hand swelled to twice its normal size when Aegis-fang connected against an orc club too far down the handle. But he willed that hand closed on the hammer shaft.

He willed his shaky legs to hold steady.

He growled and he shouted and he chopped down another orc.

He ignored the thousands still moving down from the north, focusing instead on the ones within his deadly range.

So focused was he and the dwarves that none of them saw the sudden thinning of the orc line up in the north. None noted orcs sprinting away suddenly to the west, or groups of others simply and suddenly falling to the stone, many writhing, some already dead as they hit the ground.

None of the defenders heard the hum of elven bowstrings.

They just fought and fought, and grew confused as much as relieved when fewer and fewer orcs streamed their way.

The swarm, faced with a stubborn foe in the south and a new and devastating enemy in the north, scattered.

The battle south of the mountain spur continued for a long while, but when Wulfgar's group managed to turn their attention in that direction and support the main force of Battlehammers, and when the elves of the Moonwood, Nikwillig among them, came over the ridge and began offering their deadly accurate volleys at the most concentrated and stubborn orc defensive formations, the outcome became apparent and the end came swiftly.

Bruenor Battlehammer stood on the riverbank just south of the mountain spur, staring out at the rolling water, the grave for hundreds of Felbarran dwarves that dark day. They had won their way from Mithral Hall to the river, had re-opened the halls and established a beachhead from which they could begin their push to the north.

But the cost. . . .

The horrible cost.

"We'll send forces out to the south and find a better place for landing," Tred said to the dwarf king, his voice muted by the sobering reality of the battle.

Bruenor regarded the tough dwarf and Jackonray beside him.

"If we can clear the bank to the south, our boats can come across far from the giant-throwers," Jackonray explained.

Bruenor nodded grimly.

Tred reached up and dared pat the weary king on the shoulder. "Ye'd have done the same for us, we're knowing. If Citadel Felbarr was set upon, King Bruenor'd've thrown all his boys into fire to help us."

It was true enough, Bruenor knew, but then, why did the water look so blood red to him?

PART THREE

A WINTER RESPITE

Do you know what it is to be an elf, Drizzt Do'Urden?"

I hear this question all the time from my companion, who seems determined to help me begin to understand the implications of a life that could span centuries—implications good and bad when one considers that so many of those with whom I come into contact will not live half that time.

It has always seemed curious to me that, while elves may live near a millennium and humans less than a century, human wizards often achieve levels of understanding and power to rival those of the greatest elf mages. This is not a matter of intelligence, but of focus, it seems clear. Always before, I gave the credit for this to the humans, for their sense of urgency in knowing that their lives will not roll on and on and on.

Now I have come to see that part of the credit for this balance is the elven viewpoint of life, and that viewpoint is not one rooted in falsehood or weakness. Rather, this quieter flow of life is the ingredient that brings sanity to an existence that will see the birth and death of centuries. Or, if preferable, it is a segmented flow of life, a series of bursts.

I see it now, to my surprise, and it was Innovindil's recounting of her most personal relationships with partners both human and elf that presented the notion clearly in my mind. When Innovindil asks me now, "Do you know what it is to be an elf, Drizzt Do'Urden?" I can honestly and calmly smile with self-assurance. For the first time in my life, yes, I think I do know.

To be an elf is to find your distances of time. To be an elf is to live several shorter life spans. It is not to abandon forward-looking sensibility, but it is also to find emotionally comfortable segments of time, smaller life spans in which to exist. In light of that realization, for me the more pertinent question thus becomes, "Where is the range of comfort for such existences?"

There are many realities that dictate such decisions—decisions that, in truth, remain more subconscious than purposeful. To be an elf is to outlive your companions if they are not elves; even if they are, rare is the relationship that will survive centuries. To be an elf is to revel in the precious moments of your children—should they be of only half-elf blood, and even if they are of full blood—and to know that they may not outlive you. In that instance, there is only comfort in the profound and ingrained belief that having these children and these little pockets of joyful time was indeed a blessing, and that such a blessing outweighs the profound loss that any compassionate being would surely feel at the death of an offspring. If the very real possibility that one will outlive a child, even if the child sees the end of its expected lifespan, will prevent that person from having children, then the loss is doubly sad.

In that context, there is only one answer: to be an elf is to celebrate life.

To be an elf is to revel in the moments, in the sunrise and the sunset, in the sudden and brief episodes of love and adventure, in the hours of companionship. It is, most of all, to never be paralyzed by your fears of a future that no one can foretell, even if predictions lead you to the seemingly obvious, and often disparaging, conclusions.

That is what it is to be an elf.

The elves of the surface, contrary to the ways of the drow, often dance and sing. With this, they force themselves into the present, into the moment, and though they may be singing of heroes and deeds long past or of prophecies yet to come, they are, in their song, in the moment, in the present, grasping an instant of joy or reflection and holding it as tightly as any human might.

A human may set out to make a "great life," to become a mighty leader or sage, but for elves, the passage of time is too slow for such pointed and definitive ambitions. The memories of humans are short, so 'tis said, but that holds true for elves as well. The long dead human heroes of song no doubt bore little resemblance to the perceptions of the current bards and their audience, but that is true of elves, too, even though those elf bards likely knew the principals of their songs!

The centuries dull and shift the memories, and the lens of time alters images.

A great life for an elf, then, results either of a historical moment seized correctly or, more often, it is a series of connected smaller events that will eventually add up to something beyond the parts. It is a continuing process of growth, perhaps, but only because of piling experiential understanding.

Most of all, I know now, to be an elf is not to be paralyzed by a future one cannot control. I know that I am going to die. I know that those I love will one day die, and in many cases—I suspect, but do not know!—they will die long before I. Certitude is strength and suspicion is worthless, and worry over suspicion is something less than that.

I know, now, and so I am free of the bonds of the future.

I know that every moment is to be treasured, to be enjoyed, to be heightened as much as possible in the best possible way.

I know, now, the failing of the bonds of worthless worry.

I am free.

—Drizzt Do'Urden

19

QUIET TENDAYS

Winter had already settled in far to the north, on the higher foothills of the Spine of the World. Cold winds brought stinging sheets of snow, often moving horizontally more than vertically. Drizzt and Innovindil kept their cowls pulled low and tight, but still the crisp snow stung their faces, and the brilliance of the snowcap had Drizzt squinting his sensitive eyes even when the sun was not brightly shining. The drow would have preferred to move after dark, but it was simply too cold, and he, Innovindil, and Sunset had to spend the dark hours huddled closely near a fire night after night. He couldn't believe how dramatically the shift in the weather had come, considering that it was still autumn back in the region of Mithral Hall.

The going was slow—no more than a few miles a day at most, and that only if they were not trying to climb higher along the icy passes. On a few occasions, they had dared to use Sunset to fly them up over a particularly difficult ridge, but the wind was dangerously strong for even the pegasus's powerful wings. Beyond that, the last thing the pair wanted was to be spotted by Gerti and her army of behemoths!

"How many days have passed?" Drizzt asked Innovindil as they sat for a break and a midday meal one gray afternoon.

"A tenday and six?" the elf answered, obviously as unsure of the actual time they had spent chasing Gerti as was Drizzt.

"And it seems as if we have walked across the seasons," said the drow.

"Summer never comes to the mountains, and up here, autumn and spring are what we in the lower lands would call winter, to be sure."

Drizzt looked back to the south as Innovindil responded, and that view reminded him of just how high up they had come. The landscape opened wide before him, sloping down and spreading so completely that it appeared to flatten out below him. In viewing that, it occurred to Drizzt that if the ground was bare and less broken, he could start a round stone rolling there and it would bounce all the way to Mithral Hall.

"They're getting far ahead of us," Drizzt remarked. "Perhaps we should be on our way."

"They're bound for Shining White, to be sure," Innovindil replied. "We will find it, do not doubt. I have seen the giant lair many times from Sunset's back." She motioned to the northwest, higher up in the mountains.

"Will we even be able to get through the passes?" Drizzt asked, looking back up at the steel gray sky, clouds heavy with the promise of even more snow.

"One way or another," she said. The drow took comfort in Innovindil's clear determination, in her scowl that seemed every bit as forceful and stoic as his own. "They treat Sunrise lovingly."

"Frost giants appreciate beauty."

As do I, Drizzt thought but did not say. Beauty, strength, and heart combined.

He considered all of that as he looked at Innovindil, but the thought itself sent his mind rushing back to an image of another female companion he had once known. There were many similarities, Drizzt knew, but he needn't look farther than Innovindil's pointy ears and sharply angled eyebrows to remember that there were great differences, as well.

Innovindil pulled herself up from beside the low-burning fire and began collecting her pack and supplies.

"Perhaps we can put some distance behind us before the snow begins," she said as she strapped on her sword and dagger. "With this wind, we'll not move through the storm."

Drizzt didn't reply other than a slight nod, which Innovindil was too busy

to even notice. The drow just watched her going about her tasks, enjoying the flow of her body and the sweep of her long golden hair as gusts of wind blew through.

He thought of his days immediately following the fall of Shallows, when he had hidden in a cave, rolling the one-horned helm of his dead friend in his hands. The emptiness of that time assailed him again, reminding him of how far he'd come. Drizzt had given in to the anger and the pain, had accepted a sense of complete hopelessness for perhaps the first time in all his life.

Innovindil and Tarathiel had brought him from that dark place, with patience and calm words and simple friendship. They had tolerated his instinctive defenses, which he'd thrown up to rebuff their every advance. They had accepted his explanation of Ellifain's death without suspicion.

Drizzt Do'Urden knew that he could never replace Bruenor, Catti-brie, Regis, and Wulfgar; those four were as much a part of who he was as any friend could ever hope. But maybe he didn't have to *replace* them. Maybe he could satisfy his emotional needs around the holes, if not filling in the holes themselves.

That was the promise of Innovindil, he knew.

And he was glad.

"Move swifter," Kaer'lic instructed in her broken command of the Dwarvish tongue. She had gleaned a few words of the language in her years on the surface, and with its many hard consonant sounds, the language bore some similarities to the drow's own, and even more to the tongue of the svirfneblin, which Kaer'lic spoke fluently. To get her point across, even if her words were not correct, the drow priestess kicked poor Fender on the back, sending him stumbling ahead.

He nearly fell, but battered though he was, he was too stubborn for that. He straightened and looked back, narrowing his gray eyes under his bushy brows in a threatening scowl.

Kaer'lic jammed the handle of her mace into his face.

Fender hit the ground hard, coughing blood, and he spat out a tooth. He tried to scream at the priestess, but all that came through his expertly slashed throat was a wheezing and fluttering sound like a burst of wind through a row of hanging parchments.

"With all care," Tos'un said to his companion. "The more you injure him, the longer it will take for us to be away." As he finished, the male drow glanced back to the south, as if expecting a fiery chariot or a host of warriors to rush over him. "We should have left the wretch with Proffit. The trolls would have eaten him and that would have been the end of it."

"Or Lady Alustriel and her army would have rescued him as they overran Proffit, and wouldn't he be quick in telling them all about a pair of dark elves roaming the land?"

"Then we should have just killed him and been done with it."

Kaer'lic paused and spent a moment scrutinizing her companion. She allowed her expression to show her disappointment in him, for truly, after all those years, she expected more from the warrior of House Barrison Del'Armgo.

"Obould will get nothing more from him than we have already gleaned," Tos'un said, his tone uncertain and revealing that he knew he was trying an awkward dodge. "And we will need no barter with the orc king—he will be glad that we have returned to him, even though the news we bear will hardly be to his liking."

"The news of Proffit's downfall and the reclamation of Nesmé will outrage him."

"But he is smart enough to separate the message from the messenger."

"Agreed," said Kaer'lic. "But you presume that King Obould is still alive, and that his forces have not been scattered and overrun. Has it occurred to you that perhaps we are returning to a northland where Bruenor Battlehammer is king once more?"

That unsettling thought had occurred to Tos'un, obviously, and he glanced past Kaer'lic and kicked poor Fender as the dwarf tried to rise.

"When I see Donnia again, I will slap her for leading us down this horrid road."

"*If* we see Donnia and Ad'non again, we will all need to find a new road to travel, I fear," Kaer'lic replied, emphasizing that important first word. "Or perhaps Obould continues to press and to conquer. Perhaps this is all going better than any of us ever dared hope, despite the setback along the northern

banks of the Trollmoors. If Obould has secured Mithral Hall, will even Lady Alustriel find the forces to drive him out?"

"Is that event more desirable?"

The question seemed ridiculous on the surface, of course, but before Kaer'lic snapped off a retort, she remembered her last encounter with the orc king. Confident, dangerously so, and imperious, he hadn't asked her and Tos'un to go south with Proffit. He had ordered them.

"We shall see what we shall see," was all the priestess replied.

She turned her attention back to Fender and jerked him upright from his crouch, then sent him on his way with a rough shove.

To the northeast, they could see the shining top of Fourthpeak, seeming no more than a day's march.

There lay their answers.

With pieces of orc still hanging from the ridges of his plate mail armor, it seemed hard to take Thibbledorf Pwent very seriously. But in a confusing time of regret and despair, Bruenor Battlehammer could have found no better friend.

"If we hold the riverbank all the way down to the south, then them Felbarrans and other allies might be getting across out o' the durned giants' range," Pwent calmly explained to Bruenor.

The two stood on the riverbank watching the work across the way on the eastern side, where the Felbarrans were already laying the foundation for a bridge.

"But will we be able to stretch our line?" Bruenor asked.

"Bah! Won't take much," came the enthusiastic reply. "Ain't seen no stupid orcs south o' here at all, and they can't be coming in from the west cause o' the mountain. Only way for them dogs to get down here is the north."

The words prompted both dwarves to turn and look up that way, to the mountain spur, the line of rocks sloping down to the river's edge. Many dwarves were up there, constructing a wall from the steep mountainside to the tower Wulfgar and Bruenor had taken. Their goal was to tighten the potential area of approach as much as possible so that the orc force couldn't simply swarm over them. Once that wall was set and fortified, the tower would serve as an anchor and the wall would be extended all the way to the river.

For the time being, the ridgeline east of the tower was dotted by lookouts, and held by the Moonwood elves, their deadly bows ready.

"Never thinked I'd be happy to see a bunch o' durned fairies," Pwent grumbled, and a much-needed grin creased Bruenor's face, a grin all the wider because of the truth of those words. Had not Nikwillig led the Moonwood elves south in force, Bruenor doubted that the dwarves would have won the day. At best, they would have been able to somehow get back inside Mithral Hall and secure the tunnels. At worst, all would have been lost.

The scope of the risk they had taken in coming out had never truly registered to King Bruenor until that moment when he had been battling at the riverbank at the southern base of the mountain arm, centering the three groupings of dwarven forces. With Wulfgar north and Pwent and the main force south, Bruenor had been struck by how tentative their position truly had been, and only then had the dwarf king come to realize how much they had gambled in coming out.

Everything.

"How're the ferry plans coming along?" he asked, needing to move on, to look forward. It had been a victory, after all.

"Them Felbarrans're planning to string the raft so it's not free floating," Pwent explained. "Too much rough water south o' here to chance one getting away. We should be getting it up in two or three days. Then we can get them humans out o' the hall, and start bringing the proper stones across to start building this side o' the bridge."

"And bring King Emerus across," came another voice, and the two turned to see the approach of Jackonray Broadbelt, one arm in a sling from a spear stab he'd suffered in the fighting.

"Emerus's coming?" Bruenor asked.

"He lost near to a thousand boys," Jackonray said grimly. "No dwarf king'd let that pass without consecrating the ground."

"Me own priests've already done it, and the river, too," Bruenor assured him. "And the blessings of yer own and of Emerus himself will only make the road to Moradin's Halls all the easier for them brave boys that went down."

"Ye been there, so they're saying," said Jackonray. "Moradin's Halls, I mean. A palace as grand as the tales, then?"

Bruenor swallowed hard.

"Aye, me king looked Moradin in the eye and said, 'Ye send me back to kill them stinkin' orcs!' " Pwent roared.

Jackonray nodded and grinned wide, and Bruenor let it go at that. The tales of his afterlife were flying wildly, he knew, with Cordio and the other priests shouting them and embellishing them loudest of all. But for Bruenor, there was nothing more.

Just the tales. Just the suppositions and the grand descriptions.

Had he been at Moradin's side?

The dwarf king honestly did not know. He remembered the fight at Shallows. He remembered hearing Catti-brie's voice, as if from far, far away. He remembered a feeling of warmth and comfort, but all of it was so vague to him. The first clear image he could conjure after the disaster at Shallows had been the face of Regis, as if the halfling and his magical ruby pendant had reached right into his soul to stir him from his deep slumber.

"Who'd be missing that kind o' fun?" Pwent was asking when Bruenor tuned back into the conversation.

He realized that Jackonray was hardly listening, and was instead just standing and staring at Bruenor.

"We'll be honored to see yer great King Emerus," Bruenor assured him, and he saw the Felbarran relax. "He can say his farewells to his boys and give his honor to Nikwillig o' Felbarr, right after I'm giving him the honor of Mithral Hall. 'Twas Nikwillig who won the day, not to doubt."

"It's a meeting long overdue, yerself and King Emerus," Jackonray agreed. "And we'll get King Harbromm from Adbar down here soon enough. Let's see them stupid orcs stand against the three kingdoms!"

"Kill 'em all!" Pwent roared, startling his two companions and drawing the attention of everyone nearby, and being dwarves, they of course took up the cheer.

They were all cheering again, except for Cottie Cooperson, of course, who never even smiled anymore, let alone cheered. Word had come down the tunnels that the eastern gate was open and the way would soon be clear to ferry the refugees across the Surbrin and to the tamer lands southeast. Before winter, they would all be in Silverymoon. And from there, in the spring, they could go out, free of the dark stones of Mithral Hall.

Those cheers followed Delly Curtie as she carried Colson along the corridor from the gathering hall. Inside, she had been all smiles, offering support and shoulder pats, assuring Cottie that she'd rebuild her life and maybe even have more children. She had gotten only a broken and somewhat sour look in response, for the brief moment that Cottie had lifted her teary-eyed gaze from the floor.

Out there, Delly found it hard to break any kind of a smile. In there, she supported the cheers, but outside they cut at her heart. They would all be going across the Surbrin soon, leaving her as one of only four humans in Mithral Hall.

She managed to keep her expression stoic when she entered her private chambers to find Wulfgar inside, pulling a blood-stained tunic over his head.

"Is it yer own?" Delly asked, rushing to his side.

She held Colson tight against her hip with one arm, while her other hand played over the barbarian's muscular frame, examining him for any serious wounds.

"The blood of orcs," Wulfgar said, and he reached across and gently lifted Colson from the woman's grasp. His face lit up as he brought the toddler up high to stare into her eyes, and Colson responded with a giggle and a wriggle, and a face beaming with happiness.

Despite her dour mood, Delly couldn't hold back her warm smile.

"It's secured to the river, they're saying," she said.

"Aye, from the mountain to the river and all along to the south. Pwent and his gang are finishing up any pockets of orcs even now. There won't likely be any living by morning."

"And they'll be floating the ferry then?"

Wulfgar glanced away from Colson just long enough to show his curiosity at the woman's tone, and Delly knew that her voice had been a bit too eager.

"They will begin stringing the guide ropes tomorrow, yes, but I know not how long the process will take. Are the folk of the razed lands anxious to be on their way?"

"Wouldn't ye be, yerself, if Bruenor wasn't yer own father?"

Again Wulfgar turned to show her his perplexed expression. He started to nod, but just shrugged instead.

"You are no child of Bruenor," he remarked.

"But I am the wife of Wulfgar."

Wulfgar brought Colson down to his hip, and when the toddler whined and wriggled, he set her down to the floor and let her go. He came up straight before Delly, facing her directly, and placed his huge hands on her slender shoulders.

"You wish to cross the river," he stated.

"My place is with Wulfgar."

"But I cannot leave," Wulfgar said. "We have only begun to break free of Obould's grasp, and now that we have a way beyond Mithral Hall's doors, I must learn the fate of my friend."

Delly didn't interrupt him, for she knew all of it, of course, and Wulfgar was merely reaffirming the truth of the situation.

"When the Surbrin east of Mithral Hall is more secure, have King Bruenor find you a place working out there, in the sun. I agree that we are not built as dwarves."

"The walls're closing in tight on me."

"I know," Wulfgar assured her, and he pulled her close. "I know. When this is done—by summer, we hope—you and I will journey to all the cities you long to see. You will come to love Mithral Hall all the more if it is your home and not your prison." As he finished, he pulled her closer, wrapping his strong arms around her. He kissed her on top of her head and whispered promises that things would get better.

Delly appreciated the words and the gestures, though in her mind, they hardly diminished the echoes of the cheers of the people who would soon be leaving the smoky dark tunnels of King Bruenor's domain.

She couldn't tell that to Wulfgar, though, she knew. He was trying to understand and she appreciated that. But in the end, he couldn't. His life was in Mithral Hall. His beloved friends were there. His cause was there.

Not in Silverymoon, where Delly wanted to be.

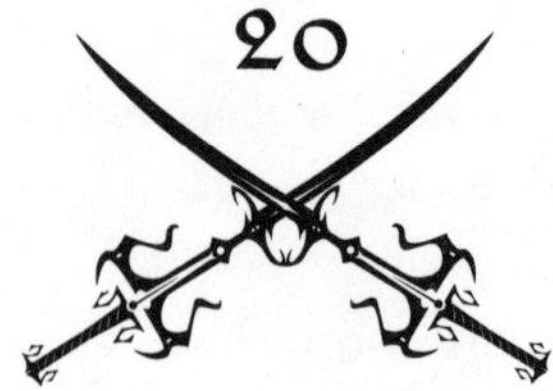

20

A FRIENDLY DOSE OF REALITY

Two thousand mugs raised in toast, the dwarven holy water foaming over the sides. Two thousand Battlehammer dwarves, every dwarf that could be spared from the work out in the east or from the tunnels, cheered, "To the Mirabarran Battlehammers!" Then as one, they drained their mugs, and invariably splashed foam on beards yellow and red and white and orange and black and brown and silver and even green.

"Oo oi!" came the shout from Pikel Bouldershoulder as soon as the toast was finished.

That a non-Battlehammer and non-Mirabarran like Pikel had so perfectly accentuated the celebration of Bruenor's clan for the immigrants from Mirabar was a point not lost on Catti-brie. Sitting beside her father's dais, propped with fluffy pillows—of which there were very few in all the halls—the woman considered the unlikely collection represented in the gathering before her.

Most of the group were Bruenor's kinfolk, of course, some dwarves who had lived in Mithral Hall before the coming of Shimmergloom the shadow dragon, and others who had been raised as Battlehammers under the shadow of Kelvin's Cairn in Icewind Dale. Others were Felbarran, coming in from the east and seeming as much at home as the Battlehammers themselves. Torgar and his boys were all there, even the many who had been wounded in

the fighting on the ridge north of Keeper's Dale or more recently in the fighting in the south. Ivan and Pikel Bouldershoulder were there, and though they weren't Battlehammers, every dwarf in the complex wanted them to become of the clan. Nanfoodle the gnome was there, along with Regis, Wulfgar, and Catti-brie.

So they were not all joined by blood, Catti-brie understood, but they were certainly all joined by cause and by common resolve. She glanced over at her father, sitting on his throne and draining another mug of mead, blessed as holy water by the priests. His toasts and his appreciation were genuine, she knew. He couldn't be happier or more full of gratitude concerning the arrival of Torgar, Shingles, and the boys from Mirabar. They had saved the day over and over again, from the northern stretches of the mountainous terrain to, apparently, the work in the south. They had fought brilliantly with Banak Brawnanvil north of Keeper's Dale, had pushed the entrenched orcs from the tunnels so that Nanfoodle could work his magic on the ridge. They had suffered terrible losses, but had done so with typical dwarven stoicism. The losses would be worth the victory, and nothing short of victory was acceptable.

It was all a reflection of her father, Catti-brie realized. Everything from Torgar's decision to leave Mirabar to Citadel Felbarr's bold, if ill-advised, attempt to cross the river was due in part to the character of Bruenor Battlehammer.

Catti-brie could only smile as she looked upon her dear father.

Eventually, her gaze went across the dais to Banak, lying more than sitting, propped in a carriage the woman feared would soon become his prison. He had given his body for the cause—even the optimistic Cordio doubted that the dwarf would ever walk again—and yet there he was, cheering and drinking and with a bright smile gleaming out from between the whiskers of his hairy old face.

It was a good day to be a Battlehammer, Catti-brie decided. Despite the tragedy in the eastern breakout and their precarious position between Mithral Hall and the Surbrin, despite the horde of orcs pressing in on them from every side and the terrible losses they all had suffered, friends and kin forever lost, it was a good day to be a Battlehammer.

She believed that with all her heart, and yet was not surprised at the feel of a teardrop running down her soft cheek.

For Catti-brie had come to doubt.

She had lost Drizzt, she believed, and only in that realization did the woman finally admit it all to herself. That she had loved him above all others. That he alone had made her whole and made her happy. So many problems had come between them, issues of longevity and children, and of the perceptions of others—there it was, all before her and hopelessly lost. All those imagined ills seemed so foolish, seemed the petty workings of confusion and self-destruction. When Catti-brie had been down on the ground and surrounded by goblins, when she had thought her life at its end, she had found an emptiness beyond anything she had ever imagined possible. The realization of her mortality had sent her thoughts careening along the notions of things that should have been. Lost in that jumble, she had pushed Drizzt away. Lost in that jumble, Catti-brie had forgotten that the future isn't a straight road purposely designed by the traveler. The future is made of the actions of the present, each and every one, the choices of the moment inadvertently strung together to produce the desired trail. To live each and every day in the best possible manner would afford her a life without regret, and a life without regret was the key to an acceptance of inevitable death.

And now Drizzt was lost to her.

In all her life, would Catti-brie ever heal that wound?

"Are you all right?"

Wulfgar's voice was soft and full of concern, and she looked up to see his blue eyes staring back at her.

"It's been a difficult time," she admitted.

"So many dead."

"Or missing."

The look on Wulfgar's face told her that he understood the reference. "We are able to go out again," he said, "and so we must hope that Drizzt will be able to come in."

She didn't blink.

"And if not, then we will go find him. You and I, Bruenor and Regis," the big man declared. "Perhaps we will even convince Ivan and Pikel to join in the hunt—the strange one talks to birds, you know. And birds can see all the land."

She still didn't blink.

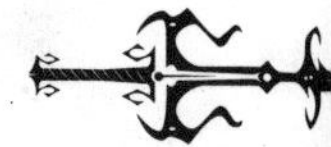

"We will find him," Wulfgar promised.

Another cheer rose up in the hall, and Bruenor called upon Torgar to come forth and give a proper speech about it all. "Tell us what bringed ye here," the dwarf king prompted. "Tell us all yer journeys."

Wulfgar's grin disappeared as soon as he looked back at Catti-brie, for her expression was no less distant and detached, and no less full of pain.

"Do you need to leave?" he asked.

"I'm weary to the bone," she answered.

With great effort, the woman pulled herself out of her chair and leaned heavily on the crutch Cordio had made for her. She began to take a shuffling step forward, but Wulfgar caught hold of her. With a simple and effortless movement, the large man swept her into his arms.

"Where're ye going, then?" Bruenor asked from the dais. Before him, Torgar was giving his account to a thoroughly engaged audience.

"I'm needing a bit of rest, is all," said Catti-brie.

Bruenor held a concerned look for a few moments, then nodded and turned back to Torgar.

Catti-brie rested her crutch across her body and put her head on Wulfgar's strong shoulder. She closed her eyes and let him carry her from the celebration.

Delly Curtie approached the audience chamber with good intent, determined to try to fit in, in the place that Wulfgar would always call home. She told herself with every step that she had followed Wulfgar out of Luskan of her own accord, with her eyes wide open. She reminded herself that her responsibilities went far beyond the issues surrounding her relationship with a man who seemed more at home beside the dwarves than with his own race. She reminded herself of Colson, and the girl's well-being.

She would have to strike a middle ground, she decided. She would take Wulfgar out of Mithral Hall as often as possible, and would stay with the folk of the neighboring and predominantly human communities for extended periods.

She caught a quick glimpse of someone coming the other way through the maze of anterooms, and from the size alone, she knew it had to be Wulfgar. Her step lightened. She would make the seemingly untenable situation work.

As she came through a half-door and moved around one of the huge vats the clerics used for their brewing, Delly caught sight of him again, more clearly.

He didn't see her, she knew, because he was looking at the woman he was carrying.

Delly's eyes widened and she threw herself behind the brew barrel, putting her back to it and closing her eyes tightly against the sudden sting. She heard Wulfgar and Catti-brie pass by on the other side, and watched them exit the small room and continue on their way.

The woman exhaled and felt as if she was simply melting into the floor.

Lady Alustriel did not need to wait for the ferries to be running in order to cross the Surbrin. The tall and beautiful woman, as accomplished in the magic arts and in the arena of politics as anyone in all the world, brought her fiery conjured chariot down on a flat stretch of ground just outside the opened eastern door of Mithral Hall, sending dwarves scrambling for cover and bringing a chorus of cheers and salutes from the Moonwood elves who held firm in their position on the mountain spur.

Alustriel stepped from the chariot and dismissed it into a puff of smoke with a wave of her hand. She straightened her dark robe and brushed her long silver hair into place, at the same time fixing a properly somber expression onto her delicate but determined features. It would be no easy visit, she knew, but it was one she owed to her friend Bruenor.

With purpose in every stride, Alustriel moved to the door. The dwarf guards fell aside, gladly admitting her, while one ran ahead to announce her to Bruenor.

She found the dwarf king with two other dwarves and an elf, drawing up plans for King Emerus Warcrown's arrival. The four stood up at her entrance, even Bruenor dipping into a low and polite bow.

"Good King Bruenor," Alustriel greeted. "It is uplifting to see you well. We had heard rumors of your demise, and truly a pall had befallen the lands of goodly folk."

"Bah, got to tease 'em a bit, ye know," Bruenor replied with a wink. "Makes my arrival all the more stunning and inspiring."

"I doubt that Bruenor Battlehammer needs aid in that manner."

"Always the kind one, ain't ye?"

Alustriel offered a quiet nod.

"I give ye Jackonray and Tred of Felbarr," Bruenor explained, pointing out the dwarves, who both nearly fell over themselves trying to bow before the great Lady of Silverymoon. "And this one's Hralien of the Moonwood. Never thought me and me boys'd be so grateful to see a bunch o' elves!"

"We stand together," Hralien answered. "Or surely we shall all of us fall before the darkness that is Obould."

"Aye, and glad I am that ye decided to come, good lady," Bruenor told Alustriel. "Torgar o' Mirabar just returned from yer victory over them stinking trolls, and he's telling a tale that yerself and Sundabar've decided to stay back."

"His words are true, I fear," Alustriel admitted.

"Aye, ye're thinking to wait out the winter, and I'm not for arguing that," Bruenor said. "But we'd be smart to set our plans for the spring soon as we can. We'll have a gnome's puzzling of it to get five armies working right." He paused when he noticed that Alustriel was shaking her head with his every word.

"What're ye thinking?" Bruenor asked her.

"I have come to confirm what Torgar has already told to you, my friend," said Alustriel. "We will hold Obould where he is, but it is not the decision of Silverymoon, Everlund, and Sundabar to wage war against him at this time."

Bruenor was certain that his chin had hit the floor, so wide did his mouth fall open.

"I have over flown the region you intend as a battlefield, and I tell you that this orc king is a wise one. He is fortifying even now, digging in his warriors on every mountaintop and preparing every inch of ground for a stubborn defense."

"All the more reason we got to get rid of him here and now," Bruenor argued, but again Alustriel shook her head.

"The cost will be too great, I fear," she said.

"But ye ran to Nesmé's aid, didn't ye?" Bruenor couldn't completely eliminate the sarcastic tone from his voice.

"We put the trolls back in the moor, yes. But they were not nearly as formidable as the force that has arrayed against Mithral Hall from the north. Tens of thousands of orcs have flocked to Obould's call."

"Tens of thousands who'll turn their weapons against yerself and yer precious Silverymoon!"

"Perhaps," said Alustriel. "And in that event, they will face a stubborn and determined defense. Should Obould press on, he will fight in ground of our choosing and not his own. We will fight him from behind our walls, not assail him behind his."

"And ye're to leave me and me kin out here alone?"

"Not so," Alustriel insisted. "You have opened the way to the river—I wish that Silverymoon could have arrived in force to aid in that."

"A few hunnerd less Felbarrans'd be lying at the bottom of the river if ye had," Tred dared to say, and his tone made it clear to all that he was no more happy with Alustriel's surprising stance than was Bruenor.

"These are trying times," Alustriel offered. "I do not pretend to make them seem better than they are. I come to you now to deliver a suggestion and a promise from Silverymoon and from Sundabar. We will help you build the bridge across the Surbrin, and we will help you to defend it and to hold open the eastern door of Mithral Hall. I see that you are constructing fortifications on the mountain spur north of the door—I will send batteries of archers and catapults to aid in that defense. I will rotate wizards up there to stand shoulder to shoulder with your warriors, offering fireballs against any who dare come against you."

Bruenor's scowl did diminish a bit at that, but just a bit.

"You know me well, Bruenor Battlehammer," the Lady of Silverymoon said. "When the drow marched upon Mithral Hall, my city came to your side. How many of the Silver Guard fell in Keeper's Dale in that battle?"

Bruenor twitched, his expression softening.

"I wish as you wish, that Obould and his scourge of orcs could be wiped from the lands for all time. But I have seen them. You cannot imagine the enemy allied against you. If all the dwarves of Felbarr and Adbar, and all the warriors of Silverymoon, Everlund, and Sundabar were to come to your side,

we would still have to kill our enemies five for every one of our own to begin to claim a victory. And even then Obould's forces swell daily, with more orcs pouring out of every hole in the Spine of the World."

"And even with that, ye're not thinking that he's meaning to stop where he is?" Bruenor asked. "If his forces are swellin', the longer we . . . the longer *you* wait, the bigger they swell."

"We have not abandoned you, my friend, nor would we ever," Alustriel said, and she took a step toward Bruenor and gently reached up to place her hand on his shoulder. "Every wound to Mithral Hall cuts deeply into the hearts of the goodly folk of all the region. You will be the spur, the one shining light in a region fallen to darkness. We will not let that light dim. On our lives, King Bruenor, my friend, we will fight beside you."

It was not what he wanted to hear from Lady Alustriel, but it seemed as if it was all he was going to get—and truly, it was a lot more than he had expected, given Torgar's sour account of Alustriel's intentions.

"Let us weather the winter," Alustriel finished. "And let us see what promise the spring brings."

21

GERTI'S DOORBELL

Snow whipped all around them, forcing both Drizzt and Innovindil to bend low and lean into the wind to stop from being blown right over. The drow led the way, moving as swiftly as he could manage, for the trail of the giants remained clear to see, but would not last for long, he knew. Drizzt continually worked his fingers in his sleeve, clenching and unclenching his fist in a futile attempt to hold off the freezing. Innovindil had assured him that Shining White, the home of Gerti, was not far away. The drow hoped that was true, for he wasn't sure how long he and Innovindil could continue in such a blizzard.

By mid-morning the trail was all but overblown and Drizzt kept moving as much on instinct as through his tracking abilities. He soldiered along as straight as he could manage, and veered from the course only when he came upon boulder tumbles or ravines that would have likely forced the giants' caravan aside.

Around one such boulder tumble, the drow saw that he was guessing right, for there in the middle of a shallow dell was a pile of manure, half-covered and still steaming in the new-fallen snow. Drizzt made for it and bent low over it. He brought a gloved hand down and separated the pieces, inspecting each.

"No blood in the stool," he told Innovindil when she crouched near him.

"Sunrise is eating well, despite the onset of deep winter," the elf agreed.

"Gerti is treating him as she would a valued pet," said the drow. "It bodes well."

"Except that we can be certain now that she will not easily give up the pegasus."

"Never was there any doubt of that," said Drizzt. "We came here to fight for our friend, and so we shall." He looked up at Innovindil's fair face as he spoke the pledge, and saw that she appreciated his words. "Come along," he bade her, and started on his way.

Innovindil gave a tug on Sunset's reins to prompt the pegasus along, and followed with a renewed spring in her step.

It didn't last long, though. The storm intensified, snow blowing across so fiercely that Innovindil and Drizzt could hardly see each other if they moved more than a few feet apart.

They got a bit of a reprieve when they passed around an eastern spur, for the wind was from the northwest and suddenly both of those directions were blocked by mountain walls. Drizzt put his back against the bare stone and exhaled.

"If we can find a suitable overhang, perhaps we should put up for the day until the storm blows over," he offered, and he was glad that he was able to lower his voice without the wind to intercept and dissipate it.

He took another deep breath and pulled the frozen cowl back from his face. He wiped the snow from his brow, chuckling helplessly when he realized that his eyebrows were iced over, and he looked at his companion to see that she was paying him no heed.

"Innovindil?" he asked.

"No need," the elf answered. "To camp, I mean."

She met Drizzt's gaze then motioned for him to look across the way.

The rock wall ran north for some distance, then bent back to the east. Along that facing, a few hundred yards from them, Drizzt saw a gaping darkness, a cave face in the stone.

"Shining White?"

"Yes," Innovindil answered. "An unremarkable entrance to a place rumored to be anything but."

The two stood there a while, catching their breath.

"A plan?" Innovindil finally asked.

"Sunrise is in there," Drizzt answered. "So we go in."

"Just walk in?"

"Swords drawn, of course." He turned to his companion and offered a grin.

He made it sound so simple, which of course it was. They had come for Sunrise, and Sunrise was inside Shining White, and so they collected themselves and moved along, staying close to the mountain wall where the snow had not piled.

A dozen feet or so before the closest edge of the cave entrance, Drizzt motioned for Innovindil to stay back and crept ahead. He came up straight at the edge of the cave, then slowly bent and turned and peeked in.

He slipped around the edge, inching into a tunnel that widened almost immediately to nearly twenty feet across. The drow froze, hearing deep and steady breathing from across the way. He quick-stepped across the tunnel to the other wall, then crept along to an alcove.

Inside, a seated giant leaned back against the wall, its hands tucked behind its head, lips flapping with every snore. A massive maul lay across its outstretched legs, the business end worked brilliantly into the design of an eagle's head, with the sharp, hooked beak comprising the back side of the head.

Drizzt crept in. He could tell that the behemoth was sleeping soundly, and recognized that he could move right up and open wide its throat before it ever knew he was there. To his surprise, though, he found himself sliding his scimitars away. Gently, but with great effort, he lifted the maul from the giant's lap, and the beast snorted and grumbled, bringing one hand down and turning sideways.

Drizzt moved out of the alcove and back to the cave entrance, where Innovindil and Sunset stood waiting.

"Fine weapon," he whispered, though it seemed as if he could hardly hold the maul.

"You killed its wielder?" asked the elf.

"Fast asleep, and no threat to us."

Innovindil's curious expression reminded Drizzt of his strange choice.

Why hadn't he simply killed the giant; would that not be one less enemy to battle?

His answer was just a shrug, though, and he put a finger to pursed lips and bade the elf to quietly follow.

The three moved past the alcove on the opposite side of the corridor. Many feet farther along, the tunnel turned sharply to the right, and there the roof climbed much higher as well. A short way from the trio beamed a natural skylight, some fifty feet or more from the floor, the gray light of the stormy day streaming in. The floor became slick and some areas lay covered in snow. Farther down, a pair of large doors loomed before them.

"Let us hope that they are not locked, and that they are well greased," Innovindil quietly remarked.

The three inched along, Sunset clip-clopping with every stride, the sharp echoes making the other two more than a little nervous. Both the drow and the elf entertained thoughts of leaving the pegasus outside, and would have had it not been for the brutal storm.

Drizzt put his ear to the door and listened carefully for a long while before daring the handle—or almost daring the handle. For as he reached up, the ring being more than two feet above his head, he noted that its inner edge was not smooth, with one particularly sharp lip to it. He retracted his hand quickly.

"Trapped?" Innovindil asked.

Drizzt motioned that he did not know. He pulled off his cloak, then loosened his enchanted, armored shirt so that he could pull one sleeve down over his hand. He reached up again and slowly grasped the handle. He could feel the sharp edge through the shirt, and he gingerly altered the angle of his grasp so that the trap, if that's what it was, would not press on his palm.

"Ready to fight?" he mouthed to his companion, and he drew out Icingdeath in his left hand. When Innovindil nodded, Drizzt took a deep breath and pulled the door ajar, immediately snapping his hand down across his body to Twinkle, sheathed on his left hip.

But the sight that greeted the two had their hands relaxing almost immediately. A warm glow washed out of the open door. Beyond the portal, that light reflected brilliantly off of a myriad of walls and partitions, all made of shining ice—not opaque and snowy, but clear and highly reflective. Images of a drow, an elf, and a pegasus came back at the companions from every conceivable angle.

Drizzt stepped in and found himself lost in a sea of reflected Drizzts. The partitions were barely wide enough to admit a giant and sorted in a mazelike manner that set off alarm bells in the wary drow's mind as soon as he recovered from the initial shock of it all. He motioned to Innovindil to quickly follow and rushed ahead.

"What is it?" the elf finally asked when she caught up to Drizzt as he paused at a four-way intersection of shiny ice walls.

"This is a defense," Drizzt replied.

He looked around, soaking it in, confirming his fears. He noted the bare stone floor, in such a sharp contrast to the walls, which seemed to have no stone in them. He looked up to the many holes in the high ceiling, set strategically from east to west along the southern reaches of the chamber, designed, he realized, to catch the sunlight from dawn to twilight. Then he sorted through his images, following the line across the breadth of the huge chamber. A single sentry at any point along the wall would easily know of the intruders.

Magic had created that hall of mirrors, Drizzt knew, and for a specific purpose.

"Move quickly," the drow said even as he started off.

He dipped and darted his way through the maze, trying to find side aisles that would reflect him in a confusing manner to any sentries. He had to hope that any guards who might be posted to watch over the hall were, like the one in the previous tunnel, less than alert.

No alarm horns had blown and no roars had come at him from afar. That was a good sign at least, he had to believe.

Around one sharp bend, the drow pulled up short, and Innovindil, leading Sunset right behind him, nearly knocked him forward onto his face.

Still Drizzt managed to hold back, absorbing the energy of the bump and skittering to the side instead of forward, for he did not want to take another step, did not want to step out onto the open, twenty-foot border of the eastern end of the cavern. That border was a river, and though it was iced over, Drizzt could clearly see the water rushing below the frozen surface.

Across the way and down to his left, the drow spotted another tunnel.

He motioned for Innovindil to carefully follow, then inched down the bank, stopping directly across from the exit tunnel. Up above him, he saw a large rope dangling—high enough for a giant to reach, perhaps, so that it might swing across.

He heard Sunset clip-clopping back away from him and turned to see Innovindil astride the pegasus, angling to line him up for a straight run to the exit tunnel. With a grin, Drizzt sprinted back to her and clambered up behind her, and the elf wasted no time in putting Sunset into a quick run and a short leap, wings going out and beating hard. With grace more akin to a deer than a horse, Sunset alighted across the frozen river in the tunnel and Innovindil quickly pulled him up to a stop.

Drizzt was down in a flash, Innovindil following.

"Do you think they know we're here?" the moon elf asked.

"Does it matter?"

Now the corridors became more conventional, wide, high, and winding, maze-like, with many turns and side passages. The enormity of Shining White surprised Drizzt, and the enormity of their task became more than a little daunting.

"Guenhwyvar will smell Sunrise out," he said as he pulled out the figurine.

"More likely to smell your blood, I suspect," came an answer from a voice that was not Innovindil's, that was far too deep and resonant to belong to an elf.

Drizzt turned slowly, as did his companion, and Sunset pawed the stone.

A pair of frost giants stood calmly some twenty feet or so behind them, one with hands on her hips, the other holding a massive hammer in his right hand patting it onto his left.

"You bring a second pegasus for Dame Gerti," the female remarked. "She will be pleased—perhaps enough so to allow you a quick death."

Drizzt nodded and said, "Aye, we have come to please Gerti, of course. That is our greatest desire."

He slapped Sunset on the rump as he finished, and Innovindil went up astride the pegasus even as it leaped away.

Drizzt turned to follow, took a few steps, then, hearing the giants charging in behind, he cut a quick turn and charged at them, howling with fury.

"Drizzt!" Innovindil shouted, and he knew by her tone that she had concluded that he meant to engage the behemoths.

Nothing could have been farther from his thoughts.

He rushed at the one holding the hammer, and as it started to swing at him he cut to the right, toward the second giant.

The first was too clever to continue its attack—an attack that likely would have struck its companion. But as the female behemoth reached for Drizzt he turned anyway again, back toward the first, his feet, their speed enhanced by magical anklets, moving in a blur. He dived into a roll, turning sidelong as he went so that he came up short and cut back to his right, which sent him rushing right between the giants. Both of them lurched in to grab at him, and the female might have had him, except that the pair knocked heads halfway down.

Both grunted and straightened, and Drizzt ran free.

Barely ten strides down the next corridor, though, the drow heard the shouts of more giants, and he had to turn into yet another perpendicular corridor so that he didn't run headlong into a behemoth.

"No dead ends," the drow whispered—a prayer if he ever heard one—with every blind turn.

He soon came into a wider corridor lined on both sides with statues of various shapes and size. Most were of ice, though a few of stone. Some were giant-sized, but most reflected the stature of a human or an elf. The detailing and craftsmanship was as finely worked as dwarven stone, and the elegance of the artwork was not lost on the drow—the statues would not have seemed out of place in Menzoberranzan or in an elven village. He had little time to pause and admire the pieces, though, for he heard the giants behind him and in front, and horns blowing from deeper in the seemingly endless complex.

He pulled his cloak from his shoulders and cut to the side, toward a cluster of several elf-sized statues.

Innovindil could only hope that the floor stayed stone and was not glazed over with ice, for she could ill afford to allow Sunset to slow the run with giants scrambling all around her. She came upon corridor after corridor, turning sometimes and running straight at others, meaning to turn at some others

and yet finding a group of enemies coming at her from that direction. . . . A blind run was the best the elf could manage. Or a blind flight, for every now and then she put the pegasus up into the air to gain speed. She had to take care, though, for airborne, Sunset could not navigate the sharp, right-angled turns. Innovindil watched ahead and behind, and looked up repeatedly. She kept hoping that the ceiling would open up before her so that she could lift Sunset into a short flight, perhaps one that would get them both out through a natural chimney or a worked skylight.

At one corner, the elf and her pegasus nearly slammed into the stone wall, for the angle of the turn proved to be more than ninety degrees. Sunset skidded to a rough stop, brushing the stone as Innovindil brought the pegasus about.

Innovindil sucked in her breath as they realigned and she prompted the pegasus to run again, for that moment of stillness left her vulnerable, she knew.

And so she was only a little surprised when she saw a gigantic spear of ice—a long, shaped icicle—soaring at her from down the previous corridor. She ducked instinctively, and if she had not, she would have been skewered. Even with the near miss, the elf was almost dislodged, for the spear shattered on the stone above her and a barrage of ice chips showered over her.

Stubbornly holding her seat, Innovindil kicked her heels into Sunset's flank and bade him to run on. She heard a shout behind her and to the side, from whence the spear had come, and she understood enough of the frost giant language, which was somewhat akin to Elvish, to understand that a giantess was berating the spear thrower.

"Do you want to hurt Gerti's new pet?"

"The pegasus or the elf?" the giant answered, his booming voice echoing off the stone behind Innovindil.

"Both, then!" the giantess laughed.

For some reason, their tone made Innovindil think that catching the spear in her chest would have been preferable.

Two giants charged down the corridor, only occasionally glancing to either side until one suddenly lurched to the left and gave a victorious shout.

The other yelled, "Clever!" when it, too, noticed the cloak on the statue—a cloak not carved of stone, but flowing as only fabric could.

With a single stride to the side, the first giant brought a heavy club to bear, crushing down on the cloak. The ice statue beneath it exploded into a shower of shards and splinters.

"Oh, you broke Mardalade's work!" the other shouted.

"T-the drow?" the first stammered and dropped its club.

"Finds you quite amusing," came an answer from behind, and both giants spun around.

Drizzt, skipping down the other way, paused long enough to offer a salute, then a smile as he pointed back behind the behemoths.

Neither turned—until they heard the low growl of a giant panther.

The two giants spun and ducked as six hundred pounds of black-furred muscle leaped over them, cutting close enough so that both threw up their hands and ducked even lower, one falling to the stone.

Drizzt sprinted away. He used the moment of reprieve to try to sort out the maze of crisscrossing corridors. He listened carefully to the sounds all around him, too, trying to make some sense of them. Shouts from unrelated areas told him that Innovindil was still running, and gave him a fairly good idea of her general direction.

He sprinted away, back to the west, then north, then west again. He heard the clip-clop of the running pegasus as he approached the next four-way intersection, and ran harder, thinking to catch hold of his friend as she passed through, and leap up behind her.

But he slowed, quickly abandoning that notion. Better that the giants had two targets, he realized.

Innovindil and Sunset crossed in front of him, head down and flying fast, with the pegasus a few feet off the ground. Though he could not help but pause and admire the elf's handling of the winged horse, Drizzt clearly heard the approach of giants not far behind. He picked up his pace again, and as a pair of giants ran through the intersection in fast pursuit of the elf, Drizzt rushed out right behind them, and managed to slash one in the back of the leg as he passed, drawing a howl of pain.

That one stopped and the other slowed, both turning to regard the running dark elf.

The wounded one then fell flat to his face, as a great panther sprang against the back of his neck, then leaped away. Three more giants poured into the intersection, and all five shouted wildly.

"Left!"

"Right!"

"Straight ahead!"

"The elf, you fools!"

"The drow!"

And all of that, of course, only gave Drizzt and Innovindil a bit more breathing room.

Around and around they went, and Drizzt crossed corridors he recognized. At another intersection, he heard the clip-clop of Sunset's hooves again, and he got there first. Again he thought of jumping up astride the pegasus, and again he abandoned the notion, for still more giants bobbed along behind his fleeing companion.

Drizzt stood at the corner, leaning out enough so that Innovindil noticed him. He pointed across the way, to the tunnel on the approaching Innovindil's left. She responded by bringing Sunset over to the right, near Drizzt, in a wider banking turn.

"Right, left, second right, and straight to the river!" the drow shouted as she thundered past.

Drizzt ducked back behind the corner. He heard giants approaching from behind him, as well as the ones coming in pursuit of Innovindil; he glanced both ways repeatedly and nervously, hoping that Innovindil's pursuit would arrive first.

His relief was sincere and deep when he saw that they would. Still focusing on the pegasus-riding elf, the giants came on at full speed, and were caught by complete surprise when Drizzt leaped around the corner beside them and shouted at them.

They stopped and fell all over themselves trying to get at him, and he ran off back the way they had come, and the confusion of all the giants increased many times over when the group previously chasing Drizzt also scrambled into the intersection in a wild tangle.

Drizzt's smile widened; he couldn't deny that he was enjoying himself!

But then he was in a storm of pelting sleet, a small black cloud roiling at the ceiling high overhead and stinging him with hailstones as big around as his feet. The stone below him grew almost instantly slick and he went into a controlled slide, holding his precarious balance.

Of course, as soon as he hit a drier spot, his foot kicked out behind him and he had to fall into a roll. He looked back as he did, and noted one of the giantesses in the tumult of the intersection staring down his way and waggling her huge fingers once more.

"Oh, lovely," the drow said. He put his feet under him and ran off as fast as he could manage on the slippery floor.

He sensed the lightning bolt an instant before it flashed, and he dived down and to the side. His fall sped along as the bolt clipped him. He had to ignore the burning and numbness in his arm, though, for the giants—both groups—came on in fast pursuit.

Drizzt ran for his life, with all speed, hoping his guess of the layout was correct. He had sent Innovindil on a roundabout course that he hoped would get him to a specific intersection at the same time as the swifter pegasus. With the ice storm and the lightning bolt, that wouldn't happen even if his quick calculations had been correct.

He saw her cross the intersection before him, in a straight run for the frozen river and the escape tunnels. She looked back as he came out right behind her, following her course.

"Run on!" he cried, for he knew that she had no time to pause and wait. Giants were on his heels, including that nasty spellcaster—and wouldn't she love to have all the intruders in a line before her in a long, straight tunnel.

"Leap it! Fly across!" Drizzt implored Innovindil as she neared the frozen river, and she did, bringing Sunset into a quick flight that carried her to solid ground on the other side. No fool, she, the elf pulled up on the reins, then turned the pegasus aside and moved down the bank, just a few feet out of the tunnel's line of sight.

Drizzt came up on the river right behind her, the giants closing fast. Not even slowing in the least, the drow dived headlong, thinking to slide across and begin his run once more. He saw Innovindil as he hit the ice on his belly, the elf calling to him.

He heard a loud grunt from the other side, to his right and up above, and

rolled onto his side just in time to see a huge rock soaring down at him, thrown by a giant who was perched upon a ledge.

"Drizzt!" Innovindil yelled.

The drow tucked and turned, and caught a handhold, for he could see that the rock's aim had been true. Slowing his progress, he avoided being crushed, but the rock hit the ice right in front of him and crashed through. The drow, helpless in his slide, went into the icy waters.

"Drizzt!" Innovindil yelled again.

Hanging by a finger, the cold current pulling at him relentlessly, Drizzt managed to offer her a single shrug.

Then he was gone.

22

INNER VOICES

Ye must do this, Delly Curtie told herself over and over again, every step of the way through the dwarven complex. As sure as she was that what she was doing was for the best—for everyone involved—Delly needed constant reminders and assurances, even from herself.

Ye cannot stay here, not a minute longer.

Bah, but she's not yer child anyway, ye silly woman!

It's for his own good more'n yer own, and she's a better woman than ye'd ever be!

Over and over, the woman played out all the rationalizations, a litany that kept her putting one foot in front of the other as she neared the closed door to Catti-brie's private room. Colson stirred and gave a little cry, and Delly hugged the girl tighter against her and offered a comforting coo.

She came up to the door and pressed her ear, then hearing nothing, pushed it open just a bit, paused, and listened again. She heard Catti-brie's rhythmic breathing. The woman had returned exhausted a short while before from the audience chamber, announcing that she needed some sleep.

Delly moved into the room. Her first emotions upon seeing Catti-brie swirled within her, a combination of anger and jealousy, and a desperate feeling of inferiority that gnawed at her belly.

No, ye put it all aside! Delly silently determined, and she forced herself closer to the bed.

She felt the doubts crawling up within her with every step, a cacophony of voices telling her to hold on to Colson and never let go. She looked down on Catti-brie as the woman lay there on her back, her thick auburn hair framing her face in such a manner as to make her appear small, almost childlike. Delly couldn't deny her beauty, the softness of her skin, the richness of her every feature. Catti-brie had lived a good life, but a difficult one, and yet, she seemed somehow physically untouched by the hardships—except for her current injury, of course. For all her battles and swordfights, not a blemish was to be found on the woman's face. For a brief moment, Delly wanted to claw her.

A very brief moment, and Delly drew a deep breath and reminded herself that her own nastiness was more a negative measure of herself than any measure of Catti-brie.

"The woman's not ever shown ye an angry look nor offered ye a harsh word," Delly quietly reminded herself.

Delly looked to Colson, then back to Catti-brie.

"She'll make ye a fine mother," she whispered to the baby.

She bent low, or started to, then straightened and hugged Colson close and kissed her atop the head.

Ye got to do this, Delly Curtie! Ye cannot be stealing Wulfgar's child!

But that was the thing of it, she realized. *Wulfgar's* child? Why was Colson anymore Wulfgar's child than Delly Curtie's? Wulfgar had taken the babe from Meralda of Auckney at Meralda's desperate request, but since Delly had joined up with him and Colson in Luskan, she, not Wulfgar, had been more the parent by far. Wulfgar had been off in search of Aegis-fang, and in search of himself. Wulfgar had been out for days at a time battling orcs. And all the while, Delly had held Colson close, had fed her and rocked her to sleep, had taught her to play and even to stand.

Another thought came to her then, bolstering her maternal uprising. Even with Colson in his care and Delly gone, would Wulfgar stop fighting? Of course not. And would Catti-brie abandon her warrior ways after her wounds healed?

Of course not.

Where did that leave Colson?

Delly nearly cried out at the desperate thought. She spun away from the bed and staggered a step toward the door.

You are entitled to the child, and to a life of your own making, said the voice in her head.

Delly kissed Colson again and stepped boldly across the room, thinking to walk away without looking back.

Should everything good happen to her? the voice asked, and the reference to Catti-brie was as clear to Delly as if it was her own inner voice speaking.

You give and give of yourself, but your own good intentions bring to you desperation, said the voice.

Aye, and empty tunnels o' dark stone, and not a one to share me thoughts, Delly answered, not even aware that she was having a conversation with another sentient being.

She reached the door then, but paused, compelled to look to the side. Catti-brie's gear was piled on a small bench, her armor and weapons covered by her worn traveling cloak. One thing in particular caught Delly's eye and held it. Peeking out from under the cloak was a sword hilt, fabulous in design and gleaming beyond anything Delly had ever seen. More beautiful than the shiniest dwarf-cut gem, more precious than a dragon's mound of gold. Before she even knew what she was doing, Delly Curtie slipped Colson down to the side, balancing her on one hip, and took a fast step over and with her free hand drew the sword out from under the cloak and out of its scabbard at the same time.

She instantly knew that the blade was hers and no one else's. She instantly realized that with such a weapon, she and Colson could make their way in a troubled world and that all would be right.

Khazid'hea, the sentient and hungry sword, was always promising such things.

She opened her eyes to see a comforting face staring back at her, crystal blue orbs full of softness and concern. Before she even fully registered who it was and where she was, Catti-brie lifted her hand to stroke Wulfgar's cheek.

"You will sleep your life away," the big man said.

Catti-brie rubbed her eyes and yawned, then allowed him to help her sit up in her bed.

"Might as well be sleeping," she said. "I'm not doing much good to anyone."

"You're healing so that you can join in the fight. That's no small thing."

Catti-brie accepted the rationale without argument. Of course she was frustrated by her infirmity. She hated the thought of Wulfgar and Bruenor, and even Regis, standing out there on the battle line while she slumbered in safety.

"How goes it in the east?" she asked.

"The weather has held and the ferry is functional. Dwarves have come across from Felbarr, bearing supplies and material for the wall. The orcs strike at us every day, of course, but with the help of the Moonwood elves, they have been easily repelled. They have not come on in force, yet, though we do not know why."

"Because they know we'll slaughter them all across the mountains."

Wulfgar's nod showed that he did not disagree. "We hold good ground, and each passing hour strengthens our defenses. The scouts do not report a massing of orcs. We believe that they too are digging in along the ground they have gained."

"It'll be a winter of hard work, then, and not much fighting."

"Readying for a spring of blood, no doubt."

Catti-brie nodded, confident that she'd be more than ready to go back out into the fighting when the weather turned warm.

"The refugees from the northern settlements are leaving even now," Wulfgar went on.

"The way out is safe enough to risk that?"

"We've got the riverbank for a mile and more to the south, and we've put the ferry out of throwing range of any giants. They'll be safe enough—likely the first of them are already across."

"How clear is it up there?" Catti-brie asked, not even trying to hold the concern out of her voice.

"Very. Perhaps too much so," Wulfgar answered, misreading her concern, and he paused, apparently catching on. "You wonder if Drizzt will find his way to us," he said.

"Or if we can find our way to him."

Wulfgar sat on the edge of the bed and stared at Catti-brie for a long, long while.

"Not so long ago you told me he wasn't dead," he reminded. "You have to hold onto that."

"And if I cannot?" the woman admitted, lowering her eyes for even voicing such a fear.

Wulfgar cupped her chin with his huge hand and tilted her head back so that she had to look him in the eye. "Then hold on to your memories of him, though I do not believe he is dead," he insisted. "Better to have loved . . ."

Catti-brie looked away.

After a moment of confusion, Wulfgar turned her back yet again. "It is better to have loved him and lost him than never to have known him at all," he stated, reciting one of the oldest litanies in all corners of the Realms. "You were lovers; there is nothing more special than that."

Telltale tears welled in Catti-brie's deep blue eyes.

"You . . . you told me . . ." Wulfgar stammered. "You said that in your years on the boat with Captain Deudermont . . ."

"I didn't tell you anything," she replied. "I let you assume."

"But . . ."

Wulfgar paused, replaying that conversation he and Catti-brie had shared during their trials out on the battle line with Banak. He had asked her pointedly about whether or not she and Drizzt had become more than friends, and indeed she had not answered directly, other than to refer to the fact that they had been traveling as companions for six long years.

"Why?" Wulfgar finally asked.

"Because I'm thinking myself the fool for not," Catti-brie said. "Oh, but we came close. We just never . . . I'm not wanting to talk about this."

"You wanted to see how I would react if I believed that you and Drizzt were lovers," Wulfgar said, and it was a statement not a question, indicating that he had it all figured out.

"I'll not deny that."

"To see if Wulfgar had healed from his torment in the Abyss? To see if I had overcome the demons of my upbringing?"

"Don't you get all angry," Catti-brie said to him. "Maybe it was to see if Wulfgar was deserving of a wife like Delly."

"You think I still love you?"

"As a brother would love a sister."

"Or more?"

"I had to know."

"Why?"

The simple question had Catti-brie rocking back in her bed. "Because I know it's farther along with me and Drizzt," she said after only a brief pause. "Because I know how I feel now, and nothing's to change that, and I wanted to know how it would affect yourself, above all."

"Why?"

"Because I'd not break up our group," Catti-brie answered. "Because we five have forged something here I'm not wanting to lose, however I'm feeling about Drizzt."

Wulfgar spent a long while staring at her, and the woman began to squirm under that scrutiny.

"Well, what're you thinking?"

"I'm thinking that you sound less like a dwarf every day," he answered with a wry grin. "In accent, I mean, but you sound more like a dwarf every day in spirit. It's Bruenor who's cursed us both, I see. Perhaps we are both too pragmatic for our own good."

"How can you say that?"

"Six years beside a man you love and you're not lovers?"

"He's not a man, and there's the rub."

"Only if your dwarven practicality makes it a rub."

Catti-brie couldn't deny his tone or his smile, and it infected her soon enough. The two shared a laugh, then, self-deprecating for both.

"We've got to find him," Wulfgar said at length. "For all our sakes, Drizzt must come back to us."

"I'll be up and about soon enough, and out we'll go," Catti-brie agreed, and as she spoke, she glanced across the way at her belongings, at the weathered traveling cloak and the dark wood of Taulmaril peeking our from under it.

At the scabbard that once held Khazid'hea.

"What is it?" Wulfgar asked, noticing the sudden frown that crossed the woman's face.

Catti-brie led his gaze with a pointing finger. "My sword," she whispered.

Wulfgar rose and crossed to the pile, pulling off the cloak and quickly confirming that, indeed, the sword was gone.

"Who could have taken it?" he asked. "Who would have?"

While Wulfgar's look was one of confusion and curiosity, Catti-brie's expression was much more grave. For she understood the power of the sentient sword, and she knew that the person who pulled Khazid'hea free of its scabbard had gotten more than he'd bargained for.

Much more.

"We have to find it, and we have to find it quickly," she said.

It is not for you, came the voice in Delly's head as she moved toward the waiting ferry. All around her dwarves worked the stone, smoothing the path from the door to the river and building their defenses up on the mountain spur. Most of the human refugees were already aboard the ferry, though the dwarf pilot had made it quite clear that the raft wouldn't put out for another few minutes.

Delly didn't know how to answer that voice in her head, a voice she thought her own.

"Not for me?" she asked aloud, quietly enough to not draw too much attention. She masked the ridiculous conversation even more by turning to Colson and acting as if she was speaking to the toddler.

Are ye daft enough to think ye should go back into the mines and live yer life with the dwarfs, then? Delly asked herself.

The world is wider than Mithral Hall and the lands across the Surbrin, came an unexpected answer.

Delly moved off to the side, behind the screen of a lean-to one of the dwarves had put together for the workers to take breaks out of the cold wind. She set Colson on a chair and started to set her pack down—when she realized that the second voice wasn't coming from in her head at all, but from the pack. Gingerly, Delly unwrapped Khazid'hea and once the bare metal of the hilt was in her hand that voice rang all the more clearly.

We are not crossing the river. We go north.

"So the sword's got a mind of its own, does it?" Delly asked, seeming

more amused than concerned. "Oh, but ye'll bring me a pretty bit o' coin in Silverymoon, won't ye?"

Her smile went away as her arm came out, drifting slowly and inexorably forward so that Khazid'hea's tip slid toward Colson.

Delly tried to scream, but found that she could not, found that her throat had suddenly constricted. Her horror melted almost immediately, however, and she began to see the beauty of it all. Yes, with a flick of her hand she could take the life from Colson. With a mere movement, she could play as a god might.

A wicked smile crossed Delly's face. Colson looked at her curiously, then reached up for the blade.

The girl nicked her finger on that wickedly sharp tip, and began to cry, but Delly hardly heard her.

Neither did Delly strike, though she had more than a little notion to do just that. But an image before her, the bit of Colson's bright red blood on the sword, on *her* sword, held her in place.

It would be so easy to kill the girl. You cannot deny me.

"Cursed blade," Delly breathed.

Speak aloud again and the girl loses her throat, the sentient sword promised. *We go north.*

"You—" Delly started to say, but she bit the word off in horror. *You would have me try to get out of here to the north with a child in tow?* she silently asked. *We'd not get past the perimeter.*

Leave the child.

Delly gasped.

Move! the sword demanded, and never in all her life had Delly Curtie heard such a dominating command. Rationally, she knew that she could just throw the sword to the ground and run away, and yet, she couldn't do it. She didn't know why, she just could not do it.

She found her breathing hard to come by. A multitude of pleas swirled through her thoughts, but they wound in on themselves, for she had no real answer to the commands of Khazid'hea. She was shaking her head in denial, but she was indeed stepping away from Colson.

A nearby voice broke her from her torment momentarily, and Delly surely recognized that particular wail. She spun to see Cottie Cooperson moving toward the ferry, where the pilot was barking for everyone to hurry aboard.

We cannot leave her, Delly pleaded with the sword.

Her throat . . . so tender . . . Khazid'hea teased.

They will find the child and come for us. They will know that I did not cross the Surbrin.

When no rebuttal came back at her, Delly knew she had the evil sword's attention. She didn't really form any cogent sentences then, just rambled through a series of images and thoughts so that the weapon would get the general idea.

A moment later, Khazid'hea wrapped and tucked under her arm, Delly ran for the ferry. She didn't explain much to Cottie when she arrived and handed Colson to the troubled woman, but then she really didn't have to explain anything to Cottie, who was too wrapped up in the feel and smell of Colson to hear her anyway.

Delly waited right there, until the pilot finally shouted down at her, "Away we go, woman. Get yerself aboard!"

"What're ye about?" asked one of the other passengers, a man who often sat beside Cottie.

Delly looked at Colson, tears welling in her eyes.

She had a fleeting thought to tear out the toddler's throat.

She looked up at the pilot and shook her head, and as the dwarf tossed the ferry ropes aside, freeing the craft into the river, Delly stumbled off the other way, glancing back often.

But ten steps away, she didn't bother to even look back again, for her eyes were forward, to the north and the promises that Khazid'hea silently imparted, promises that had no shape and no definition, just a general feeling of elation.

So caught was Delly Curtie by the power of Khazid'hea that she gave Colson not another thought as she worked her way through the workers and the guards, stone by stone, until she was running free north along the riverbank.

"Halt!" cried an elf, and a dwarf sentry beside him echoed the shout.

"Stop yer running and be counted!" the dwarf cried.

More than one elf lifted a bow toward the fleeing figure, and dwarven crossbows went up as well. More shouts ensued, but the figure was out of range by then, and gradually the bows began to lower.

"What do ye know?" Ivan Bouldershoulder asked the dwarf sentry who had shouted out. Behind him, Pikel lifted his hand to the sky and began to chatter excitedly. The dwarf sentry pointed far to the north along the riverbank, where the figure continued to run away.

"Someone run out, or might that it was an orc scout," the dwarf replied.

"That was no orc," said the elf bowman beside them. "A human, I believe, and female."

"Elfie eyes," the dwarf sentry whispered to Ivan, and he gave an exaggerated wink.

"Or might be half-orc," Ivan reasoned. "Half-orc scout might've wandered in with the others from the northern towns. Ye best be tightening the watch."

The elf nodded, as did the dwarf, but when Ivan started to continue his line of thought, he got grabbed by the shoulder and roughly tugged back.

"What're ye about?" he asked Pikel, and he stopped and stared at his brother.

Pikel held tight to Ivan's shoulder, but he was not looking at his brother. He stared off blankly, and had Ivan not seen that druidic trick before, he would have thought his brother had completely lost his mind.

"Ye're looking through a bird's eyes again, ain't ye?" Ivan asked and put his hands on his hips. "Ye durned doo-dad, ye know that's always making ye dizzier than usual."

As if on cue, Pikel swayed, and Ivan reached out and steadied him. Pikel's eyes popped open wide, and turned and stare at his brother.

"Ye back?" Ivan asked.

"Uh-oh," said Pikel.

"Uh-oh? Ye durned fool, what'd ye see?"

Pikel stepped up and pressed his face against the side of Ivan's head, then whispered excitedly in Ivan's ear.

And Ivan's eyes went wider than those of his brother. For Pikel had been watching through the eyes of a bird, and that bird, on his bidding, had taken a closer look at the fleeing figure.

"Ye're sure?" Ivan asked.

"Uh huh."

"Wulfgar's Delly?"

"Uh huh!"

Ivan grabbed Pikel and tugged him forward, shoving him out toward the north. "Get a bird watching for us, then. We gotta go!"

"What're ye about?" the dwarf sentry asked.

"Where are you going?" echoed the elf archer.

"Go send the word to Bruenor," Ivan shouted. "Catch that ferry and search the tunnels, and find Wulfgar!"

"What?" dwarf and elf asked together.

"Me and me brother'll be back soon enough. No time for arguing. Go tell Bruenor!"

The dwarf sentry sprinted off to the south, and the Bouldershoulder brothers ran to the north, heedless of the shouts that followed them from the many surprised sentries.

23

MUTUAL BENEFIT

The storm had greatly abated, but the day seemed all the darker to Innovindil as she sat on Sunset staring back at the cave entrance to Shining White. From what she could tell the giants had pursued her as far as the inner door, and the sentry out in the corridor was still contentedly snoring when she and Sunset had galloped past.

The elf knew that she should be on her way and should not linger out there. She knew that giants could be creeping out of secret passageways onto ledges along the mountain wall, perhaps very near to her and up above. She feared that if she glanced right or left at any time, she might see a boulder soaring down at her.

But Innovindil didn't look to the sides, and did not prompt Sunset to move off at all. She just sat and stared, hoping against all logic that Drizzt Do'Urden would soon come running out of that cavern.

She chewed her lip as the minutes passed. She knew it could not be so. She had seen him go into the rushing river, swept away below a sheet of ice through which he could not escape. The river didn't flow out aboveground anywhere in the area, from what she could see and hear, so there was nothing she could do.

Nothing at all.

Drizzt was lost to her.

"Watch over him, Tarathiel," the elf whispered into the wind. "Greet him in fair Arvandor, for his heart was more for the Seldarine than ever for his dark demon queen." Innovindil nodded as she spoke those words, believing them in her heart. Despite the black hue of his skin, Drizzt Do'Urden was no drow, she knew, and had not lived his life as one. Perhaps he was not an elf in manner and thought, either, though Innovindil believed that she could have led him in that direction. But her gods would not reject him, she was certain, and if they did, then what use might she have for them?

"Farewell my friend," she said. "I will not forget your sacrifice, nor that you entered that lair for the sake of Sunrise, and for no gain of your own."

She straightened and started to twist, moving to tug the reins to the right so she could be on her way, but again she paused. She had to get back to the Moonwood—she should have done that all along, even before Tarathiel had fallen to Obould's mighty sword. If she could rally her people, perhaps they could get back to Shining White and properly rescue Sunrise.

Yes, that was the course before her, the only course, and the sooner Innovindil began that journey, the better off they would all be.

Still, a long, long time passed before Innovindil found the strength to turn Sunset aside and take that first step away.

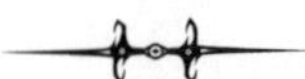

He scrambled and clawed, kicked wildly, and flailed his arms as he tried desperately to keep his face in the narrow pocket of air between the ice and the cold, cold water. Instinct alone kept Drizzt moving as the current rushed him along, for if he paused to consider the pain and the futility, he likely would have simply surrendered.

It didn't really seem to matter, anyway, for his movements gradually slowed as the icy cold radiated into his limbs, dulling his muscles and weakening his push. With every passing foot and every passing second, Drizzt slowed and lowered, and he found himself gasping water almost constantly.

He slammed into something hard, and the current drove him atop it so that he was granted a reprieve for a few moments, at least. Holding his perch

on the rock, the drow could keep his mouth in an air pocket. He tried to punch up and break through the ice, but his hand slammed against an unyielding barrier. He thought of his scimitars and reached down with one hand to draw out Twinkle. Surely that blade could cut through—

But his numb fingers couldn't grasp the hilt tightly enough and as soon as he pulled the scimitar free of its sheath, the current took it from his grasp. And as he lurched instinctively for the drifting and falling blade, Drizzt was swept away once more, turning as he went so that his head dipped far under the icy water.

He fought and he scrambled, but it was all for naught, he knew. The cold was taking him, permeating his bones and inviting him to a place of a deeper darkness than Drizzt had ever known. He wasn't seeing anything anymore in the black swirl of water, and even if there had been light, Drizzt would not have seen, for his eyes were closed, his thoughts turning inward, his limbs and sensibilities dying.

Distantly, the drow felt himself jostled about as the underground river turned and dipped. He crashed though a rocky area, but hardly felt anything as he bounced from one stone to the next.

Then the river dropped again, more steeply, as if plunging over a waterfall. Drizzt fell hard and landed harder and felt as if he had wedged up against the ice, his neck bent at an awkward angle. The cold sting knifed at his cheek and pressed inward.

Innovindil moved east from Shining White, keeping the higher mountains on her left and staying within the shadow of those peaks. For she knew she would need them to shelter her from the icy wind when night fell, and to shield the light of the campfire she would have to make.

She didn't dare bid Sunset to take to the air, for the gusts of wind could bring catastrophe. It occurred to her that perhaps she should turn south, running to the better weather and to the dwarves of Clan Battlehammer. Would they help her? Would they march beside her all the way to Shining White to rescue a pegasus?

Probably not, Innovindil knew. But she understood, though it surely pained her to admit it, that she would not likely get back to Shining White before the spring thaw.

She could only hope that Sunrise would last that long.

Drizzt's misperception surprised him when he realized he was not pressed up against the underside of the ice sheet, but was, rather, lying atop it. With a groan that came right from his aching bones, the drow opened his eyes and propped himself up on his elbows. He heard the rush of the waterfall behind him and glanced back that way.

The river had thrown him free when he'd come over that drop, and he had gone out far enough, just barely, to land upon the ice sheet where it resumed beyond the thrashing water.

The drow coughed out some water, his lungs cold and aching. He rolled over and sat on the ice, but spread right back out again when he heard it crackling beneath him. Slowly and gingerly, he crept toward the stone wall at the side of the river, and there he found a jag where he could sit and consider his predicament.

He really hadn't gone that far in his watery journey, he realized—probably not more than fifty feet or so from where he'd fallen through, not counting the two large steps downward.

Drizzt snapped his hands to his belt to feel Icingdeath, but not Twinkle, and he grimaced as he recalled losing the scimitar. He glanced back up at the waterfall wistfully, wondering how in the world he might retrieve the blade.

Then he realized almost immediately that it didn't really matter. He was soaking wet and the cold was going to kill him before any giants ever could. With that thought in mind, the drow forced himself up on unsteady feet and began inching along the wall, keeping as much of his weight as possible against the stone, and stepping from rock to rock wherever he found the opportunity. He traveled only a few hundred feet, the sound of the waterfall still echoing behind him, when he noted a side passage across the way, fronted by a landing that included a rack of huge fishing poles.

He didn't really want to move back into Shining White, but he saw no choice. He lay down on his belly on the ice, maneuvering himself so that he was clear

of all the rocks poking up through it. Then he pushed off, sliding out across the frozen river. He scraped and crawled and managed to get across then he went up to the landing and beyond, moving along an upward-sloping tunnel.

A short while later, he went back on his guard, for the tunnels became wider and more worked, with ornate columns supporting their ceilings, many of which were frescoed with various designs and artwork. At one point, he ducked back just in time as a pair of giants ambled across an intersection not far ahead.

He waited for them to clear the way, and . . .

What? he wondered. Where was he to go?

The giants had crossed left to right, so Drizzt went to the left, moving as swiftly as his still numb and sorely aching legs would allow, knowing that he needed to get to a fire soon. He fought to keep his teeth from chattering, and his eyelids felt so very heavy.

A series of turns and corridors had him moving into the more populated reaches of the complex, but if the giants were at all bothered by the continuing cold, they certainly didn't show it, for Drizzt saw no sign of any fires anywhere. He kept going—what choice did he have?—though he knew not where, and knew not why.

A cry from behind alerted him that he had been seen, and the chase was on once more.

Drizzt darted around a corner, sprinted some thirty feet, then ducked fast around another turn. He ran on, down a corridor lined with statues, and one that he recognized! On the floor lay a broken statue, along with the drow's own traveling cloak. He scooped it as he passed, wrapped it tight around him, and sprinted on as more and more giants took up the chase. He had his bearings, and he looked to make every turn one that would take him closer to the exit.

But every turn was blocked to him, as giants paralleled him along tunnels running closer to the exit. He found every route of escape purposefully blocked. He was being herded. Drizzt couldn't stop, though, unless he planned to fight, for a pair of giants chased him every stride, closing whenever he slowed. He had to turn left instead of right, and so he did, cutting a tight angle around the next corner and running on for all his life. He turned the next left, thinking that perhaps he could double back on the pair chasing him.

That way, too, was blocked.

Drizzt turned right and rushed through some open doors. He crossed a large chamber, and the two giants within howled and joined in the chase. Through another set of doors, he came to the end of the hallway, though it turned both left and right. Thinking one way as good as the other, the drow banked left and ran on—right into another large room, one sporting a huge round table where a group of frost giants sat and played, rolling bones for piles of silver coins.

The table went over, coins and bones flying everywhere, as the behemoths jumped up to leap after the drow.

"Not good," Drizzt whispered through his blue lips and chattering teeth.

The next door in line was closed, and the drow hardly slowed, leaping hard against it, shouldering it in. He stumbled and squinted, for he had come into the brightest-lit room in the complex. He tried to reorient himself quickly, to put his feet under him and continue on his way.

Whichever way that might be.

For he had come into a large oval chamber, decorated with statues and tapestries. Heads of various monsters—umber hulks, displacer beasts, and even a small dragon among them — lined the walls as trophies. Drizzt knew he wasn't alone, but it wasn't until he noted the dais at the far end of the room that he truly appreciated his predicament. For there sat a giantess of extraordinary beauty, decorated with fabulous clothing and many bracelets, necklaces and rings of great value, and wearing a white gown of fabulous texture and fabric. She leaned back in her seat and crossed her bare and shapely legs.

"I do so love it when the prey delivers itself," she said in the common tongue, her command of it as perfect as Drizzt's own.

The drow heard the doors bang closed behind him, and one of the pursuing giants graced him with an announcement. "Here is the drow you wanted, Dame Orelsdottr," the giant said. "Drizzt Do'Urden is his name, I believe."

Drizzt shook his head and brought a hand up to rub his freezing face. He reached low with the other one, pulling forth Icingdeath—and as he did, he heard giant sentries to either side of him bristle and draw weapons. He looked left and right, noting a line of spears and swords all pointing his way.

With a shrug, the drow dropped his scimitar to the floor, put his foot atop it and slid it out toward Gerti.

"Not even a fight from the famed Drizzt Do'Urden?" the giantess asked.

Drizzt didn't answer.

"I would have expected more of you," Gerti went on. "To surrender before dazzling us with your blade work? Or do you believe that you spare your life by giving yourself up to me? Indeed you are a fool if you do, Drizzt Do'Urden. Gather your scimitar if you will. Take up arms and at least try to fight before my soldiers crush the life out of you."

Drizzt eyed her hatefully, and thought to do as she asked. Before he could begin to calculate his chances of getting the blade and quick-stepping ahead to at least score a hit or two upon Gerti's pretty face, however, a low and feral growl from the side of the giantess caught his, and her attention.

Gerti turned and Drizzt leveled his gaze, and every giant in the chamber followed suit, to see Guenhwyvar perched on a ledge barely fifteen feet from Gerti, level with her pretty face.

The giantess didn't blink and didn't move. Drizzt could see her tightening her grip on the white stone arms of her great throne. She knew the panther could get to her before she could even raise her hands in defense. She knew Guenhwyvar's claws would tear at her blue and tender skin.

Gerti swallowed hard.

"Perhaps now you are more in the mood for a bargain," Drizzt dared to say.

Gerti flicked a hateful glance his way then her gaze snapped back to the threatening cat.

"She probably won't be able to kill you," Drizzt said, his freezing jaw hurting with every word. "But oh, will anyone ever look upon Dame Gerti Orelsdottr again and marvel at her beauty? Take out her pretty eye, too, Guenhwyvar," Drizzt added. "But only one, for she must see the expressions on the faces of those who look upon her scarred visage."

"Silence!" Gerti growled at him. "Your cat might wound me, but I can have you killed in an instant."

"And so we must bargain," Drizzt said without the slightest hesitation. "For we both have much to lose."

"You wish to leave."

"I wish to sit by a fire first, that I might dry and warm myself. Drow are not so comfortable in the cold, particularly when we are wet."

Gerti snorted derisively. "My people bathe in that river, winter and summer," she boasted.

"Good! Then one of your warriors can retrieve my other scimitar. I seem to have dropped it under the ice."

"Your blade, your fire, your life, and your freedom," Gerti said. "You ask for four concessions in your bargain."

"And I offer back your eye, your ear, your lips, and your beauty," Drizzt countered.

Guenhwyvar growled, showing Gerti that the mighty panther understood every word, and was ready to strike at any time.

"Four to four," Drizzt went on. "Come now, Gerti, what have you to gain by killing me?"

"You invaded my home, drow."

"After you led the charge against mine."

"So I free you and you find your elf companion, and again you invade my home?" Gerti asked.

Drizzt nearly fell over with relief upon learning that Innovindil had indeed gotten away.

"We will come back at you only if you continue to hold that which belongs to us," said the drow.

"The winged horse."

"Does not belong as a pet in the caves of frost giants."

Gerti snorted at him again, and Guenhwyvar roared and tamped down her hind legs.

"Surrender the pegasus to me and I will be on my way," said Drizzt. "And Guenhwyvar will disappear and none of us will ever bother you again. But keep the pegasus, kill me if you will, and Guenhwyvar will have your face. And I warn you, Gerti Orelsdottr, that the elves of the Moonwood will come back for the winged horse, and the dwarves of Mithral Hall will join them. You will find no rest with your stolen pet."

"Enough!" Gerti shouted at him, and to Drizzt's surprise, the giantess started to laugh.

"Enough, Drizzt Do'Urden," she bade him in quieter tones. "But you have asked me for something more; you have upped my end of the bargain."

"In return—" Drizzt started to reply, but Gerti stopped him with an upraised hand.

"Tell me not of any more body parts your cat will allow me to keep," she said. "No, I have a better bargain in mind. I will get your blade for you and let you warm before a great fire, all the while feasting on as much food as you could possibly eat. And I will allow you to walk out of Shining White—nay, to ride out on your precious winged horse, though it pains me to allow so beautiful a creature to wander away from me. I will do all this for you, and I will do more, Drizzt Do'Urden."

The drow could hardly believe what he was hearing, and that sentiment seemed common in that chamber, where many giants stood with their mouths drooping open in amazement.

"I am not your enemy," said Gerti. "I never was."

"I watched your people bombard a tower with great boulders. My friends were in that tower."

Gerti shrugged as if it did not matter and said, "I, we, did not begin this war. We followed an orc of great stature."

"Obould Many-Arrows."

"Yes, curse his name."

That raised Drizzt's eyebrows.

"You wish to kill him?" Gerti asked.

Drizzt didn't answer. He knew he didn't have to.

"I wish to witness such a battle," Gerti said with a vicious little grin. "Perhaps I can deliver King Obould to you, Drizzt Do'Urden. Would that interest you?"

Drizzt swallowed hard. "Now it would seem that you have upped your own end of the bargain even more," he reasoned.

"Indeed I have, so accept it with two promises. First, you will kill Obould. Then you will broker a truce between Shining White and the surrounding kingdoms. King Bruenor's dwarves will not seek retribution upon my people, nor will Lady Alustriel, nor any other allies of Clan Battlehammer. It will be as if the giants of Shining White never partook in Obould's war."

It took Drizzt a long time to digest the startling words. Why was Gerti doing this? To save her beauty, perhaps, but there was so much more going on than Drizzt could begin to understand. Gerti hated Obould, that much was obvious—could it be that she had come to fear him, as well? Or did she believe that the orc king would falter in the end, with or without her treason, and the result would prove disastrous for her people? Yes, if the dwarves of the three kingdoms joined with the folk of the three human kingdoms, would they stop with the orcs, or would they press on to exact revenge upon the giants as well?

Drizzt glanced around and noted that many of the giants were nodding and grinning, and those whispering amongst themselves all seemed in complete accord with Gerti's proposal. He heard naysayers, but they were not loud and dominant.

It began to make sense to Drizzt as he stood there shivering. If he won, then Gerti would be rid of a rival she surely despised, and if he lost, then Gerti would be no worse off.

"Orchestrate it," Drizzt said to her.

"Pick up your fallen scimitar, then, and dismiss your panther."

Alarms went off in Drizzt's head, suspicion twisting his black face. But Gerti seemed even more relaxed.

"Before all my people, I give you my word, Drizzt Do'Urden. Among the giants of the Spine of the World, our word is the most precious thing we own. If I deceive you now, would any of my people ever believe that I would not do the same to them?"

"I am no frost giant, so I am inferior in your eyes," Drizzt argued.

"Of course you are," Gerti said with a chuckle. "But that changes nothing. Besides, it will amuse me greatly to watch you battle King Obould. Speed against strength, a fighter's tactics against a savage fury. Yes, I will enjoy that. Greatly so." She finished and motioned toward the scimitar again.

Drizzt stared her in the eye for a long moment.

"Be gone, Guenhwyvar," he instructed.

The panther's ears flicked up and she turned to regard Drizzt curiously.

"If she betrays me, the next time you come to the material plane, seek her out and steal her beauty," Drizzt said.

"My word is not to be broken," said Gerti.

"Be gone, Guenhwyvar," Drizzt said again, and he stepped forward and retrieved Icingdeath. "Go home and find your rest, and rest assured that I will call upon you again."

24

AT THE BEHEST OF OTHERS

Drizzt led Sunrise out of Shining White the next morning, well aware that Gerti's giants were watching his every step. The air was calm and warmer, the sun shining brilliantly against the new-fallen snow.

The drow stretched and adjusted his clothing and cloak, and the belt that held both his scimitars once more. Not twenty steps from the front, he turned and looked back at Shining White, still amazed that Gerti had stayed true to her word, and that she had cut the deal with him in the first place. He took that as a hopeful sign regarding the future of the region, for Gerti Orelsdottr and her frost giant army apparently held no heart for continuing the war, and perhaps equally important, apparently held no bond of friendship with Obould Many-Arrows. Gerti wanted the orc king dead almost as much as Drizzt did, it seemed, and if that was true of the giantess, might it also be true of some of Obould's rival orc chieftains? Would attrition play on the massive army, defeating it where the dwarves could not?

That hopeful thought was quickly replaced by another, for Drizzt realized that if Gerti really could arrange for him to meet Obould, he could accelerate that disintegration of the invading force. Without the orc king as figurehead, the chaotic creatures would turn on each other, day after day and tenday after tenday.

Drizzt clenched his hands and rolled his fingers, flexing the muscles in his forearms, chasing the last vestiges of the river's cold bite from his bones. As Innovindil had killed Obould's son, so he would strike an even greater blow.

The thought of his elf companion had him shielding his eyes with one hand and scanning the sky, hoping to spot a flying horse. He wanted to spring upon Sunrise's back and put the pegasus up high to gain a wider view of the region, but Gerti had strictly forbidden that. In fact, Sunrise was wearing a harness that would prevent the pegasus from spreading wide his wings.

Gerti was offering a bargain, but she was doing it on her terms and with her guarantees.

Drizzt accepted that with a nod, and continued to scan the skies. He had the pegasus with him. He had his scimitar back from the cold waters, and he had his life. After the disaster of his foray into Shining White, those things were more than he had imagined possible.

And he might get a fight with the hated Obould. Yes, Drizzt realized, things had worked out quite well.

So far.

Gerti sat on her great throne eyeing the giants milling around in the audience chamber. She had surprised them all, she knew, and the looks that came her way reflected suspicion as much as curiosity. Gerti knew that she was gambling. Her father, the great Jarl Orel who had united the many families of giants in the Spine of the World under his iron-fisted rule, lingered near death, leaving Gerti as the heir apparent. But it would be the first transfer of power since the unification, and that, Gerti knew, was no small thing.

She had followed the advice of Ad'non Kareese and Donnia Soldou and had joined with Obould's grand ambitions, leading her people out of their mountain homes in forays that were initially intended to be low-risk and short-lived, quick strikes using orc fodder to bear the losses, and frost giants to collect the gains. Ironically, Obould's successes had upped the ante for Gerti, and dangerously so, she had come to understand as Obould had gained more and more power in their relationship. Obould was making her look

small and insignificant to her minions, and that was something Gerti knew she could ill afford. And so she had orchestrated her abandonment of Obould. But even that, she knew, had been a risk. For if the orc king had continued his conquering ways, or even if he could simply solidify and hold onto his already considerable gains, Gerti's people would have paid an exaggerated price—more than thirty frost giants had died in the campaign—for relatively minor gains in loot. The price Gerti herself would also pay in terms of stature could not be ignored.

A lone drow had given her an opening to change the equation, and she considered her bargain with Drizzt to be less of a gamble than those around her understood. The price had been nothing more than relinquishing the pegasus—true, the winged horse seemed a shiny bauble, but it was hardly of practical use to her. The gain?

That was the one variable, and the only part of any of it that seemed a gamble to Gerti. For if Drizzt killed Obould, then Gerti's abandonment of the orc's cause would seem prudent and wise, and even more so if Drizzt then followed through with his promise to relay the giantess's desire for a truce to the formidable enemies that would no doubt rush in to expel the leaderless orcs from their conquered lands. Might Gerti then salvage some practical gains from that ill-advised campaign, perhaps even the opening of trading routes with the dwarves of Mithral Hall?

The danger lay in the very real possibility that Obould would slay Drizzt, and thus gain even more stature among his subjects, if that was possible. Of course, in that eventuality, Gerti could claim to the orc king that she had delivered Drizzt to him for just that purpose. Perhaps she could even spin it to make it seem as if she, and not Obould, was truly the puppet-master.

"The winged horse was more trouble than it was worth," Gerti said to a nearby giantess who flashed her one of those suspicious and curious looks.

"It was beautiful," the giantess replied.

"And its beauty would bring an unending string of elves to Shining White, seeking to free it."

More curious looks came at her, for when had Gerti ever been afraid of the lesser races entering Shining White?

"Do you really wish to have the elves with their stinging bows sneaking into our home? Or the cunning dwarves digging new tunnels to connect to our lesser-used ways, insinuating themselves among us, popping up by surprise and smashing their ugly little hammers into our kneecaps?"

She saw a few nods among the giants as she explained, and Gerti weighed the various looks carefully. She had to play it just right, to make her maneuvering seem clever without reminding them all that her initial blunder had brought all of the risk and trouble to them in the first place. It was all about the message, Gerti Orelsdottr had learned well from her wise old father, and that was a message she meant to tightly control over the next few tendays, until the pain of losses faded.

If Drizzt Do'Urden managed to kill Obould, that message would be easier to shape to her advantage.

The same storm that had dumped heavy snows on the mountains near Shining White swirled to the southeast, bringing high winds and driving, cold rain, and whipping the waters of the Surbrin so forcefully that the Felbarran dwarves tied the ferry up on the eastern bank and retreated into sheltering caves. As anxious as they were to be on their way to Silverymoon, the human refugees did not dare to try their luck in the terrible weather, and so they, too, put up in those caves.

Cottie Cooperson made herself as inconspicuous as possible, staying in the back and at the very edges of the firelight, with Colson fully wrapped in a blanket. The others soon learned of the child, of course, and questioned Cottie.

"What'd ye do to its mother?" one man asked, and he bent low and forced Cottie to look at him squarely, demanding an honest answer.

"I seen Delly handing the child to Cottie of her own accord," another woman answered for the poor and lost Cooperson lass. "Right at the dock, and she run off."

"Run off? Or just missed the ferry?" the suspicious man demanded.

"Run off," the woman insisted. "Of her own choosing."

"She wanted the child out of Mithral Hall while they're fighting," Cottie lied.

"Then the dwarves should know they've got an adopted granddaughter of King Bruenor among their passengers," the man reasoned.

"No!" shouted Cottie.

"No," added the supportive woman. "Delly's not wanting that stubborn fool Wulfgar to know of it, as he'd be wanting the child back."

It made no sense, of course, and the man stood and turned his glare over the other woman.

"Bah! What business is it o' yer own, anyway?" she asked.

"None," another man answered. "And no one's a better mother than Cottie Cooperson."

Others seconded that remark.

"Then it's our own secret, and no business to them grumpy dwarves," the woman declared.

"Ye think Wulfgar's to be seeing it that way?" the doubting man argued. "Ye want the likes o' that one and his fierce father chasing us across all the lands?"

"Chasing us to what end?" the woman beside Cottie replied. "To get his child back? Well then we'll give him the little girl back, and no one's to argue."

"He'll come with rage in his eyes," the man argued.

"And it'll be rage he'll have to put on his wife, from where I'm sitting," said another man. "She give the child to Cottie to care for, and so Cottie's to care for the girl. Wulfgar and Bruenor got no right to anything but appreciation in that!"

"Aye!" several others loudly agreed.

The doubting man stared at Cottie's allies long and hard, then turned back to Cottie herself, who was hugging Colson as warmly as any mother ever could hold her own child.

He could not deny that the sight of Cottie with the child warmed his heart. Cottie, who had been through so very much pain, seemed content for perhaps the first time in all their trials. Even with his fears for the vengeance of Wulfgar, the man could not argue against that simple truth. He gave an accepting smile and a nod.

All construction of defenses along the mountain spur slowed during those hours of the storm, and the rain and sleet pelted the elves and dwarves who walked their patrols. They even dared to lessen those watches, for no enemies would come against them in the gale—or so they believed.

Similarly, Ivan and Pikel Bouldershoulder found their progress slowed to a crawl. Pikel's animal friends, who had guided them far north of the dwarves' position in pursuit of Delly Curtie, were still hunting at the behest of the doo-dad, but with lower and shorter flights and with very limited visibility.

"Durned fool woman," Ivan grumbled over and over again. "What's she thinking in running out o' Mithral Hall?"

Pikel squeaked to show his own confusion.

Ivan kicked at a stone, silently questioning his own decision to chase her out. They were more than a day's march from the mountain spur, and likely well behind the orc lines, though they hadn't seen any of the wretches in their march.

The dwarf truly hoped that they would not have to resort to Pikel's "root-walking" tricks to get back to Bruenor's boys.

"Durned fool woman," he grumbled and kicked another stone.

Compelled by the ever-hungry Khazid'hea, Delly Curtie was among the very few creatures wandering around outside in the cold storm. Exhausted, soaking wet, cold and miserable, the woman never entertained a single thought of finding shelter and stopping her march, because the sword would not let such a notion filter through her mind.

Khazid'hea held her, fully so. Delly Curtie had become an extension of the sword. Her entire existence was focused upon pleasing Khazid'hea.

The sword was not appreciative.

For though Delly was a willing slave, she was not what Khazid'hea coveted most of all: a worthy wielder. And so as darkness fell over the land and Delly's eyes conveyed to the sword the image of a distant campfire, the weapon compelled her to move toward it with all speed.

For hours she walked, often falling and skinning her legs, one time slipping on an icy rock so that she slammed her head and nearly knocked herself unconscious.

What am I doing out here, anyway? I meant to go to Silverymoon, or

Sundabar, and yet here I am, walking wild lands!

That flicker of cogent thought only made Khazid'hea reinforce its compulsion over her, dominating her and making her trudge along, one foot in front of the other.

Khazid'hea felt her fear some time later, when they heard the guttural voices of the encamped creatures, the language of orcs. But the vicious sword took that fear and transformed it, bombarding poor Delly with images of her child being massacred by those same orcs, turning her terror into red rage so completely that she was soon running headlong for the camp. Khazid'hea in hand she burst into the firelight, killing the nearest surprised orc with a single thrust of the fabulous blade, that drove its tip right through a blocking forearm and deep into the orc's chest.

Delly yanked the blade free and swiped wildly at the next orc in line, slashing a deep cut through the trunk of a hardwood tree as the creature ducked aside. She pursued wildly, stabbing and slashing, and the orc managed one block, which took the end off its simple spear, before falling back in fear.

Something hit Delly in the side, but she hardly felt it, so consumed was she, and she pressed forward and stuck the retreating creature in its ugly face again and again, slashing and beating it, sending lines of bright blood flying into the air. She tasted that blood and was too outraged and too consumed to be revolted.

Again something hit her in the side, and she whirled that way, thinking that an orc was punching at her. A moment of clarity led to a moment of confusion as the woman regarded her attacker, standing across the campfire from her, bow in hand.

Delly glanced down to her side, to see two arrows deeply embedded, then looked back in time to watch the orc pull back its bowstring once more.

Khazid'hea overwhelmed her with an image of that very orc biting out Colson's throat, and the woman shrieked and charged.

And staggered back from the weight of an arrow driving into her chest.

With a growl, Delly held her feet, glaring at the archer, stubbornly taking a step toward the orc. She never heard its companion creeping up behind her, never heard the sword rushing for her back.

She arched, eyes going to the night sky, and a moment of peace came over her.

She noticed Selûne then, gliding overhead, trailed by her glittering tears, through a patch of broken clouds, and she thought it a beautiful thing.

Khazid'hea fell from her grasp, its sharp tip digging into the ground so that it stayed upright, waiting for a more worthy wielder to take it in its grasp.

The sword felt its connection with Delly Curtie break completely and knew itself to be an orphan.

But not for long.

25

GERTI'S AMUSEMENT

Drizzt watched the approach of two of Gerti's messengers from a sheltered dell a mile to the east of Shining White's entrance. The drow had quickly learned the limits of Gerti's trust, for he had been told explicitly that he could not remove Sunrise's harness, and he knew well that his every move was being carefully monitored. If he tried to run away, the giants would rain boulders upon him and the pegasus.

The drow believed that Gerti trusted him, though, for why would she not? Certainly his desire to do battle with Obould was honestly placed and stated! No, all the "precautions" Gerti was taking were more a show for her own people, he understood—or at least, he had to believe. He had been around a wise leader all his life, a dwarf who knew what to do and how to present it—two very different things—and he understood the politics of his current situation.

Of course, Gerti might just be using him to get a chance at killing Obould, with no intention of ever letting Drizzt and Sunrise go after the battle, whatever the outcome. So be it, Drizzt had to accept, for he had really found no options in that chamber in Shining White. All had been lost, then she'd offered at least a glimmer of hope.

The two giants entered Drizzt's dell and tossed a bag of food and a waterskin at his feet.

"A substantial force of orcs is moving east of here, along the border of the mountains to a high pass," said one, a giantess of no small beauty.

"Sent by King Obould to aid in the construction of a large city he plans in that defensible place," the other added. Muscular and wide-shouldered even by the standards of his huge race, the male's face was no less handsome than that of his female companion, with light blue skin and silvery eyebrows that turned into a V whenever he furrowed his brow.

"Dark Arrow Keep," said the giantess. "You would do well to remember that name and relay it to your allies should you escape all of this."

The implications of the report were not really surprising to Drizzt. On his journey north to Shining White, he had seen clear signs that the orc king intended to dig in and hold his conquered ground. The construction of a major city, and one in the defensible high ground of the Spine of the World—from which more and more orcs continued to rally to his cause—seemed a logical course to that end.

"Obould is not with the caravan, though," the giantess explained. "He is moving from mountain to mountain, overseeing the work on many lesser keeps, and reminding the orcs who they serve."

"With his shamans," added the other. "And likely a pair of dark elves serve as his wider eyes—are they known to you?"

Drizzt's expression was all the answer the giants needed.

"You killed a pair of those drow, we know," the giant went on. "These two are, or were, their companions. They were sent to the south with the troll army, but they will return. They will hold a grievance toward Drizzt Do'Urden, no doubt."

"Murder and warfare are so common among my people that they just as likely won't," Drizzt replied, and he shrugged as if it didn't matter, for of course it did not. If the two drow were with Obould, then they were already his enemies.

"We will move in the morning," the giantess said. "Gerti hopes to meet up with Obould within three days."

She wants him dead before his grand designs can take real shape, Drizzt thought, but did not reply.

Every added bit of information about Obould's movements reinforced Gerti's deal with him. The giantess saw a war coming beyond anything in her

power to influence. Or, in the absence of that war, she saw her own position greatly diminishing before the rise of King Obould Many-Arrows.

Delivering Drizzt to Obould might prove a gamble to Gerti, Drizzt understood, for it was likely that Obould's stature would only climb if he proved victorious. The fact that Gerti was willing to take that chance showed Drizzt just how desperate she was becoming.

Obould was taking full control, so Gerti believed that she had nothing to lose.

The drow thought it odd that his victory over Obould would so greatly benefit Gerti Orelsdottr, a giantess he would hardly claim as an ally in any cause. He remembered the bombardment of Shallows, the callous disregard Gerti's warriors had shown for the poor besieged people of the village as they had launched boulder after boulder their way.

Yet, if he proved victorious and killed Obould, and the orc forces began to scatter and turn on themselves in the absence of a strong leader, Drizzt was then bound to parlay on behalf of those same giants for a truce.

The drow nodded grimly and accepted the notion then in his heart, as he had previously accepted it in his thoughts when his very life had been at stake. Better for everyone if the war could simply end, if the dark swarm of orcs could be pushed back into their holes and the land reclaimed for the goodly folk. What gain would there be in then pursuing an attack upon Shining White, in which hundreds of dwarves and their allies would be slain?

"Are you ready to fight him?" the giantess asked, and when Drizzt looked at her, he realized he'd been so wrapped up in his thoughts that he'd missed the question the first few times she'd asked it.

"Three days," he agreed. "Obould will die in three days."

The giant and giantess looked to each other and grinned, then walked off.

Drizzt replayed his pledge many times, letting it permeate his bones and his heart, letting it become a litany against all the pain and loss.

"Obould will die in three days," he repeated aloud, and his lips curled hungrily.

The two giants down the trail to his right kept Sunrise under close guard, but they were not holding Drizzt's attention that cold and clear morning. Up to his left, on a barren and rocky hilltop, Gerti Orelsdottr and King Obould stood in the sunlight, talking and arguing.

She had orchestrated all of it, had set Drizzt in place within an easy and swift climb to the appointed spot, then had brought Obould out here alone for a parlay.

The orc didn't seem suspicious at all to Drizzt, he appeared at ease and supremely confident. Obould had been a bit on his guard when he and Gerti first arrived at the hilltop, but after a few minutes of pointing and talking, the orc visibly relaxed.

They were discussing the construction of defenses, Drizzt knew. All the way out there, a full four days of marching south from Shining White, Drizzt had witnessed the unveiling of King Obould's grand designs. Many hilltops and mountainsides were under construction in the north, with rock walls taking shape and the bases of large keeps already set in place. On an adjoining mound to the one where the two principals stood, a hundred orcs toiled at the stone, preparing strong defenses.

Those sights only heightened Drizzt's sense of urgency. He *wanted* to kill Obould for what the orc had done to his friends and to the innocents of the North; he *needed* to kill Obould for the sake of those remaining. It was not the behavior that Drizzt had come to expect from an orc. Many times, even back in Menzoberranzan, he had heard others remark that the only thing truly subjugating goblinkind to the other races was the lack of cohesion on their part. Even the superior minded matron mothers of Menzoberranzan had remained leery of their goblin and orc slaves, knowing that a unified force of the monsters, weak as they might be individually, could prove to be an overwhelming catastrophe.

If Obould truly was that unifying force, at least in the Spine of the World, he had to die.

Many minutes passed, and Drizzt subconsciously grasped at his scimitar hilts. He glanced nervously at the adjoining hilltop, where several other orcs—shamans, they appeared—kept a watch on their leader, often moving to the closest edge and peering across at the two figures. Their interest had faltered over the past few minutes, but Drizzt knew that would likely be a temporary thing.

"Hurry up, Gerti," he whispered.

The drow stepped back into the shadows, startled, for almost as if she had heard his plea, Gerti turned away from Obould and stormed off, moving down the mountainside with swift, long strides.

So surprised was he that Drizzt nearly missed the moment. Obould, apparently caught off his guard by Gerti's sudden retreat, stood there gaping at her, hands on his hips, eyes staring out from behind that curious skull-like helm with its oversized, glassy goggles.

The drow shook himself from his hesitation and bounded up the slope, moving fast and silently. He came atop the hillock just a few strides from the orc, and thought for a moment to rush in and stab his enemy before Obould even knew he was there.

But the orc king spun on him, and Drizzt had skidded to a stop anyway.

"I had thought you would never dare to stand without an ally," the drow said, and his scimitars appeared in his hands—almost magically, it seemed, so fast and fluid was his movement.

A low growl escaped Obould's lips as he regarded the drow.

"Drizzt Do'Urden?" he asked, the growling rumble continuing through every syllable.

"It is good that you know my name," Drizzt answered, and he began to stalk to the side, Obould turning to keep him squarely in line. "I want you to know. I want you to understand why you die this morning."

So sinister was Obould's chuckle that it hardly deviated from the continuing growl. He reached his right hand up slowly and deliberately over his left shoulder, grasped the large hilt of his greatsword, and slowly drew it up. The top edge of his scabbard was cut halfway up its length, so as soon as the sword tip broke free of the sheath, Obould snapped the sword straight up then down and across before him.

Drizzt heard a shout from the other hillock, but it didn't matter. Not to him, and not to Obould. Drizzt heard a larger commotion, and glanced to see several orcs running his way, and several others lifting bows, but Obould raised his hand out toward them and they skidded to a stop and lowered their weapons. The orc king wanted the fight as much as he did.

"For Bruenor, then," Drizzt said, and he didn't piece together the implications of the scowl that showed in Obould's bloodshot yellow eyes.

"For Shallows and all who died there."

He kept circling and Obould kept turning.

"For the Kingdom of Dark Arrows," Obould countered. "For the rise of the orcs and the glory of Gruumsh. For our turn in the sunlight that the dwarves, elves, and humans have too long claimed as their own!"

The words sent an instinctual shiver down Drizzt's spine, but the drow was too wrapped up in his anger to fully appreciate the orc's sentiment.

Drizzt was trying to take a complete measure of his enemy, trying to look over the orc's fabulous armor to find some weakness. But the drow found himself locked by the almost hypnotic stare of Obould, by the sheer intensity of the great leader's gaze. So held was he, that he was hardly aware that Obould had started to move. So frozen was Drizzt by those bloodshot eyes, that he only moved at the very last second, throwing his hips back to avoid being cut in half by the sidelong swipe of the monstrous sword.

Obould pressed forward, whipping a backhand slash, then pulling up short and stabbing once, twice, thrice, at the retreating drow.

Drizzt turned and dodged, his feet quick-stepping, keeping him in balance as he backed. He resisted the urge to intercept the stabbing and slashing sword with one of his own blades, realizing that Obould's strokes were too powerful to be parried with one hand. The drow was using the moments as Obould pressed his attack to fall into his own rhythm. As he sorted out his methods, he realized it would be better to hold complete separation. So he kept his scimitars out to the side, his arms out wide, his agility and feet alone keeping Obould's strikes from hitting home.

The orc king roared and pressed on even more furiously, almost recklessly. He stabbed and stepped ahead, whipped his sword out one way then rushed ahead in a short burst as he slashed across. But Drizzt was quicker moving backward than Obould was in coming forward, and the orc got nowhere close to connecting. And the seasoned drow warrior, his balance perfect as always, let the blade go by and reversed his momentum in the blink of a bloodshot eye.

He ran right past Obould, veering slightly as the orc tried to shoulder-block him. A double-stab drove both his scimitars against Obould's side, and when the armor stopped them, Drizzt went into a sudden half-turn, then back again, slashing higher, one blade after the other, both raking across the orc king's eye plate.

Obould came around with a howl, his greatsword cutting the air—but only the air, for Drizzt was well out of range.

The drow's smile was short-lived, however, when he saw that his strikes, four solid hits, had done nothing, had not even scratched the translucent eye plate of the skull-like helm.

And Obould was on him in a flash, forcing him to dive and dodge, and even to parry once. The sheer force of Obould's strike sent a numbing vibration humming through the drow's arm. Another opening presented itself and Drizzt charged in, Twinkle cutting hard at the grayish wrap Obould wore around his throat.

And Drizzt, scoring nothing substantial at all, nearly lost some of his hair as he dived forward, just under the tremendous cut of the heavy greatsword. It occurred to Drizzt as he came around to face yet another brutal assault that his openings had been purposefully offered, that Obould was baiting him in.

It made no sense to him, and as he threw his hips left and right and back, and even launched himself into a sidelong somersault at one point, he kept studying the brute and his armor, searching desperately for some opening. But even Obould's legs seemed fully entombed in the magnificent armor.

Drizzt leaped up high as the greatsword cut across below him. He landed lightly and charged forward at his foe, and Obould instinctively reacted by throwing his sword across in front of him.

The greatsword burst into flame, but the startled Drizzt reacted perfectly, slapping Icingdeath across it.

The magic of the scimitar overruled the fires of the greatsword, extinguishing them in a puff of angry gray smoke, and it was Obould, suddenly, who was caught by surprise, just as he had started forward to overwhelm the drow. His hesitation gave Drizzt yet another opening, and the drow took a different tact, diving low and wedging himself between the orc's legs, thinking to spin and twist and send Obould tumbling away.

How might the armored turtle fight while lying on its back?

That clever thought met with the treelike solidity of King Obould's legs, for though Drizzt hit the orc full force, Obould's foot did not slip back a single inch.

Though dazed, the drow knew he had to move at once, before Obould could bring the sword around and skewer him where he crouched. He started to go, and realized he was quick enough to escape that blade.

But so did Obould, and so the orc did not focus on his sword, but rather kicked out hard. His armored foot crunched into the drow's chest and sent Drizzt flying back ten feet to land hard on his back. Gasping for breath that would not come, Drizzt rolled aside just as Obould's sword came down, smashing the stone where he'd just been lying.

The drow moved with all speed, twisting and turning, putting his feet under him, and throwing himself aside to barely avoid another great slash.

He couldn't fully avoid a second kick as the orc went completely on the offensive. The clip, glancing at it was, sent him tumbling once more. The drow finally straightened out enough to throw himself into a backward roll that put him on his feet once more, squarely facing the charging orc.

Drizzt yelled and charged, but only a single step before he burst out to the side.

He couldn't win, so he ran.

Down the side of the stony hill he went, the shouts of the orcs form the other hill and the taunts of Obould chasing him every step. He cut a fast turn around a jag in the stone, wanting to get out of sight of the archers, then cut again onto a straight descending path. His heart leaped when he saw Sunrise waiting for him, pawing the ground. As he neared, he realized that the pegasus was no longer wearing the harness.

Sunrise started running even as Drizzt leaped astride, and only a few steps off, the horse leaped into the air and spread his great wings, taking flight.

Gerti led the barrage, launching a stone that soared high into the air, not far behind the flying horse and drow rider. Her dozen escorting giants let fly as well, filling the air with boulders.

Not one scored a hit on the drow, though, for Gerti's instructions had been quite clear. As the pegasus banked, the giantess managed to catch the drow's attention, and his slight nod confirmed everything between them.

"He failed us, so why not kill him?" the giant beside Gerti asked.

"His hatred for Obould will only grow," the giantess explained. "He will try again. His role in this drama is not yet done."

She looked back to the hillock as she spoke, to see Obould standing imperiously, his greatsword raised in defiance, and behind him, the shamans and other orcs howled for him, and for Gruumsh.

Gerti looked back to Drizzt and hoped her prediction would prove correct.

"Find a way to kill him, Drizzt Do'Urden," she whispered, and she recognized the desperation in her own voice and was not pleased.

PART FOUR

THE BALANCE OF POWER

There is a balance to be found in life between the self and the community, between the present and the future. The world has seen too much of tyrants interested in the former, selfish men and women who revel in the present at the expense of the future. In theoretical terms, we applaud the one who places community first, and looks to the betterment of the future.

After my experiences in the Underdark, alone and so involved in simple survival that the future meant nothing more than the next day, I have tried to move myself toward that latter, seemingly desirable goal. As I gained friends and learned what friendship truly was, I came to view and appreciate the strength of community over the needs of the self. And as I came to learn of cultures that have progressed in strength, character, and community, I came to try to view all of my choices as an historian might centuries from now. The long-term goal was placed above the short-term gain, and that goal was based always on the needs of the community over the needs of the self.

After my experiences with Innovindil, after seeing the truth of friends lost and love never realized, I understand that I have only been half right.

"To be an elf is to find your distances of time. To be an elf is to live several shorter life spans." I have learned this to be true, but there is something more. To be an elf is to be alive, to experience the joy of the moment within the context of long-term desires. There must be more than distant hopes to sustain the joy of life.

Seize the moment and seize the day. Revel in the joy and fight all the harder against despair.

I had something so wonderful for the last years of my life. I had with me a woman whom I loved, and who was my best of friends. Someone who understood my every mood, and who accepted the bad with the good. Someone who did not judge, except in encouraging me to find my own answers. I found a safe place for my face in her thick hair. I found a reflection of my own soul in the light in her blue eyes. I found the last piece of this puzzle that is Drizzt Do'Urden in the fit of our bodies.

Then I lost her, lost it all.

And only in losing Catti-brie did I come to see the foolishness of my hesitance. I feared rejection. I feared disrupting that which we had. I feared the reactions of Bruenor and later, when he returned from the Abyss, of Wulfgar.

I feared and I feared and I feared, and that fear held back my actions, time and again.

How often do we all do this? How often do we allow often irrational fears to paralyze us in our movements. Not in battle, for me, for never have I shied from locking swords with a foe. But in love and in friendship, where, I know, the wounds can cut deeper than any blade.

Innovindil escaped the frost giant lair, and now I, too, am free. I will find her. I will find her and I will hold onto this new friendship we have forged, and if it becomes something more, I will not be paralyzed by fear.

Because when it is gone, when I lay at death's door or when she is taken from me by circumstance or by a monster, I will have no regrets.

That is the lesson of Shallows.

When first I saw Bruenor fall, when first I learned of the loss of my friends, I retreated into the shell of the Hunter, into the instinctual fury that denied pain. Innovindil and Tarathiel moved me past that destructive, self-destructive state, and now I understand that for me, the greatest tragedy of Shallows lies in the lost years that came before the fall.

I will not make that mistake again. The community remains above the self; the good of the future outweighs the immediate desires. But not so much, perhaps. There is a balance to be found, I know now, for utter selflessness can be as great a fault as utter selfishness, and a life of complete sacrifice, without joy, is, at the end, a lonely and empty existence.

–Drizzt Do'Urden

26

INTO THE BREACH ONCE MORE

He knew that Innovindil had escaped, of course, but Drizzt could not deny his soaring heart one clear and calm afternoon, when he first spotted the large creature in the distance flying above the rocky plain. He put Sunrise into swift pursuit, and the pegasus, seeming no less excited than he, flew off after the target with all speed. Just a few seconds later, Drizzt knew that he, too, had been spotted, for his counterparts turned his way and Sunset's wings beat the air with no less fervor than those of Sunrise.

Soon after, both Drizzt and Innovindil confirmed that it was indeed the other. The two winged horses swooped by each other, circled, and came back. Neither rider controlled the mounts then, as Sunrise and Sunset flew through an aerial ballet, a dance of joy, weaving and diving side by side, separating with sudden swerving swoops and coming back together in a rush that left both Drizzt and Innovindil breathless.

Finally, they put down upon the stone, and the elf and the drow leaped from their seats and charged into each other's arms.

"I thought you lost to me!" Innovindil cried, burying her face in Drizzt's thick white hair.

Drizzt didn't answer, other than to hug her all the tighter. He never wanted to let go.

Innovindil put him out to arms' length, stared at him, shaking her head in disbelief, then crushed him back in her hug.

Beside them, Sunrise and Sunset pawed the ground and tossed their heads near to each other, then galloped off, leaping and bucking.

"And you rescued Sunrise," Innovindil breathed, again moving back from the drow—and when she did, Drizzt saw that her cheeks were streaked with tears.

"That's one way to explain it," he answered, deadpan.

Innovindil looked at him curiously.

"I have a tale to tell," Drizzt promised. "I have battled with King Obould."

"Then he is dead."

Drizzt's somber silence was all the answer he needed to give.

"I am surprised to find you out here," he said a moment later. "I would have thought that you would return to the Moonwood."

"I did, only to find that most of my people have marched across the river to the aid of Mithral Hall. The dwarves have broken out of the eastern gate, and have joined with Citadel Felbarr. Even now, they strengthen their defenses and have begun construction of a bridge across the River Surbrin to reconnect Mithral Hall to the other kingdoms of the Silver Marches."

"Good news," the drow remarked.

"Obould will not be easily expelled," Innovindil reminded him, and the drow nodded.

"You were flying south, then, to the eastern gate?" Drizzt asked.

"Not yet," Innovindil replied. "I have been scouting the lands. When I go before the assembly at Mithral Hall, I wish to give a complete accounting of Obould's movements here."

"And what you have seen is not promising."

"Obould will not be easily expelled," the elf said again.

"I have seen as much," said Drizzt. "Gerti Orelsdottr informed me that King Obould has sent a large contingent of orcs northeast along the Spine of the World to begin construction of a vast orc city that he will name Dark Arrow Keep."

"Gerti Orelsdottr?" Innovindil's jaw drooped open with disbelief as she spoke the name.

Drizzt grinned at her. "I told you I had a tale to tell."

The two moved to a quiet and sheltered spot and Drizzt did just that, detailing his good fortune in escaping the underground river and the surprising decisions of Gerti Orelsdottr.

"Guenhwyvar saved your life," Innovindil concluded, and Drizzt didn't disagree.

"And the frost giants showed surprising foresight," he added.

"This is good news for all the land," said Innovindil. "If the frost giants are abandoning Obould's cause, then he is far weaker."

Drizzt wasn't so certain of that estimation, given the level of construction on defensive fortifications he had witnessed in flying over the region. And he wasn't even certain that Gerti was truly abandoning Obould's cause. Abandoning Obould, yes, but the greater cause?

"Surely my people, the dwarves, and the humans will fare better against orcs alone than against orc ranks bolstered by frost giants," Innovindil said to the drow's doubting expression.

"True enough," Drizzt had to admit. "And perhaps this is but the beginning of the greater erosion of the invading army that we all believe will occur. Orc tribes, too, have rarely remained loyal to a single leader. Perhaps their nature will reveal itself in the form of battles across the mountaintops, orc fortress against orc fortress."

"We should increase the pressure on the pig-faced creatures," Innovindil said, a sly grin creasing her face. "Now is the time to remind them that perhaps they were not wise in choosing to follow the ill-fated excursion of Obould Many-Arrows."

Drizzt's lavender eyes sparkled. "There is no reason that we have to do all of our scouting from high above. We should come down, now and again, and test the mettle of our enemies."

"And perhaps weaken that resolve?" Innovindil asked, her grin widening.

Drizzt rubbed his fingers together. Fresh from his defeat at the hands of Obould, he was quite anxious to get back into battle.

Before the sun set that very same day, a pair of winged horses bore their riders above a small encampment of orc soldiers. They came down powerfully, side by side, and both drow and moon elf rolled off the back of their respective mounts, hit the ground running and in balance and followed the thundering steeds right through the heart of the camp, scattering orcs as they went.

Both Drizzt and Innovindil managed a few strikes in that initial confusion, but neither slowed long enough to focus on any particular enemy. By the time Sunset and Sunrise had gone out the other side of the small camp, the two elves were joined, forearm to forearm, blades working in perfect and deadly harmony.

They didn't kill all twenty-three orcs in that particular camp, though so confused and terrified were the brutes at the onset of battle, more intent in getting out of the way than in offering any defense, that the devastating pair likely could have. The fight was as much about sending a message to their enemies as it was to kill orcs. Through all the wild moments of fighting, Sunset and Sunrise played their role to perfection, swooping in and kicking at orc heads, and at one point, crashing down atop a cluster of orcs that seemed to be forming a coherent defensive posture.

Soon enough, Drizzt and Innovindil were on their mounts again and thundering away, not taking wing for twilight was upon them, but running off across the stony, snowy ground.

Their message had been delivered.

The orc stared down the end of its bloody blade, to its latest victim squirming on the ground. Three swipes had brought it down, had taken its arm, and had left long, deep gashes running nearly the length of the dying orc's torso. So much blood soaked the fallen orc's leather tunic that anyone viewing the creature would be certain that it had been cut more than three times.

That was the beauty of Khazid'hea, though, for the wicked sword did not snag on leather ties or bone, or even thin metal clasps. Cutter was its nickname, and the name the sentient sword was using when communicating with its current wielder. And Cutter was a name that newest wielder understood to be quite apropos.

Several orcs had challenged the sword-wielder for the blade. All of them, even a pair who attacked the sword-wielder together, and another orc thought to be the best fighter in the region, lay dead.

Is there anything that we cannot accomplish? the sword asked the orc, and the creature responded with a toothy smile. *Is there any foe we cannot defeat?*

In truth, Khazid'hea thought the orc a rather pitiful specimen, and the sword knew that almost all of the orcs it had killed in its hands might have won their battle had the sword-wielder been holding a lesser weapon. At one point against the most formidable of the foes, Khazid'hea, who was telepathically directing its wielder through the combat, had considered turning the orc the wrong way so that its opponent would win and claim the sword.

But for the moment, Khazid'hea didn't want to take those risks. It had an orc that was capable in combat, though minimally so, but was a wielder Khazid'hea could easily dominate. Through that orc, the sentient sword intended to find a truly worthy companion, and until one presented itself, the orc would suffice.

The sword imagined itself in the hands of mighty Obould Many-Arrows.

With that pleasant thought in mind, Khazid'hea contented itself with its current wielder.

The last fight, this last dead orc, marked the end of any immediate prospective challengers, for all the other orcs working at the defensive fortification had made it quite clear that they wanted nothing to do with the sword-wielder and his new and deadly toy. With that, Khazid'hea went back into its sheath, its work done but its hunger far from sated.

That hunger could never be sated. That hunger had made the sword reach out to Delly Curtie so that it could be free of Catti-brie, a once-capable wielder who would not see battle again anytime soon, though a war waged outside her door. That hunger had made Khazid'hea force Delly into the wild North, for the region beyond the great river was mired in peace.

Khazid'hea hated peace.

And so the sword became quite agitated over the next few days, when no orcs stepped forth to challenge the sword's current wielder. Khazid'hea thus began to execute its plan, whispering in the thoughts of the orc, teasing it with promises of supplanting Obould.

Is there anything we cannot do? the sword kept asking.

But Khazid'hea felt a wall of surprisingly stubborn resistance every time it hinted about Obould. The orc, all the orcs, thought of their leader in terms beyond the norm. It took some time for Khazid'hea to truly appreciate that in compelling the orc to supplant Obould, it was asking the orc to assume the mantle of a god. When that reality sank in, the sentient sword backed away its demands, biding its time, hoping to learn more of the orc army's structure so that it could choose an alternative target.

In those days of mundane labor and boring peace, Khazid'hea heard the whisper of a name it knew well.

"They're saying that the drow elf is Drizzt Do'Urden, friend of King Bruenor," another orc told a group that including the sword's current wielder.

The sentient sword soaked it all in. Apparently, Drizzt and a companion were striking at orc camps in the region, and many had died.

As soon as the sword-wielder left that discussion, Khazid'hea entered its mind.

How great will you be if you bring Drizzt Do'Urden's head to King Obould? the devilish sword asked, and it accompanied the question with a series of images of glory and accolades, of a hacked drow elf lying dead at the orc champion's feet. Of shamans dancing and throwing their praise, and orc females swooning at the mere sight of the conquering champion.

We can kill him, the sword promised when it sensed doubt. *You and I together can defeat Drizzt Do'Urden. I know him well, and know his failings.*

That night, the sword-wielder began to ask more pointed questions of the orc who had relayed the rumors of the murderous dark elf. Where had the attacks occurred? Were they certain that the drow had been involved?

The next day, Khazid'hea in its hand and in its thoughts, the sword-wielder slipped away from its companions and started off across the stony ground, seeking its victim and its glory.

But for Khazid'hea, the search was for a new and very worthy wielder.

27

GROUSING

The audience chamber of Mithral Hall was emptier than it had been in many months, but there could not have been more weight in the room. Four players sat around a circular table, equidistant to each other and all on the diagonal of the room, so that no one would be closer to the raised dais and the symbolic throne.

When the doors banged closed, the last of the escorts departing, King Bruenor spent a moment scrutinizing his peers—or at least, the two he considered to be his peers, and the third, seated directly across from him, whom he realized he had to tolerate. To his left sat the other dwarf, King Emerus Warcrown, his face scrunched in a scowl, his beard neatly trimmed and groomed, but showing a bit more gray, by all accounts. How could Bruenor blame him for that, since Emerus had lost nearly as many dwarves as had Clan Battlehammer, and in an even more sudden and devastating manner?

To Bruenor's right sat another ally, and one he respected greatly. Lady Alustriel of Silverymoon had been a friend to Bruenor and to Mithral Hall for many years. When the dark elves invaded the dwarves' homeland Alustriel had stood strong beside Bruenor and his kin, and at great loss to the people of her city. Many of Alustriel's warriors had died fighting the drow in Keeper's Dale. Alustriel seemed as regal and beautiful as ever. She was dressed in a

 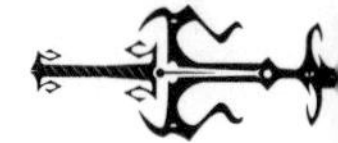

long gown of rich, deep green, and a silver circlet accentuated her sculpted features and her silvery hair. By all measures, the woman was beautiful, but there was something more about her, a strength and gravity. How many foolish men had underestimated Alustriel, Bruenor wondered, thinking her pretty face the extent of her powers?

Across from the dwarf sat Galen Firth of Nesmé. Dirty and disheveled, carrying several recent scars and scabs, the man had just come from a battlefield, obviously, and had repeatedly expressed his desire to get right back to the fighting. Bruenor could respect that, certainly, but still the dwarf had a hard time in offering too much respect to that man. Bruenor still hadn't forgotten the treatment he and his friends had found in Nesmé, nor the negative reaction of Nesmé to Settlestone, a community of Wulfgar's folk that Bruenor had sponsored.

There was Galen, though, sitting in Mithral Hall as a representative of the town, and brought in by Alustriel as, so she said, a peer.

"Be it known and agreed that I speak not only for Silverymoon, but for Everlund and Sundabar, as well?" Alustriel asked.

"Aye," the other three all answered without debate, for Alustriel had informed them from the beginning that she had been asked to serve as proxy for the other two important cities, and none would doubt the honorable lady's word.

"Then we are all represented," Galen Firth remarked.

"Not all," said Emerus Warcrown, his voice as deep as a boulder's rumble within a mountain cave. "Harbromm's got no voice here."

"Two other dwarves sit at the table," Galen Firth argued. "Two humans for four human kingdoms, but two dwarves do not suffice for only three dwarven mines?"

Bruenor snorted. "Alustriel's getting three votes, and rightly so, since them other two asked her to do their voting here. Why yerself's even getting a voice is something I'm still wondering."

Galen narrowed his eyes, and Bruenor snorted again.

"Not I nor King Bruenor would deign to speak for King Harbromm of Citadel Adbar," Emerus Warcrown added. "King Harbromm has been advised of the situation, and will make his decisions known in time."

"Now is the time to speak!" Galen Firth replied. "Nesmé remains under assault. We have driven the trolls and bog blokes from the town and pushed most back into the Trollmoors, but their leader, a great brute named Proffit, has eluded us. While he lives, Nesmé will not be safe."

"Well, I'll be sending ye all me warriors then, and right off," Bruenor answered. "I'll just tell Obould to hold back his tens of thousands until we're properly ready for greeting him."

The sarcasm made Galen Firth narrow his eyes all the more.

"We will settle nothing about our enemies if we cannot come to civil agreement among ourselves," the ever-diplomatic Alustriel put in. "Bury old grievances, King Bruenor and Galen Firth, I beg of you both. Our enemies press us—press your two peoples most of all—and that must be our paramount concern."

Emerus Warcrown leaned back in his thick wooden chair and crossed his burly arms over his barrel-like chest.

Bruenor regarded his counterpart, and offered an appreciate wink. Emerus was dwarf first, Bruenor understood clearly. The hierarchy of his loyalty placed Bruenor and Harbromm, and their respective clans, at the top of Emerus's concerns.

As it should be.

"All right then, them grievances are buried," Bruenor answered Alustriel. "And know that I lost more than a few good Battlehammers in helping Galen Firth there and his troubled town. And not a thing have we asked in kind."

Galen started to say something, again in that petulant and negative tone of his, but Alustriel interrupted with a sudden and harsh, "Enough!" aimed directly at him.

"We understand the plight of Nesmé," Alustriel went on. "Are not the Knights in Silver doing battle there even now, securing the region so that the tradesmen can rebuild the houses and strengthen the wall? Are not my wizards patrolling those walls, the words of the fireball ready at their lips?"

" 'Tis true, my good lady," Galen admitted, and he settled back in his chair.

"The trolls are on the run, and will be put back in the Trollmoors," Alustriel promised all three of them. "Silverymoon and Everlund will help Nesmé see to this need."

"Good enough, and what's yer timetable?" asked Bruenor. "Will ye have them back afore winter settles in too deep?"

The question seemed all the more urgent since the first snows had begun to accumulate that very day outside of Mithral Hall's eastern door.

"That is our hope, so that the people of Nesmé can return to their homes before the trails grow deep with snow," Alustriel answered.

"And so that yer armies will be ready to fight beside me own when the winter lets go of the land?" Bruenor asked.

Alustriel's face grew very tight. "If King Obould presses his attack on Mithral Hall, he will find Clan Battlehammer bolstered by the forces of Silverymoon, Everlund, and Sundabar, yes."

Bruenor let a long and uncomfortable moment of silence pass before pressing the point: "And if King Obould decides that his advance is done?"

"We have spoken of this before," Alustriel reminded him.

"Speak of it again," Bruenor demanded.

"By the time winter passes, Obould's army will be powerfully entrenched," said Alustriel. "That army was formidable enough when it was marching against defended positions. Your own people know that better than any."

"Bah, but ye're giving up!" King Emerus interrupted. "Ye're all thinking to leave the orc to his gains!"

"The cost in dislodging him will be terrible," Alustriel explained, not disagreeing. "Perhaps too great a price."

"Bah!" Emerus growled. He slammed a fist onto the heavy wooden table—and it was fortunate that the table was built so sturdily, else Emerus's smash would have splintered it to kindling. "Ye're going to fight for Nesmé, but Mithral Hall's not worthy of yer sacrifice?"

"You know me better than to say that, King Emerus."

Alustriel's statement did calm the dwarf, who was far more on his edge than normal after the catastrophe at the river. Earlier that same day, King Emerus had presided over the consecration of the River Surbrin, saying farewell to nearly a thousand good dwarves.

He fell back in his seat, crossed his burly arms again, and gave a great, "Harrumph."

"King Bruenor . . . Bruenor, my friend, you must understand our thinking in this," Alustriel said. "Our desire from Silverymoon to Everlund to Sundabar to rid the land of Obould and his thousands is no less than your own. But I have flown over the occupied lands. I have seen the swarms and their preparations. To go against them would invite disaster on a scale heretofore unknown in the Silver Marches. Mithral Hall is open once more—your path across the Surbrin will be assured. You are now the lone outpost, the last bastion for the goodly folk in all the lands between the Trollmoors and the Spine of the World, the Surbrin and Fell Pass. You are not without friends or support. If Obould comes against you again, he will find the Knights in Silver standing shoulder to shoulder with Clan Battlehammer."

"Waist to shoulder, perhaps," Galen Firth quipped, but the scowls of the two dwarves showed him clearly that his feeble attempt at humor was not appreciated, and Alustriel went on without interruption.

"This piece of ground between your eastern door and the Surbrin will not fall, if all of it is to be covered in layers of the dead from the three cities I represent at this meeting," she said. "We are all agreed on this. Winter's Edge will be expanded as a military encampment, and supplies and soldiers will flow through Silverymoon to that town unabated. We will relieve King Emerus's dwarves here, so that they can return to their work in securing the Underdark route between Felbarr and Mithral Hall. We will offer great wagons and drivers to King Harbromm, so that Citadel Adbar can easily enter the conflicted region as they see fit. We will spare no expense."

"But you will spare yer warriors," Bruenor remarked.

"We will not throw thousands against defended mountains for the sake of nearly barren ground," Alustriel bluntly answered.

Bruenor, wearing the same expression and seated in the same posture as his dwarf counterpart, offered a grim nod in response. He wasn't thrilled with Alustriel's decision; he wanted nothing more than to sweep ugly Obould back to his mountain hole. But Bruenor's people had done battle with the orc king and his legions, and so Bruenor surely understood the reasoning.

"Strengthen Winter's Edge, then," he said. "Work your soldiers in concert. Drill them and practice them. I wish that the Moonwood had chosen to attend this meeting. Hralien, who speaks for them, has promised his support, but from afar. Surely they fear that Obould is as likely to turn against their forest as against Mithral Hall, since they chose to enter the fray. I expect the same loyalty to them, from all o' ye, as ye're offering to Mithral Hall."

"Of course," said Alustriel.

"They saved me a thousand dwarves," Emerus agreed.

Galen Firth sat quietly, but not still, Bruenor noted, the man obviously growing agitated that the discussion had so shifted from the fate of his beloved Nesmé.

"Ye go get yer town put back together," Bruenor said to him. "Ye make it stronger than ever before—I'll be sending caravans full o' the best weapons me smithies can forge. Ye keep them damned trolls in their smelly moor and off o' me back."

The man visibly relaxed, even uncrossing his arms and coming forward as he replied, "Nesmé will not forget the aid that Mithral Hall offered, though Mithral Hall was terribly pressed at the time."

Bruenor responded with a nod, and noted out of the corner of his eye that Alustriel was smiling with approval for his generous offering and words. The King of Mithral Hall wasn't thrilled with the decisions made that day, but he well understood that they all had to stand together.

For if they chose to stand alone, they would fall, one by one, to the swarms of Obould.

"You don't know that," Catti-brie said, trying to be comforting.

"Delly is gone, Colson is gone, and Khazid'hea is gone," Wulfgar replied, and he seemed as if he could hardly stand up while uttering those dreaded words.

He and Catti-brie had sent the news throughout Mithral Hall that Khazid'hea was missing, and had made it quite clear that the sword was not to be handled casually, that it was a weapon of great and dangerous power.

It was obvious that someone had taken it, and few dwarves would be put under the spell of any sentient weapon. That left Delly, or one of the other human refugees who had set out across the river.

It had to be Delly, Catti-brie silently agreed. She had come to Catti-brie's room before, the woman knew. Half-asleep, she had once or twice seen Delly staring at her from the doorway, though out of concern or jealousy, she did not know. Was it possible that Delly had come in to speak with her and had been intercepted by the machinations of a bored and hungry Khazid'hea?

For where had Delly gone? How dare she leave Mithral Hall with Colson, and without ever speaking to Wulfgar?

The mystery had Wulfgar on the very edge of outrage. The man, battered as he had been, should have been resting, but he hadn't gone to his bed in more than a day, ever since the troubling report of Ivan and Pikel Bouldershoulder chasing after a lone figure running off to the north. The dwarves were betting it to be Cottie Cooperson, who was quite out of her mind with grief, but both Catti-brie and Wulfgar held a nagging feeling that someone else might be out of her mind, or at least that someone might have inadvertently let a malignant spirit into her mind.

"Or is it that we have been infiltrated by stealthy allies of Obould?" Wulfgar asked. "Have spies come into Mithral Hall? Have they stolen your sword, and my wife and child?"

"We will sort through all of this," Catti-brie assured him. "We will find Delly's trail soon enough. The storms have lessened and the ferry will soon be running again. Or Alustriel and King Emerus will aid us in our search. When they come out from their meeting with Bruenor, bid them to find the refugees who went across the river. There we will find answers, I'm sure."

Wulfgar's expression showed that perhaps he was afraid of finding those answers.

But there was nothing else to be done. Dozens of dwarves were searching the halls, for the sword, the woman, and the toddler. Cordio and some of his fellow priests were even using divining spells to try to help the search.

So far, there were only questions.

Wulfgar slumped against the wall.

"Obould will be dead in three days," Stormsinger the giant growled. "That was your promise, Princess Gerti, yet Obould is alive and more powerful than ever, and our prizes—pegasus, dark elf, and that magical panther he carries—have flown from our grasp."

"We are better off having Drizzt Do'Urden working toward the same goal as we," Gerti argued, and she had to raise her voice to lift it above the

tumult of protest that was rising all around her. Once again the weight of events pressed down on the giantess. It had all seemed so simple just a few tendays past: She would lend a few giants here and a few giants there to throw boulders from afar at settlements the orcs had surrounded, softening up the defenses so that Obould could overrun the towns. She would gain spoils of war for the cost of a few rocks.

So she had thought. The explosion at the ridge, where twenty of her giants had been immolated, had irrevocably changed all of that. The assault into Mithral Hall, where several more had fallen to tricks and traps, had irrevocably changed all of that. The ceremony of Gruumsh, where Obould had seemingly taken on godlike proportions, had irrevocably changed all of that.

Gerti was left just trying to bail out of it all, to let Obould and the dwarves battle it out to the last and leave herself and her kin playing on both sides of the equation so that, whoever proved victorious, the battle would not come to Shining White.

The grumbling around her showed her clearly that her kin weren't holding much faith in her or her curious choices.

If only Drizzt Do'Urden had slaughtered the wretched Obould!

"Drizzt is a formidable opponent," Gerti said, following that notion. "He will find a way to strike hard at Obould."

"And at Shining White?"

Gerti narrowed her eyes and scowled at the petulant Stormsinger. Clearly the large warrior was positioning himself as an alternative to her when the great Jarl Orel finally let go of life. And just as clearly, many of the other giants were beginning to look favorably on that positioning.

"Drizzt will not, by his word, and he will dissuade others from coming against us, should Bruenor defeat Obould."

"It is all a waste," Stormsinger groused. "We have lost friends, all of us, and for what gain? Have we more slaves to serve our needs? Have we more wealth than we knew before we followed King Obould of the orcs? Have we more territory, rich mines or wondrous cities? Have we even a single winged horse, one handed over to us and now handed away?"

"We have . . ." Gerti started to say, but a chorus of complaining rose up in the room. "We have . . ." she said more loudly, and repeated it over and over until at last the din lessened. "We have gained position," she explained. "We could not have avoided this war. If we had not joined with Obould initially, then we would likely find him as an enemy soon enough, if not already. Now that will not happen, for he is indebted to us. And now King Bruenor and all of his allies are indebted to us, despite our waging war on them, because of Drizzt Do'Urden. We have gained position, and in a time as conflicted and confusing as this, that is no small thing!"

She spoke her words with conviction and with the weight of her royal position behind her, and the room did quiet.

But they would stir again, Gerti feared, and Stormsinger, though he did not respond at that time, would not let the matter drop there.

Far from it.

28

THE WAVE OF EMOTION

"Well, that's that, then," Ivan Bouldershoulder said.

He and his brother stood over the woman's body. She was lying on her belly, but with one arm reaching up above her and shoulders turned so that they could clearly see her face.

A couple of inches of snow had gathered around the still form. Pikel bent over and gently brushed some from Delly's cold face, and he tried unsuccessfully to close her eyes.

"Poor Wulfgar," said Ivan.

"Oooo," Pikel agreed.

"But I'm not for seeing her little one anywhere near," said Ivan. "Ye think them damned orcs might've taken the kid?"

Pikel shrugged.

Both dwarves scanned the area. It had been a small camp, obviously, for the remnants of a campfire could be seen in the snow, and a collection of branches that had likely served as a lean-to. Delly's body hadn't been there long—no more than a couple of days, Pikel confirmed for his brother.

Ivan moved around the area, kicking at the snow and poking about every rock or log for some sign of Colson. After many minutes, he finally turned back to his brother, who was standing on the highest ground not so far away, his back to Ivan and looking up at the sky, shielding his eyes with one hand.

"Well, that's that, then," Ivan said again. "Delly Curtie's lost to us, and the little kid's not anywhere to be found. Let's get her wrapped up and take her back to Mithral Hall so Wulfgar can properly say farewell."

Pikel didn't turn around, but began hopping up and down excitedly.

"Come on, then," Ivan called to him, but the green-bearded Pikel only grew more agitated.

"Well, what're ye seein?" Ivan asked, finally catching on. He walked toward his brother. "Sign o' where them stupid orcs might've gone? Are ye thinking that we should go and see if the little kid's a prisoner?"

"Oo oi!" Pikel shouted, hopping anxiously then and pointing off to the north.

"What?" Ivan demanded, and he broke into a trot, coming up beside Pikel.

"Drizzit Dudden!" Pikel squealed.

"What?"

"Drizzit Dudden! Drizzit Dudden!" Pikel shouted, hopping even higher and jabbing his stubby finger out toward the north sky. Ivan squinted, shielded his eyes from the glare, and saw a large flying form. After a few moments, he made it out as a flying horse.

"Pegasus," he muttered. "Might be them elfs from the Moonwood."

"Drizzit Dudden!" Pikel corrected, and Ivan looked at him curiously. He guessed that Pikel was once again using those magical abilities that could grant him attributes of various animals. Ivan had seen Pikel imbue himself with the eyes of an eagle before, eyes that could pick out a field mouse running across a meadow from hundreds of yards away.

"Ye got them bird eyes on, don't ye?" Ivan asked.

"Hee hee hee."

"And ye're telling me that's Drizzt up on that flying horse?"

"Drizzit Dudden!" Pikel confirmed.

Ivan looked back at the far distant pegasus, and shook his hairy head. He glanced back at Delly Curtie. If they left her there, the next snow would bury her, perhaps until the spring thaw.

"Nah, we got to find Drizzt," Ivan said after a moment of weighing the options. "Poor Delly and poor Wulfgar, but many've been left out for the birds since Obould come charging down. Stupid orc."

"Stupit orc," Pikel echoed.

"Drizzt?" Ivan asked.

"Drizzit Dudden," his green-bearded brother answered.

"Well, lead on, ye durned fool doo-dad! If we find them orcs and them orcs got Wulfgar's little one, then who better'n Drizzt Do'Urden to take the kid away from them?"

"Hee hee hee."

The sentient sword had worked its way through five wielders since Delly Curtie. Using its insidious telepathic magic, Khazid'hea invaded the thoughts of each successive owner, prying from it the identity of the nearest orc it feared the most. After that, with a more worthy wielder identified, Khazid'hea had little trouble in instigating a fight among the volatile creatures, and in shaping that fight so that the more worthy warrior proved victorious.

Then news had come that the dark elf friend of Bruenor Battlehammer was working in the area once more, slaughtering orcs, and Khazid'hea found its most lofty goal within apparent reach. Ever since the companions had come to possess the sword, Khazid'hea had longed to be wielded by Drizzt Do'Urden. Catti-brie was worthy enough, but Drizzt, the sword knew, was a warrior quite different. In Drizzt's hands, Khazid'hea would find the promise of victory after victory, and would not be hidden away in a scabbard while the drow warrior fired from afar with a bow.

A bow was a cowardly weapon, to Khazid'hea's thinking.

How great will your glory be, how wonderful the riches, when you bring King Obould the head of Drizzt Do'Urden, the sword told its current wielder, a slender and smallish orc who relied on finesse and speed instead of brute strength, as was usually so with his brutish race.

"The drow is death," the orc said aloud, drawing curious stares from some nearby orcs.

Not when I am in your hands, Khazid'hea promised. *I know this one. I know his movements and his technique. I know how to defeat him.*

Even as the orc started away, heading northwest toward the last reported encounter with the drow and his elf companion, Khazid'hea began to wonder the wisdom of his course. For the ease with which the sentient sword had convinced the orc, had convinced every orc that had picked it up, was no small thing. Drizzt Do'Urden was not a weak-willed orc, Khazid'hea knew. The drow would battle against Khazid'hea's intrusions.

Unless those intrusions only reinforced that which Drizzt already had in mind, and from everything Khazid'hea had learned, the drow was on a killing rampage.

It seemed a perfect fit.

Drizzt rolled off the back of Sunrise as the pegasus set down in a fast trot. Landing nimbly, Drizzt ran along right behind the mount as Sunrise charged through the orc encampment, bowling monsters aside.

In the center of the camp, Drizzt broke out from behind, rushing ahead suddenly to cut down one orc still staggering out of the pegasus's path. Two short strokes sent that orc flying to the ground, and the efficiency of the kill allowed Drizzt to reposition his feet immediately, spinning to meet the charge of a second creature. A right-handed, backhanded downward parry lopped the tip off that second orc's thrusting spear, and while he made the block, Drizzt brought his left arm across his chest. The orc overbalanced when it felt only minimal resistance to its thrust, and Drizzt slashed right to left with that cocked blade, tearing out the creature's throat.

A thud behind the drow had him leaping about, but the threat from there was already ended, the creeping orc cut down by a well-placed elven arrow. With a quick salute to Innovindil and Sunset soaring over the camp, Drizzt moved on in search of his next kill.

He spotted a form in the lower boughs of a thick pine and rushed to the trunk. Without slowing, he leaped against it, planting his foot, then pushed off to the side, climbing higher in the air and landing atop one of the lower branches. Three quick springs brought him near to the cowering orc, and a few quick slashes had the humanoid tumbling to the ground.

Drizzt sprang down to the lowest branch again and did a quick survey. He picked a lone orc at the far end of the camp, then a trio closer and to his left. With a grin, he started for the trio, but stopped almost immediately, his gaze

suddenly drawn back to the lone figure approaching from across the way.

His heart went into his throat; he wanted to scream out in denial and rage.

He knew the sword that orc carried.

Drizzt came out of the tree in a wild rush. He held all respect for the devastating weapon set in the orc's grasp, but it didn't matter. He didn't slow and didn't try to measure his opponent. He just rushed in, his scimitars working in a blur of motion, spinning circles over his shoulder, slashing across and stabbing ahead. He cut, he leaped, and he thrust, over and over. Sometimes he heard the ring of metal as he struck the fine blade of Khazid'hea, other times the rush of air cracking over his blades, and other times the softer sound of a blade striking leather or flesh.

He went into a spin around the orc, blades flying wide and level, turning their angle constantly to avoid any feeble parries, though the orc was already past any semblance of defense. The drow stopped in mid-turn and rushed back the other way, right near the orc, blades stabbing, smashing, and slashing. Technique no longer mattered. All that mattered was striking at the orc. All that mattered was cutting that creature who was holding Catti-brie's sword.

Blood flew everywhere, but Drizzt didn't even notice. The orc dropped the blade from its torn arm, but Drizzt didn't even notice. The light went out of the creature's eyes, the strength left it legs, and the only thing holding it upright was the constant barrage of Drizzt's hits.

But Drizzt didn't notice.

The orc finally fell to the dirt and the drow moved over it, smashing away with his deadly blades.

Sunset set down behind him, Innovindil leaping from her seat to rush to his side.

Drizzt didn't even notice.

He slashed and chopped. He hit the orc a dozen times, a score of times, a hundred times, until his sleeves were heavy with orc blood.

"Drizzt!" he finally heard, and from the tone, it registered to him that Innovindil must have been calling him for some time.

He fell to his knees and dropped his bloody blades to the dirt, then grabbed up Khazid'hea, holding it across his open, bloody palms.

"Drizzt?" Innovindil said again, and she crouched beside him.

The drow began to sob.

"What is it?" Innovindil asked, and she gathered him close.

Drizzt stared at Khazid'hea, tears running from his lavender eyes.

"There are other possible explanations," Innovindil said to Drizzt a short while later. They made camp down near the Surbrin, off to the side of a quiet pool that hadn't quite iced over yet so that Drizzt could clean the blood from his hands, his face, his whole body.

Drizzt looked back at her, and at Khazid'hea, lying on a stone on the ground before the elf. Innovindil, too, stared at the sword.

"It was not unexpected," Drizzt said.

"But that didn't lessen the shock."

The drow stared at her for a moment, then looked down. "No," he admitted.

"The orc was paid back in full," Innovindil reminded him. "Catti-brie has been avenged."

"It seems a small comfort."

The elf's smile comforted him somewhat. She started to rise, but stopped and glanced to the side, her expression drawing Drizzt's eyes that way as well, to a small bird sitting on a stone, chattering at them. As they watched, the bird hopped from its perch and fluttered away.

"Curious," said the elf.

"What is it?"

Innovindil looked at him, but did not reply. Her expression remained somewhat confused, though.

Drizzt looked back to the stone, then scanned the sky for any sign of the bird, which was long gone. With a shrug, he went back to his cleaning.

The mystery didn't take long to unfold, for within an hour, as Drizzt and Innovindil brushed Sunrise and Sunset, they heard a curious voice.

"Drizzit Dudden, hee hee hee."

The two turned to see Ivan and Pikel Bouldershoulder coming into view, and they both knew at once that the bird had been one of Pikel's spies.

"Well, ain't yerself the fine sight for a tired dwarf's eyes," Ivan greeted, smiling wide as he moved into the camp.

"Well met, yourself," Drizzt replied, stepping forward to clasp the dwarf's offered hand. "And *curiously* met!"

"Are you not far from the dwarven lines?" Innovindil asked, coming over to similarly greet the brothers. "Or are you, like we two, trapped outside of Mithral Hall?"

"Bah, just come from there," said Ivan. "Ain't no one trapped here—Bruenor busted out to the east and we're holding the ground to the Surbrin."

"Bruenor?" Innovindil asked before Drizzt could.

"Red-bearded dwarf, grumbles a lot?" said Ivan.

"Bruenor fell at Shallows," Drizzt said. "I saw it myself."

"Yeah, he fell, but he bounced," said Ivan. "Priests prayed over him for days and days, but it was Regis that finally woke him up."

"Regis?" Drizzt gasped, and he found it hard to breathe.

"Little one?" Ivan said. "Some call him Rumblebelly."

"Hee hee hee," said Pikel.

"What're ye gone daft, Drizzt?" asked Ivan. "I'm thinking ye're knowing Bruenor and Regis."

Drizzt looked at Innovindil. "This cannot be."

The elf wore a wide smile.

"Ye thought 'em dead, didn't ye?" Ivan asked. "Bah, but where's yer faith then? Nothing dead about them two, I tell ye! Just left them a few days ago." Ivan's face grew suddenly more somber. "But I got some bad news for ye, elf." He looked to the sword and Drizzt's heart sank once more.

"Wulfgar's girl, she took that blade and come out on her own," Ivan explained. "Me and me brother—"

"Me brudder!" Pikel proudly interrupted.

"Me and me brother come out after her, but we found her too late."

"Catti-brie—" Drizzt gasped.

"Nah, not her. *Wulfgar's* girl. Delly. We found her dead a couple o' days back. Then we spotted yerself flying about on that durned winged horse and so we came to find ye. Bruenor and Regis, Catti-brie and Wulfgar been worrying about ye terribly, ye got to know."

Drizzt stood there transfixed as the weight of the words washed over him.

"Wulfgar and Catti-brie, too?" he asked in a whisper.

Innovindil rushed up beside him and hugged him, and he truly needed the support.

"Ye been out here thinking yer friends all dead?" Ivan asked.

"Shallows was overrun," Drizzt said.

"Well, course it was, but me brother—"

"Me brudder!" Pikel cried on cue.

Ivan snickered. "Me brother there built us a statue to fool them orcs, and with Thibbledorf Pwent beside us, we give them the what's-for! We got 'em all out o' Shallows and run back to Mithral Hall. Been killing orcs ever since. Hunnerds o' the dogs."

"We saw the battlefield north of Keeper's Dale," Innovindil remarked. "And the blasted ridgeline."

"Boom!" cried Pikel.

Drizzt stood there shaking his head, overwhelmed by it all. Could it be true? Could his friends be alive? Bruenor, Wulfgar, and Regis? And Catti-brie? Could it be true? He looked to his partner, to find Innovindil smiling warmly back at him.

"I know not what to say," he admitted.

"Just be happy," she said. "For I am happy for you."

Drizzt crushed her in a hug.

"And they'll be happy to see ye, don't ye doubt," Ivan said to Drizzt. "But there's a few tears to be shed for poor Delly. I don't know what possessed the girl to run off like that."

The words hit Drizzt hard, and he jumped back from Innovindil and turned an angry glower over the sentient sword.

"I do," he said and he cursed Khazid'hea under his breath.

"The sword can dominate its wielder?" Innovindil asked.

Drizzt walked over and grabbed the blade, lifting it before his eyes. He sent his questions telepathically to Khazid'hea, feeling the life there and demanding answers.

But then something else occurred to him.

"Get yer flying horses tacked up then," said Ivan. "The sooner we get ye back to Mithral Hall, the better for everyone. Yer friends are missing ye sorely, Drizzt Do'Urden, and I'm thinking that ye're missing them just as much."

The drow wasn't about to argue that, but as he stood there holding the magnificent sword, the sword that cut through just about anything, his thoughts began cascading down a different avenue.

"I can defeat him," he said.

"What's that?" asked Ivan.

"What do you mean?" Innovindil asked.

Drizzt turned to them and said, "I outfought Obould."

"Ye fought him?" an incredulous Ivan spouted.

"I fought him, not so long ago, on a hillock not so far from here," Drizzt explained. "I fought him and I scored hit after hit, but my blades could not penetrate his armor." He brought Khazid'hea up and sent it slashing across in a powerful stroke. "Do you know the well-earned nickname of this blade?" he asked.

"Cutter," he answered when the other three just stared at him. "With this sword, I can defeat Obould."

"It is a fight for another day," Innovindil said to him. "After you are reunited with those who love you and fear you are lost to them."

Drizzt shook his head. "Obould is moving now, hilltop to hilltop. He is confident and so his entourage is small. I can get to him, and with this blade, I can defeat him."

"Your friends deserve to see you, and your friendship demands you attend to that," said Innovindil.

"My service to Bruenor is a service to all the land," Drizzt replied. "The folk of the North deserve to be free of the hold of Obould. I am given that chance now. To avenge Shallows and all the other towns, to avenge the dwarves who fell before the invaders. To avenge Tarathiel—we'll not get this chance again, perhaps."

The mention of Tarathiel seemed to take all the argument out of the elf.

"Ye're going after him now?" Ivan asked.

"I cannot think of a better time."

Ivan considered things for a bit, then began to nod.

"Hee hee hee," Pikel agreed.

"Ye hit the dog for meself, too," Ivan remarked, and his smile erupted with sudden inspiration. He pulled out his hand crossbow, of near-perfect drow design, and tossed it to Drizzt, then pulled the bandolier of explosive darts from over his shoulder and handed them to the drow.

"Pop a couple o' these into the beast and watch him hop!" Ivan declared.

"Hee hee hee."

"Me and me brother . . ." Ivan started to say, then he paused and looked at Pikel, expecting an interruption. Pikel stared back at him in confusion.

Ivan sighed. "Me and me brother—" he started again.

"Me brudder!"

"Yeah, us two'll get back to Mithral Hall and tell yer friends that ye're out here," Ivan offered. "We'll be expecting ye soon enough."

Drizzt turned to his elf friend. "Go with them," he bade her. "Watch over them from above and make sure they arrive safely."

"I am to allow you to go off alone after King Obould?"

Drizzt held up the vicious sword, and the bandolier and crossbow.

"I can defeat him," he promised.

"If you can even get him alone," Innovindil argued. "I can aid in that."

Drizzt shook his head. "I will find him and watch him from afar," he promised. "I will find an opportunity and I will seize it. Obould will fall to this sword in my hand."

"Bah, it's not a job for yerself alone," Ivan argued.

"With Sunrise, I can move swiftly. He'll not catch me unless I choose to be caught. In that event, King Obould will die."

The drow's tone was perfectly even and balanced.

"I will not stay at Mithral Hall," said Innovindil. "I will see the dwarves there, and I will come right back out for you."

"And I will be waiting," Drizzt promised. "Obould's head in hand."

It seemed as if there was nothing more to say, but of course Pikel added, "Hee hee hee."

29

A DEEP BREATH

"I will grow weary of this travel soon enough," Tos'un Armgo said to his drow companion.

They had been on the move for days and days, finally catching up to Obould many miles north of where they had expected to find him, the western door of Mithral Hall. There too, the fight had not gone well, apparently, and the orc king seemed in little mood for any discussion of it. It was fast becoming apparent that the travels had just begun for the two drow if they meant to remain with Obould. The orc king would not set stakes anywhere, it seemed, even in the increasingly inclement weather.

One bright morning, Tos'un and Kaer'lic awaited his arrival on some flat stones outside of the foundation of a small keep atop a steep-sided hill, their first real chance to speak with Obould since their return. Obould would entertain guests only at the pleasure of Obould. All around the two drow, orcs were hard at work clear-cutting the few trees that grew among the gray stone and dirt of the hillsides, and clearing any boulder tumbles that could offer cover to an approaching enemy.

"He is building his kingdom," Kaer'lic remarked. "He has been hinting at this for so long now, and none of us bothered to listen."

"A few castles hardly make a kingdom," said Tos'un. "Particularly when we are speaking of orcs, who will soon turn their garrisons upon one another."

"You would enjoy that, no doubt," a gruff voice responded.

The two dark elves turned to see the approach of Obould, and that annoying shaman Tsinka. Kaer'lic noted that the female did not seem at all pleased.

"A prediction based upon past behavior," Tos'un said, and he offered a bow. "No insult meant to you, of course."

Obould scowled at him. "Behavior before the coming of Obould-who-is-Gruumsh," he replied. "You continue to lack the vision of my kingdom, drow, to your own detriment."

Kaer'lic found herself taking a slight step back from the imposing and unpredictable orc.

"I had figured that you two had followed your two kin to the side of your Spider Queen," the orc said, and it took a moment for the words to register.

"Donnia and Ad'non?" Kaer'lic asked.

"Slain by yet another drow elf," Obould replied, and if he was bothered in the least by that news, he did not show it.

Kaer'lic looked at Tos'un, and the two just accepted the loss with a shrug.

"I believe that one of the shamans collected Ad'non's head as a trophy," Obould said callously. "I can retrieve it for you, if you would like."

The insincerity of his offer stung Kaer'lic more than she would have expected, but she did well to keep her anger out of her face as she regarded the orc king.

"You kept your army together through a defeat at Mithral Hall," she said, thinking it better to let the other line of conversation fall away. "That is a good sign."

"Defeat?" Tsinka Shinriil shrieked. "What do you know of it?"

"I know that you are not inside Mithral Hall."

"The price was not worth the gain," Obould explained. "We fought them to a standstill in the outer halls. We could have pressed in, but it became apparent to us that our allies had not arrived." He narrowed his eyes, glared at Kaer'lic, and added, "As we had planned."

"The unpredictability and unreliability of trolls. . . ." the drow priestess said with a shrug.

Obould continued to glower, and Kaer'lic knew that he at least suspected that she and Tos'un had played a role in keeping Proffit's trolls from joining in the fight.

"We warned Proffit that his delays could pose problems in the north," Tos'un added. "But he and his wretched trolls smelled human blood, the blood of Nesmians, their hated enemies for so many years. He would not be persuaded to march north to Mithral Hall."

Obould hardly looked convinced.

"And Silverymoon marched upon them," Kaer'lic said, needing to divert attention. "You can expect nothing more from Proffit and his band. Those few who survive."

A low growl issued from between Obould's fangs.

"You knew that Lady Alustriel would come forth," Kaer'lic said. "Take heart that many of her prized warriors now lay dead on those southern bogs. She will not gladly turn her eyes to the north."

"Let her come," Obould growled. "We are preparing, on every mountain and in every pass. Let Silverymoon march forth to the Kingdom of Dark Arrows. Here, they will find only death."

"The Kingdom of Dark Arrows?" Tos'un silently mouthed.

Kaer'lic continued to scrutinize not only Obould, but Tsinka, and she noted that the shaman grimaced at the mention of the supposed kingdom.

A divisive opening, perhaps?

"Proffit is defeated, then," the orc king said. "Is he dead?"

"We know not," Kaer'lic admitted. "In the confusion of the battle, we departed, for it was obvious that the trolls would be forced back into the Trollmoors, and there, I did not wish to go."

"Wish to go?" Obould said. "Did I not instruct you to remain with Proffit?"

"There, I would not go," said Kaer'lic. "Not with Proffit, and not for Obould."

Her brazen attitude brought another fierce scowl, but the orc king made no movement toward her.

"You have accomplished much, King Obould," Kaer'lic offered. "More than I believed possible in so short a time. In honor of your great victories, I have brought you a gift." She nodded to Tos'un as she ended, and the male drow leaped away, skipping down the hillside to the one remaining boulder tumble. He disappeared from sight, then came back out a moment later, pulling along a battered dwarf.

"Our gift to you," said Kaer'lic.

Obould tried to look surprised, but Kaer'lic saw through the facade. He had spies and lookouts everywhere, and had known of the dwarf before he had ever come out to meet the dark elves.

"Flay his skin and eat him," Tsinka said, her eyes suddenly wild and hungry. "I will prepare the spit!"

"You will shut your mouth," Obould corrected. "He is of Clan Battlehammer?"

"He is," the drow priestess answered.

Obould nodded his approval, then turned to Tsinka and said, "Secure him in the supply wagon. We will keep him close. And do not injure him, on pain of death!"

That elicited a most profound scowl from the shaman, a look Kaer'lic did not miss.

"He will prove valuable to us, perhaps," said Obould. "I expect to be in parlay with the dwarves before the turn of spring."

"Parlay?" Tsinka echoed, her voice rising to a shriek once more.

Obould turned his scowl upon her and she shrank back.

"Take him now and secure him," the orc king said to her, his voice even and threatening.

Tsinka rushed past him to the dwarf, then roughly tugged poor Fender along.

"And injure him not at all!" Obould commanded.

"I had expected you to press into Mithral Hall," Kaer'lic said to the orc king when Tsinka was gone. "In truth, when we returned to Keeper's Dale, we expected to find the orc army scattering back for the Spine of the World."

"Your confidence is inspiring."

"That confidence grows, King Obould," Kaer'lic assured him. "You have shown great restraint and wisdom, I believe."

Obould dismissed the compliment with a snort. "Is there anything else you wish?" he asked. "I have much to do this day."

"Before you move along to the next construction?"

"That is the plan, yes," said Obould.

Kaer'lic bowed low. "Farewell, King of Dark Arrows."

Obould paused just a moment to consider the title, then turned on his heel and marched away.

"One surprise after another," Tos'un remarked when he was gone.

"I am not so surprised anymore," said Kaer'lic. "It was our mistake in underestimating Obould. It will not happen again."

"Let us just go back into the tunnels of the upper Underdark, or find another region in need of our playful cunning."

Kaer'lic's expression did not shift in the least. Eyes narrowed, as if throwing darts at the departing Obould, the priestess mulled over all the information. She thought of her lost companions, then simply let go of them, as was the drow way. She considered Obould's attitude, however, so disrespectful toward the dead drow and toward the Spider Queen. It was not so easy to let go of some things.

"I would speak with Tsinka before we leave," Kaer'lic remarked.

"Tsinka?" came Tos'un's skeptical response. "She is a fool even by orc standards."

"That is how I like my orcs," Kaer'lic answered. "Predictable and stupid."

Later that same day, after casting many spells of creation and imbuing a certain item with a particular dweomer, Kaer'lic sat on a stone opposite the orc priestess. Tsinka regarded her carefully and suspiciously, which she had expected, of course.

"You were not pleased by King Obould's decision to abandon Mithral Hall to the dwarves," Kaer'lic bluntly stated.

"It is not my place to question He-who-is-Gruumsh."

"Is he? Is it the will of Gruumsh to leave dwarves in peace? I am surprised by this."

Tsinka's face twisted in silent frustration and Kaer'lic knew she had hit a nerve here.

"It is often true that when a conqueror makes great gains, he becomes afraid," Kaer'lic explained. "He suddenly has so much more to lose, after all."

"He-who-is-Gruumsh fears nothing!" shrieked the volatile shaman.

Kaer'lic conceded that with a nod. "But likely, King Obould will need more than the prodding of Tsinka to fulfill the will of Gruumsh," the drow said.

The shaman eyed Kaer'lic curiously.

Smiling wickedly, Kaer'lic reached into her belt pouch and pulled forth a small spider-shaped fastener, holding it up before the orc.

"For the straps of a warrior's armor," she explained.

Tsinka seemed both intrigued and afraid.

"Take it," Kaer'lic offered. "Fasten your cloak with it. Or just press it against your skin. You will understand."

Tsinka took the fastener and held it close, and Kaer'lic secretly mouthed a word to release the spells she had placed in contingency upon the fastener.

Tsinka's eyes widened as she felt an infusion of courage and power. She closed her eyes and basked in the warmth of the item, and Kaer'lic used that opportunity to cast another spell upon the orc, an enchantment of friendship that put Tsinka fully at ease.

"The blessing of Lady Lolth," Kaer'lic explained. "She who would see the dwarves routed from Mithral Hall."

Tsinka moved the fastener back out and stared at it curiously. "This will drive He-who-is-Gruumsh back to the dwarven halls to complete the conquest?"

"That alone? Of course not. But I have many of them. And you and I will prod him, for we know that King Obould's greatest glories lay yet before him."

The shaman continued to stare glassy-eyed at the brooch for some time. Then she looked at her new best friend, her smile wide.

Kaer'lic tried hard to make her smile seem reciprocal rather than superior. The drow didn't worry about it too much, though, for Tsinka considered her trustworthy, thought Kaer'lic to be her new best friend.

The drow priestess wondered how Obould might view that friendship.

The walls of Mithral Hall seemed to press in on him as never before. Ivan and Pikel had returned that morning with the news of Delly and of Drizzt, bringing a conflicted spin of emotions to the big man. Wulfgar sat in the candlelight, his back against the stone wall, his eyes unblinking but unseeing as his mind forced him through the memories of the previous months.

He replayed his last conversations with Delly, and saw them in the light of the woman's desperation. How had he missed the clues, the overt cry for help?

He couldn't help but grimace as he considered his responses to Delly's plea that they go to Silverymoon or one of the other great cities. He had so diminished her feelings, brushing them away with a promise of a holiday.

"You cannot blame yourself for this," Catti-brie said from across the room, drawing Wulfgar out of his contemplation.

"She did not wish to stay here," he answered.

Catti-brie walked over and sat on the bed beside him. "Nor did she want to run off into the wild orc lands. It was the sword, and I think myself the fool for leaving it out in the open, where it could catch anyone walking by."

"Delly was leaving," Wulfgar insisted. "She could not tolerate the dark tunnels of dwarves. She came here full of hope for a better life, and found . . ." His voice trailed off in a great sigh.

"So she decided to cross the river with the other folk. And she took your child with her."

"Colson was as much Delly's as my own. Her claim was no less. She took Colson because she thought it would be best for the girl—of that, I have no doubt."

Catti-brie put her hand on Wulfgar's forearm. He appreciated the touch.

"And Drizzt is alive," he said, looking into her eyes and managing a smile. "There is good news, too, this day."

Catti-brie squeezed his forearm and matched his smile.

She didn't know how to respond, Wulfgar realized. She didn't know what to say or what to do. He had lost Delly and she had found Drizzt in a dwarf's single sentence! Sorrow, sympathy, hope, and relief so obviously swirled inside her as they swirled inside him, and she feared that if the balance tilted too positively, she would be minimizing his loss and showing disrespect.

Her concern about his feelings reminded Wulfgar of how great a friend she truly was to him. He put his other hand atop hers and squeezed back, then smiled more sincerely and nodded.

"Drizzt will find Obould and kill him," he said, strength returning to his voice. "Then he will return to us, where he belongs."

"And we're going to find Colson," Catti-brie replied.

Wulfgar took a deep breath, needing it to settle himself before he just melted down hopelessly.

All of Mithral Hall was searching for the toddler in the hopes that Delly had not taken her out. Dwarves had gone down to the Surbrin, despite the freezing rain that was falling in torrents, trying to get a message across the way to the ferry pilots to see if any of them had noted the child.

"The weather will break soon," Catti-brie said. "Then we will go and find your daughter."

"And Drizzt," Wulfgar replied.

Catti-brie grinned and gave a little shrug. "He'll find us long before that, if I'm knowing Drizzt."

"With Obould's head in hand," Wulfgar added.

It was a little bit of hope, at least, on as dark a day as Wulfgar, son of Beornegar, had ever known.

". . . orc-brained, goblin-sniffing son of an ogre and a rock!" Bruenor fumed. He stalked about his audience hall, kicking anything within reach.

"Hee hee hee," said Pikel.

Ivan shot his brother a look and motioned for him to be silent.

"Someone get me armor!" Bruenor roared. "And me axe! Got me a few hunnerd smelly orcs to kill!"

"Hee hee hee."

Ivan cleared his throat to cover his brother's impertinence. They had just informed King Bruenor of Drizzt's intentions, how the drow had taken the magical sword and Ivan's hand crossbow and had gone off after Obould.

Bruenor hadn't taken the news well.

Thrilled as he was that his dear friend was alive, Bruenor couldn't stand

his current state of inaction. A storm was whipping up outside, with driving and freezing rain, and heavy snow at the higher elevations, and there was simply no way for Bruenor or anyone else to get out of Mithral Hall. Even if the weather had been clear, Bruenor realized that there would be little he could do to help Drizzt. The drow was astride a flying horse—how could he possibly hope to catch him?

"Durned stupid elf," he muttered and he kicked the edge of his stone dais, then grumbled some more as he limped away.

"Hee hee hee," Pikel snickered.

"You'll only break your foot, and you won't be able to even go out to the walls," said Regis, rushing into the hall to see what was the matter. For word was passing through the complex that Drizzt had been found alive and well, and that King Bruenor was out of sorts.

"Ye heared?"

Regis nodded. "I knew he was alive. It will take more than orcs and frost giants to kill Drizzt."

"He's going after Obould. All by himself," Bruenor growled.

"I would not want to be Obould, then," the halfling said with a grin.

"Bah!" snorted the dwarf. "Durned stupid elf's taking all the fun again!"

"Hee hee hee," said Pikel, and Ivan elbowed him.

Pikel turned fiercely on his brother, his eyes going wild, and he began to waggle his fingers menacingly, all the while uttering birdlike sounds.

Ivan just shook his head.

"Boo," said Pikel, then "hee hee hee," again.

"Will ye just shut up?" Ivan said and he shook his head and turned away, crossing his burly arms over his chest.

He found Regis staring at him and chuckling.

"What?"

King Bruenor stopped, then, and similarly regarded Ivan, and he, too, began to chuckle.

Ivan stared at them both curiously, for unlike the pair, he couldn't see that his brother had just turned his beard as green as Pikel's own.

"They're thinking yerself to be amusing," Ivan said to Pikel.

"Hee hee hee."

Head down, cowl pulled low, Drizzt Do'Urden did not remain under shelter against the storm. North of Mithral Hall, it was all snow, blowing and deepening all around him, but with Sunrise in tow, the drow made his way across the uneven, rocky terrain, moving in the general direction of where he had last seen Obould. As the daylight waned, the drow ranger found a sheltered overhang and settled in, lying right along Sunrise's back to share some of the steed's body heat.

The storm finally broke after sunset, but the wind kicked up even more furiously. Drizzt went out and watched the clouds whip across the sky, stars blinking in and out with their passing. He climbed up over the jag of stone he had used for shelter and scanned the area. Several clusters of campfires were visible from up there, for the region was thick with the remnants of Obould's army. He marked the direction of the largest such cluster, then went back down and forced himself to get some much-needed rest.

He was up and out before the dawn, though, riding Sunrise, and even putting the pegasus up into a series of short, low flights.

A smile spread on the drow's face as he neared the region of the previous night's campfires, for the pennant of Obould soon came into view—the same flag he had seen flying with the orc king's personal caravan. He found a good vantage point and settled in, and soon enough, that same caravan was on the move once more.

Drizzt studied them closely. He spotted Obould among the ranks, growling orders.

The drow nodded and took a wide scan of the region, picking his path so that he could shadow the caravan.

He'd bide his time and await the opportunity.

We will kill them all, the vicious Khazid'hea whispered in his mind.

Drizzt focused his will and simply shut the telepathic intrusion off, then sent his own warning to the sword. *Bother me again and I will feed you to a dragon. You will sit in its treasure piles for a thousand years and more.*

The sword went silent once again.

Drizzt knew that Khazid'hea had sought him out purposely, and knew

that the sword had desired him as its wielder for some time. He considered that perhaps he should be more amenable to the sentient blade, should accept its intrusions and even let it believe that it was somewhat in charge.

It didn't matter, he decided, and he kept up his wall of mental defense. Khazid'hea could dominate most people, had even taken Catti-brie by surprise initially and had bent her actions to its will.

But against a warrior as seasoned and disciplined as Drizzt Do'Urden, a warrior who knew well the intrusive nature of the sentient sword, Khazid'hea's willpower seemed no more than a minor inconvenience. Drizzt considered that for a moment, and realized that he must take no chances. Obould would prove enough of a foe.

"We will kill them all," Drizzt said, and he lifted the blade up before his intense eyes.

He felt Khazid'hea's approval.

30

WHEN GODS ROAR

Kaer'lic Suun Wett nearly fell over when she saw the distinctive form of the winged horse sweeping in from the south. Orcs readied their bows, and Kaer'lic considered a spell, but Obould moved first and fast, and with little ambiguity.

"Hold your shots!" he bellowed, rushing and turning about so that there could be no mistaking him.

As he turned Kaer'lic's way, the drow priestess saw such fires raging in his eyes that they washed away any thoughts she entertained of ignoring his command and throwing some Lolth-granted spell at the pegasus rider.

That only infuriated her more as the winged horse closed and she recognized the black-skinned rider astride the magnificent creature.

"Drizzt Do'Urden," she mouthed.

"He dares approach?" asked Tos'un, who was standing at her side.

The pegasus banked and reared up, stopping its approach and seeming to hover in the air through a few great wing beats.

"Obould!" Drizzt cried, and as he had maneuvered himself upwind, his words were carried to the orcs. "I would speak with you! Alone! We have an unfinished conversation, you and I!"

"He has lost all sensibility," Kaer'lic whispered.

"Or is he in parlay with Obould?" asked Tos'un. "As an emissary of Mithral Hall, perhaps?"

"Destroy him!" Kaer'lic called to Obould. "Send your archers and cut him down or I will do it my—"

"You will hold your spells, or you will discuss this matter with Ad'non and Donnia in short order," Obould replied.

"Kill the ugly beast," Tos'un whispered to her, and Kaer'lic almost launched a magical assault upon the orc king—until good sense overruled her instinctive hatred. She looked from Obould over to Drizzt, who was taking the pegasus down lower onto an adjoining high point, a huge flat rock wedged against the steep hillside, its far end propped by several tall natural stone columns.

Kaer'lic did well to hide her grin as she looked back at the orc king, all adorned in his fine plate mail fastened by spider-shaped buckles. Though she hadn't planned on getting anywhere near to Drizzt Do'Urden, in effect, the scene was playing out exactly as she had hoped. Better than she had hoped, she thought, since she had not expected that Drizzt Do'Urden himself would prove to be the first formidable foe King Obould faced in his "improved" armor. If Drizzt was half as good as Kaer'lic had come to believe, then Obould was in for a very bad surprise.

"You intend to speak with this infidel?" she asked.

"If he speaks for Mithral Hall and they have anything to say that I wish to hear," Obould answered.

"And if not?"

"Then he has come to kill me, no doubt."

"And you will walk out to him?"

"And slaughter him." Obould's look was one of perfect confidence. He seemed almost bored by it all, as if Drizzt was no serious issue.

"You cannot do this," Tsinka said, moving fast behind her god-figure. "There is no reason. Let us destroy him from afar and continue on our way. Or send an emissary—send Kaer'lic, who knows the way of the drow elves!"

The sudden widening of Kaer'lic's red eyes betrayed her terror at that prospect, but she recovered quickly and flashed Tsinka a hateful look. When Tsinka's responding expression became concerned, even deeply wounded, Kaer'lic remembered the enchantment, remembered that she was "best friends" with the pitiful shaman. She managed a smile at the fool orc, then lifted her index finger and waggled it back and forth, bidding Tsinka not to interfere.

Tsinka continued to look at her dear, dear dark elf friend curiously for a moment longer, then happily smiled to indicate that she understood.

"This one is formidable, so I have heard," Kaer'lic said, but only because she knew she would hardly dissuade Obould from his intended course.

"I have battled him before," Obould assured her with a shrug.

"Perhaps it is a trap," Tsinka said, her voice falling away to ineffectiveness as she sheepishly looked at Kaer'lic.

Obould snickered and started to walk away, but stopped and glanced back, his yellow teeth showing behind the mouth slit in his bone-white helmet. Two strides put him past Kaer'lic, and he reached over and grabbed poor Fender by the scruff of his neck, and easily hoisted the dwarf under one arm.

"Never parlay without a counteroffer prepared," he remarked, and he stormed away.

Drizzt was not surprised to see Obould stalking from the far hilltop, though the sight of the dwarf prisoner did catch him off his guard. Other than that squirming prisoner, though, Obould was moving out alone. As he had shadowed Obould looking for the proper terrain, Drizzt had concocted elaborate ambushes, where he and Sunrise might swoop down from behind a shielding high bluff in a fast and deadly attack on Obould. But Drizzt had known those plans to be unnecessary. He had taken a good measure of the orc king in their fight, in more ways than physical. Obould would not run from his challenge, fairly offered.

But what of the dwarf? Drizzt had to find a way to make sure that Obould would not kill the poor fellow. He would refuse the fight unless the orc king guaranteed the prisoner's safety, perhaps. As he watched the approach, the drow became more convinced that he would be able to do just that, that Obould would not kill the dwarf. There was something about Obould, Drizzt was just beginning to see. In a strange way, the orc reminded Drizzt of Artemis Entreri. Single-minded and overly proud, always needing to prove himself—but to whom? To himself, perhaps.

Drizzt had known beyond the slightest bit of doubt that Obould would come out to meet him. He watched the orc king's long strides, noted the other orcs and a pair of drow creeping about in a widening arc behind the solitary figure of the great king. He had his left hand on Icingdeath, and he drew Khazid'hea from a scabbard strapped on Sunrise's side, but put the blade low immediately so as not to offer any overt threat.

We will cut out his heart, the sword started to promise.

You will be silent and remain out of my thoughts, Drizzt answered telepathically. *Distract me but once and I will throw you down the mountainside and rain an avalanche of snow and cold stones upon you.*

So forceful and dominant was the focused drow that the sentient sword went silent.

"He will win, yes? With the magic you put on his armor, Obould will win, yes?" Tsinka babbled as she moved to a closer vantage point beside the two drow.

Kaer'lic ignored her for most of the way, which only made the foolish shaman more insistent and demanding.

Finally the drow priestess turned on her and said, "He is Gruumsh, yes?"

Tsinka stopped short—stopped both walking and babbling.

"Drizzt is a mere drow warrior," said Kaer'lic. "Obould is Gruumsh. Do you fear for Gruumsh?"

Tsinka blanked, her doubts spinning around to reflect a lack of faith.

"So be silent and enjoy the show," said Kaer'lic, and so overpowering was her tone, particularly given the enchantment she still maintained regarding Tsinka, that her effect over the babbling shaman proved no less than Drizzt's dominance over Khazid'hea.

"Say what you must, and be quick," Obould said as he mounted the high flat stone directly across from the drow. Sunrise took a few quick strides and flew off the other way, as Drizzt had instructed.

"Say?" the drow asked.

Obould dropped poor Fender down onto the stone, the dwarf grunting as he hit face first. "You have come with parlay from Mithral Hall?"

"I have not been to Mithral Hall."

A smile widened on Obould's face, barely visible behind that awful skull-like helmet.

"You believe that the dwarves will parlay with you?" Drizzt asked.

"Have they a choice?"

"They will speak with their axes and their bows. They will answer with fury, and nothing more."

"You said that you have not been to Mithral Hall."

"Need I return to a place and people I know so well to anticipate the course of Clan Battlehammer?"

"This is beyond Clan Battlehammer," said Obould, and Drizzt could see that his smile had disappeared. With a growl, the orc king kicked the squirming Fender, sending the dwarf flying off the back side of the stone and bouncing down a short descending path.

The sudden surge of anger caught the drow off guard.

"You wish for a parlay with Mithral Hall?" Drizzt stated as much as asked, and he didn't even try to keep the surprise out of his voice.

Obould stared at him hatefully through the glassy eye-plates.

Questions came at Drizzt from every corner of his mind. If Obould desired a parlay, could it be that the war was at its end? If Drizzt battled the orc king, would he be showing disloyalty to Bruenor and his people, given that he might have just witnessed a sliver of hope that the war could be ended?

"You will return to your mountain homes?" Drizzt blurted, even as the question formulated in his thoughts.

Obould scoffed at him. "Look around you, drow," he said. "This is my home now. My kingdom! When you fly on your pet, you see the greatness of Obould. You see the Kingdom of Dark Arrows. Remember that name for the last minutes of your life. You die in Dark Arrows, Drizzt Do'Urden, and will be eaten by birds on a mountainside in the home of King Obould." He ended with a snarl and lifted his greatsword up before him, beginning a determined approach.

"Who is your second?" Drizzt asked, the unexpected words halting

Obould. "For when you are dead, I will need to know. Perhaps that orc will be wiser than Obould and will see that he has no place here, among the dwarves, the elves, and the humans. Or if not, I will kill him, too, and speak with his second."

Drizzt saw Obould's eyes widen behind the glassy plates, and with a roar that shook the stones, Obould leaped ahead, stabbing ferociously with his powerful sword, the blade bursting into flame as he thrust.

Out snapped Icingdeath, in the blink of a drow eye, the enchanted weapon slapping across the greatsword, extinguishing the fires in an angry puff of smoke as Drizzt hopped to the side. He could have struck with Khazid'hea, for Obould, in his supreme confidence, had abandoned all semblance of defense in the assault. But Drizzt held the attack.

The greatsword came slashing across, predictably, forcing the drow into a fast retreat. Had he taken that first opening and struck with his newfound sword, Drizzt would have scored a hit, but nothing substantial.

And in that instance, Obould would have recognized his unanticipated vulnerability.

Obould pressed the attack wildly, slashing and stabbing, rushing ahead, and on the high ground behind and to the side of the flat stone, orcs cheered and shouted in glee.

Drizzt measured every turn and retreat, letting the fury play out, using less energy than his outraged opponent. He wasn't trying to tire Obould, but rather to gain better insight into the orc's turns and movements, that he could better anticipate.

The greatsword flamed to life again with one feinted stab that became a sudden reversal into a downward chop, and had Drizzt not seen a similar distraction tactic used against the elf Tarathiel, he might have found himself caught by surprise. As it was, the descending greatsword met only the slap of Icingdeath, extinguishing the larger weapon's fires.

Obould came on suddenly and wildly, charging straight for the drow, who stepped left, then leaped back right, going into a roll as Obould started one way then threw himself back the other, slashing his sword across. That sword flamed to life again, and the rolling Drizzt felt the heat of those magical fires as the blade cut above him.

Drizzt came up to his feet and spun, then back-stepped and slid off to the side once more as Obould continued to press. Around and around they went, the orcs cheering and howling with every slash of Obould's sword, though he got nowhere close to hitting the elusive drow.

Neither did he show any signs of tiring, though.

Finally, Obould stopped his charge and stood glaring at Drizzt from behind the flames of the upraised greatsword.

"Are you going to fight me?" he asked.

"I thought I was."

Obould growled. "Run away, if that is your course. Cross blades if you are not afraid."

"You grow tired?"

"I grow bored!" Obould roared.

Drizzt smiled and faked a sudden rush, then stopped abruptly and caught everyone by surprise when he simply tossed Icingdeath up into the air. Obould's eyes followed the ascent of the sword.

Drizzt reached his free hand behind his back and brought out the loaded hand crossbow, and as Obould snapped his gaze back upon him—yes, he wanted the orc king to see it coming!—the drow gave a shrug and let fly.

The dart hit Obould's helmet in the left eye then collapsed in on itself and exploded with a burst of angry flame and black smoke. Obould's head snapped back viciously, and the orc king went flying down to the stone, flat on his back, as surely as if a mountain had fallen atop him. He lay very still.

Gasps and silence replaced the wild cheering of all those looking on.

"Impressive," Tos'un quietly remarked.

Beside him, Kaer'lic stood with her jaw hanging open, and beside her, Tsinka whimpered and gasped.

They watched Drizzt snap the hand crossbow back behind him, then casually catch the falling scimitar.

Kaer'lic noticed the approach of the pegasus, and suddenly feared that Drizzt would escape once more—and that, she could not allow.

She began casting a powerful spell, aiming for the flying horse and not

the too-lucky drow, when she was interrupted by Tsinka, who grabbed her arm, and screamed, "He moves!"

The drow priestess looked back at Obould, who rocked up onto his shoulders, arching his back and bending his legs, then snapped back the other way, leaping up to his feet.

The orcs screamed in glee.

Drizzt hid his surprise well when Obould was suddenly standing before him once more. He noted the tip of the dart, embedded in the glassteel plate of the helmet, and the black scorch marks showing over the rest of that plate, and partially over the other one as well.

He hadn't expected to kill Obould with the dart, after all, and it was a fortunate thing that the orc king's fall had caught him more by surprise than his sudden return, for Obould howled and attacked once more, slashing with abandon.

But . . .

He couldn't see! Drizzt realized as he stepped aside and Obould continued to press the attack at the empty air before him.

Kill him now! the hungry Khazid'hea implored, and the drow, in complete agreement, didn't even scold the sentient sword.

He stepped in suddenly and drove Khazid'hea at a seam in the orc king's fabulous armor, and the fine blade bit through and slid into Obould's side.

How the great orc howled and leaped, tearing the sword right from Drizzt's grasp. Obould staggered back several steps, blood leaking out beside the sticking blade.

"Treachery!" Obould yelled, and he reached up and yanked the ruined helmet from his head, throwing it over the cliff face. "You cannot beat me fairly, and you cannot beat me unfairly!"

To Drizzt's amazement, he came on again.

"Unbelievable," whispered Tos'un.

"Stubborn," Kaer'lic corrected with a snarl.

"Gruumsh!" howled the gleeful and crying Tsinka, and all the orcs cheered, for if that sword protruding from Obould's side would prove a mortal wound, it did not show at all in the great orc's pressing attacks.

"He doesn't even know when he's dead," Kaer'lic grumbled, and she launched into a spell, then, a calling to magical items she had fastened by the grace of Lady Lolth.

It was time to end the travesty.

Drizzt tried to battle past his incredulity and properly respond to Obould's renewed attacks. It took him several parries and a few last-second dodges to even realize that he should draw out Twinkle to replace his lost sword.

"And what have you gained for all of your treachery, drow?" Obould demanded, pressing forward and slashing away.

"You are without a helmet, and that is no small thing," Drizzt shouted back. "The turtle has come out of its shell."

"Only so that I can look down upon you in the last moments of your life, fool!" Obould assured him. "That you might see the pleasure on my face as your body grows cold!" He ended with a devastating charge, and turned in anticipation even as Drizzt started to jump aside.

The move caught Drizzt off guard, for it was truly an all-or-nothing, victory-or-defeat maneuver. If Obould guessed wrong, turning opposite Drizzt's sudden dodge, then Drizzt would have little trouble in slamming one or both of his scimitars down upon the back of the orc's skull.

But Obould guessed right.

On his heels, corralled and running out of retreating room, Drizzt parried desperately. So fast was Obould's sword-work that Drizzt couldn't even think of launching an effective counter. So furious was the orc king's attack that Drizzt didn't even entertain any thoughts of swinging for his exposed head. Drizzt understood the power behind Obould's swings, and he knew that he could not fend that greatsword. Not the shirt he had taken from the dead dark elf, not even the finest suit of Bruenor's best mithral stock would save him from being cloven in half.

Very simply, Obould had guessed right in his turn and Drizzt understood that he was beaten.

Both his blades slapped against the slashing greatsword, Icingdeath extinguishing the stubborn fires yet again. But the shock of the block sent waves of numbness up the drow's arm, and even with a two-bladed parry, he could not fully deflect the swing. He fell down—that, or he would have been cut in half—and scrambled into a forward roll, but he could not get fully past Obould without taking a hit, a kick at least. He braced himself for the blow.

But it did not fall.

Drizzt came around as he got back to his feet, to see Obould squirming and jerking wildly.

"What?" the orc king growled, and he jolted left then right.

It took Drizzt several seconds to sort it out, to notice that the spider clasps on Obould's armor were animating. Eight-legged creatures scrambled all over the orc, and by Obould's roars and jerking movements, it seemed as if more than a few were stopping to bite him.

As the orc thrashed, pieces of that fabulous armor suit went flying. One vambrace fell to the stone, and he kicked his legs to free himself of the tangle of flapping jambs. His great breastplate fell away, as well as one pauldron and the backplate. The remaining pauldron flapped outward, held in place only by the embedded sword—and how Obould howled whenever that vicious blade moved.

Not understanding, not even caring, Drizzt leaped in for the kill.

And promptly leaped back out, as Obould found his focus and countered with a sudden and well-timed sword thrust. Drizzt winced as he back-stepped, blood staining his enchanted shirt on the side. He stared at his opponent through every inch of his retreat, stunned that Obould had found the clarity to so counter.

Separated and with a moment's respite, Obould straightened. His face twisted into a grimace and he slapped one hand across to splatter a spider that had found a soft spot in his toughened orc hide. He brought his hand across, throwing the arachnid carcass to the ground, then reached over, growled and grimacing, and pulled Khazid'hea free of his side, taking the pauldron with it.

Wield me as your own! the sword screamed at him.

With a feral and explosive roar, Obould threw the annoying sword over the cliff.

"Treachery again!" he roared at Drizzt. "You live up to the sinister reputation of your heritage, drow."

"That was not my doing," Drizzt yelled back. "Speak not to me of treachery, Obould, when you encase yourself in an armor my blades cannot penetrate."

That retort seemed to quiet and calm the orc, who stood more upright and assumed a pensive posture. He even offered a nod of concession to Drizzt on that point, ending with a smile and an invitation: "I wear none now."

Obould held his arms out wide, and brought his greatsword flaming to life, inviting the drow to continue.

Drizzt straightened against the sting in his side, returned the nod, and leaped ahead.

Those watching the fight, drow and orc alike, did not cheer, hoot, or groan over the next few moments. They stood, one and all, transfixed by the sudden fury of the engagement, by the hum of swords, and the dives and leaps of the principals. Blade rang against blade too many times to be heard as distinguishable sounds. Blades missed a killing mark by so narrow a margin, again and again, that the onlookers continually gasped.

The confusion of the battle challenged Drizzt at every level. One moment, he felt as if he was fighting Artemis Entreri, so fluid, fast, and devious were Obould's movements. And the next moment, he was painfully reminded by a shocking wave of reverberating energy flowing up his arm that he might well be battling a mighty giant.

He let go of all his thoughts then, and fell into the Hunter, allowing his rage to rise within him, allowing for perfect focus and fury.

He knew in an instant that the creature he faced was no less intense.

Any traces of her charm spell was gone then, Kaer'lic knew, as Tsinka Shinriil, finding herself deceived by the drow's work on Obould's armor, leaped up beside Kaer'lic and began shrieking at her.

"You cannot defeat him! Even your treachery pales against the power of

Obould!" she screamed. "You chose to betray a god, and now you will learn the folly of your ways!"

Truly it seemed a moment of absolute glee for the idiot Tsinka, and that, Kaer'lic could not allow. The drow's hand shot up as she mouthed the last words of a spell, creating a sudden disturbance in the air, a crackling jolt of energy that sent Tsinka flying away and to the ground.

"Kill her," Kaer'lic instructed Tos'un, who moved immediately to see to the enjoyable task.

"Wait," Kaer'lic said. "Let her live a bit longer. Let her witness the death of her god."

"We should just be gone from this place," said Tos'un, clearly intimidated by the spectacle of King Obould, who was matching the skilled drow cut for cut.

Kaer'lic flashed her companion a warning look, then turned her focus back upon that high stone. Her eyes went wild and she began to chant to Lady Lolth, reaching within herself for every ounce of magical strength she could muster for her powerful spell. The very air seemed to gather about her as she moved through the incantation. Her hair bristled and waved, though there was no wind. She grasped at the air with her outstretched hand then brought it in close and reached with the other one. Then she repeated the movements again and again as if she was taking all of the energy around her and bringing it into her torso.

The ground began to tremble beneath them. Kaer'lic began a low growl that increased in tempo and volume, slowly at first, but then more forcefully and quickly as the drow priestess began to reach out toward Drizzt and Obould with both hands.

Thunder rolled all around them. The orcs began to cower, shout, or run away. And the ground began to shake, quick and darting movements at first that grew into great rolling waves of stone. Rock split and crumbled. A crevice appeared before Kaer'lic and charged out toward the unfazed combatants.

And the high rock split apart under the force of Kaer'lic's earthquake. And stones tumbled down in an avalanche. And Obould fell away, roaring in protest.

And Drizzt went right behind him.

31

TO BE AN ELF

Her nose was no more than a misshapen lump of torn flesh, with blood and grime caked all around it and over her left eye. Kaer'lic's spell had broken most of the bones in Tsinka's face, the shaman knew, and Tsinka was glad indeed when she had awakened to find the two drow long gone. Everyone was long gone, it seemed, for the orcs had run away from that terrible earthquake.

For many minutes, Tsinka Shinriil sat and stared at the broken rock across the way, plumes of dust still hanging in the air from the weight of the avalanche. What had Kaer'lic done? Why had Lady Lolth gone against He-Who-Was-Gruumsh? It made no sense to the poor, broken shaman.

Moving against hope, Tsinka pulled herself to her feet and staggered toward the area of disaster. She followed the same path Obould had taken on his approach to the renegade drow. She could still see some of her god's footprints in the snow and dirt before her. Half-blinded by drying blood and streams of tears, Tsinka stumbled along, falling more than once, crying out to her god.

"How did you let this happen?"

She nearly tripped over a form half-buried in the snow and rubble, then recoiled and kicked out at it when she saw it was that ugly little dwarf. He grunted, so she kicked him again and moved along. She pulled herself up on

the remains of the flat rock that had served as the battleground. The earthquake had split it in half, and the far half, where both Obould and Drizzt had been standing, had fallen away.

Tsinka wiped her arm across her face and forced herself to stagger forward. She fell to her knees and peered into the area of ruin, into the dust.

And there, only a dozen feet below her, she saw the form of a battered but very much alive dark elf.

"You!" she howled, and she spat at him.

Drizzt looked up at her. Filthy and bruised, bloody on one side and holding one arm in close, the drow had not escaped unharmed. But he had escaped, landing on a small ledge, perched on the very edge of oblivion.

"Where will you run now?" Tsinka shouted at him.

She glanced all around then scrambled to the side, returning a moment later with a rock in each hand. She pegged one down at him and missed, then took more careful aim with the second and whipped it off his upraised, blocking arm.

"Your flying horse is nowhere about, drow!" she shouted, and she hopped around in search of more ammo.

Again she pelted Drizzt with rocks, and there was nothing he could do but lift his arm to block and accept the stinging hits. He had no room to maneuver, and try as he may, he could not find any handholds that would propel him back up to the flat rock.

Every time she threw a stone, Tsinka scanned the skies. The pegasus wouldn't catch her by surprise, she vowed. The drow had played a role in destroying He-Who-Was-Gruumsh, and so the drow would have to die.

He was out of options. There was nothing Drizzt could do against the assault. He still had his scimitars and Ivan's crossbow, but the remaining darts he'd left on Sunrise, who was nowhere to be seen. Sitting on the tiny ledge, Drizzt had hoped that the pegasus would find him before the inevitable return of his enemies.

No such luck, and so all he could do was deflect the stinging stones with his upraised arms.

The orc shaman disappeared for a longer period of time, then, and Drizzt desperately looked around. No pegasus came into view—and in his rational thoughts, he knew that it would be some time before Sunrise would come back to the unstable, devastated area.

"At least Obould is gone," he whispered, and he glanced out over the ledge, where the shifting stones continued to rumble. "Bruenor will win the day."

Whatever hope that notion inspired disappeared in the realization of his mortality, as Drizzt looked back up to see the orc hoist a huge rock over her head in both hands. He glanced to the sides quickly, looking for some place he might leap.

But there was nothing.

The orc snarled at him and moved to throw.

And she lurched and went flying, both her and the rock tumbling out too far, past the surprised drow and down the broken mountainside. On the rock above, hanging over the edge, loomed a hairy and battered face.

"Well met, Drizzt Do'Urden," said Fender. "Think ye might be taking me home?"

"We will go to Gerti and determine what she is about," said Kaer'lic.

"The dwarf is gone and Tsinka is likely plotting our demise," Tos'un replied.

"If the pig-faced shaman even lives," Kaer'lic retorted. "I hope she does, that I might make her death even more unpleasant. Too much have I seen of these wretched and foul-smelling orcs. Too many tendays have we spent in their filthy company, listening to their foolish gibbering, and pretending that anything they might have to say would be of the least bit of interest to us. Gruumsh take Obould, and Lady Lolth take Drizzt, and may they both be tortured until eternity's end!"

So caught up was she in her ranting, that Kaer'lic didn't even notice Tos'un's eyes go so wide that they seemed as if they might just roll out of his face. So full of spit and anger was she that it took her some time to even realize that Tos'un wasn't looking at her, but rather past her.

Kaer'lic froze in place.

Tos'un squealed, turned, and ran away.

Kaer'lic realized she should just follow, without question, but before her mind could command her feet to run, a powerful hand grabbed her by the back of her hair and jerked her head back so violently and forcefully that she felt as if her entire body had been suddenly compacted.

"Do you recognize the foul smell?" Obould Many-Arrows whispered into her ear. He tugged harder with that one hand pulling her down and back, but not letting her fall. "Does my gibbering offend you now?"

Kaer'lic could hardly move, so forceful was that grasp. She saw Obould's greatsword sticking past her, off to the side. She felt his breath, hot against her neck, and stinking as only an orc's breath could. She had to tug back and stretch her jaw muscles so that they could even move against that incredible pull, and she tried futilely to form some words, any words.

"Casting a spell, witch?" Obould asked her. "Sorry, but that I cannot allow."

His face came forward suddenly, his jaw clamping on Kaer'lic's exposed throat. She reached up and grabbed at him and squirmed and thrashed desperately, with all her might.

Obould tore his face away, taking her throat with it. He yanked Kaer'lic back and put his bloody and battered face right before her, then spat her own flesh into her face.

"I am imbued with the blessing of Gruumsh," he said. "Did you truly believe that you could kill me?"

Kaer'lic gasped, her arms flailing wildly and uncontrollably, blood pouring from her torn throat, and bubbling from the air escaping her lungs.

Obould threw her to the ground and let her die slowly.

He scanned the region, and noted some movement on a distant ridge. It wasn't Tsinka, he knew, for he had seen her broken body on the stones as he climbed back up the mountainside.

He'd need to find a new shaman, a new consort who treated him as a god. He'd need to move quickly to reconsolidate his power, to cut short the rumors of his demise. The orcs would be fast to flee, he knew, and only he, imbued with the power of Gruumsh, could stop the retreat.

"Dark Arrows," he said with determination. "My home."

The weather broke, leaving the air fresh and clean, and with a warm south wind blowing. Bruenor and his friends would not stay inside, spending their days along the northern mountain spur, staring off into the north.

Pikel Bouldershoulder's bird scouts were the first to report a pair of winged horses, making all speed for Mithral Hall, and so it was not a surprise, but such a tremendous relief nonetheless, when the distinctive forms finally came into view.

Bruenor and Wulfgar moved a couple of paces out in front of the others, Regis, the Bouldershoulders, Cordio, Stumpet, and Pwent behind them, and Catti-brie in back, leaning heavily on a wooden cane and on the side of the tower.

Sunset set down on the stone before the dwarf king, Innovindil lifted her leg over before her and dropping quickly, turning as she went to support poor Fender through the move. Without that support, the dwarf would surely have tumbled off.

Wulfgar stepped forward and gently hoisted the dwarf from the pegasus, then handed him to Cordio and Stumpet, who hustled him away.

"Obould is gone," Innovindil reported. "The orcs will not hold, and all the northland will be free again."

As she finished, Sunrise landed on the stone.

"A sight for an old dwarf's sore eyes," Bruenor said.

Drizzt slipped down to the ground. He glanced at Bruenor, but his stare remained straight ahead, cutting through the ranks, which parted as surely as if he had shouldered his way through, leaving the line of sight open between the drow and Catti-brie.

"Welcome home," Regis said.

"We never doubted your return," offered Wulfgar.

Drizzt nodded at each, though he never stopped staring ahead. He patted Bruenor as he walked past. He tousled Regis's hair and he grabbed and squeezed Wulfgar's strong forearm.

But he never stopped moving and never stopped staring.

He hit Catti-brie with a great hug, pressing up against her, kissing her and crushing her, lifting her right from the ground.

And he kept walking, carrying her along.

"That is what it is to be an elf, Drizzt Do'Urden," Innovindil whispered as the two moved to, and through, Mithral Hall's new eastern door.

"Well I'll be a bearded gnome," said Bruenor.

"Hee hee hee," said Pikel, and Regis giggled, embarrassed.

They all were fairly amused, it seemed, but Bruenor's mirth disappeared when he glanced across at Wulfgar.

The big man stared at the path Drizzt and Catti-brie had taken, and there was a wince of profound pain to be found behind his mask of stoicism.

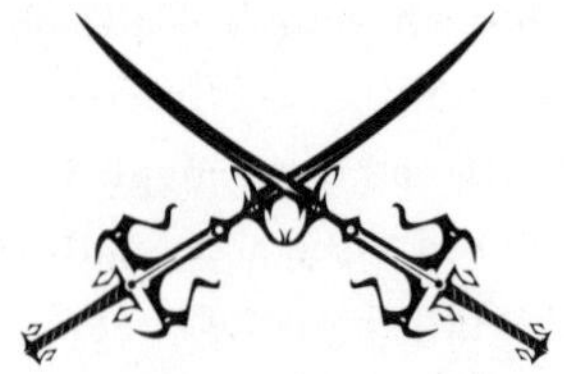

EPILOGUE

"She will understand," Drizzt said to Catti-brie, the two of them sitting on the edge of their bed early one morning, nearly two tendays after the drow's return to Mithral Hall.

"She won't, because she'll not have to," Catti-brie argued. "You told her that you would go, and so you shall. On your word."

"Innovindil will understand . . ." Drizzt started to argue, but his voice trailed off under Catti-brie's wilting stare. They had been over it several times already.

"You need to close that chapter of your life," Catti-brie said to him quietly, taking his hands in her own and lifting them up to her lips to kiss them. "Your scimitar cut into your own heart as deeply as it cut into Ellifain. You do not return to her for Innovindil. You owe Innovindil and her people nothing, so yes, they will understand. It's yourself that you owe. You need to return. To put Ellifain to rest and to put Drizzt at peace."

"How can I leave you now?"

"How can you not?" Catti-brie grinned at him. "I do not doubt that you'll return to me, even if your companion on your journey is a beautiful elf.

"Besides," the woman went on, "I'll not be here in any case. I have promised Wulfgar that I will journey with him to Silverymoon and beyond, if necessary."

Drizzt nodded his agreement with that last part. According to the dwarf ferry pilot, Delly Curtie did come near his craft before it set off for the eastern bank with the refugees from the north, and he did recall seeing the woman hand something, perhaps a baby, over to one of the other human women. He couldn't be certain who—they all looked alike to him, so he declared.

Wulfgar wasn't about to wait until spring to set off in pursuit of Colson, and Catti-brie wasn't about to let him go alone.

"You cannot go with us," Catti-brie said. "Your presence will cause too much a stir in those gossiping towns, and will tell whoever has the child that we're in pursuit. So you've your task to perform, and I've mine."

Drizzt didn't argue any longer.

"Regis is staying with Bruenor?" Drizzt asked.

"Someone's got to. He's all out of sorts since word that Obould, or an orc acting in Obould's stead, continues to hold our enemies in cohesion. Bruenor thought they would have begun their retreat by now, but all reports from the north show them continuing their work unabated."

"The Kingdom of Dark Arrows. . . ." Drizzt mouthed, shaking his head. "And Alustriel and all the others will not go against it."

Catti-brie squeezed his hand tighter. "We'll find a way."

Sitting so close to her, Drizzt couldn't believe anything else, couldn't believe that every problem could not be solved.

Drizzt found Bruenor in his audience hall a short while later, Regis sitting beside him and the Bouldershoulder brothers, packed for the road, standing before him.

"Well met again, ye dark one," Ivan greeted the drow. "Me and me brother . . ." Ivan paused.

"Me brudder!" said Pikel.

"Yeah, we're off for home to see if Cadderly can do something about me . . . about Pikel's arm. Won't be much fighting to be found up here for a few tendays, at least. We're thinking to come back and kill a few more orcs." Ivan turned to Bruenor. "If ye'll have us, King Bruenor."

"Would any ruler be so foolish as to refuse the help of the Bouldershoulders?" Bruenor asked graciously, though Drizzt could hear the simmering anger behind Bruenor's every sound.

"Boom!" shouted Pikel.

"Yeah, boom," said Ivan. "Come on, ye green-bearded cousin o' Cadderly's pet squirrel. Get me home—and no small roots, ye hear?"

"Hee hee hee."

Drizzt watched the pair depart the hall, then turned to Bruenor and asked, "Will your kingdom ever be the same?"

"Good enough folk, them two," said Bruenor. "Green-bearded one scares me, though."

"Boom!" said Regis.

Bruenor eyed him threateningly. "First time ye say 'hee hee hee,' I'm pulling yer eyebrows out."

"The folk o' the towns're going to let them stay, elf," the dwarf said, turning back to Drizzt. "Durned fools're to let the stinking orcs have what they took."

"They see no way around it, and no reason to find one."

"And that's their folly. Obould, or whatever smelly pig-face that's taking his place, ain't to sit there and argue trade routes."

"I do not disagree."

"Can't let them stay."

"Nor can we hope to dislodge them without allies," Drizzt reminded the dwarf.

"And so we're to find them!" Bruenor declared. "Ye heading off with Invo . . . Inno . . . that durned elf?"

"I promised to take her to Ellifain's body, that Ellifain might be properly returned to the Moonwood."

"Good enough then."

"You know that I will return to you."

Bruenor nodded. "Gauntlgrym," he said, and both Drizzt and Regis were caught off guard.

"Gauntlgrym," Bruenor said again. "We three. Me girl if she's ready and me boy if he's back from finding his little girl. We're to find our answers at Gauntlgrym."

"How do you know that?" Regis asked.

"I know that Moradin didn't let me come back to sign a treaty with any stinking, smelly, pig-faced orc," Bruenor replied. "I know that I can't fight him alone and that I ain't yet convinced enough to fight beside me."

"And you believe that you will find answers to your dilemma in a long-buried dwarven kingdom?" asked Drizzt.

"I know it's as good a place to start looking as any. Banak's ready to take control o' the hall in me absence. Already put it in place. Gauntlgrym in the spring, elf."

Drizzt eyed him curiously, not certain whether Bruenor was on to something, or if the dwarf was just typically responding to sitting still by finding a way to get back on the road to adventure. As he considered that, however, Drizzt realized that it didn't much matter which it might be. For he was no less determined than Bruenor to find again the wind on his face.

"Gauntlgrym in the spring," he agreed.

"We'll show them orcs what's what," Bruenor promised.

Beside him, Regis just sighed.

Tos'un Armgo had not been so alone and out of sorts since he had abandoned the Menzoberranzan army after their retreat from Mithral Hall. His three companions were all dead and he knew that if he stayed anywhere in the North, Obould would send him to join them soon enough.

He had found Kaer'lic's body earlier that morning, but it was stripped of anything that might be of use to him. Where was he to go?

He thought of the Underdark's winding ways, and realized that he couldn't likely go back to Menzoberranzan, even if that had been his choice. But neither could he stay on the surface among the orcs.

"Gerti," he decided after considering his course for much of that day, sitting on the same stone where Obould and Drizzt had battled. If he could get to Shining White, he might find allies, and perhaps a refuge.

But that was only *if* he could get there. He slipped down from the rock and started moving down the trail to lower ground, sheltered from the wind and from the eyes of any of Obould's many spies. He found a lower trail and moved along, making his way generally north.

Do not abandon me! he heard, and he stopped.

No, he hadn't actually heard the call, Tos'un realized, but rather he had felt it, deep in his thoughts. Curious, the drow moved around, attuning his senses to his surroundings.

Here! Left of you. Near the stone.

Following the instructions, Tos'un soon came upon the source, and he was grinning for the first time in many days when he lifted a fabulous sword in his hands.

Well met, imparted Khazid'hea.

"Indeed," said Tos'un, as he felt the weapon's extraordinary balance and noted its incredibly sharp blade.

He looked back to where he had found the sword and noted that he had just pulled it from a seam in Obould's supposedly impenetrable armor.

"Indeed. . . ." he said again, thinking that perhaps not all of his adventure had been in vain.

Nor was Khazid'hea complaining, for it didn't take the sentient sword long to understand that it had at last found a wielder not only worthy, but of like mind.

On a clear and crisp winter's morning, Drizzt and Innovindil set out from Mithral Hall, moving southwest. They planned to pass near to Nesmé to see how progress was going on fortifying the city, and cross north of the Trollmoors to the town of Longsaddle, home of the famed wizard family the Harpells. Long allies of King Bruenor, the Harpells would join in the fight, no doubt, when battle finally resumed. And so desperate was Bruenor to find allies—any allies—that he would gladly accept even the help of eccentric wizards who blew each other up nearly as often as they dispatched their enemies.

Drizzt and Innovindil planned to stay along a generally southwesterly route all the way to the sea, hoping for days when they could put their winged mounts up into the sky. Then they'd turn north, hopefully just as winter was loosening its icy grip, and travel back to the ravine and harbor where Ellifain had been laid to rest.

That same morning, the ferry made the difficult journey across the icy Surbrin, bearing Wulfgar and Catti-brie, two friends determined to find Wulfgar's lost girl.

Bruenor and Regis had seen both pairs off, then had returned to the dwarf king's private quarters to begin drawing up plans for their springtime journey.

"Gauntlgrym, Rumblebelly," Bruenor kept reciting, and Regis came to know that as the dwarf's litany against the awful truth of the orc invasion. The mere thought of the Kingdom of Dark Arrows covering the land to his very doorstep had Bruenor in a terrible tizzy.

It was his way of escaping that reality, Regis knew, his way of doing something, anything, to try to fight back.

Regis hadn't seen Bruenor so animated and eager for the road since the journey that had taken them out of Icewind Dale to find Mithral Hall, those many years ago.

They'd all be there, all five—six, counting Guenhwyvar. Perhaps Ivan and Pikel would return before the spring and adventure with them.

Bruenor was too busy with his maps and his lists of supplies to be paying any attention, and so he missed the sound completely when Regis mumbled, "Hee hee hee."